FROM SWITZERLAND TO THE RUSSIAN BORDER—A JOURNEY INTO TERROR, TORTURE, AND SUSPENSE.

In the locked carriage of a train speeding across the shell-scarred landscape of Europe sits the one man who can turn the tide of the war. Backed by a socialist millionaire, aided by a beautiful Ukrainian emigree, supported by the German High Command is the exiled Ulyanov—known as Lenin.

The dread assassins of the Okhrana—Czarist police—will torture mercilessly, kill cold-bloodedly to stop QUADRIGA, the top-secret German mission.

The lives of passionate men and women, the fate of nations, the future, hang in the balance. All are caught in the onrushing tide of history in a stunning novel of suspense based on fact more frightening, more startling than fiction.

"ACTION, SUSPENSE, ESPIONAGE . . . A CRUCIAL PERIOD IN 20TH CENTURY HISTORY."

—*New York Post*

BOOKS BY OWEN SELA

THE BEARER PLOT

THE KIRIOV TAPES

THE PORTUGUESE FRAGMENT

THE BENGALI INHERITANCE

AN EXCHANGE OF EAGLES

THE PETROGRAD CONSIGNMENT

THE PETROGRAD CONSIGNMENT

OWEN SELA

A DELL BOOK

for Anton Felton
guide, philosopher, friend

Published by
Dell Publishing Co., Inc.
1 Dag Hammarskjold Plaza
New York, New York 10017

ISBN: 0-440-16885-6

Reprinted by arrangement with The Dial Press
Printed in the United States of America
First Dell printing—April 1980

CONTENTS

Prologue	7
Quadriga	22
Revolution	113
Stratagem	176
The Train	222
Counterpassant	340
Coda	389

PROLOGUE

The Zahringerplatz lies in the oldest part of Zurich, an area of narrow alleys and winding streets where houses still have oriel windows and bear curious wrought-iron signs. To one side of the Zahringerplatz lies the Brunnenturm, where Lombard money changers once did business. On the opposite side stand the ancient buildings of a Dominican friary, dominated by the pointed wooden steeple of its church.

Shortly before noon on a bleak Friday in February, Commissioner Klaus Hartmann, Chief of Zurich's Foreign Police, lumbered with seeming casualness along the Zahringerplatz to where the narrow, tree-lined street joined the Predigerplatz. Hartmann was a big, square-shouldered man, whose dark Homburg was jammed firmly on a bristly, rectangular head. He walked up to a burly, potbellied Swiss stamping his feet noisily on the corner. The Swiss turned to stare at Hartmann belligerently and then, recognising him, smiled and nodded. Sergeant Hugo Spuhl had been standing on that corner for precisely seventy-one minutes.

"He hasn't come yet," Sergeant Spuhl said.

Standing parallel to the snow-covered friary wall, Hartmann looked down the Predigerplatz towards the tower of the recently completed university building half a mile away, now festooned with fronds of mist. Zurich in that third year of the war was full of foreigners. Not tourists, not strangers from the nearby cantons of Zug or Aargau or Schwyz, but Englishmen, Frenchmen, Germans, and Russians.

The Foreign Police was the nearest thing Switzerland had to a Secret Service, and it was Commissioner Hartmann's job to ensure that no foreign diplomats, agents, or political exiles living in Zurich engaged in activity prejudicial to Swiss neutrality. Which, given the size of his force, was an impossible task. Which also meant that Hartmann, being a practical man, accepted the fact that certain businessmen would take advantage of Swiss banking secrecy to enter into transactions that would be illegal between belligerents and that a certain number of Englishmen, Frenchmen, and Russians would spend their time spying on the Germans and on each other.

The Russian political exiles were a different matter. They were a noisy, disputatious rabble, whose arrival in Zurich he had unavailingly protested to Foreign Minister Grimm. They were all troublemakers, exiled from their own country for conspiring to overthrow the established order. Unlike, say, the sixteenth-century Huguenots, they had brought with them neither skills nor money. Their contribution to the economy was minute, and café proprietors often complained that they sat arguing for hours over a solitary round of coffee. Hartmann considered them parasites who should be expelled at the earliest possible moment.

The clock in the wooden steeple chimed twelve. Soon afterwards the side door of the library in the friary complex opened and a short, wiry figure emerged, clad in a shabby grey overcoat, black brimmed hat, and mountain boots.

"That's him," Sergeant Spuhl whispered. "Vladimir Ilyich Ulyanov."

Looking neither right nor left, Ulyanov thrust himself across the Predigerplatz and along the narrow alley of oak-beamed shops called the Prediger, the studs of his boots screeching on the cobbles. Slowly Hartmann and Spuhl eased away from the corner and followed. It wasn't difficult. They could hear the scrape of Ulyanov's boots twenty yards away.

According to Sergeant Spuhl's reports, the surveillance of Ulyanov had proved to be surprisingly easy. Ulyanov was a creature of habit. Every morning for the past two weeks he had left his room in the Spiegelgasse at eight thirty and walked to the library in the Predigerplatz by way of Limmat Quai. Soon after midday, leaving his books neatly aligned, he would walk home through the Prediger for lunch. At one thirty he would return to the library, to work on articles and pamphlets and to write letters to comrades, until the library closed.

Ulyanov spent most evenings at home, with only the occasional visit to the Café Adler or the Eintracht, a workmen's social club in the Neumarkt. In the past two weeks he had not travelled outside Zurich, and his only relaxation was to go for a walk on Thursday afternoons, when the library was closed.

The previous Thursday it had been snowing, and Spuhl had reported that Mrs. Ulyanov had looked ill. Even so, the Ulyanovs had walked along the lake as far as Wollishofen and had consumed two bars of nut chocolate, whose pale blue wrappers, dutifully collected by Sergeant Spuhl, showed that they had cost fifteen centimes each.

At the end of the Neumarkt, Ulyanov turned into the Spiegelgasse and began the long climb up the cobbled alley to number fourteen, where he shared a furnished room with his wife. Even from the Neumarkt, Hartmann could smell the sausage factory at the top of the hill. What the smell was like at number fourteen it was impossible to conceive.

"Two weeks," Sergeant Spuhl said, "and he's done the same thing every day. When do we stop watching him?"

"Next Wednesday," Hartmann promised.

The two men walked towards the Rindermarkt.

"Of all the Russian exiles in Zurich, why watch this one?" Spuhl asked.

"Because he is potentially the most dangerous man in the whole of Europe."

Spuhl stopped and looked from Hartmann back towards the Spiegelgasse. "Him?"

Hartmann nodded. Three weeks previously he had discovered amongst the possessions of a Russian exile illegally present in Zurich a lengthy work by Ulyanov entitled *What Is To Be Done?* Although the treatise was fifteen years old and dealt principally with a falling-out between Russian socialists, Hartmann had felt its contents were more dangerous than that. Ulyanov called for a world revolution to begin in an industrialised country in western Europe. In essence Ulyanov had written a manual for the violent seizure of power. Hartmann remembered that even though the work was fifteen years old, it had been one of the Russian immigrant's most valued possessions. And recently Ulyanov had been attempting to suborn members of Fritz Platten's Swiss Social Democrats. "Ideas cross mountains far easier than armies," Hartmann said. "Given the right opportunity, that man Ulyanov could change the world."

Sergeant Spuhl grinned. "If we let him," he said contemptuously.

Count Dimitri Kuryakin was a compact, savage-looking man, whose Tartar ancestry showed in his small, slanted eyes, waxlike slab of nose, and a long, drooping mandarin moustache. Though he was slightly under six feet tall, his heavily muscled shoulders and thick body made him look shorter. His bushy eyebrows, roughened skin, and greying fringe of thick, dark hair contrasted strongly with his formal clothes.

A former officer in the Preobrajensky, Kuryakin was a Knight of Saint George. The bleached gleam of the white cross on his lapel testified to the valour with which he had fought during the retreat from the head of the Yalu River to Mukden. That had been twelve years ago.

Count Dimitri Kuryakin was now Head of Section Four, the toughest and most ruthless branch of the Okhrana. Section Four's intelligence system and records were overwhelmingly accurate and their successes formidable. Almost entirely staffed by battle-hardened veterans of the Russo-Japanese War, their loyalty to Russia and each other was only exceeded by their loyalty to Kuryakin.

Now as he squatted on the satin-covered footstool beside the porcelain stove, Kuryakin fingered the Mauser that lay heavily in the pocket of his frock-coat. In five years the revolver had become as natural a part of his dress as his shirt and trousers. In those five years he had used the Mauser three times to gun down would-be assassins. The revolutionaries in Petrograd now believed that as long as Kuryakin carried the Mauser he could not be killed.

Ordinarily, because it was improper to bear arms in the royal presence, Kuryakin would have deposited the weapon with the venerable Count Fredericks, the Minister of the Imperial Household. But these were not ordinary times The Alexander Palace was a nest of intrigue, and there especially, because of his opposition to Rasputin, Kuryakin had enemies. Besides, he thought he might have another use for the weapon.

He stared round the tastefully furnished reception room panelled with oak and replete with three hundred years of Romanov history. On the dark walls were portraits of the Tsar's father, Alexander III, and Mueller-Norden's painting of the Tsarina as fiancée. There were two paintings by Borski of Peter the Great and a massive bust of Ivan. Before a pair of tall doors emblazoned with the golden double-eagle of the Romanovs stood a giant negro wearing a gold embroidered jacket and scarlet trousers.

As Kuryakin looked at him, the negro stiffened, the whites of his eyes showing as he grew tense listening intently to the sounds in the room behind him. Unobtrusively Kuryakin placed his hand on the outside of his coat pocket. Suddenly the negro relaxed, looked directly at Kuryakin, and nodded. Kuryakin got to his feet and snapped straight the cuffs of his jacket and the ends of his frock-coat. Then the negro bowed his silk-turbaned head and, pivoting sideways on gold-brocaded feet, extended a massive arm sideways and silently swung open the doors.

Through the open doorway Kuryakin glimpsed the bearded figure of the Tsar, standing before a desk of tooled leather, resting his weight lightly on flattened palms. He felt the Mauser tug at his coat as he went in.

"Dimitri Ivanovich," the Tsar said softly, "I have

been denied the pleasure of meeting you for too long." The Tsar spoke French perfectly, which was not surprising since French had been the official language of the court for many years. He waved Kuryakin to one of the plain leather chairs and, at the same time, took a cigarette from the box on his desk and lit it. "Do smoke if you want to."

Kuryakin sat down and, with his eyes fixed on the Tsar, took a cigarette from the box beside the chair.

"I bring the report of Minister of the Interior Protopopov," Kuryakin said in Russian. Despite his mixed ancestry, Kuryakin was passionately Russian and not wholly approving of the Western sophistication of Petrograd. "I am ordered to convey to Your Imperial Majesty the deepest apologies of Minister of the Interior Protopopov, who is afflicted with influenza." In fact the Minister was suffering from a recurrence of syphilis, which was now at an advanced stage and accompanied occasionally by paralysis of the spine.

"We trust he will soon be recovered." The Tsar sat down behind his desk.

The Tsar was ill. His face behind the heavy, grey-flecked beard looked wasted, the skin cracked and dry and covered with small wrinkles; those once deep-blue sailor's eyes were now nearly grey, and the whites were decidedly yellow.

Kuryakin unfolded Protopopov's report. Since the murder of Rasputin four weeks previously, the Tsar had abandoned his army command post at Mogilev and resumed residence at Tsarskoe Selo. Since then Protopopov, himself a Rasputin appointee, had instituted a routine of weekly audiences so that he could impress upon the Tsar the essential importance of his Ministry.

There were still bread queues in Petrograd, Kuryakin read, and political agitators were leaving the queues to raid food shops. Protopopov had instituted a survey on the food situation and now reported that there was at least four weeks' supply of bread in the city. He would issue a proclamation to that effect. There was no need for rationing.

Protopopov had also met with General Khabalov, the Military Commander of Petrograd. In the unlikely event that the agitation became serious, there were four companies, including the Don Cossacks, ready and willing to suppress the rising quickly.

Because of the requisitions of the War and Transport Ministries, there was a temporary shortage of the locomotives and cars necessary to move food into the cities. This matter was, however, being reviewed, and Protopopov expected to report more favourably next week.

Occasionally while he read, Kuryakin looked from the report to the khaki-clad figure of the Tsar. As was his custom, the Tsar was simply dressed, wearing the infantry uniform of the Preobrajensky, a loose-fitting khaki tunic which made his body look bigger than it really was, blue breeches, and long leather boots. The only badges of rank he wore were the red-and-gold striped Colonel's epaulettes, which had been awarded to him by his father, and, above his left breast-pocket, the white cross of the Order of Saint George. The Tsar was still the gentle, unpretentious man Kuryakin had known in the officers' mess at Krasnoe Selo. Except that now, in this third winter of the war, he looked desperately tired and defeated. There was a rigid, mechanical smile on his face and a disinterested, almost furtive expression in his eyes. Occasionally he looked at Kuryakin as if trying to remember where he was.

Kuryakin forced himself to concentrate on the report. That week Protopopov had ordered the arrest of the War Trade Committee. They had been spreading sedition amongst the troops, and, Protopopov implied, they had been connected in some way with War Minister Gutchov.

Even the threat to his beloved army brought no reaction from the Tsar. He stared vacantly at the table before him.

Kuryakin rapidly finished reading the report and looked up from the paper. "Minister of the Interior Protopopov also wishes to inform Your Imperial Majesty of his dream," Kuryakin said. Embarrassed, he stood up and attempted to hand the report to the Tsar.

Suddenly there was colour in the Tsar's face and a light of interest in his eyes. "Please read it." With hands that trembled, the Tsar took another cigarette from the box.

"Two nights ago Minister of the Interior Protopopov was visited by our friend," Kuryakin read. "Our friend says that in two months' time the crisis in Petrograd will be resolved."

"Two months," the Tsar repeated.

In two months it would be spring, and the better weather would ease the chaos in the Russian railway system.

"He forgives those who murdered him," Kuryakin continued.

"He was always a kind man."

"But his murderers must not be allowed to return to Petrograd. Their return will bring a great disaster upon the city." Kuryakin kept his eyes fixed firmly on the report. "There is also a message to Papa and Mama." Kuryakin was too embarrassed to look up at the Tsar and read quickly. "There is blood, rivers of blood. The Neva is thick with it. Papa must once again return to the front and take control of the offensive against the Germans. The Germans will fill the earth of Russia with blood. The war with Germany must be ended."

With averted eyes Kuryakin placed Protopopov's report on the Tsar's desk.

The Tsar sucked deeply at his cigarette. "Is that all? Did he not say anything more?"

"That's all," Kuryakin said. Holy Russia was now ruled by Rasputin's ghost.

An awkward silence enveloped the two men. Protocol forbade Kuryakin to leave until he was dismissed, and while the Tsar gazed broodingly at his desk, Kuryakin looked round the small study with its single window and its formally arranged chairs of plain leather. Near the window was a sofa covered with a Persian rug; beside it, a map table and a meticulously arranged bookshelf on which rested photographs of each member of the imperial family in Fabergé frames. On the Tsar's desk was a family photograph taken on holiday in the Crimea and, on the wall behind him, beside the row of ikons, photogravures of his parents.

The Tsar was essentially a family man. He was also deeply religious, and there was in him both a natural courtesy and a natural goodness. But at this point in Russia's history, Kuryakin knew that courtesy and goodness were not enough.

"I am perfectly well, Dimitri Ivanovich," the Tsar said suddenly. "I have not had much exercise recently. As you know, I am used to much activity. But I am perfectly all right." To demonstrate his well-being the Tsar leant forward and gave Kuryakin a haggard smile. "Tell me, Dimitri Ivanovich, what do you think of all this?"

'Kuryakin hesitated. Everyone who had spoken against the policies initiated by Rasputin and the Tsarina had been forced to resign. The Tsar was seeking not advice but reassurance. "I am only a humble policeman, sire," Kuryakin said.

"A policeman, yes," the Tsar said with a hint of laughter in his voice, "but humble, my dear fellow?—even as a subaltern in the Preobrajensky you were never that. I insist you tell me what you think of the situation in Petrograd."

It was as if they were brother officers in the mess at Krasnoe Selo and the Tsar merely the first amongst equals, but Kuryakin remembered the sad procession of good and honest men the Tsarina had driven out of office.

"I fear I would give offence," Kuryakin said.

"Since when have friends been capable of doing that?"

Did the Tsar mean that friends were incapable of giving offence or that they simply avoided giving offence? Kuryakin sighed. It was possibly the last time that anyone would be able to tell the Tsar the truth.

"The food shortage will get worse. I have no doubt of it."

"Why?"

The food shortage had to do with the war, the blockade, the uncommonly harsh winter, and transport. Because of the war fewer farm workers had to feed more people. Because of the blockade less food was being imported and cheap coal was no longer brought from Cardiff. The transport system had to cope with the movement of troops and munitions as well as food and coal from the Ukraine, and all this at a time when the number of available locomotives and freight cars had been halved. That morning Kuryakin had learned that because of the extreme cold and recent heavy snowfalls, the total number of locomotives made inoperative by burst boilers had increased to over a thousand, and that nearly eight hundred miles of railway track had been obliterated by snowdrifts.

The Tsar listened to Kuryakin's explanation with increasing impatience. He much preferred the soothing words of Protopopov.

"Sooner or later the food shortage will cause riots in Petrograd," Kuryakin continued. "And I do not share Minister Protopopov's confidence in the army."

"Every soldier has taken a personal oath of allegiance to me," the Tsar said. "For three hundred years the army has always supported the Emperor." He began to speak more quickly. "You should visit the front occasionally, Dimitri Ivanovich. You should relive the days of our youth and see for yourself the spirit of our soldiers. Why, just before I left Mogilev, the British Attaché said to me, 'Sire, I cannot help but admire the loyalty of your soldiers. They are ready to give their lives for one of your smiles.' "

The British Attaché may well have said that, Kuryakin reflected, but the army of 1917 was not the same army that had marched down the Nevsky with their dress uniforms in their kit bags ready for the victory parade down the Unter den Linden. In August 1914, Tannenberg alone had cost one hundred and ten thousand men. The end of that year had seen a quarter of the Russian Army—one million men—killed, wounded, or taken prisoner. The figure for 1915 was two million, three hundred and seventy-six thousand. And the 1916 campaign to take the pressure off Verdun had cost one million, two hundred thousand Russians.

Sadly, the best had gone in 1914. In the first five months of the war the Preobrajensky had lost forty-eight of its seventy officers. In the Russian army of 1917 there were few who remembered the old traditions and the old loyalties. But obviously these were not the things they talked about at Mogilev.

"And uprising will show which of us is right," Kuryakin said. "But by then it will be too late. The people have lost faith, sire."

The Tsar's voice became dangerously low. "Faith in what, Dimitri Ivanovich?"

"Faith in . . . your ministers, sire."

"I appoint the ministers the Duma wants."

That might have been what the Tsar believed, but everyone in Petrograd knew that the Tsar's ministers had been appointed by the Tsarina at Rasputin's behest.

Kuryakin said, "Before the Neva thaws there will be an uprising in Petrograd. It is likely that such an uprising will spread to the other cities of the empire. If Russia is to be saved, you must act now."

"Act now? What can I do now that I have not already done?"

"Give the Duma the constitution they seek," Kuryakin said urgently. "End the war with Germany. Prevent the Tsarina from involving herself in the affairs of state. We are at war with Germany, and popular indignation against Her Imperial Majesty is growing. She is German and people regard her—"

"I am aware that the Tsarina is a foreigner," the Tsar interrupted, "but I shall not abandon her. You must realise that she has no one to protect her but me, and these accusations are wicked, wicked and damnable. They are lies!"

Kuryakin sighed. The Tsar's concern with the slanders against his wife took precedence over the fate of Russia. A good family man, he thought bitterly.

"A constitution is a fundamental evil," the Tsar said. "A parliament cannot rule our heterogeneous empire. Russia needs strong and unified government; that is why I have sworn to uphold the tradition of autocracy."

The Tsar was repeating the stagnant theories of his tutor, Pobedonostsev. He was blind to the changes that were beginning to take place in the world outside Russia and believed that Russia would continue to be ruled as it had been for the past three hundred years by the twin orthodoxies of the monarchy and the church.

"There will be no end to the war with Germany until we have victory."

Kuryakin let his hand fall to the gun in his pocket. Only last week, at a lavish party at Palkin's Restaurant, Kuryakin had heard the Vladimirs, the Tsar's own cousins, planning to march on Tsarskoe Selo and seize him. But Russia needed more than the mere replacement of the Tsar by the Vladimirs; if *he* murdered the Tsar, the whole system would move to preserve the institution of monarchy. Russia needed vaster changes than that. He brought his hand up to his lapel and fingered the Cross of Saint George.

Suddenly the Tsar leaned forward and pressed his fingers to his temple. "I have such a headache," he said.

Kuryakin got to his feet and moved towards him.

"Please do not concern yourself. It is nothing. I need more exercise." The Tsar's gaze wandered disinterestedly around the room. "If what you said is true, my whole life has been a mistake."

"Mistakes have been made," Kuryakin said. "It is still not too late to remedy them."

The Tsar seemed not to have heard. He leant forward across the desk, his fingers kneading the skin of his forehead, his eyes screwed shut. He was no longer the Emperor, no longer the Autocrat of All the Russias. At that moment, the Tsar was simply a man whose spirit was breaking.

Suddenly he opened his eyes and took his hands away from his face. He looked at Kuryakin as if seeing him for the first time. Slowly recognition dawned and the Tsar got to his feet. "I am afraid I have wearied you," he said gently and walked to the window.

It was his usual way of indicating that an audience had ended.

QUADRIGA

In the Imperial German Foreign Ministry at 76 Wilhelmstrasse, Foreign Secretary Artur Zimmerman sat in a sumptuous office that had once been used by Bismarck, and looked thoughtfully from the red-bound dossier on his desk to the fat, bearded man seated opposite.

Despite his charm and persuasiveness, Dr. Alexander Israel Helphand was highly dangerous. Helphand was a socialist, a Russian immigrant, a Jew, who could most favourably be described as an ambiguous character. Yet he had come highly recommended and bearing a plan for forcing peace upon Russia.

A few days previously Zimmerman had met with the Kaiser at Pless Castle. Momentarily Zimmerman savoured again the pleasure of doors being flung open by heel-clicking officers, the brilliant glitter of uniforms, the flash of light on helmets, and the sonorous formality. Bethmann-Hollwegg, Lundendorff, Hindenberg, and the chiefs of the civil, military, and naval cabinets had also been there. At Pless they had decided to end the blockade by declaring unrestricted submarine warfare. Which meant that sooner rather than later, America would enter the war. But Zimmerman had been prepared for that. His strategy to keep

America out of the European war had already been implemented. In order to complement that strategy, he needed peace on the Eastern Front. Without American intervention and with peace on the Eastern Front, the German forces could smash through the Entente defences in a giant *blitzkrieg* that would ensure victory. And the reward for the architect of such a victory was enormous.

Chancellor Bethmann-Hollwegg, who for two years had opposed unrestricted submarine warfare, would have to be removed from office. The men of Blood and Iron would rule a Germany that would stretch from the outskirts of St. Petersburg to Biarritz, and he, Artur Zimmerman, would be chancellor of that Germany.

Before that could happen, however, Dr. Helphand's plan would have to be evaluated. But by whom?

The Under-Secretary's Committee, with their rigid code of professional diplomacy, would reject Helphand's intrigue with a barked *ausgeschlossen*. Colonel Nikolai's Section IIIb was staffed by professional soldiers who subscribed to a belief that wars were won on battlefields. The only organisation that would evaluate and support Helphand's plan was the Foreign Office's own intelligence service, the Imperial Intelligence Bureau East.

Zimmerman looked across his desk at the bloated figure sunk into the armchair. "I would like you to wait a few minutes and then repeat everything you have told me to our Political Section," he said.

Helphand looked at Zimmerman cautiously. "I have no objection to that provided the person I talk to has an intimate knowledge of Russia."

Zimmerman smiled underneath his luxuriant moustache. "You will talk to Dr. Caspar Ehrler. He has lived in Russia, and I believe he is something of a socialist."

Helphand settled back in his chair. "I know of Ehrler," he said "I am sure we can work together."

In the gloomy old Gotard building on the Jagerstrasse which housed the Political Section of the Imperial Intelligence Bureau East, Caspar Ehrler replaced the telephone on its cradle and frowned thoughtfully at the peeling grey wallpaper in his office. Longstanding Foreign Office practice decreed that all contacts between the Intelligence Bureau and the Foreign Office were made through the Head of the Political Section, Ulrich von Ketteler. As a career civil servant, Zimmerman's private secretary, von Futran, was surely aware of proper procedures. Yet he had insisted that Caspar come to the Foreign Office alone. Von Futran had also demanded that Caspar come immediately.

If only von Ketteler knew . . . , Caspar smiled wryly. Still, if the Foreign Minister himself chose to ignore Foreign Office procedure, it was not up to a mere *nachrichtenoffizier* to correct him. Shrugging his shoulders Caspar shuffled the radio intercepts he'd been working on into a neat pile, put on his overcoat and hat and set out to walk to the Wilhelmstrasse, fifteen minutes away.

Caspar Ehrler was a short, stocky, fresh-complexioned young man. He had a strong, squarish face with a snub nose, deep-set dark eyes, and high cheekbones which sometimes made him appear more Slavic than Aryan, a characteristic he cheerfully attributed to the wanderings of his Hanseatic ancestors. Caspar worried about his prematurely receding widow's peak and thinning red hair, which made him look older than twenty-five, and he occasionally attempted to grow a moustache to draw attention from the increasing width of his forehead. Fortunately, this was not one of those times.

Caspar had acquired his fluency in Russian in childhood. Between the ages of nine and fourteen he had attended school in St. Petersburg, where his father had managed the merchant bank of Hofer. On the family's return to Germany Caspar had been sent to the exclusive gymnasium at Cassel, which had included the Kaiser among its list of distinguished pupils. At seventeen he passed his *Abiturienten-Examen* with distinctions in Russian, French, and History and went on to Berlin University to read Political Science, Russian, and Modern History.

His doctoral thesis, *Capitalist Structures within a Socialist Framework,* had achieved a brief academic notoriety in that last summer of peace, and Caspar was saved from having to choose between an academic career, the Foreign Office, and Hofer & Co. by being called up for military service.

In those first weeks of the war Caspar had been part of Mackensen's XVII Corps which had been repulsed by Rennenkampf's First Army at the Gumbinnen railhead in East Prussia. During the fighting Caspar's retreating platoon had been cut off and surrounded by Russian troops. Changing into the uniform of a dead Russian officer, Caspar had made his platoon surrender to him and then paraded them back to safety through the Russian lines.

That exploit had earned him an Iron Cross, Third Class, and made his superiors aware of his academic qualifications and fluency in Russian. After Tannenberg Caspar had been transferred first to Military

Intelligence and then, as the Russian military threat dwindled, to the Imperial Intelligence Bureau East.

At the Foreign Office he was hurried from the spacious entrance hall into a private elevator and then conducted by the urbane, frock-coated von Futran to a conference room on the second floor.

The room was small, filled with a green baize-covered table and upright chairs, a large painting by Franz Kruger on one wall and a photograph of the Kaiser on a low sideboard. Through the tall windows there was a view of the ordered Foreign Office gardens, which seemed to stretch almost to the Tiergarten.

"His Excellency will see you shortly," von Futran announced. "Meanwhile, he would be grateful if you would deal with this." From inside the immaculately tailored frock-coat von Futran drew out a heavy linen envelope embossed with the personal seal of the Foreign Secretary. Extending it between two elegant fingers, he gave it to Caspar. "With His Excellency's compliments," von Futran said, and noiselessly left.

Caspar ripped open the envelope.

Dr. Alexander Helphand has been warmly recommended to me by Count Brockdorff-Rantzau. I have had very interesting discussions with Dr. Helphand, who has outlined to me a strategy for bringing peace on the Eastern Front. Please evaluate this carefully and report to me in person before you leave here. Zimmerman.

Caspar sat down and rested his palms on the green baize. Helphand was an intrigant, a member of the German Social Democrats, to whom he had been a frequent cause of embarrassment; the source of his fortune had given rise to rumour and conjecture. During the 1905 uprising in St. Petersburg he had, together with Rakovsky and Trotsky, led the Soviet. As a boy in St. Petersburg Caspar had seen Helphand led to the Nicholas Station to begin his exile in Siberia. Handcuffed to a soldier, Helphand had walked at the end of the long, shambling line of prisoners, a burly, heavily bearded figure incongruously dressed in a lounge suit and cloth cap, carrying a bundle over his shoulder. At the time Caspar had been struck by the hopelessness of his expression, especially when constrasted with the demeanour of Rakovsky who had marched wearing his prison tunic as if it were a uniform and, despite the handcuffs and the guards, managed to wave defiantly to the crowd.

Helphand had escaped from exile and returned to Germany where he had involved himself with the German Socialists. Working successively and sometimes simultaneously as a journalist, publisher, author, and pamphleteer, he had risen high in the socialist movement before finally being banished from Prussia. Sometime around 1910 Helphand had gone to Turkey, and later returned a millionaire. Now, in addition to his journalistic and publishing activities, he was director of an impressive list of companies in Germany, Sweden, Denmark, Bulgaria, and Turkey. He owned an Adler limousine, a house in Charlottenberg, and maintained a permanent suite at the Kaiserhof. The previous January he had been granted Prussian citizenship.

Caspar remembered that two years ago Helphand had involved the foreign Office in a grandiose scheme to paralyse Russia with a series of strikes. There were rumours that most of the two million marks the Foreign Office had contributed toward that venture had remained in Helphand's pockets. Any plan proposed by Helphand, Caspar decided, would have to be evaluated very carefully.

With a discreet knock on the door, von Futran entered. "Dr. Alexander Helphand," he announced, and stood aside to allow a stubby, bullnecked, bearded figure in a frock-coat and vivid choker to enter the room.

Since Caspar had last seen him, Helphand had grown grotesquely fat, his body almost too cumbersome for his short legs. He seemed to be pedalling furiously across the room, his pudgy hands glittering with rings and pumping like pistons as he struggled to keep his immense bulk upright over his tiny, pattering feet. "Pleased to meet you, pleased to meet you," he carolled, before finally stopping, sweating lightly and grasping the back of a chair.

Bustling, obese, overdressed, Helphand reminded Caspar of a performer in one of those shabby caberets behind the Kufurstendamm. He seemed more likely to tell a joke and draw a string of coloured handkerchiefs from his mouth than secure peace between Germany and Russia.

Helphand repeated, "Very pleased to meet you, sir." Sighing audibly, he drew the chair away from the table and sat down.

"I have been asked to evaluate your plan for bringing peace to the Eastern Front," Caspar said.

Helphand took out a leather case and carefully selected a long, thick cigar. Over the flame of the match his eyes caught Caspar's. "I read your doctoral thesis with considerable interest. It would seem we have fundamentally similar political attitudes."

Caspar stared down at the table. "I believe Foreign Secretary Zimmerman is anxious to have our discussions completed today."

"Yes. Oh, yes. You're quite right." Helphand drew deeply at his cigar. "As an expert in Russian affairs you obviously know that there is little food or fuel in the cities of Russia. You know that the people are on the verge of starvation and that they are desperate and seek to end their suffering. You are aware that Russia is ready for revolution."

Accurate information from inside Russia was hard to come by. But from his work with the radio intercepts, Caspar knew that the Russian Army was hopelessly disorganised. This had to be a reflection of the situation inside Russia.

Helphand thrust his heavy body across the table. "We must use that revolution to bring peace. That sounds crazy, doesn't it? A revolution to bring peace? But I tell you, Dr. Ehrler, the only way Russia can be eliminated from this war is by internal conquest. Even Napolean was halted before Moscow."

Helphand's plan was a repetition of 1915 but more carefully thought out and on a much larger scale. In four days Helphand was leaving for Zurich, where he would arrange a conference of all the Russian political exiles, who would be asked to pledge their authority and the co-operation of their supporters inside Russia to bring about a revolution.

The revolution itself would be started by groups of agitators whom Helphand was training in institutes in Stockholm and Zurich. These agitators would be assigned to St. Petersburg, where they would bring out the Baltic, Putilov, and Obnuhov factories on strike.

At the same time, with the support of the exiles, Helphand would stop the railways and isolate St. Petersburg and Moscow from each other and from the front. Supplies of arms and munitions would be halted, and food would remain in storehouses and at railway sidings. Inevitably this would increase the choas within the cities and lead to further industrial strife.

Then Helphand would bring out the ethnic minorities of Russia. The leaders of the Ukrainian peasantry, the Spilka, were in Zurich, and Helphand had already obtained guarantees of support from representatives of the Latvian, Estonian, Lithuanian, Polish, and Finnish independence movements.

Helphand had no doubt that once the ethnic minorities joined the revolution, Siberia, with its controlling army moved to the front and already exposed to the liberal ideas of political exiles, would support the revolution.

And then, Helphand announced with a flourish, the army would come out.

Caspar remembered how in 1905 the Cossacks had lashed the mobs of St. Petersburg into submission. "The Russian Army will never support a revolution," he said.

"You do not yet know enough about Russia, young man." Helphand chuckled to take away the sting of his remark. "The army is demoralised and disillusioned. It would desert or fight its superiors than its own people. I have seen letters sent to Rakovsky by certain influential officers confirming this."

"I'd like to see the letters," Caspar said, but Helphand was off again.

The effect of this widespread unrest, Helphand continued, would leave the Tsarist government with only two choices: indulgence, which would encourage the revolution, or repression, which would increase the bitterness of the people and compel them to support the revolutionaries; which would force the government to withdraw troops from the front, leaving Russia open to German conquest.

"Whatever they do," Helphand said triumphantly, "they lose." He looked at Caspar for confirmation.

Helphand's enthusiasm was contagious. Caspar had no doubt that if everything went according to plan, the Tsarist government would be overthrown and somehow there would be peace in the East. He forced himself to think analytically.

"The success of your plan depends on the co-operation of the revolutionary exiles," Caspar said.

Helphand smiled and shook his head. "Without the co-operation of the revolutionary exiles, success merely becomes more difficult. Once my people have started the revolution, the exiles have no choice but to support it—if they want to take part in the government of the new Russia."

"How much do the exiles know of your plans?"

"Very little, yet. But I am assured of support from the most important faction. Rakovsky, who worked with me on the Petrograd Soviet, is certain."

"Will the Mensheviks support you?" Caspar asked.

"I've always had a good relationship with Uritsky, Martov, Dan, and Plekhanov. The Mensheviks have always been susceptible to reason. I feel sure they will join us. As for the others, the Jewish Bund, the Social Revolutionaries—" Helphand shrugged. "I am hopeful."

"What about Ulyanov?" Caspar asked. He felt Helphand's whole attention focus on him, his eyes in their little pouches of fat growing passionless and immobile.

"Ulyanov is not important," Helphand rumbled.

"Without a revolutionary theory, there cannot be a revolutionary movement," Caspar said, quoting Ulyanov. "I believe Ulyanov is extremely important. He will give your uprising the moral and philosophical stature it needs to make it a proper and permanent revolution. He will turn your revolution into something big and good and wonderful that will mean much more than the mere disposal of the Tsar. He will use your revolution to build a new and inspiring world." Caspar became aware of Helphand's staring at him curiously. "Apart from that, Ulyanov and his Bolsheviks are the only people who are determined enough and dedicated enough; through Vikzhel, Ulyanov controls the All-Russian Committee of the Union of Railway Employees. Ulyanov is the only one who can bring the railways around Petrograd to a halt."

"Ulyanov will join us," Helphand said. "I have known Ulyanov for many years. Once he and Nadya lived with me in Munich, and even now I help him with money and communications with Petrograd."

Caspar smiled approvingly. "How much is all this going to cost?"

"One hundred and twenty million gold marks," Helphand said.

"One hundred and twenty mill—"

"I have left the details with Foreign Secretary Zimmerman."

"But that is half the cost of building our submarine fleet!"

"Or the cost to Germany of two days' war." Helphand drew deeply at his cigar before stubbing it out. "Young man, you are buying peace at bargain prices. Take care, the offer may never be repeated."

"It's still a lot of money," Caspar said. "Why do you need so much?"

Forty-five million marks were needed to buy arms and explosives for the agitators, to pay for their transport into Russia, to finance the conference of exiles, to acquire newspapers and establish a propaganda machine, to support the various revolutionary factions that would join the uprising, and to reimburse Helphand for expenditures he had already incurred on his institutes in Stockholm and Zurich.

A further forty million marks was to be spent on strike pay and raising a People's Militia to resist the Tsarist forces.

"The remaining thirty-five million," Helphand said, "is to ensure that Rakovsky's Social Patriots become the new government of Russia."

"Why them?" Caspar asked.

"Because Rakovsky is the only revolutionary leader with the vision and tolerance necessary to rule Russia after the revolution. Because, from the German point of view, Rakovsky is the only revolutionary who stands unconditionally for an end to the war."

But with Rakovsky, Caspar thought hopelessly, the revolution would end in Russia. A government led by Rakovsky would be hopelessly bourgeois, liberal, and privileged. It would do nothing for the Russian peasants or the Russian workers. It would not change the world.

"Rakovsky might make peace," Caspar said, "but he could never preserve it. In order for there to be an enduring peace, there must first be an end to the exploitation of the proletariat."

"I agree completely," Helphand said softly. "But to end the class struggle will take many years. The formation of the Rakovsky government is only the first step. It will bring peace between Germany and Russia and allow you and others like you to devote your energies to making social changes in your own countries. Peace is what we all need now, before the Entente and their American allies tear Germany apart."

"You're quite right," Caspar said, getting to his feet. "I will consider everything you have said most carefully and then make my report to Foreign Secretary Zimmerman."

Helphand struggled to his feet and stood leaning against the table. "This is probably the most important decision you will make in your life," he said. "Please be very careful." He extended a beringed hand to be shaken. "His Excellency the Foreign Secretary knows where to find me if I can be of any further use."

Immediately after Helphand left, von Futran came into the room with the dossier Helphand had left with Zimmerman. Caspar was mildly astonished to see that the dossier had already been indexed, referenced, classified Top Secret, and code-named Quadriga. Zimmerman, for one, seemed certain that the operation would proceed.

The dossier repeated all Helphand's arguments with more detail and a greater persuasiveness. Caspar studied it carefully for over an hour and, by the time he'd finished, he felt the plan could work.

The only problem was whether Helphand could be trusted with one hundred and twenty million marks.

"My predecessor, von Jagow, also distrusted Helphand," Zimmerman said.

Caspar was seated across the leather-topped mahogany desk in Zimmerman's office, a magnificent room on the third floor with wainscoting and a beamed ceiling, a large portrait of the Kaiser, and paintings by Cranach and Mathias Weyer. At one end of the room, surrounded by low sofas and armchairs of soft leather, was an ornate fireplace adorned with the Hohenzollern coat of arms.

Caspar had just told Zimmerman how Helphand, who'd once been Maxim Gorky's literary agent, had not paid Gorky a pfennig in royalties for his play *Lower Depths*, which had run for over five hundred performances in Berlin alone and for four years throughout Germany. The German Social Democrats had investigated Gorky's complaint and found Helphand negligent, evasive, and financially untrustworthy.

"Circumstances," Zimmerman rumbled, "compel us to look afresh at the man and his situation."

Zimmerman was a ruddy, sandy-haired man of fifty-eight, with bulbous blue eyes and a bushy moustache. With his veined nose, big, red hands and a gold watch chain spread across his ample paunch, he reminded Caspar of a provincial mayor.

"That Gorky story has been around for years," Zimmerman continued. "Helphand tells me he has offered to pay Gorky whatever the disputed sum is, but Gorky prefers to refuse the money and slander him. In any case Helphand will not recieve any money until *you* are certain that his plan will work. I want you to go to Zurich with Helphand and confirm that he has adequate support from the exiles. If he has adequate support, I want you to remain in Zurich until the conference. I want you to run Quadriga and report directly to me."

Caspar felt his mouth dropping open in surprise and quickly shut it. He felt a spasm of excitement twist his stomach. Zimmerman was giving him a great opportunity, not only to bring peace to the Eastern Front and achieve a German victory but to create a true and just socialist state.

However, Zimmerman had not yet heard his other objections. Zimmerman was a cautious man, a non-von who had reached the highest position in the Foreign Service through diligence, industriousness, and a gregarious affability. Four years ago he had allowed Gottlieb von Jagow to become Foreign Secretary, because Germany had then been on the brink of war and the Kaiser's tempestuous interference in foreign affairs had made the job of Foreign Secretary untenable. Now, only three months after his appointment, Zimmerman was thrusting himself at the Helphand plan with the recklessness of a compulsive gambler.

"Where do we find the money?" Caspar asked.

"It is there, in the so called Reptile Fund in Zurich." The Reptile Fund went back to the beginnings of the Intelligence Service, unvouchered funds whose expenditure was not subject to query or audit. "You will ensure that as little as possible sticks in Helphand's pockets."

"That would not be easy, Excellency. Arms smugglers do not give receipts."

"I said as little as possible," Zimmerman snapped. "I am aware of the problems. The important thing is to get peace in the East. If Helphand is going to make thirty million out of it, so be it."

Caspar said, "There is another point I would like to make, Excellency. Helphand feels that this revolution should be led by Rakovsky. The Russian Socialists have always followed intellectuals. Rakovsky is a former army officer whose entire political philosophy is a reaction against the military administration that allowed his entire company to be slaughtered at Nanshan. The others will not follow him."

"According to Helphand, the army will support Rakovsky."

"He will get some support from the army, Excellency. But the revolutionaries will only follow someone like Ulyanov. If the peace we achieve is to be permanent, then it is essential that we spend our money on supporting a proper revolutionary government, not Rakovsky."

"After we have secured peace in the East," Zimmerman rumbled, "and after we have won in the West, I do not care a damn who rules Russia. The important thing, Ehrler, is peace now. And I want you to understand this very clearly. Your mission is limited to securing that peace by whatever means possible. You will not be concerned with what happens in Russia afterwards. That is a direct order."

Caspar looked away from Zimmerman's flushed face to the deep pile of the carpet between his feet. "Yes, Excellency."

Zimmerman's tone became softer. "Now let us make arrangements for the money."

He pressed a buzzer on his desk and, to Caspar's surprise, von Futran led in Ulrich von Ketteler. Ulrich von Ketteler was an erect, bristle-headed, monocled Junker, whose cheek was livid with a duelling scar won at Bonn University. A former cavalry officer, von Ketteler had been appointed Head of Imperial Intelligence Bureau East, because he'd been the only Junker available and because someone had wrongly assumed that since von Ketteler's family estates were in the easternmost part of Prussia, he knew how to deal with Russians.

Von Ketteler glared angrily at Caspar and, giving Zimmerman a brief nod, sat down.

"Dr. Ehrler has just given his approval to a plan for bringing peace with Russia," Zimmerman said, smoothly. "We will need to utilize the Reptile Fund."

Von Ketteler stared angrily from Zimmerman to Caspar and back again. "How much of the fund does Your Excellency require?"

"All of it," Zimmerman said, and pushed some papers across the desk towards Ulrich. "Please sign these authorisations. I already have."

Von Ketteler took the papers and read them, fountain pen poised. "Who will be responsible for the monies?"

"Dr. Ehrler. He will report directly to me. Also, will you please make arrangements to have Dr. Ehrler relieved of all duties. He is being sent to Zurich on a mission for me."

Von Ketteler paused in his signing. The scar on his cheek grew red, and he fixed Zimmerman with a cold, basilisk, Junker glare. "Your Excellency, I protest."

"Your protest is noted," Zimmerman said, equably.

Caspar, peering over von Ketteler's shoulder, saw that he was about to sign a document authorising the bank in Zurich to immediately exchange the entire sum of gold and marks for roubles. He coughed and said, "Excellency."

"Yes, Ehrler."

"One hundred and twenty million marks is more than the total note issue of Switzerland. If the bank complies with that instruction, there will be an enormous fall in the value of the mark."

Zimmerman looked at Caspar thoughtfully, then he smiled. "I forgot, you come from a family of bankers. Perhaps we will sell half now and the rest later. You can make the detailed arrangements in Zurich."

"Even the sale of sixty million will cause the mark to drop," Caspar said.

"That cannot be helped," Zimmerman snapped, and

Munster Kirche and the town hall, through narrow side streets with medieval-looking shops, to the broad swathe of Zurich's main thoroughfare with its crowds and clanking trams. It was a pleasant afternoon, overcast but dry, the air, even in the middle of the city, exhilaratingly fresh. At the door of the Cantonal Credit Anstalt, he stubbed his cigar in the thoughtfully provided ashtray and asked to see Dr. Rasch.

Ten minutes later Dr. Rasch emerged and ushered Maugham into a private conference room. "I am sorry I have kept you waiting. If you had phoned. . . ."

"No matter. No matter. I was just walking by and saw something in your window that made me curious. The doctor tells me that a walk after lunch"—Maugham coughed noisily—"might do some good."

Dr. Rasch winced in sympathy. This war would leave only the maimed. Apart from the cough, the British agent had a strange, waxlike pallor.

Maugham lit an Army Club cigarette. "I was hoping you would allay my curiosity. I was looking at the blackboards in your window, with the chalked prices of foreign currencies. Are you aware, Dr. Rasch, that the mark has fallen a whole two points and, even more extraordinary, that the rouble has risen?"

Dr. Rasch kept a vacuous expression on his face and began to think very quickly. Exchange rates were hardly a matter in which the British agent had previously expressed interest. Rasch quickly calculated the niceties of banking ethics against the value of an account just slightly in excess of three million sterling.

"There is usually only one reason for a currency showing a marked fall, while another increases—especially if both currencies are, shall we say, weak. If you were to ask me to make an informed guess, I'd say that somebody was selling marks and buying roubles."

"Yes," Maugham said, "I thought it might be something like that. Who?"

Once again Dr. Rasch made a rapid mental review of banking ethics. "I can find out for you in a few minutes," he said. He left the room and made a couple of quick telephone calls. The British agent did not appear to notice that the currency had hardened, or that he, Dr. Rasch, was divesting himself of nearly a quarter of a million marks. He returned to the conference room, rubbing his hands. "There appears to be one large seller," he said. "The Handel Credit Bank."

"How very interesting. Tell me, Dr. Rasch, how many marks would they have to sell to bring the price down by two points?"

"Oh, that's difficult to say precisely. But if you were to ask me to make an informed guess, I would say about seventy-five million."

Over three million pounds, Maugham thought. Half the German Reptile Fund. Most interesting. He thanked Rasch profusely and walked to the Central Post Office on Stadthaus Quai, where he sent a coded cable to Wetherby.

Opinion here is that Germans are liquidating Reptile Fund in preparation for massive operation against Russia. Believe this to be connected with arrival in Zurich today of German agent Helphand. Under these conditions request restrictions against overt action in Switzerland be immediately lifted.

An hour later Maugham was seated in the starky furnished Hohnerstrasse office of Commissioner Hartmann, with his hands resting lightly on the knob of his gold-topped cane, and saying, "I wondered if you knew that Helphand, the German agent, is arriving in Zurich today."

Hartmann, heavily built and cautious eyed, considered his reply carefully. "I am aware of it," he said. "In fact if Helphand did *not* advertise his arrival, I would be concerned."

Maugham supposed that if, like Helphand, one happened to be Russian, Jewish, and also Prussian, one could not quite avoid exhibitionism. "I was wondering if you knew what brings him to Zurich at this time of the year?"

"It could be for his health," Hartmann said. Maugham, whose slender fingers were khaki with nicotine, had frequently implied that his chronic smoker's cough was really the aftermath of tuberculosis and that he lived in Switzerland because of its salubrious climate. "However, Helphand's visa application states that it is for business."

"I see," Maugham said. "Pharmaceuticals, I suppose."

"We Swiss also make excellent watches," Hartmann said.

Maugham cleared his throat. "I understand Helphand is being accompanied by a German assistant." Maugham smiled. "You will, of course, be keeping both of them under some kind of surveillance?"

"If I were doing so, I would not discuss it with you," Hartmann grunted. He hadn't known about Helphand's assistant, and it was unusual for Maugham to refer so overtly to his real occupation. "Why do you want to know if we will be watching Helphand?"

"Because we thought we'd keep a friendly eye on him, old boy, and we wouldn't want our people falling over yours."

Hartmann breathed out slowly. Maugham was asking for clearance to tail Helphand. There could be some advantage in that. "I cannot stop your people sitting around in hotel lobbies or catching your deaths of cold in unheated doorways," Hartmann said. He would have said the same thing to Helphand, had he wanted to tail Maugham.

Maugham's fingers slid down the cane with relief. Hartmann wasn't going to interfere as long as his people behaved themselves. "Tell you what, old boy, if we find out anything, we'll let you know."

"And if we find out anything," Hartmann said, "we will keep it to ourselves."

Maugham smiled, coughed once, and got to his feet. "Ta ta, old boy. I'll keep in touch."

"*Wiedersehn,*" Hartmann said and, watching Maugham limp out of the room, smiled. As everyone in Zurich knew by now, Maugham's two most vivid recollections of the summer of 1914 were the sight of Jack Hobbs getting 266 at the Oval and the sensation of Boche shrapnel lacerating his thigh.

Late that afternoon Caspar and Helphand arrived in Zurich and went straight to the Handel Bank. Their journey had taken two days, and Helphand—or Parvus, the little one, as he preferred to be called—had proved to be an absorbing, if tireless, travelling companion.

As they drove along the restrained sufficiency of the Bahnhofstrasse, Caspar peered inquisitively through the fading winter light at the discreetly lit shop windows with their displays of embroidered cotton, silks, men's suits, watches, jewellery, and furs. They had many things there that were not available in Germany: gramophones, sewing machines, perfume, Kodaks, and, most of all, food. Despite feeling slightly liverish from the vast meals Parvus had arranged on the train, Caspar gazed wide-eyed at the meats and cheeses and fruit, at coffee and soap, and at a wondrous array of cakes and chocolates and glazed cherries in Meyer's Confiserie.

At the bank an earnest-looking manager greeted them effusively. Over strong, black, nonersatz coffee, letters of authority were presented, mandates altered, and instructions given for the preparation of sight drafts and for the sale of gold and marks to continue at a diminished pace.

On the way to the Baur Au Lac, where it had been decided that Caspar would stay until Parvus had left for Stockholm, Parvus said, "You handled that very well. If I might say so, you have a natural flair for business. You should consider working for me."

Staring out of the cab window at the dull sheen of the lake, Caspar thought there was no likelihood of that. He was engaged to Helga Hofer, the pretty, blonde, vivacious daughter of Manfred Hofer, whose family owned Hofer & Co. The match was exactly what both families wanted, and as soon as the war ended Caspar would marry Helga and become a junior partner in the bank. It was a future he looked forward to with a certain detachment.

"There is still a war on," Caspar said to Parvus, "and I am still a soldier."

Parvus laughed. "The war will be over in weeks. I'll wait."

They turned onto a long drive that led them past bare, wintry gardens to the hotel entrance. A flurry of uniformed porters descended on the cab and scurried away with their luggage. As they crossed the spacious lobby, Parvus said, "Let's have dinner tonight. There are some people I want you to meet. Come to my suite at eight."

Caspar felt his stomach heave at the thought of yet another of Parvus' gargantuan meals. Yet he gave Parvus a sickly smile of agreement.

At seven o'clock that evening Caspar went downstairs to the Alcove Bar, carrying the briefcase. As he pushed through the swing doors, he felt himself being scrutinised. There was an attractive girl seated alone at the bar counter, a man four stools down from her staring sadly into the mirror behind the rows of bottles, a group of men talking animatedly together and, in one of the upholstered chairs against the wall, a big, square-headed man, nursing a gin-and-tonic and reading a newspaper.

Caspar sat at a secluded table and ordered a beer. The Bureau had been reluctant to have him cross borders carrying the Quadriga dossier and had sent it to Zurich by diplomatic courier. They had also arranged that his Section IIIb contact would deliver the dossier to him in the bar, in a briefcase identical to Caspar's own. That hadn't been such a good idea, Caspar felt. Everyone in the bar must know what he had come to do. He felt exposed, guilty, and quite ridiculous.

The girl at the counter was tall and slender, with an assured, withdrawn look that Caspar found attractive. He could see her long legs from ankle to knee, shapely in their high-heeled patent leather shoes. The girl caught him staring at her legs and smiled. Caspar looked away blushing, his mouth drying despite the beer, his heart thumping with irresolution.

He stared steadily at his beer for a while, feeling the condensation mingle with the sweat in his palms. The girl had finished her drink and was expecting him to buy her another. All he had to do was walk over and ask her what she wanted. His breath caught at the thought and he sneeked a glance at that serene, controlled face. He wondered what it would be like to go to bed with a woman like that. It would be an experience . . . and he needed experience.

A belligerent, grey-suited man sat noisily opposite him and thrust a briefcase identical to Caspar's on the floor. "Dr. Ehrler?" he asked accusingly.

Caspar nodded.

"Emil von Dichter."

Emil von Dichter was in his mid-forties, a bustling man with reddened, bulbous eyes and thin moustaches that were oiled and twisted and protruded across his narrow cheeks like strands of firmly rolled wire. Emil von Dichter was the controller of Section IIIb's network in Zurich. He ordered a schnapps and turned back to Caspar. "I came myself because I wanted to find out what kind of an operation you people are running in Zurich."

Caspar looked down at his beer. Quadriga was an Intelligence Bureau matter, at least until it became necessary to involve Section IIIb.

"I see," von Dichter snapped, managing to drop his voice two octaves. "It's your piddling little operation, is it? Well, let me tell you something, boy. You'll get no co-operation from us. And without co-operation from us, you will fail."

"The matter has been cleared between Foreign Secretary Zimmerman and Colonel Nikolai," Caspar said.

Von Dichter tossed back his schnapps and grunted. "Where did they find you?" he asked.

"On the Russian Front," Caspar said.

"And they sent you to Zurich to exchange marks for roubles. Don't look so surprised. That's public knowledge now. Everyone knows that you people are mounting an operation in Russia. What is your involvement with Helphand?"

"I'm unable to tell you," Caspar said.

"You're trying to come to some arrangement with the socialist exiles, aren't you?"

Caspar stared at him blankly.

"You don't want to involve yourself with those damned socialists," von Dichter said. "Today they want to overthrow the Romanovs and tomorrow it's the Hohenzollerns. I tell you, it's madness."

"I'm under orders," Caspar said.

Von Dichter stared at him. "No good will come of this," he warned. "What assistance do you need?"

"I'll need communication facilities and, in a day or so, a discreet and anonymous hotel."

"If you're looking for discretion and anonymity, boy, you won't find it in an hotel. What you need is an apartment."

Section IIIb had an apartment in the characterless industrial area northeast of the station. It was far enough from what von Dichter termed the fleshpots of the Bahnhofstrasse and separated by both the rivers Limat and Sihl from the university area where most of the revolutionaries lived. He arranged to send the keys round and for the receipt and dispatch of coded cables to Zimmerman; then, snorting angrily, he picked up Caspar's briefcase and left.

From behind his newspaper in the Alcove Bar, Hartmann saw von Dichter pick up the wrong briefcase and go. Standard German procedure for delivery of documents, he reflected, had been for years and wouldn't change until he decided to catch someone in the act. He eyed Helphand's assistant. Young and obviously unused to this type of work. Hartmann climbed to his feet and lumbered across the bar to where Caspar was still staring at his beer.

"Commissioner Hartmann, Foreign Police," Hartmann said, and sat down heavily. Most visitors thought the Foreign Police were the same thing as the Tourist Police. This young man obviously didn't. He had gone pale.

"Passport, please." Hartmann held out a hand like a sideplate of meat topped with bananas.

Caspar gave him his passport.

Hartmann breathed heavily over it and with a heavy twisting movement brought out a notebook and began to write. When he finished, he placed the passport on the table between them. "What are you doing in Zurich?"

Hartmann had a square, no-nonsense face, a square, no-nonsense head, and he was looking at Caspar with very square, very no-nonsense eyes.

"Tourist," Caspar said. That was one of the cover stories they'd selected in Berlin.

Hartmann heaved a patient sigh. "With a war on, a young man like you should be fighting, not touring." The massive hand shot out. "Military papers."

Fortunately the Jagerstrasse had provided for that eventuality. Caspar gave him the papers.

Hartmann breathed at them. "Discharged," he muttered and looked at Caspar suspiciously. "But you are young and well. . . ."

"And shell shocked," Caspar finished.

"You are travelling with Dr. Helphand?"

Caspar nodded.

"What business do you have with Dr. Helphand?"

"Family business. I am connected with Hofer & Co."

"And you also have business with the Handel Bank?"

Caspar nodded again.

"What business do you have with the bank?"

"Why don't you ask the bank?"

Hartmann's expression grew stony. Where Swiss banks were concerned, even Commissioners of the Foreign Police had to tread softly. "You are concerned with Dr. Helphand's Swiss companies?"

Caspar didn't know that Helphand had any Swiss companies. "No. Not exactly."

Hartmann allowed himself to look disappointed. "So you are not concerned with buying Swiss pharmaceuticals?"

"No. Not exactly."

"And yet you are in Switzerland on Dr. Helphand's business." Hartmann went silent.

Caspar, feeling trapped and a lot less fluent, went silent, too. Hartmann lit a cigar. Caspar fiddled with his hat. The silence became uneasy, then embarrassing. Finally Hartmann asked, "How long are you staying in Switzerland?"

"I plan to stay for four weeks."

"If," Hartmann said, "we let you." He rose slowly to his feet, giving Caspar plenty of time for that to sink in. "Now, let me give you a formal warning. Switzerland is a hospitable country. It is also a neutral country. Anyone breaching that neutrality will have to serve a few years in a Swiss prison before being deported." He turned and, for such a big man, walked very quickly to the door. "I shall," he promised, "be watching you."

* * *

After locking the dossier away in the hotel safe Caspar went to Parvus' suite. Parvus lay fully stretched on a softly upholstered sofa before the fire, his tiny shoes placed side by side on a garish oriental carpet. Beside him in a large winged armchair was a girl. She was reading to him and, as she read, with her left hand she gently massaged the throbbing blue filaments of vein at Parvus' temple. When Caspar entered she stopped.

"I'm sorry," Caspar said. "I didn't know—"

"It's quite all right," the girl said, putting her notes and a large sketchbook into a valise. "We've finished." She rose and moved lithely across the room towards him, one slender arm outstretched. "You must be Casper Ehrler. I am Sonya Karpinskaya. I work with Parvus."

That was obvious, Caspar thought, drily. Her hand was soft and light in his, and Caspar felt a momentary excitement as it rested briefly in his own. She was as tall as he, with a slender body that even her peasant blouse and long skirt could not conceal. Her face was dark and long, with high cheekbones, large black eyes, and a full, sensuous mouth. A mass of straight blue-black hair hung heavily to her shoulders. Dinaric, Caspar thought, embarrassed by the rapid thudding of his heart; passionate and very lovely. Her Russian had the hardened labials and final consonants of the Ukraine. She was, Caspar thought, the loveliest girl he had ever seen.

From the sofa Parvus asked, "Caspar, is it time for dinner?"

Caspar looked at his watch. "I'm early." Sonya was looking at him with a bright curiosity. "I have to talk to you."

"I'll leave," Sonya said, picking up her valise.

"Stay," Parvus said, echoing Caspar's sentiments.

"Sonya has been arranging our meetings. She knows about Quadriga."

Caspar hesitated. He wanted her to stay, but whatever Parvus had told her, it would not be proper for him to discuss Quadriga in her presence.

As if realising his conflict, Sonya said, "I must go. I don't want to be too late getting back to Meilen." She went over and kissed Parvus lightly on the cheek, and Caspar felt a quick pang of jealousy. She turned and smiled at him, saying, "I suppose I will see you again." Before Caspar could reply she was gone.

Parvus struggled into a sitting position and bent over his shoes. "I don't want to be late for my guests," he said, a trifle breathlessly.

"Quadriga is exposed," Caspar said.

"What the devil do you mean?"

Caspar told him about Hartmann.

Parvus seemed unconcerned. "Hartmann gives that warning to everybody," he said. "If he really wanted to stop Quadriga, he would have tried to frighten me." Parvus walked to the bathroom and returned, wiping his face. "Now let's forget Hartmann and go to dinner. The people you will meet are vital to Quadriga."

Caspar woke the next morning with the now familiar sensation of having eaten too much and having drunk a little unwisely. Parvus' dinner party had been lavish and mostly concerned with business. There'd been a Frenchman from Schneider-Crousot, a bleak Viennese from Skoda, Fritz Platten, the Secretary of the Swiss Social Democrats, a lecturer from the Institute at Meilen, a printer, and a newspaper proprietor. Whilst Quadriga had never been openly discussed, everyone Caspar met was ready to make some contribution to it.

Caspar rolled over on his side and looked at his watch on the bedside table. Twenty minutes to nine. The first of the revolutionaries was due in Parvus' suite at nine. Caspar groaned, stood up, walked somnolently to the bathroom, and stuck his head under the cold tap. The chill flamed his cheeks. The shock stopped his breathing, stopped also, the drumming inside his head and doused the twin circles of fire embedded in his eye sockets. Hair still dripping, he dressed. Before leaving his room he glanced quickly at the newspaper that had been thrust under his door. The British were advancing on both banks of the Ancre, and on the Eastern Front the Russians had been repulsed south of Kieslin. On the back page were hastily set banner headlines. America had severed diplomatic relations with Germany.

Full of a sense of challenge Caspar went up to Parvus' suite.

Precisely at nine o'clock the first revolutionary arrived, a nervous little man with a hungry face and a twist of beard. His name was Deshin and he represented the Social Revolutionaries, whose support lay mainly with the Russian peasantry.

Helphand dealt with him cursorily. As he explained to Caspar afterwards, the Social Revolutionaries were political sycophants and had representation in the Duma. The exiles had little influence over party affairs, and Deshin's ambiguity towards peace with Germany should be discounted.

Ziv Rakovsky came next, advancing across the room with shoulders thrown well back before succumbing to an outbreak of Russian enthusiasm and lifting Parvus out of his chair and kissing him noisily on both bearded cheeks. "Alexander, it's good to see you! So it's going to be like 1905 again!"

"Better," Parvus said, freeing himself from the embrace and looking rather overwhelmed.

"You mean this time we will travel first class to Siberia?"

"This time," Parvus said, "the train stops at Tsarskoe Selo." He introduced Caspar and told Rakovsky they could continue speaking in Russian.

The exile years had been kind to Rakovsky. The unfashionably long thatch of brown hair was only sparsely threaded with grey, and when he sat down Caspar noticed that his stomach curved lutelike against the tailored grey waistcoat. Beneath the steel-rimmed glasses, well-fleshed cheeks glistened, and in his tailored morning-coat, striped trousers, monogrammed cufflinks, and pigskin briefcase, Rakovsky looked more like a successful businessman than a revolutionary.

While Helphand detailed the plan, Rakovsky sipped champagne and leafed through the Quadriga dossier, raising his head occasionally to peer closely at Helphand over the rims of his spectacles when something especially pertinent was said. Caspar noticed that he'd folded down the page detailing the arms requirements. Old military habits, Caspar supposed, died hard.

"It's an excellent strategy, Alexander," Rakovsky said when Helphand had finished, "except for one fundamental flaw. Your strategy places too great a reliance on the efficacy of the strikes. As you know, even these days there are always four army divisions kept in Petrograd. If those divisions were all brought out on the first day, they would smash your strikes."

"But there will be strikes throughout Russia," Parvus protested.

Rakovsky tapped the Quadriga dossier. "According

to this, everything begins in Petrograd. In any case, if you haven't got Petrograd, you haven't got Russia. What you need to do, Alexander, is bring out a People's Militia on the first day."

"You're talking about a military putsch, not a revolution," Parvus said.

"I'm talking about the most efficient means of seizing power," Rakovsky said. "That's what the use of force is all about. Efficiency, economy, success." Those were the lessons he'd learned at Russia's most exclusive military academy, the Corps of Pages, and nothing that had happened since had given him any reason to change his views. "Power lies in Petrograd," Rakovsky continued. "Power lies here." He placed the Quadriga dossier on the floor and took from his briefcase a map of Petrograd marked in red and green. Rakovsky pointed to an area immediately southeast of the Bolshaya Neva. "The Winter Palace and the Admiralty—that is the administrative heart of Russia." His finger traced round the map. "The General Staff Building, the Kazanskaya Radio Station, the Okhrana Headquarters, the Arsenal, these Police Stations, here, here, and here," his finger racing over Petrograd, "and the bridges, all these must be taken and held before your uprising is successful."

Rakovsky was right, Caspar thought. One seized the centres of administration and power, and because Petrograd was a city built on marshes and all of it joined together by bridges, you seized the bridges also.

"We haven't got the men," Parvus said.

"I have the First Cadet Corps and three thousand veterans from 1905," Rakovsky said. "With the kind of money you have available, arming them is no problem. The only difficulty is getting the arms into Finland. If that is done, I can make arrangements for them to be stored near the border and taken into Petrograd." He reached into his briefcase and produced a sheaf of closely typewritten papers. "Here are my detailed plans and requirements." Rakovsky seemed certain that his proposals would be accepted and that without him there would be no revolution.

Caspar asked, "Is acceptance of your plan a condition of your support for Quadriga?"

"No," Rakovsky said. "But my plan is the one most likely to succeed."

"That's true. If the military putsch coincides with the strikes, then success is inevitable," Parvus said.

And that would leave Rakovsky and Parvus masters of Russia. "What kind of government would there be afterwards?" Caspar asked.

Rakovsky looked quickly at Parvus before answering. "A democratic government, of course, with free elections, freedom of speech, freedom of association, freedom of the press. There will be minimum wages, a forty-five-hour week–"

"And if the people of Russia reject you?"

"In that unlikely event, I will abide by their decision."

"What support do you have amongst the other exiles?" Caspar asked.

It was Parvus who answered. "That will be decided at the conference."

Caspar walked across the room and poured himself some champagne. "What is your attitude to peace?"

"Peace," Rakovsky said. "You'd be better off enquiring into my attitude to war. It is very clearly set forth in my book, *Where I Stand*. I will send a copy round to your hotel."

"I have read your book," Caspar said. "It deals with

your reaction to a previous war. What is your reaction to this war?"

Rakovsky flung out his arms in exasperation. "I have said time and time again, this war is senseless. It must be stopped."

"Would you agree to indemnities and annexations?"

"There is no point in discussing peace terms until we are in a position to procure peace."

"Our only interest in supporting Quadriga is to effect peace with Russia."

"I realise that," Rakovsky said. "I am for such a peace."

Boris Uritsky, who came next, was a typical Russian. Big and tall with flat cheekbones and deep-set eyes, he was voluble, argumentative, obstinate, and overbearing. Uritsky represented the Mensheviks.

Fourteen years previously the Social Democrats, Russia's largest Marxist party, had split over what was nominally a dispute over who should control the party magazine but which was in reality a struggle for control of the party. Uritsky's faction had lost by a mere two votes. Nevertheless, by the weird intricacies of Russian socialist politics, they had kept control of the magazine and still remained the largest Russian Marxist party.

"We will lead the revolution," Uritsky said, "because, afterwards, we will be the majority party in the Duma."

Rubbish, Caspar thought. The leaders of the revolution would be those who were prepared to take risks now.

"The revolution has already started," Parvus said. "I need your support to win."

"Are you asking us to underwrite your plan and support your candidature for Tsardom?"

"No. I am asking you to participate, lead if you like, but help us to win. I am only the fuse. You are the gunpowder."

"Exceedingly well put," Uritsky laughed, "but then you always had a way with words." The deep-set eyes narrowed, and the heavy brows knitted together in a suspicious frown. "Whom else have you approached?"

"So far, only the Social Revolutionaries and Rakovsky. But I intend talking to everyone else. Only if all of us are united can the Tsarist government be overthrown. I plan to hold an all-party conference here in Zurich on the nineteenth."

"For what reason? Two weeks of argument, seventeen different opinions, and forty-two ways of running a revolution?"

"I was hoping that, for once, we could work together towards one objective."

Uritsky laughed. "If we could have done that before, we would be ruling Russia now!" Uritsky lit one of Parvus' cigars and stared at its glowing end. "Have you asked Ulyanov Bonaparte?"

"Yes."

"You realise you may have to choose between him and us."

"Boris, for fourteen years your arguments have split the Socialist cause. Now it is time for you to forget your differences and work together for the sake of Russia."

"Work with Ulyanov! You must be joking. No one works with Ulyanov. Everyone works for him. I'd like to kick his little mongol backside all the way back to Simbirsk."

"It will be much easier to do that if we were all back in Russia. Please join us. Please go to Paris and persuade Martov, Dan, and Plekhanov to attend the conference."

"We do not need a conference. We can be ready in twenty-four hours." Uritsky stood up and looked at his cigar. "You're a rotten bloody socialist, Parvus, do you know that, smoking such expensive cigars."

"Even worse," Helphand replied. "I buy my own."

Uritsky walked to the door. "I'll bring the others," he said. "But remember, we are the gunpowder."

After Uritsky came Rosenblum and Aisenblud, representing the Jewish Socialist Bund, silent, suspicious men saying little and observing much. They were interested in the revolution but would not be compromised. They would support Helphand but would not be bound by any decision taken by the conference.

"No wonder the Romanovs have lasted three hundred years," Helphand snorted after the Bundists had left. "Everyone opposes them in their own way."

The elderly, professorial-looking Mikhail Saratov of Spilka opposed the Romanovs in every way. His small, dedicated Ukranian movement would work with anyone who would give them their independence. He listened quietly to Helphand, pledged his support, agreed to attend the conference, and informed Caspar that an independent Ukraine would make peace with Germany.

"Well, what do you think of it?" Helphand asked.

"They'll never work together," Caspar said. "They need a leader, one man who will force unity on them."

Parvus laughed, "Don't worry, Caspar. They're just being Russian. Once the revolution begins, they'll be one with us, and afterwards they'll be so busy arguing that they will make peace with Germany just so that they can carry on arguing undisturbed."

"We want more than that," Caspar said, sombrely.

"You may want, but you'll have to make do with what is available."

There was a brusque knock on the door.

"Ulyanov," Parvus said.

Caspar felt a tremor of excitement. At last he would meet the man whose ideas had so dominated his student days.

Sonya strode in and flung her slender frame onto the sofa. "Ulyanov isn't coming," she said. There was a long silence. Then Parvus cried to no one in particular, "Why must Vladya always be so difficult? I suppose he doesn't like this filthy, capitalist hotel. I suppose I'd better go and see him. Where is he?"

"He doesn't want to see you," Sonya said.

"But didn't you tell him—"

"Quote, he will not see you here or anywhere. He will not see you in public or in private. He will not see you now or ever. He wants nothing to do with you or your revolution. Unquote."

"But he still wants to use my people to get his letters and magazines to Russia." Parvus pulled fiercely at his cigar. "My God, in fifteen years the man hasn't changed. He is still the same bloody-minded Vladya."

Caspar stared at the carpet. Without Ulyanov the uprising wouldn't succeed. He thought despondently of the headline he'd seen in his room that morning. In a few weeks there would be American troops in Europe, and with Germany's forces scattered on two fronts Germany would be defeated. It was better to start making alternative plans to deal with that threat now than waste time and money on a revolution that was destined to fail.

"I'll stop his messages into Russia," Parvus rumbled. "I'll stop Ganetsky financing his organisation. I'll force him to join us."

Sonya said, "You know as well as I do that Ulyanov will only join us when he wants to."

"So we'll do without him. We don't need him. Perhaps it's better that he keep out of things. He's always been a contrary-minded, divisive force. Caspar, you heard what Uritsky said about him. The others will combine better without his arrogant polemics. Forget Ulyanov."

Sonya said, "You have to include him, Parvus. He'll only make trouble afterwards."

"If he wants to be included," Parvus snarled, "then let him beg."

The train barrelled through the long tunnel under the Zurichberg with hollow metallic reverberations and the fluttering of yellow patches of light against rock. If he wasn't so concerned about the contrary-minded Ulyanov, Caspar thought, it could have been romantic. He eyed Sonya, thrust deep into the buttoned cushions opposite him, self contained and withdrawn with none of the animation she'd demonstrated at lunch when Parvus had shown surprisingly little appetite.

They were on their way to Meilen, half an hour from Zurich, where Sonya was to show him Parvus' Institute for the Study of the Social Consequences of War. There were enough trained and dedicated revolutionaries at Meilen, Parvus said over lunch, to convince Caspar that the uprising could succeed without Ulyanov. Ulyanov was a pig-headed, arrogant, unprincipled pamphleteer, who, in twenty years, had contributed nothing to the progress of the revolution. They were, Parvus had emphasized, much better off without him.

The thought had ocurred to Caspar that Parvus protested too vehemently and that not only had Ulyanov's refusal been unexpected but that Parvus had been deeply hurt by it. Nevertheless he had agreed to visit Meilen, so that when the time came to recommend the cancellation of Quadriga, Parvus could not plead that the alternatives had not been properly examined.

The train rumbled out of the tunnel into bright wintry sunlight, passing rows of narrow, terraced houses whose steeply pointed roofs were covered with snow.

"What is between Parvus and Ulyanov?" Caspar asked.

Sonya shook her head with a flutter of dark hair. "Parvus and Ulyanov have been loving and hating each other for years. Parvus always gets upset when Ulyanov rejects him."

"Why doesn't Ulyanov like Parvus?"

"Oh, I think Ulyanov likes Parvus, but he won't work with him. Ulyanov doesn't believe Parvus is a proper revolutionary; he thinks Parvus is too rich and too ostentatious." She coloured prettily. "And that he does too many nonsenses with women. Ulyanov feels that anything Parvus does must end in failure."

"What do you think?"

Sonya laughed. "I don't think about these things."

"Surely you must have an opinion?"

She looked at him seriously, suddenly elfin and childlike. "I think Parvus is a very clever man. I have read his books."

"So you are a Parvusite?"

Her eyes widened in puzzlement. "A Parvusite?" Then she laughed, remembering that there had been a party of Parvusites soon after the 1905 revolution.

"Oh, no. I don't belong to any party. Not even Spilka."

"Why do you work for Parvus then?"

"Because he trusts me."

She took out her sketchbook and began to draw. "Parvus is a good man," she said, sketching busily. "He was very kind to me when I first came to Switzerland. Even now he helps me with my drawing and gives me work at the Institute." She looked from the sketchbook to Caspar and then back again. "I teach Ukrainian history and literature. I tell the students of revolutions that took place six hundred years ago."

And become Parvus' whore whenever he is in Zurich. Caspar felt unaccountably cheated. It was an old story, he supposed, the young, lonely, impoverished artist and the rich, powerful, elderly patron. He remembered the way she had stroked Parvus' forehead and how she had kissed him when she'd left the suite. "And I suppose you are still kind to Parvus," he blurted out before he could stop himself.

Sonya stopped sketching and looked at him. "You're a silly little man," she said. "Don't move your head." She raised her pencil and held it vertically at arm's length before her face. Then she returned to her sketching. "I don't belong to Parvus," she said softly.

"I am sorry. I didn't mean what I said."

"It doesn't matter. Most of the exiles think we are lovers."

"And are you?"

"For a short time, when I first came to Zurich, yes. Now we are close friends. Underneath all that ostentation, he is a good man. He is generous to all the revolutionaries. He allows himself to be used. I suppose he asks me to do these secret and important things for him because he knows I am the only one who wants nothing from him, and I am not concerned with politics." She looked up quickly from her sketchbook. "What about you, Caspar? You have a girlfriend in Germany?"

"Yes–no–"

Sonya laughed.

"I had," Caspar said firmly.

The train slowed and stopped at Zurich-Stadelhofen. There was a clattering of doors as people got on or off. No one came into their compartment. Few people travelled first class to Meilen.

As the train moved away, Caspar asked, "If you're not a socialist, what are you doing in Zurich?"

She began shading her drawing furiously. "I don't want to talk about that. It's not very interesting."

"Did you try to blow up someone?"

She ignored him and concentrated on her drawing.

Caspar looked out the window and fidgeted, unable to think of anything to say. He knew he was happy to be staying four weeks in Zurich. He knew with absolute certainty that, when the war ended, he would not marry Helga Hofer or work in the bank. It would be nice to stay on at the Foreign Office and be sent somewhere warm like West Africa. Sonya would make an interesting consort to an ambassador, he thought, as the train lumbered past villas and gardens and tiny huddling villages.

"What are you drawing?" he asked.

"You," she said, without looking up from her sketchbook. "Did anyone tell you that you look like Ulyanov?"

Caspar remembered the photographs he'd seen of Ulyanov and decided it was a very ambiguous compliment. "No," he said, and went to sit beside her. His own face stared placidly up at him from the sketchpad. Above his head Sonya had sketched in a Bolshevik hammer and sickle. "I like that," he laughed.

"You have a very interesting head. It isn't German at all and there is something about your face." She put down the sketchpad and looked at him. "Something wild, something stubborn, something gentle." She smiled. "I am glad Parvus brought you."

The train plunged into the Riesbach Tunnel. Sonya's eyes became suddenly luminous in the changed light. Caspar felt her body brush against his. He reached out clumsily and kissed her. In the clattering darkness she stiffened with surprise, then went limp, tilting her head back and letting him kiss her. Caspar pulled her body against his, feeling her lips soft and vulnerable under his as she allowed him to explore her mouth, and then she started to tilt her head from side to side so that his lips touched her cheeks and forehead and eyes and hair. The train charged through the tunnel with a sustained clattering, and Caspar was filled with a fierce excitement that made the blood pound in his head. He loved Sonya. It was as simple and as wonderful as that. He hoped the train would never reach the end of the tunnel. As long as they were in the tunnel, she was his and they were safe. He heard the sketchpad fall to the floor and then the train thundered into daylight. Sonya pulled herself away, turning sideways to stare out of the window and from time to time touching her face wonderingly with slender fingers.

They sat in spellbound silence until the train slowed. As it stopped Sonya got to her feet and looked down at him, as if she had never seen him before. "Welcome to Meilen, little spy," she said, smiling. "I suppose I'd better show you the Institute."

* * *

Meilen was a pleasant village, some twelve miles from Zurich, nestling on the right bank of the Zurichsee, beneath the snow-capped Pfannestiel. The Institute for the Study of the Social Consequences of War was situated in a large, three-storyed house just beyond the entrance to the village, standing in its own grounds beside a factory which manufactured temperance beverages.

He would only meet idealistic students, Caspar thought as he followed Sonya up the steps that led to the house. They were greeted at the door by Paul Chernikov, the lecturer Caspar had met the previous night. In daylight he was even more eager and toothy than ever and kept bobbing around them in his English tweed jacket and flannels, full of anxious explanations and a desire to discuss Caspar's thesis.

The Institute itself had the grim, earnest, striving atmosphere of most places of adult education, an impression that was heightened by the rows of impassive, Slavic-faced students and the cold enthusiasm of their instructors. The curriculum—political economy, theory and practise of Socialism, development of Marxism and the agrarian question—was limited, Caspar thought.

"We teach all versions of Marxism," Chernikov said proudly, "even that of Ulyanov."

Caspar saw Sonya wince and wondered what all this had to do with blowing up railway bridges and organising strikes. They had sixty students, the indefatigable Chernikov informed them, many of them respondents to recent advertisements in the exile press. And there was a waiting list.

"The Institute is organised like a commune," Chernikov announced moving between them. "Everyone has to do his fair share, even the teachers."

Caspar wished Chernikov would go and do his fair

share somewhere else, but as he appeared ready to launch into a dissertation on communes, Caspar asked, "Where does everyone live?"

Ten of the students lived in. The others were boarded out amongst the villagers.

"Isn't that indiscreet?"

"There are four thousand people in Meilen," Chernikov said. "The villagers think we are training Russian schoolteachers." He added that Slavic infiltration was commonplace in this area. Ten miles down the road was Rapperswil, which had a large Polish colony and a museum containing some of Poland's national treasures.

"Where do you live?" Caspar asked Sonya.

"I rent a room nearby."

Caspar became rapidly bored and out of breath from the continual trooping up and down stairs, and Chernikov's perpetual perkiness was beginning to grate. Caspar failed to see how a group of part-time socialists who were experts on the agrarian question could start a revolution. "You'd be better off teaching the students to shoot," he finally said, exasperated.

Chernikov momentarily swallowed his toothy grin. "But we do," he said and asked Sonya to take Caspar to Boris.

Boris was in a shed in the back garden, outside of which seven students practised a vague form of infantry manoeuvre while inside five more students watched Boris field-strip a Schmidt & Rubin carbine. Boris was a wide-shouldered, swarthy, bearded man, wearing a grubby uniform jacket bereft of insignia. As they entered, he rushed up to Sonya, crying, "Hello, darling, give us a kiss," and, wrapping his arms around her in a massive bear hug, attempted to kiss her on the mouth.

Sonya twisted her head away and elbowed herself free.

Caspar saw that Boris was slightly drunk. As Sonya introduced them, Boris said, "You see, she doesn't appreciate my barbaric Russian ways. But one day she will. One day she will." Laughing crudely, he gave Caspar a huge wink and took his hand in a crushing grip. "I am a deserter from the Russian Army," he announced with pride.

"I'll leave you to talk of guns," Sonya said. She looked at Caspar. "I'll wait for you in the house."

Boris, swaying slightly, watched her go, pursing his mouth in an obscene kiss.

Caspar snapped, "Deserter or not, learn to behave properly. You are training these students to be soldiers. Button up that uniform and, for heaven's sake, wash it!"

Boris glowered dangerously at him, shaking his head from side to side as if he had been hit. "Who the hell do you think you are?"

"I am an officer in the German Army. If the rest of the Russian Army is like you, it's no wonder that you lost Tannenberg." Caspar strode over to the table and examined the dismantled gun. "Is this all you have to train these people with?"

Boris shambled after him. "I have a couple of Mausers, two Luger pistols, and my own Mosin-Nagant."

"They'll certainly be versatile. But what the hell good is all this, if they're going to use Lebels and Mannlichers in Russia?"

"Then get us Lebels and Mannlichers," Boris said. "Find someone to field-strip them, too. I only know these weapons."

Caspar remembered that he was meeting with the representatives of Schneider-Crousot and Skoda the next morning. "I'll send you some tomorrow. And if necessary, I'll come and demonstrate them myself."

Boris moved closer to Caspar. "Can you get weapons other than rifles?"

"I imagine so."

Boris placed a massive hand on Caspar's shoulder. "Come, my friend, I want to show you something."

Boris led him across the garden into the cellar of the main house. This was obviously Boris' part of the house, and it was surprisingly neat and clean and free from damp. It was sparsely furnished with a bed, a wooden table, a chair. There was a large metal chest in the centre of the room and, on the walls, posters calling for support of the Second International. Perhaps, Caspar thought, Boris was a good soldier—when he was sober.

Boris unlocked the chest and, from underneath the pistols and rifles, took out two stick grenades and a Mills bomb. "These are all right for trench warfare," he said, "but we need the kind of things the Austrians have been using on the Eastern Front." He rummaged in the box and brought out two flat, smooth-sided, flasklike objects whose tops were fitted with fulminate of mercury fuses and firing pins. "Offensive grenades," Boris said, "no fragmentation, greater blast. The casing contains a pound of TNT and it can be attached to a timing device. If I detonate it here, it could bring down the building. Can you get me a dozen of these?"

"What on earth for?"

"For bridge supports, railway lines, and, if necessary, buildings. Also, if I have these, I won't have to teach the students how to use dynamite."

"I'll see what I can do," Caspar promised.

"Do that, German," Boris said. "And perhaps you

will find that Russian soldiers are of some use after all."

A pensive-looking Sonya was waiting for him when he got back to the house.

"Come and have a drink," Caspar said.

She hesitated and then said, "Oh, all right."

Walking down the street, she said, "I can't stand Boris when he's drunk. Sober, he's quite a nice person, but when he's been drinking he behaves like a peasant."

"Does he get drunk often?"

"About once a month. But he is very good at teaching the students to shoot."

Caspar said, "He'd better be. Once they get into Russia, people are going to be shooting back at them." He kicked at the snow with his foot. "I think we're going to have a hard time winning a revolution with this lot."

They turned into a bar, further down the street, filled with workers from the factory that made temperance beverages. Caspar sat her down at a table and bought two glasses of the local white wine.

"I want to meet Ulyanov," Caspar said.

Sonya looked at him thoughtfully over her glass. "Why do you want to see Ulyanov?"

"To persuade him to join us."

"You'll never do that," she said flatly. "If he won't do it for Parvus, whose help he still needs, he won't do it for you."

"Still, I'd like to try."

"He won't see you, Caspar. You are a German. Ulyanov is very aware of the political consequences of dealing with Germans."

"In that case he will never join us. And without him there cannot be a revolution."

"There are others," Sonya said.

"Uritsky," Caspar said, "like everyone else, is a talker. The Mensheviks will act only when they are certain of success. They are experts at leading from behind. Rakovsky thinks this is only a military exercise. If we are to succeed, we need people who are more dedicated than that. People who know what they are doing and why they are doing it and who keep doing it all the time. Ulyanov and his followers are Nechayev men. Men who practise revolutionary passion every moment of the day until it has become habitual. Men whose one pleasure, one reward, one satisfaction, is the success of revolution. We need those men, Sonya. We need Ulyanov. Please take me to him."

For a long while Sonya stared into her glass. Then she said, "Caspar, I think two things: first, that you are looking for more from this revolution than peace with Germany, and second, that you will be disappointed in Ulyanov."

"If Ulyanov does not participate, I shall have to tell Zimmerman to abandon the operation."

"It will not be easy," Sonya said, "but I can arrange it. However, I will have to ask Parvus first."

"Let's go back to Zurich and ask him together."

Sonya shook her head. "No," she said. "I will talk to Parvus from here. It will be better that way. If Parvus agrees, I will see you tomorrow."

Early the next morning the strident jangle of his bedside telephone woke Caspar from voluptuous dreams of Sonya. "Who is it?" he murmured, still lost in his dream. He came awake as he recognised Zimmerman's flat tones.

"Good morning, Ehrler, did I wake you?"

"Yes—no, of course not, Excellency." Caspar sat up in bed, swearing as the receiver was wrenched from his hand and swung squawking above the floor on its two feet of cord. Still swearing, Caspar dived after it and then, lying face down across the bed, placed it to his ear.

"Are you there, are you there? Ehrler, are you there?"

"Yes, Excellency."

"What happened? I thought I'd lost you."

You did, you silly bugger, Caspar thought. "Interference on the line, Excellency."

There was a moment's silence, then Zimmerman asked, "Are you alone?"

Caspar looked round the room. He should be so lucky. "Yes, Excellency."

"I received your cable. I have also spoken with Helphand. Quadriga must proceed."

"But Excellency, without the support of a certain person our strategy will fail."

"Reflect on history, Ehrler," Zimmerman said. "Think about the year 1905. Which of the famous people you know started that?"

The 1905 revolution had begun with a march of one hundred and twenty thousand workers on the Winter Palace. None of the revolutionary parties, none of the revolutionary leaders, had ever known about the march until days after the palace guard had opened fire. The strikes and disorganisation that had followed had been a spontaneous expression by the people, and if they had been led by anyone at all, it was not by the likes of Ulyanov but by an Orthodox priest who had no knowledge of Marx and the fact that the uprising had no place in the didactic of history.

"All we need to do is ignite the spark," Zimmerman

said. "As in 1905, the professionals—all the professionals—will join in afterwards."

Caspar reflected that both the 1905 revolution and Parvus' attempt at an uprising ten years later had failed.

"Is that Helphand's view, Excellency?"

"Yes."

"Helphand has always felt that the participation of a certain person was vital," Caspar said euphemistically.

"It would appear, then, that on reflection he has changed his mind. We must be guided by experts in this matter, Ehrler, and time is not on our side. The reason I am calling you is that, at your meetings this morning I want you to approve the necessary requisitions and make available to Helphand the funds he requires."

"But, Excellency—"

"I have no time to argue, Ehrler. The pressures on us are enormous. Quadriga must proceed as quickly as possible.

Quadriga, Caspar thought despondently, was a chariot drawn by four horses pulling in different directions. "Yes, Excellency," he said.

There was a short pause, a crackle on the line. Then Zimmerman said, "Ehrler, I want you to know that your work is much appreciated. I look forward to reading your future reports."

The phone whirred in his ear and went dead. Caspar slammed down the receiver. Parvus had no business going over his head like that. Parvus had no business misleading Zimmerman like that. Damn Parvus. Angrily, Caspar dressed and strode up to Parvus' suite.

Parvus, wrapped in a glittering silk dressing-gown, his beard flecked with egg yolk, was just finishing an enormous breakfast. "You're up early, dear boy. What's wrong? Rocks in your bed?" He poured out coffee. "Want something to eat?"

Caspar shook his head and sat down, the anger hard and tight within him, a solid pain in the middle of his chest. "I hear you've been giving Zimmerman history lessons."

Parvus studied Caspar carefully while he chewed. "And that has upset you." He thrust a newspaper at Caspar. President Wilson had followed up the severance of diplomatic relations with Germany by demanding further powers from Congress "to enforce the obligations imposed by the laws of nations." "What is more important, Caspar? Your feelings or the fate of Germany?"

Put like that, there was only one answer. But it was an unfair question. The proper question was whether Parvus' revolution would work without Ulyanov. "You agreed with me in Berlin that Ulyanov was vital. Why have you changed your mind?"

"I am afraid I allowed my love for Vladya to influence my judgement. I've known Ulyanov a long time. Seventeen years ago when he left Russia, he stayed with me in Munich. I helped him found *Iskra.* I've helped him get his work published. I've given his party money, and I run his communications for him. I know Ulyanov, Caspar. Believe me, he isn't important."

"I want to see him."

"So Sonya told me. But he is a difficult man to see. It will take time. We cannot wait that long. You've seen the newspapers. You know we must go ahead with Quadriga."

Caspar shook his head and moodily stirred his coffee. He was being treated like a small boy who'd had a fit of temper. "What do you want, Parvus? The return of your investment in the revolution? Is that why—"

"You're a damned idiot!" Parvus spluttered, slopping coffee into his saucer. "What do I want with money? Three million marks! Is that a sum that would concern me, boy? Don't you know that I am the sole supplier of coal to Denmark? That I sell the Danes German coal in my own ships and make a profit of seventy million marks a year from that alone! What is three million marks compared to that? If three million marks were that important, I wouldn't have risked it in the first place."

"So you want power," Caspar said. "You want to control Russia through Rakovsky. You want to create your own form of socialist state."

"And what's wrong with that?" Parvus demanded angrily.

"Your ideas do not go as far as Ulyanov's," Caspar said. "Admit it, Parvus. You're secretly glad that Ulyanov will not join us. You're jealous of him. You want to keep him out."

"Nonsense," Parvus rumbled. "Ulyanov is welcome to join us. I want him to join us. But I will not allow opportunity to pass me by because Ulyanov cannot make up his mind."

"Arrange for me to see him," Caspar insisted. "I'll persuade him."

"You don't know Ulyanov," Parvus said. "I'm not stopping you from seeing him, Caspar. Ulyanov is the one who will not see you."

"Sonya says she can arrange it."

Parvus' smile grew wider. "Yes," he said thoughtfully, a stubby, ringed finger stroking his beard. "Yes.

It isn't going to be straightforward, you know. One simply doesn't telephone Ulyanov and ask for an appointment."

"Fix it," Caspar said, "and I'll agree to all the requisitions and all the money you want!"

Parvus still had that strange smile on his face. "All right," he said, then picked up the phone and spoke to Sonya. When he had finished he turned to Caspar. "Sonya says it will take her a day or so to make the arrangements. She will contact you when she is ready. She said to tell you that you have her word on that."

Caspar laughed. "Fine." He reached over the table and poured himself more coffee. "When we see the gentleman from Skoda, we are going to need some of those new nonfragmentation grenades they're using on the Eastern Front."

"You shall have them, my friend," Parvus cried. "You shall have enough grenades to blow up the whole of Russia!"

On the train to Zurich, Badmayev had shaved off his moustache in order that his description would fit the French identity papers he was using. It was an extraordinarily boyish Badmayev who went direct from the Bahnhof to the house on Gessner Alee where Poidvosky awaited him with considerable trepidation and two assistants.

That anyone should come from Paris was worrying enough. That it should be Badmayev himself was terrifying. Badmayev had clawed his way to the top of the Okhrana not only by intelligence work, organisation, and diligence but by a series of perfectly planned murders. Poidvosky liked living in Zurich and had worked hard to build up a good relationship with the Swiss authorities. He worried that Badmayev's sudden arrival would change all that.

He heard the imperious ring of the doorbell and hurried to open the door, staring puzzledly for a moment at the stranger who strode past him into the house, leaving Poidvosky to carry his bags to the two interconnecting bedrooms behind the stairs which served as offices.

As Badmayev entered, the two assistants jumped to their feet and saluted. Badmayev ignored the salutes, sat down behind the desk, and demanded the agents' action reports for the previous fortnight.

For the seventy minutes it took him to study the reports, Badmayev didn't say a word. Wtihout comment he drank the coffee he was offered and kept Poidvosky and his subordinates seated round the office, frozen in attitudes of polite attention. When he finished, Badmayev folded the files neatly and placed their edges in a line with the desk. He looked at all of them with eyes that were warm and brown as a spaniel's.

"Where's Parvus?"

Poidvosky looked uncomfortable. It was one of the assistants who answered. "He left Zurich two days ago."

Badmayev sighed. "I want to meet our people in Meilen in an hour."

"It will–"

"Arrange it."

Badmayev stared into space until one of the officers left the room to make the arrangements. Then he raised his head. "I wish to stay in this house," he announced, looking directly at Poidvosky.

"Of course, director. We have a large bedroom on

the top floor with bathroom *en suite,* and there are cooking facilities—"

"Unnecessary. Are you sure Parvus did not meet with Ulyanov?"

Poidvosky nodded vehemently. "As sure as anyone can be, under the circumstances."

"Why didn't Parvus see Ulyanov?"

Poidvosky's frantic nodding became a just as frantic shaking of his head from side to side. "I don't know."

"It is your business to know such things."

"We were concerned to see whom Parvus met, not whom he did not meet."

Badmayev gave a small sigh. "Is there anything new about Ulyanov?"

Poidvosky managed to shake his head and shrug his shoulders. "Nothing. He still lives by the sausage factory, works at the library most days, goes for long walks on Thursdays, and occasionally visits Zinoviev in Berne. I believe they are producing a paper. He has—"

"Is he still living with his wife?"

"Yes."

"And still bedding the Armand woman?"

"She is in Clarens. He hasn't visited her for three months."

"So nothing's changed, except that he has fallen out with Parvus. Do you know why?"

Poidvosky shuffled his feet and looked down at his shoes with the expression of a man who has discovered he is wearing different-coloured socks.

"What about Parvus' assistant?"

"He has moved out of the Baur Au Lac and rented an apartment on the Konradstrasse. He visited Meilen with Sonya Karpinskaya."

So, Badmayev thought, the Karpinskaya woman was

helping to prepare a revolution in Zurich and consorting, in every sense of the word, with the enemy. He remembered her naked and defiant in Kiev, her supple body writhing under the lash. There she had organised student demonstrations, and that day, though bound and helpless, she had won a kind of victory. In Zurich it would be different.

The assistant came into the room and said that arrangements had been made for a meeting at the Goldenes Kreuz at Erlenbach, nine miles from Zurich, and that they should leave at once. Badmayev got to his feet and strode to the door. Poidvosky hurried after him. "I'll have your bags taken upstairs," he said. Underneath the stairs he cleared his throat diffidently.

"What?"

"The Swiss are very touchy about neutrality. If there is any violence, they are likely to arrest us all and close down our operation."

"In that case we will have to start again."

Poidvosky looked concerned. "There isn't going to be any violence, is there?"

"No," Badmayev said. "Not tonight."

In the half-dark of the late winter evening Caspar paced about his apartment, wondering if Sonya would come. He hadn't seen her since she had taken him to Meilen, five days ago. Yesterday, when he had taken the rifles to the Institute, he had hoped she would be there. But Chernikov had said she'd gone to Zurich looking for a venue for the conference. That morning she'd phoned and promised to see him early in the evening, about Ulyanov and visas for the students travelling to Russia through Germany.

Fifteen minutes to eight and she still hadn't come.

She wasn't coming. She'd conspired with Parvus to make him believe that she would take him to Ulyanov and had then done nothing. A kiss and a show of friendship, an he'd let himself be duped. Caspar stared angrily at the dimly lit street outside with its patches of grimy, yellow snow underneath the street lamps. On this side of the Limmat the streets were empty, with only the bar opposite showing any signs of animation.

It was too late to stop Quadriga now. Twenty million marks had been sent to Stockholm where the German Minister, Lucius, would supervise its transfer to Parvus. Another ten million had gone to Bucharest and the arms dealers; the newspaper proprietors and sellers of newsprint had all been paid. Damn Parvus, damn Ulyanov's stubbornness. Damn Sonya.

He remembered the way she'd looked in the railway carriage, staring out of the window, impressing the memory of his kisses on her fingertips. Even then she'd been planning to cheat him. Remembering how she'd looked and felt, he tried to believe it was not so. But without her presence, trust was disconnected. Caspar decided to return to Berlin and persuade Zimmerman to abandon Quadriga.

He recognised her knock on the door and rushed across the lounge in four giant strides, his breath catching in his throat. She stood framed in the doorway, gamine and slightly dishevelled, her face peering out from between a glistening pillbox hat of black fur and the raised-collar of her reindeer-skin overcoat. She was carrying her valise in one hand and, in the other, a bulky shopping bag from which the necks of two wine bottles protruded.

"I'm sorry I'm so late," she said as he drew her into the apartment. "I had to do some shopping, and this

Ulyanov business took longer than I thought." Underneath her coat she wore one of the newly fashionable calf-length skirts, with high, buttoned boots and a square-necked, embroidered blouse, cut just low enough to reveal the tiny beginning of the division between her breasts. She thrust the shopping bag at him. "Food and wine for you. It's an old Malorussian custom, the first time you visit a new house."

Caspar was numb with relief. Silently he took the bag and kept looking at her with mad, bubbling happiness.

Sonya looked round the lounge with its worn carpet and staid, anonymous furniture. "How many bedrooms do you have?" she asked.

"Just the one."

He showed her the small bedroom with the large bed, the kitchen, the bathroom, and the alcove in the lounge which served as a dining room.

"And you have steam heating. It's so lovely and warm. My room only has a coal fire." Her cheeks were flushed with warmth after the cold of the street outside.

Caspar went into the kitchen, opened the Dole she had brought, and came back with two glasses.

"No, thank you, Caspar. I will not drink until I have finished what I have to do. Is there somewhere I can sit and write?"

Caspar pointed to the dining table and, still carrying the bottle and glasses, followed her as she sat down and took some letters, papers, and a bottle of milk from her case. "I don't want to be watched while I'm doing this," she said. "Boris tells me you were a soldier. Why don't you go into the kitchen and prepare the food I brought."

In so many ways that was better than going out. "All right," Caspar said. "What are you doing?"

"I'm forging a letter to Ulyanov."

An hour later, while they ate, she told him that Parvus and the revolutionaries occasionally used her artistic talent to forge documents. The letters she had forged that evening would introduce Caspar to Ulyanov.

"That's dangerous," Caspar said. "We cannot afford to antagonise Ulyanov."

"I know." She gulped at her Dole and looked at him, urchin-eyed over the rim of her glass. "It will be all right. You'll see." She didn't want the letters spoilt by food stains and promised to show them to him after they had eaten.

During dinner Sonya told him about her family and her life in the Ukraine. She had three brothers and four sisters, and they'd lived on a small farm outside Kiev. She was twenty-two and had studied art and literature at the Catherine Institute in Kiev. While she missed all her family, most of all she missed her father, a lawyer who had given up a practice in Kiev for the land and had instilled in all his children an abiding love for Ukrainian poetry, history, and national aspirations. Once again, when Caspar enquired what had brought her to Zurich, she refused to talk about it, and after a minute's darkling contemplation she began to ask him about his life in Berlin and his military service on the Russian Front.

When they'd finished eating, they sat on the floor before the fire Caspar had made, and she showed him the letters. The first was short and to the point.

Vladya, this is Rihma. Trust him as you would me. Kuba.

Sonya hurriedly put the letter away because she said the second communication was written in milk on its reverse.

"This is lunacy!" Caspar exclaimed.

Sonya explained. Ulyanov had been greatly disturbed by Parvus' suspension of his communications with Russia. Absence of regular communications not only denied him information but made him feel impotent and isolated. He would also shortly have ready the latest issue of *Sotsial Demokrat*, and without Parvus' help there was no way anyone in Petrograd would read it.

Sonya showed Caspar the ink-written fair copy of the second letter. It described Caspar as a courier who had done excellent work for Kuba and who had now established a safe line of communication between Zurich and Petrograd. Because if was essential that Ulyanov maintain contact with Russia, Kuba had decided to ignore Parvus' embargo. It was essential also, and the word essential was underlined three times, that Ulyanov talk to Caspar. Parvus' plan for revolution was a reality and Ulyanov should not let his contempt for Parvus affect a momentous historical decision.

"Who is Kuba?" Caspar said.

"Ganetsky," Sonya told him, "the managing director of Parvus' companies in Stockholm."

Ganetsky was a Pole who had worked closely with the Russian Social Democrats for fifteen years and who had formed a mutual attachment with Ulyanov. He was highly regarded by the Bolsheviks and had been chairman of the tribunal that had investigated the activities of Roman Malinovsky, the Okhrana spy and friend of Ulyanov's who had once represented the Bolsheviks in the Duma. At the outbreak of the war Ganetsky had also secured the release of Ulyanov from the Austrian prison into which he had been consigned as an enemy alien. Sonya did not know whether it was Ulyanov who had infiltrated Ganetsky into Parvus' organisation or whether Parvus had picked Ganetsky because of his closeness to Ulyanov. All she did know was that Ganetsky was the confidant of both men and that Ulyanov went to great lengths to preserve his relationship with Ganetsky.

"How do I get Ulyanov's messages to Petrograd?" Caspar asked. "Doesn't Ganetsky know we are at war with Russia?"

Sonya laughed. "Don't worry, you won't have to go anywhere near Petrograd. All you will have to do is have Ulyanov's material delivered to Stockholm."

That sounded simple enough. Switzerland and Sweden were both neutral countries, and there would be no problem conveying the material through Germany.

"What if Ulyanov wants to know what I did for Ganetsky?"

"Tell him that is personal. Ulyanov is a very private man and he will not pry into your relationship with Ganetsky."

"What if he wants to know how I will get his papers to Petrograd?"

"He won't. He has no energy or time to waste on matters like that. All that concerns him is that they get there."

"What's all this about Rihma?"

"That's your code name. Every revolutionary has a code name. Ganetsky's is Kuba, Helphand is Parvus, mine is Karin, and yours is Rihma."

Caspar wondered what the purpose of having code names was, if everyone knew everybody else's. "Rihma is a strange name," he said. "Does it mean anything?"

"It's the Finnish word for thread. It means that you will have no difficulty in getting through."

"And presumably have an easier time getting to heaven than a camel. . . . When do we see Ulyanov?"

"Tomorrow. He will be with Zinoviev in Berne, working on his magazine. We will surprise him there."

Caspar reached across and kissed her. As she had done in the train, she leaned lightly against his arms, tilted her head back, and allowed herself to be kissed.

"Caspar, promise me you won't be disappointed in Ulyanov."

"That's very unlikely."

"Not as unlikely as you think. Everyone admires Ulyanov. Everyone says he is a great thinker, but they forget that he is human, that as a man he is not like his ideas. He selects ideas from Hobbes to illustrate untenable theories. Because he is so intellectually dishonest, I believe he is essential to us."

"I don't understand you, Caspar."

"Ulyanov has demonstrated that the end justifies the means. To Ulyanov facts are only useful so long as they help the revolution. He is a man beyond conventional morality, the man we need to destroy the old order. He borrows the ideas of others and uses Marx to bolster up his arguments. But Ulyanov is no Marxist. He is a disciple of Nechayev."

He told her about Nechayev, the larger-than-life revolutionary hero who, forty years ago, had led the Tsarist Police in a fine dance and made people believe he controlled a vast terrorist organisation. He was finally arrested for a particularly sordid murder and died at the age of thirty-five in the Peter and Paul Fortress.

"Nechayev wrote the Revolutionary Catechism. In three pages he said everything Ulyanov has ever said or ever will say." Caspar quoted Nechayev. "The revolutionary is a doomed man. He has no personal interests, no business affairs, no emotions, no attachments, no property, and no name. Everything in him is wholly absorbed in the single thought and the single passion for revolution. The revolutionary has no friendship except for those who have proved by their actions that they, like him, are dedicated to revolution. The revolutionary will not hesitate to destroy any position, any place, or any man in this world."

"But Caspar, that *is* Ulyanov."

"And that is why we need him."

Sonya stayed with Caspar that night, and in the big bed in the narrow room he made love to her slowly and tenderly, kissing every inch of her, feeling her nipples harden against his chest, aware of her slender body spread out below him and her wide-open eyes looking into his face, her hair spread out like a sea of ink on the pillow, easing her into a long shuddering climax punctuated with sharp little cries. He had never made love to anyone like that before, not violating but communing, not taking but giving.

The next morning he remembered that when he had kissed the weals that spread thick as fingers across the smooth skin of her back, she had cried.

But she had told him nothing.

* * *

At eleven o'clock the next day, after two hours on the train, they reached Berne, that most Swiss and patrician of cities, a hard conglomeration of brown sandstone buildings crowding into a loop of the River Aare. They took a hansom from the station to the old quarter where, amongst gaily painted fountains and low, vaulted roofs, Gregori Zinoviev lived.

Walking up the narrow, well-scrubbed wooden stairs to the Zinoviev apartment, Caspar felt nervous. He was not artful in deceit and his finger wavered as it hovered over the bell.

Sonya pressed his elbow encouragingly as if they were engaged in some childish conspiracy. Caspar jabbed at the bell.

There was a silence, followed by a shuffling of feet before the door opened, held by a short length of chain. In the resulting gap there materialised one dark eye, a mop of curly hair, and half a fleshy face. Gregori Zinoviev was making a typical appearance.

Caspar took a deep breath. "I am from Ganetsky," he announced.

The single dark eye blinked nervously. Then Zinoviev said, hoarsely, "Wrong address."

"Ganetsky," Caspar repeated, "from Stockholm."

"Nothing to do with us," Zinoviev said.

Sonya thrust Caspar aside and lowered her face level with Zinoviev's. "Gregori," she said in a low and ominous voice, "open that door before I scream you're making bombs in there."

"We're not making bombs. We don't believe in individual acts of terrorism."

"So you believe in mass terrorism. I'll scream that you're running a bomb factory." Before Zinoviev's surprised eye, Sonya's breasts lifted as she took a deep breath. "One, two. . . ."

Zinoviev visibly hesitated. Then with a great deal of fumbling he released the chain and let them in. He took them into a crowded reception room filled with shabby, overstuffed furniture, and with books and papers scattered everywhere, even on the ragged carpet. A picture of Marx hung over the fireplace, and the mantelpiece was covered with dozens of family photographs. The room was suffocatingly hot. Zinoviev obviously believed that if one wasn't sweating, one was dying of exposure.

"Where's Ulyanov?" Sonya asked.

Zinoviev licked pendulous lips. "Who wants to know?"

"You're becoming more like Nadya every day," Sonya said. She had told Caspar that it was to avoid Nadya's fussy protectiveness that they had come to meet Ulyanov in Berne. Sonya turned to Caspar. "Give Gregori the letter."

Very theatrically Caspar slit the lining of his jacket and gave Zinoviev the letter.

Zinoviev took it and hesitated. The letter was addressed to Ulyanov, the most private of men, who did not like having his mail opened. But without opening the letter Zinoviev could not know whether to admit to Ulyanov's presence in the apartment or not. A fine dialectical problem that Marx, writing in the British Museum, had never had to cope with.

"What has Ganetsky to say?" Zinoviev demanded.

"Read the letter," Sonya said.

Zinoviev hesitated. Then with a sudden quiver of decision he tore open the envelope.

"There is more on the back," Sonya said.

Zinoviev looked at them suspiciously and scurried into the kitchen, returning a few minutes later, having heated it and brought out the writing in brown squiggles. "So you are from Ganetsky," he said scornfully. "What are your political beliefs?"

"I do not believe in this war," Caspar said.

"And why not, my friend? Every other socialist does." Zinoviev's tone was hectoring and aggressive, as if compensating for his earlier timidity.

Caspar said, "The war has to do with the Tsar and his cousins, George and Wilhelm. It has nothing to do with me or the people of Russia."

"Do you believe it is an imperialist war?"

"If you say so."

"But what do *you* say, Mr. Courier? Is it an imperialist war or not? Does it carry the seeds of revolution within it or not?"

Caspar shrugged. "Whatever you say."

"Have you no opinions of your own? Have you not read Marx or Ulyanov? Or has your education been confined to the works of Parvus—"

In the corridor outside, his ear pressed to the door, Ulyanov waited, silently cursing the bourgeois Swiss, amongst whose stolid virtues was the construction of solid doors. As soon as he'd heard the doorbell he'd picked up his overcoat and bowler hat and run to the back of the house. For twelve years the unexpected ring of a doorbell had brought on palpitations and shortness of breath, a horrible dryness in his mouth and a blinding pain in his head. How many times had he told people they should not call unexpectedly.

Ever since his escape from Russia he'd known that the Okhrana wanted him, and for twelve years he had awaited their arrival with mixed feelings. Part of him wanted to be a martyr. Most of him wanted to be safe. There was nothing wrong with safety. After all, Nechayev himself had written that the real revolutionary should regard himself as capital consecrated to the triumph of revolution; capital that should not be senselessly squandered. And what use would Ulyanov be to anybody dead or incarcerated in the Peter and Paul Fortress?

He pressed his ear to the door. He could only hear occasional words, scattered phrases. Ganetsky—Ganetsky had sent someone. He knelt down and peered through the keyhole. He recognised the woman. Sonya something or another, an Ukrainian, one of Saratov's people. Hadn't she been Ganetsky's mistress at one time? The thin lips under the untrimmed red beard split in a mocking smile. Yes, she had been Ganetsky's mistress all right. Ganetsky had taken his fill of her before handing her on to that fat cuckold Parvus. Oh, Ganetsky was a lovely man. He always did the right things.

It was Ganetsky who had spoken to Adler and got him out of Austria when he'd been arrested as a spy. It was Ganetsky who had arranged his last meeting with Elizabeth; Ganetsky who maintained his courier service and from time to time gave him bits of Parvus' money; Ganetsky who spied on Parvus, for him.

He'd come to Berne that day to prepare an issue of *Sotsial Demokrat* for distribution, knowing that Parvus had withdrawn his facilities and that in all likelihood no one in Petrograd would see the paper. But he had come because he had a compulsive need to work. He had not hoped that something like this would turn up, and here was Gregori berating Ganetsky's messenger. Really, Gregori had no judgement. Mentally he added Gregori's name to the lengthy list of people who could not be relied upon: Krassin, Bogdanov, Valentinov, Martov, Plekhanov, Brilliant, Gorky. He was better than they. Even at school he had taken all the prizes. He was the leader. He had a duty to prevent others from making incorrect decisions. He had a duty to the revolution not to waste his incomparable qualities of leadership.

Ganetsky's messenger sounded simple and young, not an intellectual. Good. Gregori was mishandling everything. He would have to intervene. Ulyanov slipped out of his coat and hat, hung them up neatly, wrenched open the door, and went in.

"For heaven's sake, Gregori! The man is a worker. He has not had the time or the opportunity to read."

Vladimir Ilyich Ulyanov bustled into the room interrupting Zinoviev in full flow, stocky and aggressive. Caspar had an impression of a large bald head, a ragged beard that jutted forward, eyes that were dark and slanted, and cheekbones that were flat and faintly Mongoloid. Ulyanov wore a soft-collared shirt and tie, a shabby waistcoat, an ill-fitting jacket, baggy brown trousers, and studded workman's boots. He looked, Caspar thought with disappointment, like a jobbing builder calling on a customer with a quotation.

"I didn't want your work to be interrupted, Vladya." Zinoviev's pendulous lower lip had gone into a wet droop and his brown button eyes were glued unctuously on Ulyanov.

"There are interruptions and interruptions. News from Ganetsky is not an interruption." Ulyanov spoke with a certain testiness, and for a public speaker his tone was surprisingly unvaried, with a guttural sounding "r." He turned to face Caspar and Sonya. "I am Ulyanov." The little slanted eyes focused on Sonya. "I know you."

"Sonya Karpinskaya."

Yes, she had been Ganetsky's friend all right. Ulyanov walked up to Caspar and extended a stubby, compact hand. "Ulyanov."

"Rihma," Caspar said, feeling slightly ridiculous.

Ulyanov's eyes widened momentarily. At close quarters the effect of those eyes was amazing. They seemed to penetrate right into the middle of Caspar's skull and to challenge every thought that rested there.

"You come from Ganetsky?"

"Gregori has the letter," Sonya said.

"So Ganetsky sent a letter." Ulyanov gave them a little mocking smile before turning and taking the letter from Zinoviev's quiescent fingers. He peered at it closely, frowning, turning it over and looking at the squiggle of brown milk on the reverse. It was in Ganetsky's writing. His friend Ganetsky had sent him a courier. Ganetsky was even risking a break with Parvus because it was essential that he, Ulyanov, maintain communication with Russia. Such devotion was touching. Except Ulyanov didn't believe in devotion. Ganetsky's letter said the courier had news of Parvus' plans for revolution. Ganetsky was even suggesting he should help Parvus in that!

He raised his head to look at the young man who called himself Rihma. Short, slightly built, with a freckled, impudent face and thinning red hair. He would discuss Parvus' plans with the young man. But there were more important things to be done first. Ulyanov pointed towards a pile of *Sotsial Demokrat* on the floor. "Can you get those to Petrograd?"

That was more like the Ulyanov Caspar had expected, the person who summarised every situation and went for the essential things first. "That's why Ganetsky sent me," Caspar said.

"The important thing is, can you do it regularly?"

Caspar nodded vehemently.

"Good." Ulyanov gave him a cursory smile. "Take those with you."

"But, Vladya, we haven't investigated this—"

Ulyanov froze Zinoviev with a glare. "Ganetsky's word is good enough," he said, and turned to Caspar. "How is Ganetsky?"

"Very well."

"I am glad to hear it."

They looked at each other awkwardly. Finally Caspar said, "Vladimir Ilyich, I have a message from Ganetsky."

Ulyanov's eyes narrowed. It was not necessary that Zinoviev should know of Parvus' revolution yet. "Let us go for a walk," he said. "Walking keeps one healthy, and it is essential for a revolutionary to be healthy. Who knows when he might have to run from the police or be imprisoned under terrible conditions."

The chances of Ulyanov suffering either fate in Switzeralnd were remote. Nevertheless, accompanied by the squeak of his studded boots on the cement floor of the arcades, they walked.

The arcades were raised above street level, formed by low-vaulted roofs extending to the pavement where they were supported on sturdy fifteenth-century pillars. As they walked past confiseries and watchmakers, embroiderers and lacemakers, small bookshops and vendors of souvenirs, Caspar outlined Parvus' plan for the conquest of Russia.

Ulyanov listened intently. The plan was worthy of Parvus, imaginative, grandiose, and original; using the

Germans to start a world revolution was a brilliant idea. The only problem was Parvus.

"He is ostentatious," Sonya agreed, "but how better to enjoy wealth. It's the same as being healthy. Parvus looks upon it as a natural good. Not everyone can be as dedicated as you, Vladimir Ilyich."

Ulyanov kept on walking, arms thrust deep into his pockets, bowler hat tilted forward. In the last resort he accepted that wealth was a private matter. Wealh and ostentation were only the more obvious reasons for his dislike of Parvus. The truth was Parvus' loose morals and his friendship with the Germans made him a dangerous ally for an international revolutionary. But there was more to it than even that.

Always Parvus had been first. Before anyone else he had campaigned for an eight-hour day; before anyone else he had dared to use strikes as offensive weapons. It was Parvus who had led the last revolution. Ulyanov remembered with bitterness those frantic directives he'd sent from Geneva: Seize the banks! Seize arms! Kill the rich! Everything according to Clausewitsz and Gustave-Paul Cluseret who had actually fought in the Paris Commune. And yet when he got to Petrograd there had been no blood on the cobblestones. Parvus and that young whelp, Trotsky, had everything under control. They were running the revolution and going to the theatre in the evenings! And they called themselves Socialists.

Their kindness, after they had conspired to deprive him of his proper historical place, had been galling. It was for that and for his brilliance that Ulyanov would never forgive Parvus.

Now Parvus was asking him to help start another revolution, a revolution which would be *led* by Parvus, his friend Rakovsky, and perhaps even Trotsky!

Parvus was asking him to co-operate with the Mensheviks for that! Parvus was asking him to lend his stature to a revolution that was taking place at the wrong time, in the wrong country, and for the wrong principles—and being led by the wrong people. He would have none of it.

"Why come to me?" Ulyanov asked. "You have the money, you have the support of others."

"We need your people in Moscow and Petrograd and Kiev and Odessa. We need the railroads and factories your people control to ensure success."

They were walking along the Kramgasse, with its row of beautiful guildhouses and the Zahringer Fountain. Ulyanov couldn't believe it. They wanted his organisation! Didn't they know that nearly half his organisation in Petrograd had been arrested because Parvus had sent them morphine instead of money? Didn't they know that at no time was the organisation completely under his control because his communications with Petrograd were sporadic, existing only through the courtesy of people like Parvus and the Estonian, Keskuela? Didn't they know that his main support was Vikhzel and his railway union, and that Ulyanov had no idea how Vikhzel had been affected by the Okhrana arrests?

Now, as in 1905, all he had to contribute to a rebellion was the power of his intellect and the strength of his will. Now, as in 1905, any contribution he made would reveal how puny his party was. But how to admit that to this naive woman and her fresh-faced companion? He needed their help to maintain contact with Russia, with Ganetsky. He had to conceal his impotence.

"I will not compromise," Ulyanov announced. "I

will not make peace with the Mensheviks. I refuse to work with Rakovsky."

"What good have your ideological differences achieved for Russia?" Sonya asked.

Ulyanov gave her a crooked grin. "There is such a thing as honour," he said.

"Honour, Vladimir Ilyich, you surprise me. Does not the true revolutionary exclude all sentimentality and romanticism? All private hatred and revenge? Does not the true revolutionary always obey, not his personal impulses, but only those which serve the cause of the revolution?"

Ulyanov's deep-set eyes glinted warmly. He had written that to Parvus once. He wondered how good she was at chess. She had nearly trapped him. Nearly. "The Mensheviks are heretics," he said. "Rakovsky is a charlatan. The cause of the revolution is best served by opposing them."

"What if the Mensheviks will support you?" Caspar asked.

"If the Mensheviks, Rakovsky, and Parvus support the true revolution, then of course I will join with them."

"Why don't you attend the conference and persuade them to support you?" Caspar asked.

"That would be like asking the waves of the sea to remain still. Their ignorance is boundless. The gap between us is too vast. They lack the will and the courage to fight for the cause of the true revolution."

"History could pass you by a second time, Vladimir Ilyich," Sonya said. "And this time it could be permanent."

Ulyanov glowered at her from underneath his thick eyebrows. "The laws of history as set out by Karl

Marx do not provide an illustrious future for the Mensheviks," he said.

"What are you waiting for, then?" Caspar asked.

The steady, screeching rhythm of Ulyanov's walk faltered. He turned from Sonya and fixed Caspar with a piercing stare. Then he walked on, again slightly ahead of them. All his life he had been waiting. His life now was no different from what it had been twelve years ago, or twenty years ago. A life of constant work, constant effort, and constant betrayal. And what had he to show for it? Didn't they realise that if he could have started a revolution he would have done so already? Twenty-three years a revolutionary and he was still waiting for the historical imperative that would sweep him to power. But that was not an answer he could give the young man.

"Parvus is brilliant, but wrong," he said. "It is not dialectically correct to begin a revolution in Russia at this time. And because it is not dialectically correct, it will fail." He had their attention now. They followed him round the corner, walking towards the casino and the Zytgloggeturm. "The revolution must start in a more advanced country, where it can spread like a bush-fire through Europe. It must start where people are more ready for it, where they are cruelly hungry every day, where they risk being thrown into war and killed, where people are shamefully exploited by massive financial organisations, where democratic rights are daily trampled upon. That is where we start the revolution. Then we take it to Russia."

"When?" Caspar asked. "And where?"

"In a few months," Ulyanov said. Then, Caspar could hardly believe his ears. There, beside the clock-tower in Berne, surrounded by wealth and tradition and proud bourgeois values, in Berne where politics had long ago been abandoned in favour of government, Vladimir Ilyich Ulyanov said, "Tell Parvus that the centre of world revolution is here—in Switzerland!"

Above them the hour struck. A cock emerged from the clocktower and crowed.

In the train returning to Zurich Sonya said, "Don't you agree with Parvus now? Ulyanov is quite mad, and quite unnecessary."

"On the contrary," Caspar replied. "Ulyanov still has the finest socialist mind. He is suffering from frustration. All his adult life he has lived and thought and worked for a revolution, and now for three years he has been stuck in Switzerland and looks like he'll be here forever. Under those circumstances, what else can a professional revolutionary do but plan revolution in Switzerland?"

Sonya looked at him thoughtfully. "But he will not join you, Caspar."

Caspar smiled. "In the end he will."

Sonya leaned forward across the compartment and kissed him lightly on the cheek. "I love you," she said, "and I am happy you weren't disappointed."

As soon as the couple left, Ulyanov rushed back to the Zinoviev apartment and told Gregori the news. He insisted that a meeting of the party be called to ratify his decision and to agree how to deal with this new threat to world revolution. Ulyanov had insisted also that Zinoviev accompany him back to Zurich.

Now flanked by Nadya and Zinoviev he sat at his favourite table at the rear of the Café Adler, his clothes rumpled from the hard seats of the third-class carriage and his face lined and strained as he looked round the table and saw that all six Party members were present. They divided neatly into the old and the young, he reflected—Kharitonov, Ussievich, and Zinoviev, the old faithfuls; and the new young Dantons: Boris, who'd deserted from the army; Kyril, who until recently had been distributing the paper in Petrograd; and Kaufman, renegade from the Swiss Social Democrats.

They were all looking at him expectantly. Ulyanov cleared his throat and began to speak. "As you all know, Parvus has been in Zurich, meeting with the leaders of the so-called Socialist parties and seeking their co-operation to create an uprising in Russia. This afternoon representatives of Parvus met with me and invited me to join them. On behalf of the Bolshevik party I informed them that we would not support Parvus, nor support an uprising in Russia at this time."

"Why not?"

Ulyanov, about to embark on the dialectical reasons for his refusal, stopped. It was Boris who had interrupted him. A new recruit, unused to party discipline. Boris would have to learn. Ulyanov's eyes glinted. "There are two answers to your question. I will give you the simpler one." He waited for the appreciative titter of laughter to die and said, "The uprising is being financed with German money. As you all know, Russia is at war with Germany."

"What difference does it make whose money it is? You have said that this is an imperialist war, a war to save the tottering capitalist regime and oppress the workers. You have said that it is not our war."

Ulyanov glared at Boris' unshaven face and bull-like body. His jacket was clean for once, but his breath smelt of alcohol. "Neither is Parvus' uprising our revolution. If Parvus' uprising succeeds, Russia will be controlled not by true revolutionaries but by a gang of social-chauvinists, by lackeys of Imperial Germany like Parvus, by spineless stooges like Rakovsky, and by bankrupt Marxists like Plekhanov. The success of Parvus' uprising will be victory for the vacillators and the betrayers of the true revolution!

"Further, if Parvus' uprising succeeds, it will bring peace between Russia and Germany. And what would such a peace mean? I will tell you. It will mean a German victory! A victory for the Kaiser who is the cousin of our beloved Nicholas and whose hands are just as bloody!"

Boris looked down at the table. It was always like this with Ulyanov. You disagreed with him and then, logically, relentlessly, he proved you wrong. Even if you knew inside that you were right, Ulyanov proved you wrong.

Zinoviev said, "Parvus' so-called revolution will begin and end in Russia. We Bolsheviks are dedicated to world revolution." He turned and looked at Ulyanov. "What happens to us if Parvus' uprising succeeds?"

"I will give you five reasons why it will not succeed." Ulyanov counted them off on stubby fingers—"Parvus, Rakovsky, Plekhanov, Deshin, Rosenblum"—and was rewarded by another round of laughter. "But seriously, comrades, Parvus is not the stuff of which revolutionaries are made. You have all seen him, so fat he can hardly walk and staying, if you please, at the Baur Au Lac. Parvus is too fond of his own carcass."

Boris listened captivated as, in turn, Ulyanov dealt

with each of the others. Rakovsky believed that revolutions were made with elegant phrases. He was a *poseur* who lacked the courage to be even a Menshevik. Everyone was surprised to hear that Plekhanov was still alive, especially Plekhanov himself. Deshin represented the Social Revolutionary Party. Did anyone present know of a party with that name? As for Rosenblum, the Bundists had been expelled from the party twelve years ago.

Next Ulyanov embarked on the dialectical and Marxist reasons for the certain failure of Parvus' uprising. Boris was still captivated, though he found certain parts difficult to understand. Then a vote was taken. It was unanimously agreed that Vladimir Ilyich had done the right thing.

A round of coffees was bought and Ulyanov, looking very sly, said, "Even if the laws of history will not, I will stop Parvus." He waited, still looking mischievous, till Zinoviev asked, "How?"

"Simple," he said, serious again. "I will publish a critique of their plans in the next issue of *Sotsial Demokrat*."

Kaufman the Swiss said, "But that's hardly fair."

Ulyanov turned on him. "What does fairness have to do with it? And what is fairness? Is it not a bourgeois quality? What are you, a revolutionary, doing asking us to participate in such bourgeois feeblemindedness? Parvus' uprising has to be stopped. It is the wrong time for it and the wrong place for it—and it interferes with the progress of the true revolution."

Kaufman looked away, reddening behind misted spectacles.

Boris said, "The next issue of *Sotsial Demokrat* will not be ready for weeks. Parvus' uprising will be over by then."

"No," Ulyanov said. "He is calling a conference of all the revolutionary parties first. They're going to discuss revolution and take majority decisions. That is going to take more than a few weeks."

"But what if Parvus sees *Sotsial Demokrat* and impounds it?"

"How many copies can he impound? All we need is a dozen copies of the paper in the right places and his uprising is finished."

On his way home from the meeting an hour later Boris decided that he could not wait for Ulyanov to publish the next issue of *Sotsial Demokrat.* Parvus' uprising was far more dangerous than Ulyanov wanted to believe. It had to be stopped, permanently and immediately. Boris knew he had to act now, even if, as a result, he was exposed as an Okhrana spy.

He went into a call-box and made a long, reverse-charge call to the house in Gessner Allee, where he was both surprised and relieved to be able to talk directly with Peter Badmayev.

That night Sonya and Caspar had dinner at the Veltliner Keller and afterwards went back to the apartment where they made love with a frantic urgency, Sonya wrapping her long legs around him and responding to his furious thrusts with rapid gyrations until they both climaxed, then holding him inside her until he was hard again and loving her deliciously, slowly and easily.

Afterwards Caspar lay beside her, his cheek nuzzling the small, firm roundness of her breasts, stroking the smooth and slender length of her body. Caspar said, "I want you to stay with me."

He could feel her thinking, staring up at the darkened ceiling. "Won't that interfere with what you have to do?"

"The conference, and getting Ulyanov to join?"

"And after your conference, and after your revolution?"

"You'll be back in Russia, and I suppose I'll be back in Germany."

"I won't go back to Russia," Sonya said.

"Why not? In a few weeks Russia will be at peace and there will be an independent Republic of the Ukraine."

"That will never happen, especially with Ulyanov. The Ukraine is too valuable to let go, and all government is about not letting go."

"Ulyanov represents freedom," Caspar said. "He wants to free the Indians from the British, the Africans from the French, Germans, and Italians, the Latvians, Luthuanians, and Estonians from Russia. Ulyanov is going to build a Russia where all men are equal, where they will have the right to work and have enough food and proper homes, a Russia where people will not exploit one another and which will be a shining example to the rest of the so-called civilized world."

"Ulyanov is a destroyer," Sonya said softly. "You said that yourself. How can he build anything?"

"That is the genius of the man. That is why he is superior to Rakovsky, Uritsky, and all the others. He is a thinker and a doer. He will do everything that is necessary to destroy the old world, and then, with equal determination and dedication, he will do everything that is necessary to build something new and lasting and infinitely better."

"Caspar, you're such a romantic! Ulyanov is not like that. He is a tiny, petulant opportunist who is obsessed with power. Look how he dominates his fellow Bolsheviks! Look how he bullies Nadya! Ulyanov has no feeling for people, and that is very dangerous in a ruler. He will use you, Caspar, as he uses everything and everybody else. And he will build his own Russia which will not be your ideal socialist state. It will be a dictatorship far more terrible than anything you can ever imagine."

"You're talking nonsense, Sonya. You haven't read Ulyanov so you cannot know what he believes." He kissed her softly between her breasts. "If you don't like Russia, you can always come and live with me in Berlin. I would like you to be with me, always."

Later that night she told him about the scar on her back and how she had come to Zurich. It had happened four years ago; the students had protested the banning of Ukrainian in schools. Everyone had taken part and the demonstrations had gone on for two weeks. Whilst there had been little violence, the suspension of order had embarrassed the government and they had sent a man from St. Petersburg to end the demonstrations. He had adopted new tactics. He'd taken the army and police off the streets, and just when the students thought they had won, he ordered his men to arrest the leaders. Sonya, who had read the poetry of Taras Shevchenko at two of the meetings, had also been seized.

"It was horrible," Sonya said, describing how she had been beaten over the head, bundled into a car, and taken to a police station.

Twelve of them had been arrested, nine men and three women. They had been stripped naked and crowded into a single cell, with their hands bound to the bars above their heads and their legs pinioned together. They had been forced to stand there for hours, unable to move, with neither food nor water, and they'd had to relieve themselves where they stood. It was in the summer; the stench of bodies and sweat and human waste had been overpowering and the pain from their stretched and stiffening limbs excruciating.

One of the other women had broken first, then a man, crying out that they would do anything to be spared further pain. Late in the evening, when four of them had recanted, all of them were released from the cell. But before they were allowed to go home, each one of them had been taken, still naked, into a large room filled with policemen and officials, tied face down onto a table, and flogged.

Sonya said, "The worst thing was not their crude jokes or the humiliation of being naked and helpless, not even the pain of the lash or the burn of the ropes on my wrists and ankles. It was this man from St. Petersburg who stood at the head of the table and kept looking at me all the time I struggled and tried to stop myself recanting. He stood looking at me in this strange, passionless way and made me feel I had been used. They beat me till I fainted, and all the time his eyes were warm and brown, like a spaniel's."

She was trembling. Caspar put his arms round her and held her. "What happened after that?"

"They let us go. There were no more demonstrations."

"Weren't there protests?"

Of course there had been protests. Three days later Sonya had been arrested again. This time she was neither ill-treated nor humiliated. Instead she was charged with making seditious speeches and threatened with a sentence of six years exile in Siberia.

"There was nothing I could do. Hundreds of people had heard me read from Taras Shevchenko. My father humiliated himself before the police and agreed that if the charge was dropped, he would send me away from Russia. Saratov arranged for me to come to Zurich."

"And this policeman," Caspar asked, "what happened to him?"

"I don't know. I suppose he went back to St. Petersburg. His name was Badmayev."

In his room overlooking Gessner Allee, Badmayev sipped his coffee and glanced thoughtfully at the newspapers. The morning was more than usually dismal, with patches of smoke-grey mist drifting off the lake and curling against the window; with the persistent fall of light snow that turned to slush as soon as it touched the street. The newspapers were full of the great German retreat from Serre, Miraumont, Pyr, and on an eleven-mile front north and south of the Ancre. The war, like Parvus' uprising, would be over soon.

Badmayev's conversation with Boris the previous night had proved he'd been right to come to Zurich. Had Boris spoken to Poidvosky, Poidvosky would have cabled Paris and St. Petersburg, and by the time orders found their way through the bureaucracy of the Okhrana, Parvus' uprising would have started. Badmayev knew that the uprising could never be allowed to start. The situation in Petrograd was so tense that any distrubance, however small, could lead to a full-scale rebellion, and a rebellion at this stage would mean an end to the rule of the Romanovs. Badmayev was a fervent Tsarist. He had sworn an oath of loyalty, and it was in pursuance of that oath and his duty that he was going to act now.

He finished his coffee and changed into hose, knee breeches, a woollen shirt, and sturdy boots. After putting on a heavy sweater and a snap-brimmed alpine hat, he pulled the knapsack he had packed the previous night over his shoulders and walked through the mist to the Bahnhofplatz, where he caught a number seven tram.

Badmayev stared at the street as the tram trundled along the Bahnhofstrasse and Bleicherweg. Lights from shop windows and banks glowed feebly. Dark figures scurried along the snow-covered pavements with lowered heads and turned-up coat collars. Badmayev thought that, for him, it was the right sort of day to go climbing mountains.

After they passed the railway tunnel, the buildings grew fewer and the mist over open fields more impenetrable. The tram clanked and hummed and hissed out fat blue sparks as it climbed the lower reaches of the Uetliberg.

Half an hour later the tram stopped at the terminus, a dripping, green-roofed platform in the centre of the road, with a skein of tram lines around it disappearing into the mist. Badmayev got out and walked beyond the tram lines to where the road ended and the path began.

The narrow path was steep and caked with snow. On either side the trunks of trees were wreathed in mist. Badmayev walked seemingly surrounded by a moving column of clear air which enabled him to see the snow-compacted path for about seven yards ahead. Beyond that shadows loomed and the path disappeared in an overwhelming greyness.

The snow was soft and cold and wet, rising moistly over his boots, chilling his feet, and saturating his hose. Walking in it was uncomfortable and hard work. The squelch of boots, the rustle of clothing, and his steamy breathing all sounded unnaturally loud in the opaque silence.

Head down he trudged determinedly upwards. After a hundred yards he was breathing strenuously and sweating lightly. A hundred yards further and the climb became steeper. He passed a wooden bench and a small hut. He walked round a corner and the forest thickened. The light became strange and insubstantial, not night or day or evening but as if the mist-shrouded world was in eclipse. Below him, the mist was an immobile sea, mingling with the lake, while the trees stood beside him like dark sentinels.

A house loomed out of the greyness, dark and ominous, its pointed roof covered with snow, its timbers soft, and its windows blankly opaque. A large van stood underneath the wooden piles. Badmayev had been walking for fifteen minutes. He was nearly there.

He stepped off the path and went into the forest. Carefully looking round so that he would remember the place, he wriggled the knapsack from his shoulders and took from it a priest's soutane and hat. Putting them on over his walking clothes, he walked a further thirty yards up the track and settled down to wait.

Forty minutes later he heard the squelch of footsteps and laboured breathing, saw a shadow loom out of the mist. Badmayev recognised the tall, erect figure with the feathered hat, brown-checked overcoat, and leggings. From the folds of the soutane he took out a Luger. Then he crossed himself and prepared to step out onto the track.

Struggling up the hill, Rakovsky dragged a gloved hand across his perspiring face. Late last night a Bolshevik had informed him that Ulyanov wanted to meet him secretly at the Pension Uto-Staffel, two thousand five hundred misty feet up the Uetliberg.

The messenger had insisted that Rakovsky come alone and that he not take the train from Selnau Station but the tram to the Albisgutli Terminus and then walk along the path to the pension.

Knowing Ulyanov's passion for walking in the mountains and knowing also his passion for secrecy and intrigue, Rakovsky had come alone as requested, expecting Ulyanov to set down conditions for joining in the uprising.

Now he saw the dark figure of a man emerge from the mist. Ulyanov had got some sense into his Mongol head and was coming down the path to meet him. Rakovsky slowed and, as the figure moved into the patch of clear air before him, he saw that it was not Ulyanov but a priest.

What on earth was a priest doing in the mist of the Uelti—

The priest had stopped in the middle of the path, his feet braced wide apart. Not only that, he was carrying a heavy revolver. With his right arm extended, and left hand grasping his right wrist, the priest levelled the revolver at Rakovsky. Rakovsky heard the safety catch come off, as he fumbled in his pocket for his own weapon; then the priest fired—once, twice.

The shots cracked out with a narrow, flat sound. Rakovsky weaved to the right, gun spinning from his hand. There was a neat hole in the shoulder of his brown coat and an even neater hole above his left eye. His eyes were glazing as he fell.

Quickly Badmayev walked up to the fallen man. Rakovsky lay on his side, a streak of blood across his forehead, spattering the snow. No Rakovsky, he thought looking down at the body with his warm spaniel eyes, no uprising. His work in Zurich was finished.

* * *

Three hours later it was still snowing on the Uetliberg, a rapid stream of thick, darting flakes that blinded the eye, settled heavily on clothing, and obliterated everything that did not move. Huddling massively into his coat, Chief Inspector Hartman stared grimly at Rakovsky's body; the outflung coat tails were already buried under the snow and his pale, haughty cheeks and deep-set eye sockets were filled with it. Already buried up to the shoulders, Rakovsky's body looked like an abandoned bundle of clothes.

It was obvious how Rakovsky had died. The tiny puncture on his forehead, with the worm of blackened blood encrusted against the damp skin, must have been instantly fatal. Any footprints left by the murderer had long since been obliterated by the policemen, their attendant experts, and more falling snow. Finding the murderer was a matter for the Kriminalpolizei, and Hartmann had only been told of the killing because the victim was a known revolutionary, one of Hartmann's flock, as Chief Inspector Grenzel so inappropriately put it.

Rakovsky had been one of the more pleasant revolutionaries. Dignified, austere, still a military man, he had lived peaceably with four colleagues in a pension near the Kantonsspital. He had never been in any kind of trouble and there was nothing to indicate what he had been doing up on a mountain in inclement weather.

Rakovsky had come armed, but he had not fired his own weapon. So the other person had fired first. Which meant that the killing had been premeditated. Which meant, also, that it could not be the consequence of a falling-out amongst revolutionaries: They were given to violent argument, not physical violence. If a shooting had to take place at all, it would be in a café in the centre of Zurich with half a dozen witnesses present. This murder had been planned, which meant that one of the intelligence agencies had organised it.

Hartmann felt personally aggrieved by that. More so than the revolutionaries, the intelligence agencies were his flock. He had been betrayed. With a sense of impartiality Hartmann decided to move against all of them, to hinder all their activities in every possible way, until someone divulged, if not the name of Rakovsky's killer, the reason for his death.

Two hours later, when, in response to a frightened phone call from his assistant, Karl Muren, Maugham arrived at his office in the Weinbergstrasse, he found six policemen there, two sitting on either side of a petrified Muren while the others neatly packed his papers in wooden boxes.

"What's going on?" Maugham demanded, tapping the worn carpet with his cane.

Hartmann appeared, filling the doorway of the cubicle that Maugham used as his private office. With a massive, curling finger, Hartmann beckoned him inside.

"You have no business—" Maugham protested, standing beside his desk.

Hartmann placed a sheet of paper between them. "I have a warrant."

Maugham did not bother to look at it. "These papers are the property of the British Consulate."

"Then they should be in the British Consulate," Hartmann replied testily. He had not taken off his coat and in the narrow room looked more massive than ever. There was also a frighteningly impersonal expression on his face. Hartmann was not only doing his duty but liking it.

"Herr Muren has very kindly stored these papers for us while certain building alterations are being made at the Consulate."

"Herr Muren," Hartmann said, "has already admitted being an agent for British Intelligence."

Maugham lit a cigarette and sat down. "Let's be reasonable, my dear fellow. Why us?'

"Why Rakovsky?" Hartmann asked.

The news had been in the afternoon papers, which was the first Maugham had known of it. "It has nothing to do with us," Maugham protested. "Why don't you talk to the Russians."

"I will," Hartmann said nastily, "but until then, this office remains closed and your papers stay with me."

Hartmann had less luck with the Russians. The house in the Gessner Allee was embassy property and could not be searched. Poidvosky himself was almost incoherent with fear and quite obviously knew nothing about the killing.

Emil von Dichter of Section IIIb was unable to accept Hartmann's invitation to the offices on the Hohnerstrasse. Von Dichter was returning to Berlin, and with Junker haughtiness he informed Hartmann that the Germans had no interest in socialist revolutionaries.

REVOLUTION

The Duma Committee Room looked like an office with rows of chairs and tables arranged one behind the other, two or three armchairs in the middle and, surprisingly, no central table where everyone could gather round. Kuryakin was trying to decide if and where he should sit when Michael Rodzianko came in as urgently as his bulk would allow.

Rodzianko was a massive man, well over six feet and weighing nearly three hundred pounds. His large head was thrust forward from the silk collar of his frock-coat, and his pointed beard jutted aggressively at a point a few inches above Kuryakin's head. "I am sorry to have to see you here, Count Kuryakin," he rumbled in a deep bass. "But you see, my office—" He flung powerful hands above his head in a theatrical gesture of despair. "Chaos, people, confusion."

Kuryakin suppressed a smile. If he had met Rodzianko in his office, everyone would have known of his visit. Here, in an anonymous committee room, Rodzianko could pretend he was passing by. "I understand, Monsieur President," Kuryakin said, and placed his briefcase on a desk. It was obvious they were not going to sit.

"You said it was a matter of urgency and discretion."

"Yes. I have in my case a warrant for the arrest of Alexander Kerensky."

Rodzianko's massive shoulders slumped. His hand reached up and absently stroked his beard. "I expected this," he said, despondently.

That morning Kuryakin had been summoned to the Ministry of the Interior. Protopopov had been in a vile mood, angry and frightened, his small, sleek body now cowering behind his enormous desk, now advancing across the room with precise dancer's steps. "Kerensky has committed treason," he'd cried. "He must be arrested and imprisoned immediately."

Alexander Kerensky was a lawyer who, since leaving the University of St. Petersburg twelve years previously, had travelled to every part of Russia, defending political prisoners. A member of the Social Revolutionary Party, he had been elected to the Third and Fourth Dumas and headed the commission of inquiry into a police massacre at the Lena Goldfields which had resulted in the resignation of a former Minister of the Interior.

He was now only thirty-six. He had been born in Simbirsk, which, interestingly enough, was also the birthplace of Protopopov. His father had been the Principal of Simbirsk High School and had instilled in his son a passionate love of Russia and a deep respect for personal freedom. In contrast to many other alumni of St. Petersburg University, Kerensky had rejected the austere, foreign dogma of Marxism in favour of the Narodnik movement, rooted in the soil of Russia, indistinct and inconsistent but overwhelmingly humanitarian and entirely Russian. For twelve years Kerensky had been a thorn in the side of the Tsarist Government. But he had never broken the law, and the Okhrana had never tried to arrest him.

"What exactly has Kerensky done?" Kuryakin asked.

"Yesterday in the Duma—here, let me read it to you." Protopopov minced over to the desk and picked up a copy of Kerensky's speech, parts of which were heavily underlined in red. *"The Ministers are but fleeting shadows.* That's a fine way to talk about the Tsar's most loyal servants."

"But it isn't treason."

Protopopov looked up angrily from the copy of the speech. "Treason—well, this is treason: *To prevent a catastrophe, the Tsar himself must be removed, by terrorist methods if there is no other way.* Incitement to assassination of the Tsar is treason, is it not?"

Kuryakin took the copy of the speech from Protopopov and read it quickly. There was no doubt that Kerensky had committed treason. There was also no doubt that, privately, Kuryakin agreed with Kerensky. He reread Kerensky's closing sentence: *If you will not listen to the voice of warning, you will find yourselves face to face with facts, not warnings. Look up at the distant flashes that are lighting the skies of Russia.*

Kuryakin said, "Kerensky is a member of the Duma. He has parliamentary immunity. We cannot arrest him."

"But he has committed treason!" Protopopov cried.

"He is immune to arrest for treason, murder, rape, fraud, and anything else you care to name."

Protopopov sat down behind his desk, black eyes glaring. "Arrest him," he said. "Take twenty of your men and arrest him. Your elite Korean veterans are more feared than the Cossacks. You could arrest the whole Duma and no one will lift a finger against you."

"You overestimate the power and reputation of my men," Kuryakin said.

Protopopov closed his eyes and shook his head. "No, no. Go to the Duma. Bring me Kerensky. In the name of the Tsar of All the Russias, I demand it. I demand it, do you hear! The Tsar demands that Kerensky shall be arrested!"

"It would be politically expedient," Kuryakin said, "to obtain the consent of the President of the Duma first."

Protopopov looked at him suspiciously for a moment. Then he said, "Yes, do that. But whether Rodzianko agrees or not, I want Kerensky!"

Now Kuryakin asked Rodzianko, "You agree, then, that Kerensky has committed treason?"

The giant President of the Duma half-turned to face Kuryakin. "If I were a lawyer, I would say yes. But as a patriotic Russian, I would say that Kerensky spoke the truth and that such truth is necessary. Either the Tsar acts now or there will be a revolution."

"Have you told the Tsar that, Monsieur President?"

Rodzianko sighed heavily. "I saw the Emperor five days ago. I told him that all Russia is unanimous in wanting a change of government and the appointment of a responsible premier. I told him that the Empress is universally hated and that all circles are clamouring for her removal. I told him that revolution is imminent."

"What did he say?"

"Nothing. Would you believe it, he simply sat there and stared at me in that hopeless, sick way of his and said nothing. I finally said, 'Sire, it is my duty to express my profound foreboding and conviction that this will be my last report to you.' At that he became petulant and asked me to leave. He is a doomed man, and I am afraid we are doomed with him."

"What effect will the arrest have on Kerensky?"

"It will kill him. He is not a well man. And if there is going to be a revolution, we are going to need all the Kerenskys there are."

"There's only one Kerensky," Kuryakin said. "Will you agree to his arrest?"

"What difference does it make? You are under orders. It is not your duty to think of political consequences. How many of your men have you brought?"

Kuryakin said, "I've come alone."

Rodzianko looked at him in surprise and then slowly raised his massive head from his chest. A smile split his beard and he threw back his head and laughed. "Let us go and talk to Kerensky," he said.

"Don't worry, Alexander, we will never give you up."

Rodzianko, Kerensky, and Kuryakin were in one of the smaller committee rooms on the left side of the palace, huddling round a bubbling samovar. They had decided that Kuryakin would inform Protopopov that in anticipation of an illegal arrest, the security forces around the Duma had been doubled and were too many even for Kuryakin's seasoned elite. Further, if any attempt were made to arrest Kerensky without due process of law, the entire Duma would take to the streets in a massive demonstration, the like of which would never have been seen in Petrograd. They were confident that the twin spectres of a massive demonstration and a unified Duma would force Protopopov to consider the matter constitutionally.

"And by then there will be no Protopopov," Kerensky said. He was a thin, clean-shaven man of medium height with a marvellous kestrel head, a coxcomb of bristly hair, a sharp nose, and hooded eyes. He was young, alert, and slightly amused at the furor his speech had caused.

Kuryakin raised a glass of steaming black tea to his lips. "How certain are you of that?"

"If I might quote from my speech of yesterday–"

"Don't," Rodzianko said. "We already have enough problems with your speech of yesterday."

"If we do not listen to the voice of warning, we will find ourselves face to face with facts," Kerensky quoted, imperturbably. "And the simple fact is that the people will not put up with the present state of government much longer. There will be an uprising within the month."

"Do your sources confirm this?" Rodzianko asked Kuryakin.

"Yes. I also have information that the uprising, when it comes, will be German financed."

"That's rubbish!" Kerensky cried. "Monarchist propaganda! The Germans have–"

"Been buying into roubles. And my agents in Zurich report a vast increase in activity amongst the exiles there."

"All the more reason for the Tsar to grant us a proper constitution now. A revolution, especially a German-financed one, will see the end of the monarchy."

"Will *you* support a German-financed revolution?"

"The question is meaningless. If the Germans want to start a revolution, then let them. All they're doing is hastening an inevitable process."

"And if German stooges seize power?"

"Never!" Kerensky said. "We are at war with Germany, a war supported by all political parties. Admittedly, the people and the army are temporarily disenchanted with the war, but that is only because the war is blamed for the incompetence of the Tsarist ministers. If the government is changed, internal problems will be resolved. Then the people and the army will once again combine to prevent the spread of Pan-Germanism. Anyone who has achieved influence by trading with the Germans will be lucky not to be lynched."

Kuryakin put down his glass and got to his feet. "I hope you're right."

The others rose, too. "I've heard a lot about you and your Japanese veterans," Kerensky said, taking Kuryakin's hand. "I thought we were destined to be enemies. But there is more to you than I dreamed possible. Thank you for your consideration, and thank you for what you have done for me."

Kuryakin smiled, grimly. "My feelings for Russia had something to do with it as well," he said.

Outside, the Potemkinskaya was buried deep under a heavy covering of snow. The street was empty and silent, the temperature thirty-five degrees below zero. Wrapped in furs, his earflaps tied underneath his chin, Kuryakin emerged like a squat, black shadow onto the street and hailed a *droshky* to take him back to his office in the Moika. Idly watching his breath steam in front of him, Kuryakin thought he'd never before disobeyed an order as direct as Protopopov's. He was a soldier, used to a chain of command, and even in disobeying a syphilitic nincompoop like Protopopov, there was a sense of betrayal. But the old systems were breaking down. The time had come for all patriotic Russians to declare themselves, to choose between the Tsar—the little father, the divinely appointed ruler of the Russian people—and Russia itself.

And if he, with his deeply imbued sense of tradition and military discipline, his inbred loyalty to the monarchy, and sense of history, was prepared to oppose the Tsar's legally appointed minister, what of the others?

The English Club in the Place Michel had been founded in 1770 by an English merchant named Gardener. It was a large, impressive, and secluded place, a replica of those sober institutions dotted around St. James. Even though no Englishman had been a member for at least thirty years, it still received foreign newspapers and was still known as the English Club. Kuryakin thought there was some irony in arranging to meet the chief agent of the British Secret Service in Petrograd there.

Kuryakin waited in the reading room, which was only called that because newspapers were available there, and sipped a glass of tea as he looked across the Neva at the solid embankment walls and thin, gold spire of the Peter and Paul Fortress. If things did not work out, that could be his home for the next twenty years. His visitor interrupted that uncomfortable train of thought.

Richard Hain was an elegant young man wearing a modishly fashioned shirt and a large velvet bow. Tall and slim, with a fine head of dark brown hair and a moustache that gave his lean face an air of youthful bravado, Hain could well have passed as a regular Guards Officer. He was also the only person at the British Embassy who spoke Russian.

"Tea?" Kuryakin enquired, looking into Hain's harrassed face. "Or vodka? I'm afraid that the English Club does not run to crumpets."

"Tea," Hain said, and flung himself into a chair

opposite Kuryakin. "Dimitri, what the devil are your people up to in Zurich?"

"Nothing unusual," Kuryakin said.

"You mean killing Rakovsky was usual?"

"Oh, that," Kuryakin said. "Unfortunate, wasn't it?"

Hain gulped at his tea and spluttered.

"You have to be Russian to drink tea quickly," Kuryakin said.

Hain patted his scalded mouth with his handkerchief. "The Swiss have closed down our whole operation in Zurich. Dimitri, you've got to do something about it."

Kuryakin smiled. "It's very tempting. I would like to sacrifice Poidvosky. But, at this time, I can't." He leant forward across the low table, suddenly serious. "Parvus is running a big operation through Switzerland. He is trying to start an uprising here, with German money. Yesterday, three students from his institute in Zurich were arrested on the Finnish border at Haparanda, carrying gold, guns, and morphine."

"Morphine, for God's sake!"

"Morphine manufactured in Switzerland, which, when sold to the Russian Red Cross, brings a profit of six hundred percent. I think Rakovsky's death is only the beginning. I would like to be able to tell my people in Switzerland that they can rely on the help of the British."

Hain stirred his tea and looked thoughtfully at it. "We had three telephone calls today enquiring what were we doing about getting rid of the German woman."

Kuryakin's voice became harsh. "And what are you doing about it, Richard?"

"We said that she is your empress, old boy. She is

your problem. In fact, Rakovsky, Parvus, this whole bloody mess is your problem." He lifted his glass and sipped more delicately at his tea.

"It is our problem," Kuryakin said firmly. "If anything happens in Petrograd and the Tsarist government is overthrown, Russia is going to be out of the war so damned quick you won't even be able to say Lloyd George."

"The Russian parties in the Duma support the war."

"Try telling that to Parvus and his German friends in Zurich. The moment there is an uprising, they will all be over here—Plekhanov, Uritsky, Ulyanov, the lot. I don't believe you will find them anxious to continue the war."

"My hands are tied, old boy," Hain said. "You know it is not British policy to interfere in the internal affairs of other nations."

"Stop being so bloody sanctimonious. We need your help, Richard. We need troops. The Petrograd divisions are unreliable. We need arms; even we Okhrana loyalists do not have enough. We need open British support."

"To openly support the Tsar now would compromise HMG's position, if the Tsarist government fell. Besides, HMG cannot find support at home for giving the Tsarist government anything other than purely military aid. HMG will not help you resolve your internal problems, Dimitri."

"But your confounded HMG has no hesitation in demanding that half a million untrained, unsupported Russian soldiers be sent into battle in order to protect British positions on the Western Front!"

"That is how governments work."

Kuryakin smiled bitterly. "I suppose at the appropriate time you will make diplomatic protests."

"We're very good at that," Hain admitted. "I'm sorry. No one in London listens to me. Over there they live in a world of unreality. They will not let me help you, but if in a small way there is anything I can do. . . ."

Kuryakin patted Hain on the shoulder. "I'll remember that," he said.

Afterwards Kuryakin went to Palkin's Restaurant, where his assistant, Serge Chudnovsky, stood outside, shivering in the lightly falling snow. The Nevsky was quiet, and they had to walk up to the Moska Hotel to find a *droshky*. "Come with me," Kuryakin said. "I want to show you something."

They rode down the Nevsky towards Znamenskaya, the horses' hooves muffled by the thick carpet of snow. In the square they turned by the church, whose large dome looked grey and ghostly against the midnight sky, drove past a row of anonymous streets, and stopped at one called 5th Rozhdestvenskaya. Kuryakin paid off the *droshky* and they walked down the street, past the Customs House and the Nativity Church. Just past the church Kuryakin opened a series of locks and they passed into a darkened house.

As Kuryakin turned on the lights, Serge noticed that the windows were lined with heavy black curtains, drawn so that no light seeped onto the street. It was a typical house of the area, with servants' quarters and a wine cellar below street level, two reception rooms, a dining room and a kitchen on the ground floor, and four bedrooms upstairs.

In the wine cellar was a barricaded armoury, with

Nagant rifles, Mauser pistols, grenades, ammunition boxes, and a Maxim machine gun. The pantry and part of the dining room next door had been converted into a provision store, with enough food to last twenty men three weeks. The entire ground floor had been subdivided into smaller rooms, each furnished with rows of tables and chairs that were typical of a Russian office, and two of the upstairs rooms had been brought together to form a dormitory. Kuryakin led Serge to one of the other bedrooms. Immediately Serge recognised the Germano-Russian style of furniture Kuryakin liked and his favourite reproductions of Gauguin and Bakst.

"Our secret headquarters," Kuryakin said. "For when the revolution comes."

"We will fight the revolution from here?"

"Not fight it," Kuryakin said. "Survive it." He sat behind the desk and lit a cigarette. "All new governments feel constrained to dispose of the Secret Police. By the time they realise their mistake, it is too late. We will ensure that if there is a new Russian government, it does not suffer too greatly from its mistakes."

"There will be a new Russian government?"

"Very likely. We cannot count on any help from the British, and we must assume that some of Parvus' people will get through."

Serge said, "So we are finished, then?"

"We are not finished. We will survive, whatever government seizes power. But the days of the Tsar are numbered. Serge, I want you to go back to the Moika and prepare our files for transport to Finland. I propose to take them across myself, tonight."

"But we cannot work without those files."

"We will not survive without them, either."

* * *

Later that evening Kuryakin returned to his office on the Moika and looked at the files Serge had extracted for transit to Finland. The files were, by tradition, his personal property, but they had a significance much greater than that.

Those meticulously referenced and cross-indexed files contained information going back fifteen years: details of the Okhrana's assassination of Prime Minister Stolypin; reports from agents who had infiltrated the revolutionaries who worked as double agents; the revelations of Josef Dzhugashvili, a leading Bolshevik known as Stalin; details of the weaknesses of and scandals involving members of the Duma, grand dukes, army officers, and ministers; the names of certain noble ladies who had given themselves to Rasputin.

The files were the dross of Secret Police work. Dross that was essential to the continuation of that work. Dross that would enable the owner of the files to exert strong pressures on whoever seized power. Kuryakin was determined that the files should not fall into the wrong hands. He was determined to use the information contained in them to ensure that *his* political section could work unhindered for the benefit of Russia.

Carefully he packed the files and the indices into the heavy canvas sacks Serge had provided. Then, just as carefully, he carried them downstairs and loaded them into the boot of the waiting car.

Snow fell thickly as he snaked towards the Nevsky Prospekt. Kuryakin drove slowly, cautiously. He had no margin for delay or accident.

He emerged on to the Nevsky opposite the mute magnificence of the Kazan Cathedral and turned left, in the direction opposite to that in which he had to go. Deserted, the Nevsky looked more vast than usual, wide and anonymous, its Rastrelli palaces and pastel façades barely lit and uniformly white with snow. Kuryakin leaned forward, peering through the windscreen and wiping it frequently with the back of his gloved hand. In a city where transport was mainly by carriage or electric tram, the car would be noticed. But, as the murderers of Rasputin had shown, a car was extremely convenient for transporting that which was best kept hidden; and because there were so few cars in Petrograd, he was unlikely to be stopped by a police patrol.

Opposite the shuttered Gostiny Dvor, he turned left onto Sadovaya and drove towards the Troitsky Bridge. The patrol waved him across. Soon afterwards he was on Petersburg Island, driving past the forbidding bastions of the Peter and Paul Fortress. On his right as he went up the Kameno-Ostrovsky Prospekt was the palace of Mathilde Kschessinskaya, larger and more splendid than the little house on the Admiralty side where she had once entertained the Tsar. He wondered what would happen to her and all her well-known royal alliances. For that matter, he wondered what would happen to him.

The bridge at the end of Petersburg Island was deserted, and he raced along it, driving quickly across the eastern tip of Apothecary Island. Petrograd, the city of Peter the Great, was built on water, spread over nineteen islands and linked by a tracery of bridges, the surly waters of the Neva hemmed in by massive granite quays. Petersburg Island and the Admiralty side were the most populous, and already, as he crossed Apothecary Island, the houses were noticeably fewer and less grand. The snow squeaked as it was crushed against the windscreen by the slowly moving wipers and piled into a thick curtain above the swept and streaky arcs.

Kuryakin slowed for the narrow bridge across the Great Neva which joined Apothecary Island to the mainland. After crossing it he turned west, heading for the furthest part of Petrograd. Suddenly there was a vivid blue flash. Curtains of electric blue light swept across the sky and swirled amongst the domes and towers of Petrograd in sudden, coruscating brilliance. Kuryakin skidded to a stop, nearly blinded. Afterwards he remembered that the Northern Lights were a good omen.

When he could see again, he drove on, still travelling west, past shabby houses and timber yards and deserted, cheap summer villas, heading to where Russia ended amongst the bleak flats and marshes of the Gulf of Finland. He still drove slowly, feeling the car twist and shudder under him, its wipers moving agonizingly across the screen, the sound of the engine a long, constant murmur filling his ears.

Shortly before three o'clock he reached Staraya Derevnya, "the old village," which consisted of a few huts and timber yards surrounded by frozen marshland. With the wind hurling snow off the gulf, it seemed the bleakest place on earth.

Just beyond the village Kuryakin stopped at a small timber yard, drawing up before the barred gate, watching the snow dance in his headlamps as he pressed the horn twice, gently. Moments later a dark, fur-clad figure emerged into the beams of the headlamps, shoulders hunched against the snow, and opened the gate. Kuryakin followed the figure across the yard to a large storehouse. The man opened the door and motioned Kuryakin to drive in.

Inside it was absurdly clear, absurdly dry, and, when Kuryakin switched off the clattering engine, absurdly silent. He felt the pressure of that silence in his ears and pressed his hands to his head before stretching luxuriously and stepping down from the car. Already melted snow was dripping onto the floor and transparent spears of ice had formed on the underside of the car.

"Vasili," Kuryakin said going up to the man, both hands extended. "I am grateful."

All that could be seen of Vasili Romanovitch was his leathery face, wet from the snow, and clear blue eyes under bushy white eyebrows. "You have no need to be grateful. I am repaying a debt." The blue eyes studied Kuryakin carefully. "Things are going bad for you?"

"Bad for all of us. And getting worse. Is everything ready?"

"Yes. But you will have to hurry. He has been waiting since midnight."

"How much?" Kuryakin asked.

"Too much. One hundred roubles, but you must leave quickly; otherwise you will be trapped by the sunrise."

Kuryakin asked Vasili to help him unload the sacks, which they dragged across the yard into Vasili's hut. Inside, a fire burned smokily and a tall, big-boned, bearded man lay snoring on a bunk. He woke as they entered, glaring at both of them. "What's the time?" he asked.

"Twenty after three," Kuryakin replied. Under the patchy beard the man's face was wolfish, his eyes sharp and set close together. The man was a food smuggler, who had brought a sled full of butter, cheeses, and meat across the ice from Finland. "It's too late," the man said flatly.

"It will not be light before seven," Kuryakin said. "By then we could be in Finland." Vasili had told him that this man was the best of the smugglers. He brought the most food, knew the route intimately, and had the fastest horses. But Vasili had warned Kuryakin that the man was not to be trusted.

"It's too late," the man repeated.

With a good horse and reasonable weather conditions, Kuryakin knew the journey could be done in just over three hours. "You're being well paid," he said.

"I'll be just as well paid tomorrow."

"Tomorrow you might have competition." A hundred roubles was three times as much as any smuggler earned on the run from Finland.

The man picked up his hat and pulled it well down over his ears. "Enough talk," he said. "Let's go."

They went across to a barn where the man had kept his horse and sled. The sled was a *drovny*, broad and low and filled with hay, the kind mostly used for farm haulage. Kuryakin threw the sacks into the sled and arranged the hay over them. The man climbed into the seat and drove slowly out of the barn. Kuryakin took Vasili's hand. "Thank you. I will see you in two days."

"I look forward to it. God go with you."

Kuryakin ran after the sled and threw himself into the hay. They drove slowly out of the yard and along the tiny steeet, the sound of the horses's hooves muffled by the snow. Outside the village the man soon turned towards the sea; the runners of the sled grated as they bounced across the frozen marshland. Kuryakin stretched to full length and looked up at the still-falling snow, remembering drives under the winter stars on nights gone by, when someone used to ride ahead on horseback with a torch to frighten away any prowling wolves. His childhood had been lovely, he thought, safe, protected. Always there had been his father, big and strong like he himself now was, a hunter like he had been. It was a strange experience, Kuryakin reflected, being one of the hunted.

The sled bounced awkwardly down a sharp incline and stopped. Kuryakin raised himself on one elbow and looked. Before him was an immense grey expanse, blurred with whirling snow. "The money," the man said.

Kuryakin gave him fifty roubles. The man looked at it and said, "The price is one hundred."

"You'll get the balance on the other side." He reached into his pocket and took out his Mauser. Aware of the man watching him, he cocked it. "And if you have any ideas of collecting an extra ten roubles by handing me over to the border police, you'll never live to spend it."

The man spat. Then with a shout and a crack of the whip he urged the horse over the ice. Kuryakin was thrown backwards, and in a moment they were travelling at breakneck speed out into the Gulf of Finland.

There was about a half inch of frozen snow on the surface, which gave the horse's hooves sufficient grip. The sled ran smoothly, its runners singing like a sawmill. Kuryakin worried about the noise, but there was no help for it. They had to move quickly or not at all. The mainland of Russia faded in blurring whorls of snow.

It was still snowing and they were still travelling quickly an hour later when Kuryakin saw the beam of the searchlight sweeping the ice ahead of them. They were approaching the island fortress of Kronstadt and the searchlight played across the belt of ice separating the islands from the shore in order to detect smugglers. Kuryakin heaved himself up and tapped the man on the shoulder. "Can they see us through the snow?" he shouted.

The man turned a white-rimmed face to him. "Who knows?"

Nevertheless the man turned the sled inland, hoping to merge the sled with the darkness of the forest that lined the shore. Then, as if to thwart them, as they approached the narrows between Kronstadt and the wooden pier of Lissy Nos, the snow stopped. The man urged the horse faster. The singing of the runners became louder, the beat of the horse's hooves a rapid staccato gallop.

Kuryakin looked over the side of the sled. He could see the trees! Damn it, they were too close! The guards on the mainland shore must surely hear them. He reached up and tapped the man again on the shoulder. "Slower," he demanded.

The man swore. "At this spot we have to go quickly."

Perhaps the man was right. After all, he had done this journey many times before. Suddenly the sled was bathed in light. Kuryakin could make out the grain of the wood, the huge bolts in the crossbeams. They were seen! It was over! The next moment they were surrounded by blackness.

He heard the crack of the whip as the man urged the horse to even greater efforts. The sled was bouncing and careening over the ice, swaying from side to side, threatening each time it hit a mound of snow to hurl itself sideways and capsize, dragging the horse down with it. Kuryakin felt his hands clench over the butt of the Mauser, his body grow rigid with fear and helplessness.

The light came on again. He could make out the wooden pier of Lissy Nos jutting into the gulf like an extended finger, its ugly, squat guardhouse looking over the frozen sea. He prayed that it would be too cold for anyone to be standing outside. The sled swayed and bucked and bounced, the continual hum of its runners like a long, wailing cry of desperation.

Then they were past it, moving once more out into the sea, the flashes of light growing fainter and fainter until once more they were surrounded by blessed darkness.

Two hours later they were in the railway yard at Terioki, the last station in Finland. Kuryakin hauled out the sacks and gave the man the rest of the money. "Thank you," he said.

The man spat.

It was a lazy, torpid Sunday afternoon, cold and grey with the snow flickering down from the sky like soiled lint. Caspar lay warm, content, and heavily somnolent with his cheek on Sonya's naked shoulder, her arm wrapped comfortably round his body. They were lewd, lascivious, wanton libertines, Caspar thought, mouthing each word silently and kissing Sonya's blue-veined breast.

She stirred sleepily.

"Darling."

"We should leave soon."

"Of course."

They were due to hear Ulyanov speak at the Volkshaus.

"We can meet him afterwards."

"But he might say something important."

Sonya pulled Caspar to her and reached a hand down between his legs. "It won't matter if we're a little late."

"He might notice us."
"We'll tell him we got lost."
"Did we?"
"Aren't we?"
"Mmmmm. . . ."
"What about Ulyanov?"
"Who?"
"Mmm. . . ."

They got to the Volkshaus late, wet, bright-eyed and flushed. Ulyanov glared at them from the low platform from which he was addressing half a dozen earnest-looking Swiss, dressed as if for vespers, and a similar number of Ulyanov's less formally attired supporters. He was well on with the Swiss Revolution and had the undivided if perplexed attention of Fritz Platten, the Secretary of the Swiss Social Democrats.

The Swiss Social Democrats were being exhorted to make sacrifices in the interests of mankind. It was their duty as socialists to stir up hatred of the government which supported the tourist industry and thereby encouraged bourgeois practises, a government which oppressed the masses and proclaimed a neutrality which aided the imperialist warmongers. That government had to be destroyed. If the Social Democratic Party refused to do it, then those here must. If necessary, those committed revolutionaries present must split the party. It was superfluous to speak of solidarity amongst revolutionaries. The true revolutionary had only one aim—the success of the revolution. And to achieve that, everything must be destroyed. The party was not sacred. The majority was not sacred. If the majority was stupid then a resolute minority must act.

"Nechayev."

"Sssh."

They should seize the banks and railway stations. Also the post office. They should seize weapons. The reason why Switzerland would be the centre of world revolution was because weapons were so easily available. It was the only country in the world whose soldiers took their guns home with them. The soldiers must be propagandized. . . .

In his monotonous voice, Ulyanov rumbled on and on, linking logical statement to logical statement, idea to slogan, and then repeating everything. Obviously if a thing was worth saying, it was worth saying twice. The Swiss began to look more puzzled, and even the expressions on the faces of his own supporters became faintly glazed. They'd heard all this before. Only for Petrograd substitute Zurich. Nevertheless, when an hour and a half later they left for the Café Adler, Caspar felt quite certain that there was no immediate danger of barricades along the Bahnhofstrasse.

Accompanied by Nadya, Ulyanov came to the Café Adler, his face wan and furrowed under the yellow electric light. As he spotted Caspar and Sonya, he released Nadya's arm and forced himself to walk unaided between the tables to them.

He lowered himself into a chair and pressed his hands to his temples. His head felt as if it were being compressed by a red-hot steel band.

"Coffee, Vladimir Ilyich?" Sonya asked.

Eyes screwed shut against the pain, Ulyanov nodded.

"Vladya, are you all right?" Nadya came up and sat beside him. Ignoring Caspar and Sonya, she began stroking him firmly along the back of his neck. If they had been in private, she would have stroked his head until the pain went, but Vladya had ruled that no one must know of his headaches. He was strong and only temporarily exhausted. He'd been exhausted before. He would recover.

"It's only tiredness," Ulyanov explained, opening his eyes and looking at Caspar and Sonya. "It is very exhausting to talk for so long."

Nadya said, "Drink your coffee, and we will go."

"Did you bring the letters?" Ulyanov asked.

Yes, ever-reliable Nadya had brought the letters. Surreptitiously Ulyanov handed them to Caspar. He felt he should say something to the couple. He reminded himself that the party needed young recruits and that these two were his only link with Russia. "What did you think of the lecture?" he asked.

Caspar said, "I believe that Russia is more prepared for revolution than Switzerland."

Nadya's fingers were drawing the pain from his head. It was easier to think. He had to correct the young man. "Not yet," Ulyanov said. "Every revolution implies a class shift. Unless the time is right for such a class shift, no revolution is possible. In Russia the power is held by very few, and the only opposition is not the workers but the liberal bourgeois. The revolution must, therefore, be in two stages: the first when the bourgeois take power and the second when the revolutionary proletariat seize power. That is not the case in Switzerland where you have an advanced industrial proletariat, ready and able to seize power."

"Don't you believe in a Russian revolution, then?" Sonya asked.

"Believe in it! I have spent my whole life waiting

for it. But I will not be there to see it." He paused and smiled tiredly. "After all, I am forty-seven now."

"Nonsense, Vladya. You will lead the revolution," Nadya said.

Ulyanov's smile became mocking. "I hope you are right," he said, and looked at Caspar. "Meet me here in four days. I will have more letters for you." Holding onto the table for support, Ulyanov got to his feet and then, with a surprising burst of energy, left.

Afterwards, in the apartment, Caspar carefully steamed open Ulyanov's letters. The first letter was to an organiser in Petrograd. There were no specific instructions, only the familiar revolutionary diatribe. *From the point of view of the working class the least evil is defeat of the Tsarist monarchy.* So Ulyanov still did not care if the Russians were defeated, as long as the revolution triumphed. *The smart exploiters of the leading capitalist country, England, are for peace in order to strengthen capitalism, but we should not be confused with the petty, sentimental liberals, etc. The era of the bayonet has come. The imperialists should not profit by the slogan of peace.* Quite right, too! *Our slogan is civil war. Peace does not benefit the revolutionary proletariat.* That was the Ulyanov he admired, the stubborn, defiant Ulyanov who would tear Russia apart.

The other letter was personal, to his sister Maria. It appeared that for most of his forty-seven years Ulyanov had been supported by his mother. Her death had deprived him of his allowance, though Maria had recently sent him eight hundred and eight francs. *Please write and let me know what this money is. I cannot understand where so much money comes from;*

Nadya says jokingly that I must have been pensioned off. Ha ha! The joke is a merry one, for the cost of living makes one despair and I have desperately little capacity for work because of my shattered nerves. Often they only had oatmeal for lunch, which Nadya managed to scorch. *We have roasts every day,* Ulyanov had written with black humour, on the verge of despair. *There are no changes here. We live very quietly and Nadya is often poorly.*

The Reptile Fund could change all that, if it only could be diverted from Parvus to Ulyanov. But first Ulyanov had to be persuaded to join—then there would be a revolution worth talking about.

Petrograd with its repetitious façades and homogeneous baroque palaces was a tedious panorama of featureless white. Sleds slipped noiselessly along the *prospekts* where the snow made it impossible to distinguish the pavements from the roads. There were few trams, and the food queues were longer and more malevolent as rumours of imminent starvation swept through the frozen city.

Serge showed Kuryakin leaflets that had been distributed in the Vyborg area. GIVE US BREAD! DOWN WITH THE WAR! The Russians no longer cared about Constantinople. All they wanted was food and the return of their men from Bukovina, Lemburg, and Przemysl.

Also, Serge informed him, the socialists were holding a parade for International Women's Day. "You think there'll be trouble?" he asked.

"There aren't many women socialists," Kuryakin said.

He looked at the papers on his desk. The giant Putilov steelworks in the Moscow-Narva district was on strike. A minor dispute over the dismissals of some men had grown into a statement of grievance, accompanied by wage claims. Now all the Putilov factories were closed, and the management had imposed a lockout.

Kuryakin lit a cigarette, gloomily. Thirty thousand able-bodied, aggrieved men with time on their hands. It was the kind of situation that could spark off a revolution.

"From today, bread will be rationed," Protopopov announced. "I have made a proclamation."

Kuryakin stared grimly out of the window at the Neva, frozen solid between granite quays, and at the line of dark, huddled figures scurrying across the ice from Vasileyvsky Island. Beyond them, sepulchral in the dead winter light, he could see the Doric columns of the Exchange Building flanked by the twin navigation towers of the Strelka. The murder of Rakovsky, the arrest of the students and members of the Social Patriots in Petrograd, had undoubtedly affected the German plans for an uprising within Russia. Now the rationing of bread would change all that.

"There will be protests," Kuryakin said. March was the worst time for an uprising, with no possibility of isolating the Centre or Petersburg Island by barricading the bridges.

They were in the offices of General Khabalov, the Military Commander of Petrograd. "That is what we are here to discuss, Count Kuryakin." Khabalov was a short, barrel-chested man with a pronounced widow's peak and blunt, commonsense features. He was not the kind of general who wanted to command a city while there was a war going on.

Kuryakin sighed and walked into the centre of the room. Khabalov's office in the Admiralty was large, with sombre furnishings and a huge portrait of the Tsar over his desk. A curtain, now drawn, showed a comfortably furnished lounge, with map tables and large sectional maps of Petrograd on the walls.

"The problem is one of time," Khabalov said. "When do I bring out my Cossacks?"

Too soon or too savage and the demonstration could turn bitter and grow into a rebellion. On the other hand, too late. . . .

"It should be a police operation," Kuryakin said, "at least in the beginning. We should aim for containment. The demonstration will not only start but be the most violent here." He walked over to a map and pointed to the Vyborg side, separated from the Centre and Petersburg Island by the Liteiny and Grenadorsky Bridges. "We must aim at cutting Vyborg off from the rest of Petrograd."

"They'll only come over the ice," Protopopov said.

"Not with three machine-gun crews at each bridge," Khabalov said. "You will need detachments of mounted police and uniformed men lining the Vyborg side of the embankment. They should retreat if pressed. Your reserves, who will not retreat, can be held on our side of the Neva."

"Purely defensive?" Kuryakin asked.

Khabalov and Protopopov looked at each other. The Minister said, "Yes. We want to avoid unnecessary provocation." To change the subject he asked Kuryakin, "What about your people in Section Four?"

"They are more useful providing intelligence than attacking demonstrators with sabres."

"We need fighting men."

"In that case, use soldiers. I cannot have my people facing a crowd in uniform, because after all this is over, they will have to go back onto those streets without uniform, unarmed and masquerading as civilians, not knowing if they have been recognised and which of their contacts had been betrayed because of that recognition."

"He is right, Minister," Khabalov said. "If another thirty or forty men are going to make a difference, you'll need the army anyway."

They spent the rest of the morning discussing the disposition of forces and how and where the protests would begin and if they would grow, and deciding exactly when to call in the army.

Afterwards Kuryakin left, depressed.

It was bitterly cold on the prison roof, and despite his fur-lined gloves, Kuryakin's hands trembled as he raised the Zeiss field glasses to his eyes. March and no sign of spring, the streets below him covered with straggling ribbons of brown-stained snow, the communal street-fires glowing a vivid orange in the dismal light. Eleven o'clock in the morning and the sun buried deep in cloud, and all along the Nyustadtskaya and trams clanging drearily through a press of pedestrians, wagons, omnibuses, and open-sided drays.

The Vyborg side, where dreary factory buildings dominated with their yards full of arid storehouses and windowless dormitories, was strewn with debris and the chimneys billowed black smoke at the winter sky. Away from the Arsenalskaya Embankment and the sooty, arched roofs of the Finland Station, the streets narrowed, houses huddling together in cracked and blistered façades. Here people crowded seven to an apartment if they were lucky, or four to a cellar, living near where they worked a soulless twelve-hour day. Most of them were men, peasants come to work in the factories, and even at that hour of the morning, a hollow-eyed prostitute plied her trade, flitting out of doorways and pausing to mutter momentarily to waiting wagon drivers and *izvoshchiks*.

It was bad, but right in the heart of the city it was worse. He looked across the Liteiny Bridge towards Kazanskaya, where beds were rented five times a day and men were grateful to have an *ugol*, a corner of a room, or sleep on a wooden pallet in a night shelter, crowded two hundred to a room from floor to ceiling. Petrograd had grown too quickly, industrialized too rapidly, without thought. From the Vyborg side one could see the mean and squalid factories crowding behind the impressive Nevsky, making the air hazy with their smoke, burying their waste under the ice of the Neva. From the Vyborg side Petrograd was grim and without hope.

He heard the frail chanting and turned to look up the Nyustadtskaya where the women marched in a dark and ragged phalanx down the centre of the street. At the head and alongside the procession were policemen, their twin rows of buttons shiny on their black uniforms, pill-box hats pulled squarely down on their heads, and guns tucked away under the calf-length overcoats, acting more like shepherds than guard dogs. The trams and wagons stopped. Passersby lined the pavement watching the parade move down the snow-covered street like a giant clot. There was about two thousand of them, mostly dressed in black, their heads shrouded with the inevitable shawls, waving untidy, handwritten banners. As they came nearer, Kuryakin heard them crying for bread, crying for peace. He noticed that there were a few men amongst them, self-conscious and staring belligerently at the watching crowd.

"Come, comrades, join us!" one of the women cried.

No one moved.

Kuryakin watched them pass below him, a mass of shawls and peaked worker's caps, leather jackets and long, shapeless dresses, moving through the chill morning light towards the Arsenalskaya and the Liteiny Bridge.

He lowered the glasses and watched the demonstrating workers stream away from him. So far all was well. Even though the city was under martial law, the only soldiers in evidence were those guarding the Arsenal.

He heard more chanting and saw banners flutter to the left of him. He raised the field glasses to look. Another procession was winding out of the plaza before the Finland Station, moving along the Arsenalskaya to meet with the procession of women before the Liteiny Bridge. There were a number of women in the second procession. Textile workers, Kuryakin thought, leaving their factories and marching out in support. Also, a large number of men. Strikers from the Putilov Works.

What were the police doing? They should be heading off the two groups. But they had taken Protopopov's directive to avoid unnecessary confrontations too literally and stood lined against the further side of the embankment, allowing the two processions of workers to meet.

They met before the Liteiny Bridge in a dark, solid throng, blocking the entire Arsenalskaya and pushing back into the streets beyond. The shouting and the cheering and the chanting doubled in intensity but died while the leaders discussed what to do; then the crowd was moving towards the bridge. Hesitation once more. Single figures crossed the pavement or stood before the policemen. Then, with a frantic waving of arms, the crowd tried to rush the bridge.

There was a violent convolution of bodies. Banners flailed. Stones and bricks and shafts of wood sailed darkly through the air like dust sucked up by a strong wind. Then the crowd was pushed back from the centre, curving saucerlike. Mounted police dashed out, laying about them with the flat of their sabres. No chanting now, only isolated screams. The crowd scattered and broke, the once solid mass now running fragmented, rushing into doorways, falling onto snow. It was the police who then moved forward in a tight cordon, batons smashing into skulls, running down disoriented figures with galloping horses, leaving bodies fallen, black, and huddled on the snow.

Kuryakin watched people run past and lose themselves in the everyday ordinariness of the Nyustadtskaya. It was over, at least for now.

That evening the machine-gun detachments were replaced by small groups of mounted police, and it was only in the Vyborg area that the patrols were doubled. Soldiers, apart from those guarding the Arsenal and the Winter Palace, were confined to barracks, and within the city itself everything appeared normal.

In the Admiralty building, Protopopov met with General Khabalov, and they congratulated themselves on controlling a dangerous situation. There was a party at the French Embassy, and the guests discussed ballet and the merits of Pavlova, Karsavina, and Kschessinskaya. In the Duma they discussed a proposal that for three days there should be no trains other than those transporting food. From the British Embassy, Sir George Buchanan reported by cable: *Some disorders occurred today. But nothing serious.* With only twenty-eight policemen slightly injured and not a shot fired, it seemed a fair summary.

In Moika, however, Kuryakin brooded. The day had shown the police to be irresolute and the demonstrators to be imbued with a quality of self-perpetuating spontaneity. It was a disastrous combination. There would be more demonstrations tomorrow, and more industrial disruption. Also, the leaders of the socialist parties would have realised by now that if they did not organise the crowds, other leaders would spring from the unrest and supplant them.

If only Stalin were free. Stalin would know what the Bolsheviks were planning and that would have given Kuryakin an indication of what the others were doing. Kuryakin looked at the stack of agents' reports on his desk. No one knew who had called out the textile workers. No one knew what was being planned for the morrow. Patiently Kuryakin sieved through the reports again. There was only a slight glimmer of hope. Fyodor, the youngest of his men, only four months with the Okhrana, had reported that one Karasov had indicated there would be another protest by the women the following day.

Karasov. Kuryakin remembered that any information he might have on Karasov was in Finland. He looked at his watch. Despite the unrest, Protopopov had ruled that no special measures should be taken. At that time of the evening most of his men would be at home, the offices run by a skeleton staff of seven. Fortunately, Fyodor was amongst them.

Fyodor entered Kuryakin's office, fresh faced and

nervous. He came from a family of wealthy sugar merchants who had used their money and influence to get him into the police instead of the army. He was a quiet, determined lad with enough grace to be embarrassed at his exemption from military service.

"Karasov," Kuryakin said, tapping the reports on his desk. "Who is Karasov?"

Fyodor swallowed nervously, "He is a Social Patriot, sir. A veteran of Nanshan. He used to be one of Rakovsky's adjutants."

Kuryakin remembered. Ten days previously Fyodor had requested that Karasov be excluded from the arrests that had thrown most of the Social Patriots into prison. Karasov was a useful contact, and it was better to allow the rump of the Scoail Patriots to regroup around him.

"I want to see him tonight," Kuryakin said.

Still looking nervous, Fyodor glanced down at the desk. Surely Kuryakin as head of Section Four was aware that no agent liked his contacts meeting with other members of the Okhrana.

As if to confirm that knowledge, Kuryakin said softly, "It is important, Fyodor, or I wouldn't have asked."

"He's at work now," Fyodor said. "He is a foreman on the night shift at the Svetlana Copper Works on the Vyborg side. He won't be finished until midnight."

"I can wait till then," Kuryakin said.

In Berlin, Zimmerman apprehensively watched von Dichter stride across the floor of his office. Much depended on the reaction of this potbellied, bowlegged man marching across the room to meet him in a field-grey coat decorated with red piping and gold buttons, whose high, red collar was embroidered with gold. Von Dichter was fortyish, with severe blue eyes, greying closely-cropped hair, and an expression of unbridled ferocity. He was, Zimmerman decided, going to be troublesome.

It was von Dichter who had phoned him from Zurich and told him of Rakovsky's murder. It was von Dichter who had made a formal protest at whatever operation the Imperial Intelligence Bureau East was running in Switzerland and who had threatened to raise the matter not only with Colonel Nikolai but with General Headquarters.

Zimmerman had suggested that Caspar Ehrler brief von Dichter on Quadriga and that, as soon as possible afterwards, von Dichter should see him in Berlin. Now he bade von Dichter welcome, walked over to the tulip-wood secretaire, and poured himself a glass of Moselle. "A drink, Major?"

"Thank you, no." Von Dichter stared primly across Zimmerman's empty desk at the bleak Foreign Office garden.

"Did you have a comfortable journey?"

"Very comfortable, thank you."

The clipped, military speech, the erect posture, and the hands clasped sanctimoniously in von Dichter's lap augured ill for Quadriga. Zimmerman sat behind the desk and twirled the glass idly in his hand. He had always intended that once the operation was fully under way, Section IIIb, General Headquarters would never give Quadriga its final approval. All that the murder of Rakovsky had done was to make him want to involve Section IIIb earlier. Except, as von Dichter's resolute expression made clear, Section IIIb did not want to be involved.

"Let me explain to you," Zimmerman said, "why the success of Quadriga is so vital. We are about to lose this war. When last week's British Blockade Order begins to take effect, we are going to have less food, less materials, less armaments. We will lose this war not because the German Army will be defeated in the field but because, in the long run, we will not have the materials with which to fight.

"As you know, things have not gone well for us this last month. In the West, our forces are retreating and regrouping behind the Siegfried Line. In Asia, Kut has been evacuated by the Turks, who are retreating to Baghdad. And in America, Mr. Wilson is trying to force Congress to declare war.

"I have made certain plans to postpone America's involvement in the war. But sooner or later, they will become involved. And before that, we must obtain a decisive victory over the Entente powers. The only way we can achieve such a victory is by utilization of all our forces and all our war materials against the West. For that we must have peace in the East. I would like you to think about all this very carefully before you give me your opinion on Quadriga."

"I have considered the matter," von Dichter said. He looked at Zimmerman levelly. "Your plan will not work, Excellency."

Zimmerman moved the glass of wine away and picked up a pen and a large notepad. "Your reasons, Major von Dichter."

"Ehrler must return to Berlin at once."

"You are dissatisfied with Ehrler?"

"No. He is a most intelligent young man. A trifle inexpreienced perhaps, but if Quadriga were to go ahead, it would not do so without Ehrler. He is the only one with all the contacts amongst the Russian exiles. However, Rakovsky's killing must lead us to assume that Quadriga has been blown. And if Quadriga has been blown, then Ehrler is exposed. If Ehrler is exposed and remains in Zurich, he will certainly be killed."

"One life," Zimmerman said piously, "for so much. Ehrler is a soldier. He is taking no greater risk than any other young man in the trenches."

"If Ehrler is killed, you cannot replace him. Further, the Swiss have already closed down the English operation. If Quadriga continues, they will close us down, too. That will not only wreck your plan but also wreck a number of operations we are running. It cannot be allowed to happen. We do not want to start a war on Swiss territory."

"If the matter is handled properly," Zimmerman said, "I see no reason for any further violence."

"Matters are now out of control," von Dichter said, drily. "Rakovsky's death proves that. We also have other objections. Helphand may have excellent connections amongst the revolutionaries but his political and financial reputation is dubious."

"The money is securely within our control," Zimmerman pointed out.

"The whole operation is also too expensive."

"You're talking of one hundred and twenty million marks," Zimmerman said. "For one hundred and twenty million marks we are buying peace on the Eastern Front. And if you think that is expensive, talk to the mothers of the boys serving there. Two hundred and forty marks for the life of each German soldier is very cheap."

"With respect, Excellency, my view is that this war can and will be won on the battlefield."

"You do not have the facts to support such an opinion," Zimmerman snapped. "This war can now only be won by conspiracy."

"Conspiracy to overthrow a monarch! A conspiracy to overthrow the cousin of our own Kaiser!"

"We are at war with the Kaiser's cousin," Zimmerman said.

"We're also helping to create a government of socialists! We are playing with political and social forces we neither understand nor control. We are acting as midwives at the birth of a monster!"

"A calculated risk, if you don't mind my saying so. Once the Russian people have learned that monarchs and governments can be overthrown, then an extremist government, whether of right or left, can only have a limited life. I genuinely believe that six months after the peace the Tsar will be back on the throne. After all, the Romanovs have ruled Russia for three hundred years. They will not find anyone with that collective experience to replace Tsar Nicholas."

"History," said von Dichter, "will judge which of us is right. But by then it will be too late."

"You still do not approve?"

"We would approve, if it was a matter of last resort. But we have a choice—"

The door opened and Zimmerman's secretary entered, carrying a copy of the previous day's London *Times* on a silver slaver. "Forgive me, Your Excellency, the Reichskanzler insists you see this immediately."

Zimmerman picked up the paper. The headlines were bold and black. One could almost sense the staid newspaper bursting with self-imposed restraint.

GERMANY SEEKS ALLIANCE AGAINST U.S.
ASKS JAPAN AND MEXICO TO JOIN HER.
FULL TEXT OF PROPOSAL MADE PUBLIC.

The story began, *The Associated Press is able to reveal that Germany is seeking an alliance with Mexico to declare war against the United States. Germany has promised the Mexicans considerable support and the return to Mexico of the former lost territories of Texas, New Mexico, and Arizona. Upon conclusion of the alliance with Mexico, the Germans seek a similar alliance with Japan. Meanwhile, they expect England to sue for peace within months, due to the unleashing of unrestricted submarine warfare.*

In confirmation of the story was a telegram sent by the Foreign Office in Berlin to the German Ambassador in Mexico City. The telegram was signed "Zimmerman."

Von Dichter looked at Zimmerman, horrified. "Of course, Your Excellency will deny this story."

"I cannot deny it," Zimmerman said. "It is true." He closed his eyes in anguish. Not only Quadriga, but his scheme to keep America out of the war had collapsed. There was no doubt now that America would come into the war, bringing into the conflict its massive resources of men and materials. The vicious stalemate on two fronts would end. Instead there would be a savage onslaught from the West. God help Germany!

God help Germany! von Dichter thought. He did not understand the machinations of politicians and ministers, but as a military man he realised that Russia had to be eliminated from the war immediately. "Under the changed circumstances, Excellency," he said, "our objections to the Helphand operation are withdrawn. Section IIIb is at your disposal. I will speak to Colonel Nikolai myself and obtain the necessary approvals."

Above the Svetlana Works the night sky was tinted red from the glow of the smelters, and the massive chimneys belched thick, dark columns of smoke against the dappled backdrop of central Petrograd. Powerful lamps bathed the high factory gate and walls in a bright yellow glare. Scrawled along the wall was a slogan in red paint, POWER TO THE PEOPLE.

Kuryakin sat in the back of a car on an unlit side street facing the factory. The beat of machinery accompanied by a light, metallic clanging carried on the night air, and before the immense, locked factory gate, four armed guards stamped their feet in the snow.

Faintly across the frozen Neva, over the sounds of the factory, he heard the churches of central Petrograd chime the hour, followed by a sharp blast on a siren. Almost immediately the street filled with figures, streaming through the side gates set in the wall, hurrying out of the floodlit glare to the all-night tram stop beside the Arsenal. Kuryakin saw Fyodor in a long overcoat and fur hat move into the crowd and approach a leather-jacketed man of medium height who wore a peaked cap. They spoke together urgently and then both men walked out of the light and were lost in the shadows of the side streets.

Kuryakin heard them come, with a measured crunch of footsteps on the crusted snow. He opened the car door, saying, "Get in." He felt the car lurch as the man climbed in, lit a cigarette so he could examine Karasov in the flame of the lighter. A compact, powerful-looking man, with flat cheekbones, a sharp nose, small eyes, and an expression of impassivity.

"You know we killed Rakovsky," Kuryakin said as the flame went out.

Beside him Karasov remained very still. "We heard."

"So your party is finished."

"We would cease to be human if we ceased to hope."

"Hope for what, Karasov? To rule Russia? Even if we let you alone, with Rakovsky dead and most of your party members in prison, your fellow socialists will turn on you like the wild dogs they are and finish you off." Kuryakin pulled deeply at his cigarette and looked at Karasov in the faint red light. Karasov's face was still impassive. "That is, if we didn't finish you first by arresting the rest of your group tonight."

Karasov thought that if Kuryakin had wanted to do that, he wouldn't be sitting talking to him in the back of a car. "We are useful to you."

"You call giving my young men information they can read in the newspapers being useful? If you want to stay free, Karasov, we want much more than that."

"I do my best," Karasov said.

"I want hard facts. What are the Bolsheviks and Social Democrats up to? How do they intend to exploit the demonstrations? Which factories will join in tomorrow? Who is organising this women's demonstration you speak of?"

Karasov sat silent.

"You have to choose," Kuryakin said, "between them and us. We have the power, we have the guns, we have the army. In the long term, we will win. Then we will remember our friends . . . and our enemies."

"The arm of the Okhrana is long," Karasov said, his voice as impassive as his expression. "A Revolutionary Committee has been formed. We have been invited to participate. There will be a meeting tomorrow to co-ordinate all the demonstrations."

"Where?" Kuryakin asked excitedly. If he could arrest all the revolutionary leaders in Petrograd at the same time, that would be the end of the demonstrations.

"I don't know yet. I will be told tomorrow. When I know, I will inform Fyodor."

"Inform me," Kuryakin said.

The next morning Kuryakin looked about him with more than usual interest as he was driven from his home in the Maximillianovsky Pereulok to the Moika. There were a few more policemen than usual outside the Mariinsky and the yellow and white Quarenghi-designed Yousoupoff Palace where Rasputin had been murdered. Apart from that, however, the embankment looked normal. At the intersection with the Nevsky Prospekt, Kuryakin had the driver turn towards the Admiralty. The upper part of the Nevsky, with its mixture of old-world buildings and modern commercial blocks, was peopled with more soldiers. Peering down the Morskaya at the dark red archway of the General Staff Headquarters Building, he saw that the guard had been doubled. Two hundred yards before the Alexander Garden they were stopped.

Here the military was out in force, sentries crowding under the Roman arches of the Admiralty and soldiers patrolling amongst the fountains and monuments of the Garden. Kuryakin calculated that there were about two thousand men there. Whatever happened, Khabalov meant to ensure the safety of the capital's administrative centre and his own command post.

Satisfied, Kuryakin returned to the Moika Embankment and then cut across, past the Pavlovsky Barracks to the Troitsky Bridge. At the bridge he was stopped again, but on producing his pass was allowed to cross.

On the Petrograd side, the Kameno-Ostrovsky, dominated by the grim bastions of the Fortress, was quiet. Kuryakin turned into the Petrovskaya Ulitza, passed the scaffolded Troitsky Cathedral and the wooden cottage that was the first house built in Petrograd, and drove towards the wooden Samsonovsky Bridge. A hundred metres short of the bridge he dismissed the carriage and walked up to the heavy guard of policemen. On the further side, he could see the crowds gathered on the Samsonovsky Prospekt surrounding the Pirogoff Museum and the Military Hospital. He produced his Okhrana pass and was allowed to cross.

On the Vyborg side it was chaos. All traffic had stopped and the street was full of workers. Banners waved, the occasional red flag fluttered, but no one was making any attempt to brave the police with their machine guns.

Kuryakin attempted to walk down the Samsonovsky to the Liteiny. A man caught him by the arm.

"I saw them let you through, comrade."

"They're letting everyone through who works on this side." Kuryakin eyed the unwashed, bearded face, whose eyes were thick with matter. "I am going to the Svetlana."

"We're from the Putilov Works," the man said. "All the way across Petrograd from Moscow-Narva. When are you coming out to join us?"

"There is a meeting of the Revolutionary Committee today," Kuryakin said. "After that we will know. How did you get across the bridge?"

"Early this morning they weren't concerned."

Kuryakin left the man and pushed through the

crowd. Dressed like one of them, in a leather jacket and roughened trousers, wearing a peaked cap and heavy boots, he attracted no attention. As he reached the Military Hospital and the Pirogovskaya the crowd grew thicker. There were banners and flags, much excited shouting, and the heaving of bodies. Movement was difficult.

"Whom are you pushing, comrade?"

"Where do you think you're going?"

Pushing less vehemently, Kuryakin studied the banners. One said simply, NEMKA! Others protested, DOWN WITH AUTOCRACY!—DOWN WITH THE GERMAN WOMAN! —HANG THE MINISTERS!—DESTROY THE PUTILOV EXPLOITERS!—and Kuryakin's favourite, the only slogan directed against the Tsar, JALKA! JALKA! CHTO-NICOLI SPEAT! "What a pity Nicholas sleeps!"

"Stop pushing, comrade!"

"I have to get to work."

"Work! What do you mean, work? We're all on strike." An angry, pinched face peered suspiciously at Kuryakin.

Kuryakin dropped his hand to the Mauser in his pocket. "I have five mouths to feed," he muttered.

"We're all starving, comrade. Why should you be different?"

Still gripping the Mauser, Kurakin stared levelly at the man. "Traitor," the man muttered, but he let Kuryakin pass.

As Kuryakin pushed his way to the front of the crowd, movement became easier. The crowd was spread across the Pirogovskaya, from the walls of the hospital to the Neva Embankment, less dense at the front and stretching inexorably to within thirty yards of the Liteiny where a semicircle of mounted police protected the bridgehead.

Suddenly, for no reason and without warning, the crowd charged. One moment Kuryakin was surrounded by a press of bodies, the next he was being swept in a ragged run towards the line of policemen. There were shouts of "Seize the bridge!"—"To Kazan!"—"Burn the Pharoahs!" ("Burn the Police!")—"Kill!"

A splatter snow-trapped footsteps, a mad flash-fire of excitement, a long, persistent ululation. Against the vast accompaniment of sound, missiles rose blackly silent through the air.

The police advanced with a great clip-clopping of hooves, the ominous whirring of the flats of their swords becoming sharp thwacks as sheathed metal met flesh. The crowd turned and ran back towards the hospital, their banners trampled into the snow. Panic-stricken bodies cannoned into Kuryakin as he tried to make for the safety of the embankment.

The police came on and on, in a wide, puissant row, filling the street, the horses' hooves raising powdery flurries of snow, the policemen leaning sideways out of their saddles like polo players, their swords scything the air between them.

"God have mercy!" The crowd surged back, leaving behind their wounded, creating a clear, snow-covered gap between them and the advancing police. Suddenly the leading policeman swung upright, raised his hand high and shouted, "*Stoi!*"

With a skidding of hooves and a showering of snow, the horses stopped, flanks sweaty and heaving, nostrils streaming smoke. They stopped, except for one who did not hear or had lost control. Still tilted sideways, a lone policeman charged into the crowd.

The crowd broke. Kuryakin glimpsed a young, anguished face sideways above the snow, eyes wide with surprise or fear. It was not a man but a boy, he thought, as the rider sawed frantically at the reins and tried to get upright.

Then someone jabbed a stick into the horse's eye.

The horse whinnied, reared, then slid splaylegged on the snow. The rider was thrown helplessly sideways, arms outflung. For a moment he lay still, huddled on the ground. Then the crowd was all over him.

Kuryakin saw the row of mounted police trotting back to the bridge past the straggled lines of wounded lying on the bloodstained snow; he looked at the wounded horse, the stick still dragging from its head, limping after them, and saw the heaving mass of bodies to his left. With sudden horror he realised that, as if warned of their own fate, the policemen had abandoned their colleague. Shouting, "Let me get at him, too!" Kuryakin thrust away from him and plunged into the crowd.

The demonstrators were all round the fallen policeman, fists and sticks rising and falling in a deadly rhythm. There were grunts from the men as they swung frenziedly, a soft, solid thudding as the blows landed on limp flesh. The policeman lay on his back, his face already swollen and bloody, his uniform torn open, his body jerking like a puppet's as each blow connected.

Kuryakin took out the Mauser, pointed it at the sky, and fired twice.

The loud explosions at close range made them stop. Some ran back into the crowd. "Comrade," cried one, "give me the gun and let me finish him."

"A waste of bullets," Kuryakin said. "The pharaoh is already dead."

Twenty yards away the police were hesitantly regrouping. A hand reached out for the gun. Kuryakin elbowed the man in the throat. "They're coming," he cried, as the row of policemen moved hesitantly forward. The crowd ran back, leaving Kuryakin beside the limp and lifeless body.

"I'm from the Okhrana," he cried as the first policeman reached him. "Get this man out of here and cover me till I reach the bridge."

Afterwards Kuryakin took a police carriage to the Admiralty. Khabalov received him immediately, looking quizzically at his workman's attire and then turning back to the window where he was surveying the University Quay through binoculars.

"You must bring the troops out now," Kuryakin said.

"And why is that, my dear fellow?"

"Because the time to quell the rising is now, before more people come out onto the streets. Before they have time to organise."

Still looking through the binoculars, Khabalov pointed at the baroque, red Menshikoff Palace, occupying a whole third of the University Quay. "Everything seems normal there."

"It isn't so normal on the Vyborg side," Kuryakin snapped. "And Protopopov's directive has left the police huddling round the bridgeheads like old women, not sure whether to attack or defend."

"And how will the army change that?" Khabalov put down the binoculars and turned to look at Kuryakin.

"It will demonstrate firmness. It will give the police tangible support. It will free them from defending the bridges and allow them to force the crowds off the streets."

Khabalov walked up to his desk. "I have my orders. You should raise this at the conference with Protopopov tomorrow."

"Protopopov is determined to play down this rising. He doesn't want to admit to the Tsar that his reports have been wrong all along."

Khabalov shrugged. "My dear Kuryakin, we are nothing but the servants of our political masters."

"Damn it, man, you are the military commander of Petrograd. The ultimate responsibility for the safety of the city is in your hands."

"I'm glad you mentioned that," Khabalov murmured. "I was beginning to think the responsibility was yours." He moved away from the window, drawing himself erect, and looked directly at Kuryakin. "Nothing you have told me so far has given me any reason to doubt Minister Protopopov's judgement. The disturbances are small, local, and temporary."

Kuryakin strode up to the desk and began to write. "I am formally advising you that the crowds on the Vyborg side are immense and that the bridges cannot be held. I am advising you that things are bad and will get worse. I am advising you that we are on the verge of a major uprising, and I am requesting that troops be brought out to assist the police." He thrust the paper at Khabalov.

Khabalov glanced down at it. "You realise, of course, that you are placing me in a most invidious position. If I bring out the troops against the Minister's orders, I will be cashiered. If you are right and if we survive the holocaust you foretell, then I will be hung."

"Something has to be done," Kuryakin said.

"And I will do it," Khabalov said. He picked up the telephone and spoke to Protopopov. When he had finished, he said, "The Minister has authorised the use of the Don Cossacks."

Kuryakin felt the tension drain out of his body. The Don Cossacks were the Tsar's most loyal and most fearless warriors. Victors of numerous street battles, it was they who had swept the crowds off the streets in 1905.

"But they will not be allowed to use their whips," Khabalov added.

Kuryakin felt his jaw drop in surprise. Cossacks without whips were soldiers without ammunition. Since time immemorial those long, flailing whips had beaten the crowds of Petrograd into submission. "What is the good of that?" he asked disgustedly.

"The Minister feels that at this stage the presence of troops should only be symbolic."

Back in the Moika, Kuryakin asked Serge, "How quickly can you get all our people together?"

"Give me ninety minutes. I've been running a tight check on them all morning, in case we need to move quickly after Karasov's call."

"Bring them in," Kuryakin ordered. On the way back from the Admiralty he'd noticed groups of restless men wandering down the Nevsky, for the moment uncertain of what to do or what would happen next. There had also been reports of more fighting on the Vyborg side, of streets barricaded and a police station sacked.

"You have heard from Karasov?"

Kuryakin said, "I want to march on Tsarskoe Selo. We get into the Alexander Palace pretending to be the Okhrana detachment sent to guard the Tsar. Then we seize him. Then I talk to him."

"Then we all get hung," Serge said.

"The Tsar and I were brother officers in the Preobrajensky," Kuryakin said.

"And that, my friend, was a long time ago."

"That is the risk I have to take. I will persuade him to dismiss the ministers, to give the Duma the constitution they want, to exclude the Tsarina from the affairs of state, and, somehow, anyhow, to bring food into Petrograd."

"It won't work," Serge said. "The Tsar is not in the Alexander Palace but in Mogilev. He left yesterday. I have copies of the movement orders in my office."

"But that's absurd!" Kuryakin cried. "Which of his sycophantic nincompoops advised him to go? The Tsar is needed here. He is the one person who can persuade the people to leave the streets."

"It looks like he wants to win the war first," Serge said.

Kuryakin buried his head in his hands. "There isn't time for that," he said softly. "The Tsar is finished."

It was bitterly cold, and huddling beside Fyodor in a doorway Kuryakin felt his bones had turned to solid shafts of ice. Early that evening Karasov had called. "You will find what you're looking for at eleven o'clock tonight. The first floor apartment at 32 Smironova Ulica."

"Why so late?" Kuryakin had asked.

"Be there." An obviously frightened Karasov had rung off.

Kuryakin knew why the Revolutionary Committe was meeting so late at night. It was a well-known fact that in the winter the police found it too cold to maintain all-night vigils. Also, they would have a lot to talk about, and in the morning they could leave unrecognised, joining the crowds of people going to the factories.

Smironova Ulica was a dingy street on the Vyborg side, crowded with narrow houses let as rooms and *ugols* and run-down apartments, whose basements were always damp and often covered by six inches of water. The street smelt of cabbage soup and rotting fish.

Parked across the ends of the street were two black Okhrana cars, carrying six men from Section Four. Since midnight, no one had been allowed into the Smironova Ulica, and in the street behind it was another detachment from Section Four, keeping watch on the back of number thirty-two.

Kuryakin turned his head stiffly and looked down the street. They were waiting for Isakoff, the oldest of his men, who had been sent to the local station to bring a uniformed policeman so that entrance to the building would be made easier. Perhaps it had been a mistake to send Isakoff, Kuryakin thought. The police attitude to Jews, even those in the service of the Okhrana, was well known and they were just as likely to imprison Isakoff as accompany him.

Kuryakin eased out of the shadow of the doorway and glanced down the street. His men were well hidden. He tried to smile approvingly and felt his lips hurt as the thin film of ice covering them cracked. He was using more than half of his veterans on this operation. It was risky exposing so many of them at the one time, but it was a chance that had to be taken. The arrest of the Revolutionary Committee would keep the workers disorganised for a few more days and hopefully buy enough time for the rising to die down of its own accord.

He heard the sound of footsteps and saw Isakoff's

diminutive figure trotting along the street, the white armband on his leather jacket startlingly clear. "Where's the policeman?" Kuryakin whispered.

"The street before the police station has been barricaded off. The police station has been destroyed by fire bombs. There are no policemen."

That must have happened after they'd left the Moika, Kuryakin thought. He'd remember to tell Protopopov about it at their meeting tomorrow, in order to compel him to bring out the troops. "Get into position and give us cover," Kuryakin said, and slipped back into the doorway beside Fyodor.

Moments later he told Fyodor, "Let's go," and, giving a low whistle, raced across the street, bracing himself against the wall beside the entrance to number thirty-two. Fyodor spread himself on the opposite side of the entrance, and four others spread fanlike for a moment across the street before disappearing into shadow.

Taking out his Mauser with his right hand, Kuryakin pounded on the door with his left. "Help! Help! There's been an accident! We need help! Open quickly!"

Standing with his face pressed against the icy wall, Kuryakin heard the sound of bolts being drawn, confused mutters and the scrape of a warped door on cement. Quickly he stepped before it.

A frail, rumpled porter peered through the narrow opening. "What is it?" he muttered, querulously.

"There's been an—"

In one smooth movement Fyodor kicked the door open. The old watchman staggered backwards. Kuryakin pushed the door wider and they rushed in through the crowded hallway, full of dripping overcoats and rows of mud-stained boots.

Kuryakin grabbed the porter round the neck and pressed the revolver into his face. "Okhrana," he said. "Where are they?"

The old man twisted his head away from the gun barrel. "Upstairs," he gasped. "Third door on the left after the stairs."

Two more men ran through the open doorway and joined them. Fyodor, gun in hand, was already pounding up the uncarpeted stairs. The others followed.

"How many are there?"

"I—I—don't know. Six or seven."

Kuryakin released the porter and raced up the stairs. On the landing he stopped. Something was wrong. The porter had not been dressed in nightshirt and dressing gown—he had been wearing an overcoat. Now, as Kuryakin turned and looked, he saw the porter shambling through the open doorway, jamming a fur hat onto his head with both hands. Hands still clasped to his head, the old man began to run.

"Wait!" Kuryakin cried, then turned to look along the narrow, dimly-lit corridor: two men spread out against the wall on either side of the entrance to the apartment, Fyodor beginning a short run from across the corridor to kick the door open. "Don't!" Kuryakin screamed as Fyodor swung.

Fyodor's foot hit the door above the lock. There was a harsh, tearing sound, followed by a loud, shattering explosion. Holding his head in his arms Kuryakin, preparing to roll down the stairs, felt himself lifted and flung headlong onto the coats and boots in the hallway below. The breath slammed out of him as he landed and slid across the open doorway.

He lay there breathless, his ears still ringing with the sound of the explosion.

Then, seconds apart, the sound of three other explosions filled the street. Hands still about his head, Kuryakin rolled out of the doorway. Though all the street lamps had gone out, the street was a bright orange, and from each end came the sensation of heat and a fierce crackling. Feeling the salty tang of blood trickling through his mouth, Kuryakin raised his head and looked. At each end of the street his cars were on fire, and the air he was sucking so greedily into his lungs were fetid with the reek of burning human flesh.

A hand grasped him by the back of the collar. "Dimitri, are you all right?"

"Get down, Isakoff." Already people were crowding into the street. "Take off your armband. Kick your rifle away." They lay side by side in the snow as people ran up to the house.

Slowly Kuryakin raised himself onto his knees.

"Are you all right, comrade?"

"We were passing by," Kuryakin muttered. "An explosion . . . people inside. . . ." With Isakoff's help he stood upright, swaying. People ran through the open doorway. In the hallway Kuryakin could see a severed leg, the trouser torn in ragged spirals as if it had been dragged through barbed wire, and, in the centre of the bloodied heap, a bone glinting evilly in the firelight.

"Let's get out of here," he muttered and moved back into the surging crowd.

"I will not have you running about Petrograd at this time on a personal vendetta," Protopopov said, his sleek head bobbing behind the desk like that of a snake about to strike.

Kuryakin stared dully across the room, feeling the

lump of crusted blood in his mouth. He had arrived late for the ministers' conference and still wore the soiled, bloodstained clothes of the previous night. His head ached and he felt tired and drained. His report of the events and the situation on the Vyborg side had been received with mild incomprehension. "It is not a question of vendetta," he said, tiredly, though he knew that was not true. Last night he had lost eighteen of his men. It had been simply, even beautifully done. Three well-aimed grenades into each of the cars and nearly half of Section Four had been eliminated. "The Revolutionary Committee exists. They have access to the latest weapons. Those bombs they used last night are the latest type, being used by the Austrians. If they use them against the bridgehead, the police won't have a chance."

"I can't agree with you," Khabalov said. "We've heard stories about this new Austrian grenade. But how can any Revolutionary Committee get enough of them into Petrograd? I'm sorry you lost so many of your men, but quite obviously if the Committee you speak of existed, they would have used these new weapons by now against the Winter Palace and the Admiralty."

"You must agree, Kuryakin, our policies are working," Protopopov added.

"Someone," Kuryakin said, "has called a general strike. That morning Petrograd had been frozen in deathly stillness, fossilized in rays of brittle sunshine. Travelling to his meeting with Protopopov, Kuryakin had come across a Nevsky deserted and vastly empty. There had been no trams, no smoke from the factories. Petrograd had looked abandoned.

Khabalov said, "Someone is *trying* to organize a general strike. But it will not take place. I have issued a proclamation banning all public meetings and another proclamation demanding that the strike end in three days."

"Three days! But that's when the workers have said they will go back."

Khabalov shrugged. "We can wait. They have neither the strength nor the financial means to stay out longer than that."

"Meanwhile," Protopopov said, "we don't want you upsetting the delicate balance that exists between us and the people of Petrograd. You will not make any more forays onto the Vyborg side. You will not spread these exaggerated stories of violence. I am confining you and your men to barracks. You will remain there until you are given fresh orders by the city perfect."

"Minister! The intelligence we collect is vital! If our advice had been acted upon earlier—"

"You acted on your intelligence and lost half your men," Protopopov sneered. "Now get back to the Moika and stay there."

All that morning Kuryakin and the remnants of Section Four remained cloistered in the Moika while Morse radio messages and news bulletins confirmed that the situation in Petrograd was deteriorating. The strike had brought out over one hundred thousand people in the central area alone, and, apart from the Arsenalskaya, the entire Vyborg side was under the control of the mob. Police stations had been burned, streets barricaded with trams and telegraph poles, and the Liteiny bridgehead taken.

Soon after midday, Khabalov brought his troops out into the streets. They heard the sound of sporadic firing and reports of massive demonstrations outside the

Kazan Cathedral. At four o'clock they were ordered to the Kazansky Bridge on the Nevsky.

The sight that greeted them was frightening. About three hundred policemen and horses milled between the stone balustrades of the bridge, whilst a row of ambulances stood beside the Catholic Church of St. Catherine on whose steps lay policemen, wounded and dying. About two hundred yards further down the Prospekt between the City Hall and the old, covered market of the Priny Ryad, the street was a solid mass of people. Banners and red flags waved. Stones and pieces of ice landed harmlessly in the space between. Suddenly, from one of the buildings beside the Armenian Church, came the crackle of rifle fire. Kuryakin saw two policemen fall, then the order was given to charge.

The police went down the Prospekt in a rough semblance of order, running beside the horses and swinging their batons. Running stiffly along the snow, Kuryakin saw that, unlike the one on the Vyborg side, this crowd was not dispersing. Checking that Serge and the rest of his detachment were still with him, he plunged into the crowd.

His hand jarred as his baton bounced off a fur-covered head. A man grabbed him by the collar and Kuryakin slammed the baton against a straightening elbow, hearing the bone snap. He swung the baton in a wide sweep in front of him. A woman fell at his feet and tried to grab his ankles. He kicked her hard in the face and then stepped over her prostrate body, turning round briefly to glimpse Serge clubbing a man savagely on the back of the neck. Someone hit Kuryakin across the face, and he felt the wound in his mouth reopen. Feeling himself seized by the shoulders, he jabbed the baton into a heaving stomach and was rewarded by an explosion of breath.

The mob was fleeing now. Filled with a savage bloodlust, Kuryakin kept after them, grabbing people from behind, clubbing them fiercely, until opposite the Gostiny Dvor he stopped, panting and exhausted.

The Nevsky was littered with bodies. Windows had been smashed, shops emptied. In the crowd, forty yards before him, he could see people carrying loaves of bread and sides of smoked beef. A woman was making for the Sadovaya carrying a tray of jewellery. He spat a mouthful of blood into the snow. "I'm getting old," he said to Serge.

No sooner did they return to the Moika than they were ordered out again. Revolutionaries had seized the Great Northern Hotel on the northern side of the Znamenskaya and had fired on the police guarding the Nicholas Station opposite, killing the inspector and half a dozen of his men. Ordering his men to change out of uniform, Kuryakin asked Khabalov for transport and then issued rifles, ammunition, and six grenades to each. They raced down the Nevsky, abandoned now except for the dead lying in black, huddled heaps on the snow, and, cutting across the Ligovskaya, drove to the embankment beyond the station.

He ordered everyone to climb over the embankment onto the railway line and went into the station, from the platform.

The police detachment was now under the command of a young constable. The revolutionaries had seized the top floor in the eastern wing of the hotel, from where they had been shooting into the station, and no trains had been able to come in for the past three hours. The army had sent a squad from the Volinsk Regiment, but they had been reluctant to charge across the open square.

Accompanied by Serge and the constable, Kuryakin went up the platform steps to the main building. The entrance hall was covered in glass, and the bodies of dead policemen lay in neat rows, their faces covered with bloodstained handkerchiefs. Kuryakin peered through the broken glass. The vast square was empty, with the dumpy statue of the arch reactionary Alexander III seated plumply in the middle. As if to warn him of the impossibility of crossing that vast emptiness, a hail of bullets ripped through the entrance hall.

"In fifteen minutes," Kuryakin said, "I want you to open a barrage of fire. Have the Volinsk join in, too. I don't care if you hit anything, but I want you to make as much noise as possible."

Fifteen minutes later Kuryakin had taken his men round the station and round the Znamenskaya and were waiting, crouched in the Orlovsky Pereulok behind the hotel. The moment he heard the crackle of rifle fire, he shouted, "Let's go."

They ran across the road through the gate of the courtyard. At the rear entrance were two men with rifles, looking just like Kuryakin's own detachment. Without changing stride, Kuryakin grabbed a grenade from his belt, pulled out the pin with his teeth, and hurled it. It exploded in a yellow ball of flame, sending splinters of glass and wood everywhere.

They stormed past the shattered door along a wide corridor, into the massive lobby. Kuryakin had a glimpse of high, chandeliered ceilings, of dim lighting and huge circular carpets, of empty comfortable chairs and the staff grouped round the desk. There were two armed men at the foot of the stairs and two more on the landing. As they fired, he hurled himself flat along the carpet.

There was a smell of cordite, cries of pain, then a rapid exchange of fire. Seeing the guards crumple, he abandoned his rifle for the Mauser and pounded up the stairs. There were three men at the top of the stairway. Kuryakin fired, hearing the explosion of weapons behind him. Panting as he reached the top of the stairs, he ran after the retreating men and saw them run into a room facing the square.

Hurriedly he opened the door. There were about ten men crowded into a large room. He nodded to Serge. After Serge lobbed the grenade through, he pulled the door shut and flung himself onto the floor.

The explosion made the building rock. Plaster showered from the ceiling. The door sagged. Serge got to his feet and tore it open.

"It's over, chief," he said. "We've got our revenge."

An hour later the mob attempted to storm Znamenskaya from the east. From his vantage point on the top floor of the hotel Kuryakin saw the police arrange themselves across the entrance to the square, kneel, and fire into the crowd. The Volinsk Regiment behind them, he noticed, fired into the air.

All that night they remained at the hotel. On Sunday morning the crowds were out early. From his top-floor window Kuryakin could see them milling about the Nevsky, uncontrolled, with hardly a policeman in sight. There were sounds of firing from all over the city. At about ten o'clock he glimpsed a row of army vehicles, racing around the Fontanka Canal flying red flags.

He asked Serge, "Can you find out what's happening?"

"There's no answer from headquarters," Serge said. "We've been trying them all morning."

An hour later two armoured cars rolled into the Znamenskaya under a swarm of people carrying rifles and waving red banners. More people crowded behind them, all armed, rushing straight for the detachment of policemen at the entrance to the Nicholas Station. There was a brief exchange of fire, and then the police were overwhelmed. Frozen with horror, Kuryakin saw men beaten to death with rifle butts and bodies dragged through the mob, beaten senseless, and torn apart. In a futile gesture of rage and anguish he opened fire on the crowd.

He kept firing for twenty minutes, the gun bucking against his shoulder, the muzzle warm in his palm. But now the crowd had support; rifle fire raked the hotel room, followed by the dull thump of an artillery shell. Hurling the last of his grenades into the square below, Kuryakin ordered his men to disband. Running out of the back of the hotel, accompanied by Serge, Igor, and Tihon, Kuryakin made his way to the house in Rozhdestvenskaya, five hundred yards away. For them, the revolution was over.

For the next two days they listened to radio bulletins as regiment after regiment went over to the revolution. The Volinsk, the Pavlovsky, his beloved Preobrajensky. Impotent, they listened as the Duma took control and formed a Provisional Government.

* * *

Three gleaming cars and a mud-stained army truck stood in an ominous line beside a private siding at Tsarskoe Selo. On the platform above the vehicles a ragged line of soldiers stood, and, a little apart from them, was Captain Kotzebue, recently appointed commander of the palace.

It was a grey, dismal morning. As they waited, the soldiers smoked and chatted amongst themselves. Recently the Soviet had issued Order Number One, and they now had the right to elect their officers. If Kotzebue didn't like them slouching around, then they would dispose of him.

At the first sounds of the train they crowded to the front of the platform, peering along the line at the moving column of black smoke. Soon they could discern the murky, cylindrical outline of the black engine. As the train drew closer and they saw that the royal emblems were obscured by crossed red flags, they let out a cheer.

"Troops, fall in! Attention!"

They made some semblance of falling in and standing at attention, one or two of them extinguishing cigarettes minutes after the order had been given. They still stared down the track as the noise of the train grew louder and the rails in front of them began to vibrate. The noise of chugging steam grew louder, the rumble of wheels incessant, and then the great, gleaming bulk of the engine drew past, pulling a line of royal-blue salons. It stopped with a gigantic hiss of steam and grinding of brakes. For a moment there was silence, broken only by the sound of escaping steam. The soldiers looked impassively at the massive gold double-eagle emblems on the doors of the carriages. Then, with a slight clatter, the doors of the last carriage opened and four men dressed in frock-coats got out and walked up to Captain Kotzbue. They spoke softly for a few minutes until the door of the leading carriage opened.

A frail, bearded figure stood at the top of the steps, dressed in a plain grey uniform, the pale white cross of the Order of Saint George pinned proudly to his breast. The soldiers looked dispassionately at the man who until a few days ago had been their Tsar. With a brief nod of acknowledgement, Nicholas walked briskly down the steps and joined Kotzebue and the four frock-coated representatives of the Duma. Another figure, also in uniform, left the royal compartment and joined them. Prince Vasily Dolgorusky was the only member of the royal entourage who had decided to share the fate of his former sovereign.

Brief introductions were made. The members of the Duma Committee then stood aside as Nicholas, flanked by Kotzebue and Dolgorusky, walked along the platform. Hurriedly the troops formed two columns around them. Accompanied by the pounding of booted feet, Nicholas went down the steps to the waiting line of cars.

By the car he hesitated; then Dolgorusky opened a door and he climbed in. Kotzebue got in with him. Soldiers rushed into the first and third cars, clambered onto the running boards and launched themselves over the tailboard of the lorry. In a few minutes, the whole convoy was driving quickly to the palace.

The tall, iron gates to the Imperial Park were locked and barred. The car containing Nicholas and Kotzebue stopped.

A burly officer with his jacket unbuttoned came and stood before the gates. "Who goes there?"—the traditional cry of every sentry.

"His Majesty the Emperor!" Dolgorusky replied.

The officer beckoned to the sentry and they walked round the car, faces pressed to the glass like inquisitive dogs. "Don't know any Emperor," the officer shouted, walking back to the gates. He stopped and turned. "Who goes there?"

"Citizen Romanov," Kotzebue said.

The officer laughed and signalled for the gates to be opened. "Let Citizen Romanov pass."

STRATAGEM

Caspar woke and stirred lazily under the sheets, thinking drowsily that everything was going extremely well. The furor over Rakovsky's death had faded, and there was now speculation amongst the revolutionaries that it had nothing to do with Quadriga. Zimmerman and Parvus had agreed that he should stay on in Zurich, and they all hoped that at the conference a natural leader would emerge. Sonya had found a venue in the centre of Zurich for the conference and enough cheap, clean accommodation for the delegates in establishments that would be tolerant of their predilection for free love. Caspar's usefulness to Ulyanov had grown, and they now met every three days or so to exchange letters. Caspar had even been able to persuade him to allow Zinoviev to attend the conference as an observer. Even von Dichter had turned out well, showing himself to be the ideal control, always willing to offer help and advice but otherwise leaving Caspar to run Quadriga as he saw fit.

Caspar opened his eyes and looked at Sonya, turned on her side away from him, her black hair spread over her face and pillow and the twin mounds of her firm buttocks pressing warmly into his belly. The strands of hair about her face fluttered as she breathed, the folded wings of long lashes lay quiescent on her high cheeks. She looked vulnerable and innocent, and Caspar gazed at her entranced. He loved her more than anything in the world. He wanted her more than anything in the world.

He gently placed his hand between her half-bent knees and stroked the silky inside of her thighs, gradually moving his hand higher until he was touching the downy moistness between. Sonya stirred sleepily. "*Liebchen*," she muttered. Caspar had spent the past two days trying to perfect her atrociously-accented German.

He reached across and turned her on her back, baring her shoulders and one creamy breast. As he spread her legs apart and moved over her, she shook her head in sleepy protest. But when he kissed her, her mouth responded to his, her tongue titillating the insides of his lips and running against his teeth. She sighed softly as he entered her and began to move lubriciously with him, bringing her hands around him and pressing his body to hers, her head now thrown back away from him, her eyes fast shut, moving more and more quickly now, giving and taking pleasure, quicker and faster and harder until suddenly she opened her eyes and looked into his with a rapt expression of wonder as they both climaxed.

Caspar lunged forward on his elbows and buried his face in the pillow beside her head. He lay there at peace, idle thoughts floating through his mind. He'd already written to Helga and broken off their engagement. He'd written to his parents and told them he wanted to marry an artistic Ukrainian revolutionary. He drowsed happily. He was cocooned in happiness, concupiscently cuddled. He was at peace.

Minutes, hours, years later he woke to the ticking of a clock, a rhythmic, insistent, annoying sound. He could feel Sonya beneath and beside him, the warm flutter of her breathing against his ear, a strand of her hair in his mouth. Concupiscently cuddled. If only that damned clock would stop. What did you expect in Switzerland, though? Cuckoo clocks and cocooned cuddles. Cuddled cuckoos. Cuckoo cuddle—

It wasn't a clock. Someone was knocking at the door.

Sonya muttered as he rolled across the bed, groping for his dressing gown.

Someone was pounding at the door. Some idiot was trying to break the door down.

He struggled into his dressing gown, then wandered blearily across the lounge and opened the door one inch.

Von Dichter opened it three feet and walked in. "*Gott in Himmel!* You're still asleep!"

Caspar ran a hand before his eyes and shook his head. What the hell was von Dichter doing waking people up at this time in the morning?

"It's eleven o'clock," von Dichter snorted.

From beyond the open door Sonya murmured, "*Liebchen,* come back to bed."

A great time for her to practise German.

Von Dichter snorted.

Caspar could feel him thinking, *fleshpots.* "It's Sonya," he explained. "She's a revolutionary and very nice. We're going to get married."

Von Dichter snorted again and stared at Caspar from under bristling eyebrows. "There's been a revolution in Russia!"

Caspar felt his knees quiver. He sat down, then realised he was more than decently exposed and stood up again. "Where?" he asked.

"In Russia."

Where else would there be a revolution but in Russia. "Of course. But—"

Very clearly and very slowly, von Dichter said that while everybody had been frigging around in Zurich, there'd been a revolution in Russia.

"Parvus—"

"Nothing to do with it." Zimmerman had woken von Dichter at three o'clock that morning to tell him that. He thrust a newspaper at Caspar. "Here, read all about it. Then find out what your revolutionary friends are doing and report to me."

There was a small paragraph on the back page of the *Neue Zurcher Zeitung*. There'd been a spontaneous uprising. The Tsar had abdicated. A new government had been formed by gentlemen with unfamiliar names: Lvov, Gutchov, Kerensky, Milyukov, Rodzianko. And all the while Caspar had been organizing conferences and Ulyanov babbling about the Paris Commune to the watchmakers of Chaux-de-Fonds.

Clutching the newspaper, Caspar returned to the bedroom and whipped the sheets off Sonya.

"Caspar, what the hell—"

"There's been a revolution in Russia!" he cried. "Read all about it." Throwing her the newspaper, he struggled into his trousers.

All that morning Ulyanov had worked in the library, writing the pamphlet that would, if only he could get it printed and secretly distributed in time, bring out the whole European proletariat on the first of May.

As usual at midday he stopped working, arranged his books neatly on his desk, thrust his notes into his battered briefcase, bade the plump, bespectacled Swiss librarian behind the desk a polite good afternoon—he'd been born bourgeois and these things came out unintentionally; besides, imperialist lackey or not, she was sometimes useful—and walked the usual way back to the Spiegelgasse for lunch.

He was still eating when there was a thunderous knocking at the door. His heart surged, his mouth went dry and the food inside it turned into a sticky lump. Instinctively he jumped up and put on his coat and hat. How many times had he told the Kammerers that no one was to be allowed up to his room without being announced? The knocking continued, loud and insistent. Perhaps the Kammerers had not been given a chance to announce this visitor. He stood by the table, white-faced. See, he was only a writer, finishing his lunch and going back to the library to work. He was innocent, harmless.

Knock, knock, knock. He indicated to Nadya that she should open the door. Bronski, that overgrown Polish student, bounded into the room, panting with excitement. "Ilyich, have you heard the news? There's been a revolution in Russia! I ran all the way to tell you."

Revolution in Russia? Impossible! Everyone knew that the Russians were not yet ready for revolution. According to the inexorable laws of history, the centre of the revolution was here, in Switzerland. "Are you certain?"

"Yes, it's in the newspapers."

Ah, that was it. German newspapers. A desperate attempt by Parvus to unite all the revolutionaries without the risk of a schismatic conference. It was a ploy to get him, Ulyanov, embroiled in Parvus' intrigue. "What newspaper? What did it say?"

"The *Neue Zurcher Zeitung.* On the back page." Bronski hesitated. He couldn't remember exactly what the paragraph had said and Ilyich always wanted to know things exactly. "It said . . . that there has been a revolution."

"What else?"

"I'm sorry, I can't remember what else."

Idiot. Imbecile. This was the material with which he had to create a permanent, world revolution.

"I think . . . I'll run and tell the others."

Ulyanov dismissed him with a nod.

Without speaking a word Nadya had taken off her apron and put on coat, boots, and headscarf. The latest newspapers were always on sale in the Bellevueplatz. In silence they hurried down the stairs into the street.

Outside, in the streets of the city that was the centre of world revolution, it was snowing lightly.

By the time Caspar had got to the Bellevueplatz, the news had spread. The exiles were jostling round the newsstands, talking excitedly in Russian. "They will send transport for us."—"Rubbish! In ten days the Romanovs will be back and that lot will be hung!"—"Igor Pavlovich, have you heard the news?"—"Who is Lvov? I thought it was a place."—"At last, freedom!"—"At last, we can go home!"—"Evgini Constantinovich, we should celebrate. Do you by any chance have any vodka?"

Caspar plunged through the crowd and bought *The Times, Le Temps,* and *Berliner Tageblatt.* All were the previous day's editions and only the *Tageblatt* carried a stop press item about disturbances in Russia.

Back into the crowd again. The *Neue Zurcher Zeitung* had nothing fresh to say.

There was a momentary lull in the hubbub of excited Russian chatter as Ulyanov approached with the barrel-shaped Nadya. No one moved to greet or acclaim him. None of his Bolsheviks were there, and Ulyanov was known only by reputation to most of those present: known as a man of great intellectual ability; a private, reserved person who never had time to talk to people or drink with them in the club on the Culmannstrasse.

Caspar watched Ulyanov walk up to the newsstand, pick up the papers, scan them rapidly, and emerge with a *Neue Zurcher Zeitung.* Standing very still, slightly away from the crowd, he read the paragraph on the last page, slowly, word by German word. It was true!

"Well, Ilyich," someone called, "isn't it good news?"

Ulyanov started as if he had been struck. Good news! Another revolution had taken place without him! For a moment he gazed unseeingly at his questioner, his mouth beneath the ginger beard twisting in frustration and envy. Finally he spoke. "Yes. It is good news. But I must get back . . . we must all get back to Russia . . . before the others . . . before they betray the revolution." His hesitant gaze fell on Caspar and he rushed forward, leaving Nadya by the newsstand. "Rihma, just the fellow I wanted to see."

He placed his arm around Caspar's shoulder and drew him away, walking Caspar towards the Quai Brucke. Beyond the bridge and the lake and the Belvoir Park, the Zurichberg was shrouded in mist. Light snow was still falling. "You must get me back to Russia," Ulyanov said. "Ganetsky will know how. I am needed there."

"We're already making plans. It will take a few days to arrange."

"It must be done now, immediately, if the revolution is to be saved. Ganetsky will understand. Gutchov, Lvov, Kerensky. I tell you, they are insincere. They have seized power from the workers, and now, I know for a certain fact, they will restore the monarchy. Don't you see, I have to go back. I have to save the revolution. Zinoviev had better come, too. Arrangements must be made."

"As soon as I can," Caspar promised.

"Come, come, Rihma, it isn't that difficult. All we need are two neutral passports. With neutral passports we can go anywhere. That's it. Two Swedish passports. I could shave my head and wear a wig. We can travel through France and England as Swedes."

It was an idea, neither very good nor original, yet still a possibility.

"You both speak Swedish?"

"No, but that doesn't matter. Don't you see, we could always pretend to be dumb."

"Two dumb Swedes touring Europe together. How jolly."

"Well, why not? Dumb people have the right to travel. Look into it, for me, Rihma. Come and see me later at the Café Adler. I will have letters. I must send directives to Petrograd." And leaving Caspar at the bridge, he turned and hurried back towards the newsstand.

Nadya was walking towards them, accompanied by Fritz Platten, wearing the inevitable broad-brimmed hat and silk scarf. Ulyanov hurried towards them and then stopped to talk.

As Caspar passed them unnoticed, he heard Ulyanov

say, "I must get Gregori here. Better send him a telegram. Fritz, you must somehow get us back to Russia."

In the Russian Club where Caspar went next, there was a party. High noon, and more Russians than he'd ever imagined were in Switzerland crowded into an overheated little room, drinking more vodka, more wine, more beer, more tea than he'd known existed. He spotted Sonya at the far end of the room, laughing and gesticulating amiably with a bottle of wine while a little man in front of her mimed a hanging Romanov.

Someone proposed a toast to Lvov. Caspar drank. A toast to Kerensky. Caspar drank. A toast to Milyukov, to the Duman, to the Petrograd Soviet. Caspar's glass paused in midair. What was that? Didn't the comrade know? A Soviet had been formed.

A smiling, glowing Sonya, hair all awry, proposed a toast to the Independent Republic of the Ukraine. Caspar drank to that; he drank to Estonia and Lithuania as well and wondered how they were all getting back to Russia.

"Not through Germany, comrade," a squat, bandy-legged, bearded figure informed him. Russia was at war with Germany. Anyone who travelled through Germany was a traitor. The government had said that anyone who travelled through Germany would be hung. Caspar drank what tasted like a mixture of paint stripper and vodka. Long live Kerensky.

Across the room he spotted Aisenblud, from the Jewish Bund, bearded, solemn, thoughtful, watching the growing boisterousness of his compatriots with alarm. Long live Gutchov. Aisenbuld eyed him warily.

"How's everyone going to get back?" Caspar asked.

"There'll be a way. But first the government has to declare an amnesty."

"Oh, yes, an amnesty. . . . There won't be a conference now, you know."

"I thought so."

"Perhaps Helphand can arrange transport through Germany."

"Germany." Aisenblud's heavy lips drooped. Germany, England, France, what did it matter? It wasn't the war of his people.

"Wouldn't you like to go back to Russia?"

Of course. Wasn't he eager to go back to Russia, to Kiev, to Odessa; wasn't he desperate to read the Protocols of the Elders of Zion again; wasn't another pogrom all he lived for? But if the war ended, the Swiss would ask them to leave. "We will go back," he said. There was nowhere else to go.

"Shall I ask Helphand to make arrangements?"

"In principle," Aisenblud said.

From the Russian Club Caspar hurried to the apartment in the Ramistrasse where Uritsky lived. There was a party going on there, too, and, surrounded by Mensheviks spread-eagled on a sofa, and bellowing Cossack marching songs, Uritsky was quite drunk. "Well, little one," he cried, interrupting the music and dragging Caspar onto the sofa beside him. "We did it! We finally knobbled Nicholas Romanov!"

"The job's got to be finished," Caspar said, dabbing vodka off his trousers.

"Don't worry, we'll do it. We the Mensheviks will rule Russia!"

"But first you've got to get back to Russia. How are you going to do that?"

"That's no problem," Uritsky assured him. "I have already made arrangements with the British. Next week we leave for France, and from there they will arrange to take us to Petrograd by boat."

Caspar shook his head. "There are many German submarines in the Baltic," he said. "I hope you can swim better than Lord Kitchener."

"It's a chance we'll have to take," Uritsky said, sitting up, suddenly quite sober. "The risk of drowning is better than the certainty of being hung for treason. Give Parvus my regards and tell him that one day we hope to see im in Petrograd." He laughed and clasped Caspar round the shoulder. "Have a drink, little one. We're friends. We're in a neutral country."

In von Dichter's office Caspar obtained a priority call to Berlin, and while he spoke to Zimmerman, von Dichter listened on an extension.

Zimmerman's voice had the tone of a man expecting more bad news. In a few days, Zimmerman was due to appear before the Reichstag to defend himself over the telegram. As economically as possible Caspar told Zimmerman about Utrisky and the British and that most of the revolutionaries would not travel through Germany for fear of being tried for treason.

There was a long, crackling wait before Zimmerman replied. "It's all over, Ehrler. Cancel the conference. Clear up your affairs in Zurich and return to Berlin as soon as possible."

"Ulyanov wants to return to Petersburg, Excellency."

"Ulyanov?" There was another silence. Caspar felt tremulous with hope. Then Zimmerman said, "Ulyanov is too small to be of any help to us. However, tell him if he wishes to travel through Germany, we will not oppose it."

"Excellency, Ulyanov must travel through Germany. We must support Ulyanov!"

"I know your feelings about—"

"Excellency, we can save Quadriga! Please let me explain."

After a moment's hesitation Zimmerman said, "All right, Ehrler, say what you have to say."

"We have information here that a Workers' Soviet has been formed in Petersburg. If that is so, then the Provisional Government does not govern Russia. It can only rule with the consent of the Soviet. He who controls the Soviet, controls the government."

"I'm not sure I understand you completely, Ehrler."

"If the Soviet is anything like it was in 1905, it will be a large, unco-ordinated, amorphous, divisive body, prone to discussion, revenge, and socialist ideals. Because it has no experience of exercising power, for the present it will co-operate with the Provisional Government; in time, it will be absorbed by that governemnt. But the Soviet and the government stand for different ideals. If, before the Soviet were absorbed, we infiltrated into it someone opposed to the Provisional Government, someone opposed to the continuation of the war, someone dedicated, ambitious, and talented enough to take over the Soviet and fight the Provisional Government. . . ."

"Ulyanov can do that?"

"I believe so, Excellency. With our money and our support Ulyanov can split the Soviet right down the middle and take it over. He can take over Russia and give us peace."

"Interesting," Zimmerman said. "I am expecting Helphand here at any moment. I will discuss this with him and come back to you."

"But Excellency—"

"Meanwhile, you are authorised to do everything possible to assist Ulyanov to return to St. Petersburg. I will cable von Dichter and Minister Romberg in Berne to give you whatever assistance you need. But I emphasize one thing, Ehrler. You will be discreet. We have certain problems here. We must not be seen to be supporting the revolutionaries. It is essential, therefore, that however you arrange it, it should appear that Ulyanov is seeking our assistance and not that we are seeking his."

Later that evening, still faintly crapulous from the revolutionary celebrations, Caspar and Sonya trudged through the persistently accumulating snow to the Café Adler. Ulyanov was at a large table at the back of the café, seated before bare wood and glasses of unfinished tea, flanked by Zinoviev, Nadya, and half a dozen other disciples. Not enough to either betray or crucify him, Caspar thought, drawing up chairs to the outside of the circle. From across the table Boris, still wearing his anonymous military gear, smiled and blew a kiss at Sonya. Ulyanov's eyes flickered suspiciously, then, recognising them, became indifferent. He returned to his exposition of the revolution.

"That the revolution succeeded so quickly is only due to the fact that, as a result of an extremely unique historical situation, absolutely dissimiliar currents, absolutely heterogeneous class interests, absolutely contrary political and social strivings have merged in a strikingly harmonious manner."

Caspar realised that unlike the other revolutionaries, the Bolsheviks had not been celebrating. All of them, Boris included, were resolutely stone-cold sober.

Ulyanov went on remorselessly. The revolution had

been created by a conspiracy of Anglo-French imperialists who impelled Milyukov, Gutchov, and others to seize power for the purpose of continuing the imperialist war, for the purpose of conducting that war more ferociously, for the purpose of slaughtering millions of Russian workers!

A waiter sidled up to Caspar. He ordered coffee for Sonya and himself.

The whole reason for the revolution was the fear of the British and the French that Nicholas was privately seeking a separate peace with Germany! And now that the British and French had got what they wanted, Gutchov, Milyukov, and the others were conspiring to replace Nicholas with another Romanov! "Such," Ulyanov said, "and only such is the way the situation developed."

Caspar sipped his coffee thoughtfully. Ulyanov was quite beside himself trying to fit the revolution that had occurred into a Marxist framework, and everyone, Boris included, was following Ulyanov's words as if they were scripture. Never mind; get him into Germany, give him one hundred million marks, and he would be a different man. The razor-sharp intellect would be honed; he would no longer seek to explain the superfluous. Ulyanov would breathe fire and inspire men's souls.

Ulyanov was now onto the great and glorious achievements of the Party during the revolution of 1905. "Facts," he said, "are stubborn things."

Caspar ordered more coffee. Ulyanov continued, repetitive, persistent, remorseless. Caspar had more coffee, his face stiff with attention. Ulyanov began to heap invective on the leaders of the revolution. He must, Caspar thought, be nearing the end.

"What kind of revolution is this? A revolution led

by a prince! And what kind of foreign policy can we expect from a university professor!" He glared round the table. "Kerensky!" Ulyanov spat out the word. "A Russian Louis Blanc! A verbal Republican! A political swindler!"

Perhaps, Caspar thought, only he knew why Ulyanov had singled out Kerensky for special abuse. Kerensky was everything Ulyanov was not: ten years younger, a lawyer who had stayed in Russia to defend victims of Tsarist oppression, a splendid orator, a dilettante who had achieved power. To make matters worse, both Ulyanov and Kerensky came from the same village, Simbirsk, where Kerensky's father had taught Ulyanov and rendered many kindnesses to the Ulyanov family. That private jealousies were being transformed into political ideology was a confirmation of how desperate Ulyanov was.

Crying, "We must go back and deal with the traitor, Kerensky," Ulyanov ended his speech.

Immediately everyone began discussing how they should return. Boris produced a copy of *Volksrecht*. "There is an advertisement here," he said tapping the paper with his forefinger. "*Steps are being taken to organise the return to Russia. Contact S. Bagocky, Klusstrasse 30, Zurich*. Perhaps we should do that."

Ulyanov looked thoughtfully. Then he exclaimed, "Mensheviks! We will not travel with them."

Good, Caspar thought.

"It's an Okhrana plant," Zinoviev said.

The discussion meandered on. Ulyanov did not participate, sitting there watchful, patient, like a tolerant schoolteacher allowing children time off from their lessons. A couple of Bolsheviks, pleading the lateness of the hour, excused themselves and left.

Ulyanov said, "There are things I must discuss with Rihma."

Accompanied by Zinoviev, he walked to another table. "I have heard from Kollantai," he said, sitting down. "She is returning to Petrograd, and she is asking for directives."

"What did you say to her?" Zinoviev asked.

"No trust. No support of the government. Kerensky especially is suspect." He turned to Caspar. "I have letters. They must get to Petrograd immediately."

Caspar took the letters and put them away in an inside pocket. "It is possible," he said, "for both of you to get back to Russia. You can leave in two days. You will have to travel through Germany."

"Impossible," Zinoviev said. "Whether we approve of it or not, Russia is at war with Germany. To travel through Germany would be treason."

Ulyanov looked thoughtful.

"Perhaps, under the circumstances," Caspar said, "you can get permission from Petrograd to travel through Germany."

"And what," Ulyanov demanded, "will the Kerenskys and Milyukovs and Gutchovs make of such a passage?" As always, Ulyanov was considering the political implications.

"We shall have to approach the British," Zinoviev said.

"And tell them you're returning to Russia to make peace." Caspar looked suitably incredulous. "It would be better to stay in Zurich than go to the British. At least you'd be more comfortable in Zurich than in a British prison."

"The British wouldn't do that," Zinoviev exclaimed.

"More comfortable in Zurich than at the bottom of the Baltic," Caspar said.

"The fact is, we must somehow get back to Petrograd," Ulyanov snapped.

"Passage is available," Caspar said.

"For how many?"

"The two of you."

Ulyanov shook his head. "Impossible," he said. "Nadya must come, too."

"And perhaps Lilina, my wife," Zinoviev said.

Ulyanov blushed. "And Inessa."

Five people, and Zimmerman had said at any cost. "If you can give me photographs," Caspar said, "I will arrange the passports."

"How long will it take?"

Caspar calculated rapidly. "Not more than a week."

In the house on Gessner Allee, Badmayev also analysed the revolution. It wouldn't last, he said. As soon as the generals were able to divert troops from the front, they would march on Petrograd and the short reign of the Provisional Government would be over.

"That was what happened in 1905," he said, brown eyes gazing mildly at Poidvosky.

Poidvosky wasn't convinced. There was something about this revolution that looked permanent.

"There are always revolutions in Russia," Badmayev said. "The historical fact is that none of them have lasted. Out problem is what we do meanwhile." He looked at Poidvosky's two assistants, including them in the discussion.

No one said anything. Badmayev had sounded very assured, and if he was right, anything they said would undoubtedly be used against them in the future.

"Obviously we can't return to Petrograd."

Obviously. Poidvosky did not want to return to Petrograd, even if Gadmayev was right. He knew that sooner or later there would be another revolution and that in every revolution at least half a dozen police agents were torn apart by the crowd. Poidvosky shuddered. He definitely did not want to return to Petrograd.

"Equally obviously, we cannot sit here and do nothing."

"There is nothing to do," Poidvosky said. He liked doing nothing.

The taller of the two assistants cleared his throat and added helpfully, "The Parvus Institute has been closed and the conference abandoned."

"Even so, Ulyanov continues to meet with Parvus' agent."

"An amnesty has been declared," the shorter assistant said. "The exiles are no longer wanted by the Russian government."

"The Provisional Government," Badmayev corrected stonily. "We own no loyalty to the Provisional Government. On the other hand, we have all sworn oaths of loyalty to the Tsar." The brown eyes studied the faces of each of the other men. "We will find out what the hell Ulyanov and Parvus' agent are up to and stop it."

"All Ulyanov is trying to do is get back to Russia," Poidvosky said.

"Only get back to Russia," Badmayev repeated. "What do you think he is going to do when he only gets back to Russia? He and all the others?" Badmayev answered his own question. "They will make the revolution permanent."

The tall assistant said, "Perhaps we should allow

Ulyanov to return. The only way he can return to Russia is through Germany, and that should have a lot of propaganda value."

"I'm glad to see that some of us here haven't yet given up."

"Before we do anything," Poidvosky said, "we should obtain a directive from Petrograd. Without an authority from Petrograd, we have no status. We are merely individuals, exiles even. We can only do what you want if you represent a government."

"What happens if we do not hear from Petrograd?" Badmayev asked.

"Then, obviously, we can do nothing." Poidvosky suppressed a smile.

Badmayev's chiselled features froze. "I will get you instructions from Petrograd," he said tersely. "Until then, we carry on as usual."

Straight from Stettin Station, Parvus hurried through the dismal early morning light to the Foreign Office. He'd been in Stockholm when the first news of the Petrograd rising had filtered through, and he remembered that his chief reaction had been annoyance that something so unplanned, so obviously destined to fail, should endanger his own more deliberate effort.

But the uprising had succeeded. All the way through Germany he'd been hounded by telegrams telling him that. Lvov, Rodzianko, and Kerensky had seized power. The Tsar had abdicated. And Zimmerman wanted to see him at the Foreign Office, as soon as he set foot in Berlin.

Clutching his batch of telegrams, sitting in the Foreign Office limousine, Parvus gazed thoughtfully past von Futran's chiselled profile at the magnificent, modern buildings of Berlin, immense, looming presences towering above the glow of the street lamps. If he failed to deliver peace to Zimmerman, Parvus knew he would be finished in Germany. Germany would be finished, too. He somehow had to wrest victory from defeat.

Only the desk lamps were on in Zimmerman's room, and he crouched behind them, a large, rumpled, untidy figure, his tweed lounge suit shapeless and crumpled, his hair uncombed, his broad face heavy with fatigue. He waved tiredly at the papers littering his desk. "My speech for the Reichstag," he said by way of explanation. "Ehrler reports from Zurich that Ulyanov is prepared to co-operate with us. He recommends that we support Ulyanov with the Reptile Fund. What do you think?"

Parvus considered the problem carefully. With Rakovsky dead, Ulyanov *was* the only alternative. Ulyanov must realise that, too, and Ulyanov would do anything to seize power. And given German support, he could do it.

Money was the key to it. Without money, Ulyanov was nothing. But after he seized power he would show neither gratitude nor faith, not would he be amenable to persuasion. Afterwards, it would be Ulyanov's Russia, unless he, Parvus, could control Ulyanov; unless he, Parvus, controlled the source of Ulyanov's power, the Reptile Fund.

He already had some control over the arms and the newspapers and the arrangements, the gold and the monies in Stockholm and Bucharest. Neither Zimmerman nor his Ministers could work overtly with Ulyanov, and until Ulyanov seized power and gave Germany peace, Caspar Ehrler could not enter Russia.

So the German control had to be himself, the Russian Prussian. And if the prize was Russia, Ulyanov would accept that control.

"Ehrler is right," Helphand said. "We must support Ulyanov. I shall return to Stockholm at once and vary certain arrangements to accommodate him."

"Stockholm!" Zimmerman cried. "Shouldn't you be going to Zurich to talk to Ulyanov?"

Helphand shook his head. "No, Excellency. If I appeared in Zurich to persuade Ulyanov, he would realise how badly we need him and he would become impossible to deal with. It's better if Ehrler continues to handle it. He has done an excellent job so far."

Kuryakin, Serge, and the three other survivors from Section Four remained safe in the house on Rozhdestvenskaya Street while the revolution spluttered and died around them. The radio brought them news of the formation of the Provisional Government, its recognition by Britain and America, and the offer of a loan of one hundred million dollars. When for three days there had been no reports of any disturbances, Kuryakin sneaked out of the house to find out more of what was happening.

He had shaved off his moustache, but his cheeks were covered with unsightly stubble. He wore a soiled Preobrajensky uniform and trailed a Mosin-Nagant rifle despondently behind him. As he walked to the Nevsky Prospekt a car raced past, showering snow as it skidded round a corner and nearly throwing off the two soldiers standing on its running boards. The Nevsky was more empty than usual, the pavements still covered with shattered wood and broken glass. A few small groups of people wandered aimlessly, looking at the empty, broken shop windows, and here and there were a few groups of soldiers in ragged uniform, unwilling or unaware of the request—there were no orders now—to return to barracks. At the tram stop was a long queue.

Kuryakin joined the queue and was greeted warmly by the waiting passengers. Where had he fought? What was he doing now? Did he know what would happen next? Things were getting better, he was told climbing into the tram, though everything ran spasmodically. Sometimes there was power and sometimes not; sometimes there was fuel and sometimes not. And the trams were more unreliable than usual.

Along the Nevsky only the cheaper tea houses were open, and a few stalls in the Gostiny Dvor.

Halfway along the Nevsky the tram stopped. There was a sound of music and the tramp of marching feet. Everyone crowded to the windows and watched as ten yards ahead the Pavlovsky Regiment crossed the Nevsky.

They were going to the tauride Palace, someone informed Kuryakin. They were going to present themselves to the Duma.

Led by their officers the Pavlovsky streamed across endlessly. The entire regiment must have been there, and the tune they marched to was the *Marseillaise*. Between each section were red banners bearing slogans: WAR TO TOTAL VICTORY!—LONG LIVE THE PROVISIONAL GOVERNMENT AND THE SOVIET OF WORKERS!—LAND AND FREEDOM!—DON'T FORGET YOUR BROTHERS IN THE TRENCHES!—CONQUER OR DIE!

"The first of the Petrograd regiments," someone said with pride.

Kuryakin smiled at him, watching the vivid scarlet and black parade, the brittle winter sun glinting off the magnificent gold and blue mitre hats.

He walked back to the house from the top of the Nevsky. Things were settling down but still confused. In a few days he would have to act. Until then he was content to wait.

A week later Caspar had listened to Ulyanov's exposition of the causes of the revolution, he returned to the Café Adler carrying a large envelope in which were five passports and an identity card for the Zinoviev boy. It was nearing the end of March and there were only threadbare patches of snow on the streets and ruffled lines of broken ice in the shaded places. All along the Bahnhofstrasse the trees were sprouting tiny leaves.

Ulyanov and Zinoviev were at their usual table at the back and greeted him without any warmth. No Nadya, Caspar thought; no Lilina, no Inessa. Pity, he had been hoping to see Inessa in the flesh. Despite five children, two husbands, imprisonment, and a strained affair with Ulyanov, she was still beautiful, with a wide Russian face, eyes that photographed like pools, and a soft-looking, vulnerable mouth. Oh, well, there would be other times. He took out the envelope and placed it on the table. "They're all there," he said. "When do you want to go?"

"We cannot go," Zinoviev said.

"What do you mean, cannot go? You have the passports. You have visas acknowledging your neutral status."

"Travelling through Germany is treason," Ulyanov said, as if he'd only just realised it.

Caspar frowned. What had happened to turn Ulyanov into a patriot?

"We can only travel if we get approval from Petrograd," Zinoviev said, adding usefully, "We have written."

"But that would take weeks, months," Caspar protested. "By the time you get to Petrograd. . . . Why, Tsar Nicholas might be back on the throne . . . with Kerensky as Prime Minister."

"Better than being hung for treason," Ulyanov said. "In any event our enemies will make so much propaganda out of our journey through Germany that we will be ruined."

"So you'll go through England? You will risk being torpedoed?"

"We have considered travelling by neutral ship," Ulyanov informed him.

"And what if the English or the French arrest you?"

Ulyanov shrugged. He remained silent, sitting perfectly still, staring past Caspar towards the front of the café where a group of old men in shabby suits were playing cards. "It would be different if there were more of us," he murmured.

"How different?"

"It is very easy to indict Ulyanov the well-known revolutionary for treason. But not so easy for a revolutionary government to charge Ulyanov and sixty or seventy other ordinary working people."

"Who, unable to return to their country by any other means, used to only method available," Zinoviev added.

"The only method available for Ulyanov," Ulyanov said grimly. "It is impossible for us to return through the Entente countries. Either all of us go or all of us remain."

Caspar took the envelope with the passports and put it back into his pocket. "How many people do you wish to take with you?"

"As many as possible, sixty or seventy. It should be a mixed party of Social Revolutionaries, Mensheviks, Bundists, everybody." He looked directly at Caspar and rested his hands on his bowler hat in a gesture of formality. "I have been asked by the Zurich Committee of Russian *Émigrés,* most of whom are in favour of peace, to request means of immediate return to Russia. I am asked to point out that travel through the Entente countries is impossible, because of the danger of submarines and because the Entente will only allow those émigrés to travel who are in favour of continuing the war. After their return to Russia the Zurich Committee of Russian *Émigrés* pledges to work for the release of a similar number of German prisoners."

Caspar thought quickly. Organising the return of sixty or seventy revolutionaries was not something that the Imperial Intelligence Bureau East could do alone. The military, the railways, and other organizations would have to be involved. There was no possibility that such a journey could be kept secret; and if the transport of Ulyanov and his Bolsheviks was to be a public matter, then it was best that, as Zimmerman had directed, they appear to be seeking German assistance in the matter.

"You will have to make a formal request," Caspar said.

"A formal request! What do you mean a formal request? I have told you what I want, haven't I?"

Caspar shook his head. "You'll have to make an application to the German Ambassador in Berne. I have no standing with the German government. Neither has Ganetsky or Parvus."

Ulyanov flung his hands up wide. "This is impossible! I cannot approach the Germans!"

"Perhaps," Caspar said, "Fritz Platten can."

* * *

One of the curious features of the March Revolution was that neither side had sought to control the telephone and telegraph system and that right up to the end, when the system finally failed because most of its staff were unable to get to work, it continued distributing messages from monarchist and revolutionary with equal impartiality. Two weeks after the Tsar's abdication the system functioned more or less normally, with the exception of certain areas where telephone poles had been used as barricades.

Similarly, after the first, vengeful storming of government offices and police stations, the buildings were left abandoned. The old had passed away, the new was not yet born, and in the interim the Post Office regularly delivered letters and telegrams addressed to people who were either dead or missing.

During his ambulations about Petrograd Kuryakin had taken to visiting the Moika offices at irregular intervals and collecting messages and reports.

Which was how he received the telegram from Badmayev.

Walking along the Nevsky he thought about the problem that raised. Badmayev was still operational, and in Zurich Parvus was still meddling in Russian affairs. When the time came for Kuryakin to meet with Kerensky, it would be useful to be able to reveal Parvus' plans. Meanwhile Parvus was trying to arrange the repatriation of Ulyanov.

For years the Okhrana had left Ulyanov alone because his mere presence served to keep the socialists divided. But at this time, when who controlled the government was an open question, Ulyanov's presence in Petrograd was undesirable, especially as he was working for the Germans. Ulyanov was an extremist, with no respect for liberty or democracy. He was a megalomaniac, who would use every opportunity to seize power. And with German support he could do it.

On the other hand if he returned to Petrograd and his German connections could be publicly proved. . . .

Kuryakin crossed the Nevsky and walked to the telegraph office in the Gercena Ulica. The final decision must rest with Badmayev.

The girl behind the counter smiled warmly at him. "Preobrajensky," she said, "shouldn't you be in the parade that is marching to the Duma?"

"We've just returned from the front," Kuryakin said.

"I have a boyfriend in the parade," she said. "He didn't say there were any comrades at the front."

"We're not allowed to discuss the war," Kuryakin said. Soon a solitary figure in army uniform, trailing a long-barrelled rifle along the streets of Petrograd, would become as conspicuous as a nobleman in furs and jewels parading in a carriage-and-four. In future he would have to adopt the disguise of a factory worker.

The girl looked up from the telegram. "I don't understand it," she said.

"It's a business code," Kuryakin said. "It's for my father. Because of the uprising, he hasn't been paid by the Swiss."

The girl still looked puzzled, but she sent it.

The Bolsheviks took a week to present their request to Gisbert von Romberg, the German Ambassador in Berne. Mortally afraid of being compromised, they had approached Platten so indirectly that the poor man had arranged for the Swiss Social Democrats to buy Ulyanov and Zinoviev two one-way tickets to Berlin before the centime dropped. By then, Platten, too, became infected by their paranoia. He could not talk to Romberg without implicating the Bolsheviks. They talked round the matter for two more days, then decided to approach National Counsellor Grimm, who in turn approached Federal Counsellor Hoffmann, who finally spoke to Romberg.

A whole week of pusillanimous pussyfooting, Caspar thought impatiently, reading the telegram from Romberg to the Foreign Ministry summarising the meeting with Hoffmann. Since the whole matter had become official, he was being given copies of Foreign Office telegrams, which made him feel quite important. Romberg, he read, had recommended that a special train be organised, and arrangements for this were being made with the military authorities.

In the house on the Gessner Allee, Badmayev read Kuryakin's telegram slowly for the third time. *You must do as you see fit.* And there was a new address to which he should send future reports. Kuryakin was leaving everything to him. He had to decide what to do with Ulyanov. How nice. He had already made his decision, secure in the knowledge that he had been right all along. The counterrevolution was on. The counterrevolution would win.

Poidvosky was dubious. "They're hiding like terrorists."

"Look at the signature, man. Kuryakin. Kuryakin the hero of the Russo-Japanese war. His whole unit consists of veterans. Why, twenty of them are as good as two hundred Cossacks. If Kuryakin is around, we don't have to worry."

But Poidvosky remembered that the Russo-Japanese war had ended in defeat. And Poidvosky worried.

At the Alexander Palace the Tsar of All the Russias wished to take a walk. It was no simple matter. Permission had to be obtained, a route planned, sentries posted, and finally the private apartments unlocked.

When he was finally allowed out, some two hours after the request, he walked briskly across the park. Suddenly a soldier blocked his path. Surprised and nervous, the Tsar turned and walked in a different direction. Another soldier appeared and ordered him back. The Tsar hesitated and made to protest. Within seconds he was surrounded by half a dozen soldiers, who pushed him with their fists and prodded him with their rifle butts, crying, "You can't go there, Gospodin Polkovnik."—"You can't go here, Gospodin Polkovnik."—"Stand to attention, Gospodin Polkovnik."—"Stand at ease, Gospodin Polkovnik."—"Quick march, left, right, left, right."

The Tsar broke away and, with what dignity he could muster, walked back to the house, very disturbed.

The tea house on the Demidov Pereulok was quiet, with two ex-soldiers seated at one table, beggars' licences dangling from their necks; a fierce-looking pilgrim occupied another table and, at the large table in the centre, the usual half dozen or so pavement hawkers and veteran ex-militiamen in faded uniforms sat playing cards. It was stiflingly hot and the single window was opaque and dripping with condensation.

Kuryakin carried two scalding glasses of tea and a herring on a piece of black bread over to a vacant table and settled down to wait. Two days previously, while checking the Moika for news from Badmayev, he'd come across a message from Hain.

Hain came in shortly afterwards, far too well dressed for a teahouse. He looked about him apprehensively until he saw Kuryakin wave.

"I say, I'd never have recognized you if you hadn't waved."

Kuryakin, tearing hungrily at the bread and herring, said, "I didn't want to be recognised." He pushed the second glass of tea towards Hain.

"Are you on a job?"

"A few of us managed to avoid being massacred at the Moika."

"Are you all right? Do you need food, clothes, that sort of thing?"

"We have enough," Kuryakin said. "Why did you want to see me?"

Hain looked around the teahouse with noncommittal curiosity. "The revolution is over," he said. "HMG has recognised the Provisional Government. Where does that leave you, Dimitri?"

Kuryakin finished eating and took a large gulp of tea. "There is still time before I have to recognise the Provisional Government."

"It's all over. We're even helping to ship some of the exiles back."

"Exiles? What exiles?"

"Plekhanov and the Mensheviks from France. The Social Revolutionaries from Switzerland."

"And Ulyanov?"

Hain lit a cigarette. "We have been approached by people purporting to represent Ulyanov. But we will not let him through."

"In that case, he will travel through Germany. What are you going to do about it?"

"We will make a formal protest."

Kuryakin laughed harshly. "A lot of good that will do you. If Ulyanov comes, he will come with German support. He will come to take Russia out of the war."

"The policy of His Majesty's Government is to seek accommodation with the new régime. There is nothing we can do to stop him. There is nothing more you can do, Dimitri. Your world has changed. It is time for you to change and choose another side."

Kuryakin pushed away his empty glass of tea and lit one of his black Russian cigarettes. "What is it you want, Richard?"

"Were your files destroyed when the mob stormed the Moika?"

Kuryakin laughed. "My files are safe."

"We will buy those files from you. We will give you a capital sum and arrange for you and as many others as you want to leave Russia. We will give you employment. We will give you the protection of the British Empire."

Kuryakin threw his cigarette into his empty glass. "I don't need the British Empire as long as I have the files."

It was nearly three weeks since the Provisional Government had been formed and Caspar had recommended that the resources of Quadriga be placed behind Ulyanov. "Cables," von Dichter cried, "they're driving me mad with cables!" In different ways all the cables asked the same question: *What the hell was happening with Ulyanov?* And they all uttered the same warning: *The Entente has already begun to work against their moving Ulyanov out of Switzerland.*

What the hell *was* happening with Ulyanov? Ten days ago he'd asked Caspar for a train to ship sixty or seventy of his Bolsheviks to Petrograd. Three days ago he'd finally got Grimm round to the German Embassy. Grimm's request had been formally approved. After that, not a word from Grimm, from Ulyanov, from Platten, or from the entire confounded Zurich Committee.

"You've got to do something," von Dichter urged.

Caspar went to see Platten at the offices of the Swiss Social Democrats in the Ramistrasse.

Platten stroked his big, doughy face with thick white fingers and said distractedly, "They don't know whether they're coming or going."

"Coming or going or staying," Caspar said, feeling inclined to give a von Dichter-like snort.

"They're frightened to leave without permission from Petrograd."

"I thought that with sixty or seventy people travelling, they didn't need permission from Petrograd."

"Zinoviev is certain they will be shot as soon as they arrive. He has suggested that they travel through Germany in a sealed carriage, without stops."

"That can be arranged," Caspar said. "Is that the only problem?"

It wasn't. Ulyanov did not have sixty or seventy supporters in Switzerland. There were only about thirty of them, so it was essential that everyone travelled, whether they were of military age or not.

Caspar thought it would be ironic if, after all the

trouble they were having getting Ulyanov back, he was put into uniform, given a rifle, and marched to the front.

"He is exempt," Platten said. "He is the eldest surviving male of the family."

So if his brother had not been executed, Vladimir Ilyich Ulyanov might actually have been summoned to the colours and, being essentially a law abiding man, might well have gone. Caspar chuckled at the thought of Ulyanov in the trenches.

"There is also the question of identity documents," Platten said. Apart from Ulyanov and Zinoviev, none of the others had documents of any kind. Would the Germans make special arrangements to get them across the frontier?

"Difficult," Caspar said. "How will we know whether the passengers are political exiles or Russian spies?"

"I intend travelling with them as far as Stockholm," Platten said. Apparently he wanted to open an information bureau there. "I can have the Swiss Social Democrats guarantee that each passenger is a political exile."

"You should talk to Romberg about that," Caspar said. Romberg was officially in charge of the arrangements and had better means of communication with Berlin than Caspar. "Go and see him in Berne at once. I'm sure he will do everything you want."

Platten saw Romberg the next day; that evening Caspar received a copy of Romberg's cable to Zimmerman. Romberg seemed to be growing increasingly enthusiastic about the whole project. Not only had he recommended that Platten's proposals be accepted but that the train should be made available within forty-eight hours, by Friday, the sixth of April.

* * *

The Tauride Palace, the centre of government of all the Russias, was a babble of chaos and confusion. Soldiers from diverse regiments who had been asked to guard the palace stood around in unbuttoned uniforms and alternately rigorously checked some persons' credentials while allowing others to pass through. From time to time a group of men would commandeer a car or an armoured vehicle and careen down the Potemkinskaya on some urgent mission. Kuryakin, dressed in the uniform of a front-line infantryman and trailing his rifle, walked past them unchallenged.

Inside the palace there were soldiers everywhere, wandering around like lost sheep. The right wing was the seat of the Provisional Government, and in the left wing was the Soviet. Already the struggle between them had its territorial counterpart.

Kuryakin walked past room forty-one, where the Military Commission sat examining the former Tsarist ministers and police officials. Beyond that was the Catherine Hall, where he glimpsed Milyukov in temporary, lonely splendour. In addition to the idling soldiers, there were representatives of the insurrectionary units, delegates from Moscow and the country. Kuryakin was looking for Kerensky.

He found him seated tiredly behind a desk, with a queue of people standing beyond the open door. Kerensky spoke to each one for a couple of minutes, smiling wanly before summoning the next. Kuryakin joined the queue and shuffled forward. When he came to the desk, Kerensky looked up at him without recognition. "I have come to place my services at the disposal of the Provisional Government," Kuryakin said in a low voice.

"Yes," Kerensky said. "What services can you provide?"

"I am Count Dimitri Kuryakin, Head of the Political Section of the Okhrana." The pencil between Kerensky's slender fingers dropped. He looked up at Kuryakin; his whole face impassive.

"There is a warrant for your arrest," he said softly.

"You may not think you need the services of men like me now," Kuryakin said. "But you do."

Kerensky picked up the pencil and scribbled a note. "Go and wait in my office," he said. "You won't be disturbed there. I'll see you as soon as I can."

Kerensky came in two hours later, hollow eyed, his complexion waxy, his slender frame drooping with fatigue. "We do not need an Okhrana anymore," he said, throwing himself into a chair. "We do not need a Political Section. This government is founded on the principle of freedom."

"Freedom has to be protected," Kuryakin said. "All governments, however liberal, need a means of obtaining information and need an organisation to act sometimes in illiberal ways. I have files, information on everyone who can and will endanger these freedoms you speak of. I have the nucleus of the counterintelligence agency your government requires."

"We have no use for Okhrana files," Kerensky said. "We have no use for informers and turncoats. We are above that sort of thing. In short, Kuryakin, we have no use for people like you." He paused, drawing a hand across his face. "I know it is harsh. But it is the truth."

"Use me," Kuryakin said. "At least you know I am a patriot, that I care as much as you do about freedom. And like it or not, believe it or not, you will need a secret police. You don't yet know the realities of power."

"Who can take power away from us now?"

"Ulyanov is returning through Germany. He is being supported by Parvus and the German government. He will not be as idealistic as you are."

"If you have proof of your allegations, then produce it, and in due course we will bring Ulyanov to trial for treason. If he is found guilty, he will be executed. That is what is meant by the rule of law. That is what the new Russia is all about."

"So you will not try to stop him?"

Kerensky shook his head. "A man is free to do what he pleases. Ulyanov is an important socialist thinker. He has suffered for the cause. Let him come. The revolution is big enough to accommodate him."

"For the sake of Russia, I beg you, be practical. Men like Ulyanov are not bound by your bourgeois fantasies. They will take away everything you have fought for."

"You don't understand, do you? Freedom, liberty, democracy, these things are bigger than you or me or Ulyanov. They will always survive, because they are right and proper and because enough people believe in them. Now that Russia has tasted freedom, no one can take it away."

"Words," Kuryakin said, "empty words. With two divisions of my Japanese veterans, I could prove to you that the freedom you speak of is not self-perpetuating."

"But you won't be given a chance to try. There is a warrant for your arrest. A platoon of Ismailovsky have orders to surround a certain house in Rozhdestvenskaya Street in three hours' time. Incidentally, how many of you are there?"

"Five," Kuryakin replied. "Why are you telling me this?"

"Because I owe you a favour," Kerensky said. "And because I know you are a better person than you have been given credit for. Also, you have helped us. Despite that, it is impossible for the Provisional Government to accept your offer of service. It is also politically impossible for you to remain at liberty. Too many socialists want your head." Kerensky stood up. "Perhaps in a year or two when things have become more settled, when old grievances are buried. . . ."

"You are ordering me to leave Russia?"

"You are free to do as you wish," Kerensky said.

Kuryakin hurried back to the house on Rozhdestvenskaya Street. They had to flee.

"A strategic retreat," Serge said, perpetually optimistic.

They would leave in two groups, disguised as recalcitrant soldiers. Serge would go with Peter and Igor across the ice from Staraya Derevnya. Kuryakin and Tihon would take the train to Grusino and, from there, walk across the border. They would regroup at Valinkoski, near the Imatra Falls, where Kuryakin had a summer villa.

They left within twenty minutes of each other, taking nothing but rifles and ammunition. Even though it was a risk, Kuryakin and Tihon took a *droshky* all the way to the Okha Station.

The station was crowded, because trains were still running irregularly, but they were able to buy second-class tickets and find seats in a crowded carriage.

Tihon was a young-looking thirty-six, a former student of psychology in Vienna, a cheery individual who had been one of the Political Section's most skilled interrogators. "Think of someone in a worse situation than you," he advised, as the train made one of its interminable stops at a wayside station.

"Like whom?"

"Tsar Nicholas, for example."

Tsar Nicholas was being exiled, too, or so it was rumoured. He was being taken to Murmansk and being sent on a British destroyer to England. The Germans had agreed not to torpedo the ship.

"You think they will really let him go?"

"Kerensky will. He is no Marat."

"The others want blood," Kuryakin observed, as the train began to move. "They want to see him tried and pilloried and humilated before they kill him." The more he thought about it, the more pointless it seemed. A living Tsar, even in England, could not form the nucleus of a dissident group. He remembered the broken man he had seen in Tsarskoe Selo. Tsar Nicholas was finished. If Russia was to be saved, someone else would have to do it.

The train travelled slowly. At one end of the carriage some peasants returning to their farms on the border began to sing old folk songs. Near Toksovo, two railway officials asked Kuryakin for his travel papers.

"We shot our officers," Kuryakin said. "There is no one to give us travel papers. We are going to visit our families at Grusino."

The officials took in Kuryakin's savage expression of brooding menace and decided not to make an issue of it.

Two hours later they were in Grusino.

In the town they bought thick, brown leggings and tunics, over-coats, preserved meat, and sugar. They booked into a cheap hotel where they ate, slept, and changed. Soon after dark they left the hotel and, crossing the railway line, took a narrow track that led away from the town and into the forest.

When he had first worked with the Okhrana, Tihon had been attached to the Border Patrol and knew the places where crossings were possible, because the border guards relied on natural hazards to prevent them. They walked steadily, stopping from time to time to check their bearings and to ensure that the narrow lake was to the west of them. In about five hours they would reach the border, if they didn't lose their way or get buried in a snowdrift.

At the end of the first hour they stopped, ate some meat, and sucked the sugar.

"Ironic," Kuryakin said softly. "Here we are creeping out of Russia while the Plekhanovs and the Ulyanovs are greeted with massed bands."

"Wheels of fortune," Tihon said. "The wheels of fortune, going round and round, ever changing, ever changeable."

"Like people," Kuryakin said. "Sometimes one thing, sometimes the other."

"Oh, no," Tihon said. "People can be changed much more permanently than that."

Kuryakin did not believe it. It made interesting conversation though, when after ten minutes they started to walk again.

Soon after the second hour they came across a clearing with three or four huts and tumbledown outhouses, black and silent. A dog barked as they skirted the clearing and walked steadily onwards to where the forest ended and the marshland began.

The marsh was frozen, covered with deep snow, riddled with gullies and snowdrifts, underneath which was a fragile platform of ice and deep, dark, motionless water. They left the forest track and plunged immediately into deep snow, struggling across open ground with snow coming up to their knees and coming away in soft handfuls as they struggled for something that would give them leverage.

Each step took an interminable time, demanding prodigious effort, and they did not dare rest even for a moment for fear of sinking deep into the snow forever.

It was too late to worry now whether they could be seen or whether their tracks were being followed. It took all their energy to struggle against the all-pervading, cloying white mass. It took them over an hour to reach the forest on the far side of the meadow.

Inside the forest the going was easier. They'd lost the lake now, but if they kept going west, they would come to the river which marked the border. They walked quickly, firmly, ignoring aching, tired muscles. They had to keep going. To rest now would only bring on lethargy and permanent, snowbound sleep.

They sucked the sugar as they went and tore at the meat, not speaking. A low moon was rising as they followed the track out of the forest, crossed another open space, and came to a narrow, rickety bridge.

They walked on for two more hours, winding in and out of the forest, crossing fields. Twice they had to jump across ditches, once to walk down and climb up the other side. They were both very tired, legs no longer sensitive to that sudden softness which indicated a snowdrift. They walked on. They had no choice.

Sometime later Tihon began to recognise landmarks, a gully, a hut. They were approaching the border and the trail grew more familiar. Now Tihon insisted they walk more cautiously, pausing between each step to listen for the crashing of a sledge or voices, straining their eyes for the movement of human figures.

A hundred yards from the river the forest ended. Before them was open land with no cover, a forest on the far side. They stayed motionless for a whole five minutes, watching and listening. Nothing moved except the wind in the branches.

"Let's go," Tihon said.

They set out carefully, trying to spot the softer patches of snow. They came to a bridge which they crossed thankfully. Every step brought them nearer to the border river. It was a hundred yards away, then eighty, then sixty. Suddenly Kuryakin's feet shot straight under him and he plunged through cold snow, straight through the ice.

The snow covered his face, filling his nostrils with burning cold. He moved and sank up to his waist in chill water. Tihon stood above him, helpless. If he did not get out within minutes, he would freeze to death.

Kuryakin had fallen into a dyke and the question now was whether to go forward or back. Numb with cold he decided to go forward and leant on the snow, bringing the weight of his shoulders onto his arms. The snow gave, and he fell, widening the gap made by his original fall. He thrashed frantically, beating forward all the time, trying to lift his body and get it parallel to the ground. The soft snow gave under him. He fell forward. He felt his legs lift clear and then he plunged face down into the water.

Snow cascaded down after him. Kuryakin struggled and heaved and dragged, covering himself now with water, now with snow. His desperately flailing hand found a pole wedged into the side of the bank. He grabbed it, swivelled his body round. Then Tihon's hand was reaching down to him, pulling. Bracing his body against the side of the bank and pushing against the pole, he dragged himself up, wet and cold.

They ran to the bank of the river. Some twenty yards away a wooden plank had been thrown across it, and, still running, they crossed and threw themselves down beside the black-and-white post that indicated they were in Finland.

They didn't stay long. Without movement, Kuryakin knew he would freeze death, and they still had a long way to go. They set off into the forest and walked southwest, parallel to the river.

Kuryakin's clothes had barely dried when they reached a little hamlet, which in the old days, Tihon said, had been a well-known smugglers' base. The villagers were used to wet and bedraggled visitors at all hours of the night, and they asked no questions. They were given food and, Kuryakin, a change of clothes, and in exchange for forty gold roubles they were provided with a sledge and horses to take them to Terioki.

Badmayev's conviction that the revolution was only a temporary phenomenon was now shared by everyone except Poidvosky. Kuryakin's cables, while short on fact, at least proved that the revolution was not yet accomplished. More significantly, the cables were evidence of the existence of counterrevolutionary forces, and in Russia all the precedents were on the side of counterrevolution.

Because of that, because of the loyalty of his agents, and because certain organisational aspects were impossible to hide, Badmayev knew that the Germans were transporting the Bolsheviks to Russia. He'd seen the directives Ulyanov had sent to Lausanne, Geneva, Chaux-de-Fonds, Berne, and Zurich. All party members should arrive in Berne no later than Friday, the sixth of April. Each person was restricted to a maxium of three baskets and they should bring what food they could for the journey. Party treasurers were instructed to send any excess money they had to Zinoviev. Before boarding the train each person would be issued with a pass, provided by the Swiss Social Democrats, which would enable them to cross the border into Germany.

It was simple, down to earth, and practical. Badmayev smiled. Ulyanov hadn't a hope in hell of returning to Russia.

In his apartment in Zurich, Caspar put down his coffee and slit open the envelope which had been rushed round from von Dichter. In it was a copy of a telegram timed at four o'clock that morning, from the Foreign Ministry to the German Ambassador in Berne. *General Staff agrees. Frontier crossing at Gottmadingen. Understanding Officer will take charge of train from Gottmadingen to Sassnitz. . . . No passport formalities of any kind at frontier crossing. Luggage will be sealed. Safe transit guaranteed.*

That would thrill Ulyanov.

For technical reason maximum number to travel sixty.

Provisionally two second-class express carriages will be ready at Gottmadingen on Saturday evening.

Caspar went to the kitchen and poured himself a celebratory Stafner. The journey was finally on. He scribbled a note for Sonya, and decided to go over to the Spiegelgasse to make certain that Ulyanov knew.

Ulyanov knew all right. From behind the Kammerers' door came the soothing clink of cutlery against china. Upstairs, from behind the Ulyanov's door, there was the far from benign voice of Nadya Constantinova, high pitched and angry. "If you must, go on your own. I'll leave tomorrow."

Then, Ulyanov's voice, deeper, also angry. "You stupid woman, we have to get to Berne today. There is a lot to be done."

"Then go and do it. I will not leave before I have packed."

"What is there to pack? Inessa, who has more goods than all of us, is ready."

"Then go with her, Vladya. I will come to Berne tomorrow."

"If we don't leave now, there'll be no reason to pack. We will be spending the rest of our lives in this miserable little room."

Casper turned and walked out of the house. Nadya was having to be the practical one. She obviously realised that things would be difficult enough if they were turned back at the Russian border, much worse if all their possessions were in Zurich.

Caspar walked across the Neumarkt. The brisk air, the Stafner, and the walk had made him hungry. He ate some bread and Schublinge sausage, washed it down with beer, and then went back to the boarding house.

The row had phased down to a low rumble. Gingerly, Caspar knocked.

Ulyanov snatched open the door and stood there in his braces, glowering. "What do you want?"

"I've been told the train will be ready tomorrow evening."

"We already know that. We are taking the three o'clock train to Berne."

So, not unsurprisingly, Ulyanov had won. Peering behind him, Caspar saw a red-faced Nadya, bending over baskets, stuffing them with clothes, newspapers, and files. "I just wanted to be certain you knew," Caspar said apologetically.

Ulyanov started to close the door. Then suddenly he opened it wider and came out onto the landing. "Will you be coming to Berne?"

"No. I have a few things to do in Zurich."

"Good. Excellent. There is something you can do for us in Zurich. You can canvass the socialists here and have them sign a petition approving our journey." He darted into the room and came out with a typewritten sheet of paper.

Believing that the only morality and the only duty of the true revolutionary is to further the triumph of the revolution, and being aware that the unreasonable and immoral attitude of the Entente powers have forced you to travel through Germany, we approve of such a journey.

Nechayev again, Caspar thought.

"Get as many people as you can to sign it," Ulyanov urged. "If enough people here approve of the journey, there is nothing they can do to us in Russia. We are hoping to get international approval of our journey in Berne."

Herr Kammerer came up the stairs and stood beside Caspar, awkwardly twisting a leather cap in his hands. "My wife tells me you are leaving, Herr Ulyanov," he said. "I came to say good-bye."

"Now that there has been a revolution, they need us back in Russia," Ulyanov said.

"Yes," Herr Kammerer said. "I read about the revolution in the newspaper. My wife and I have been happy to have you in our house. We hope you will have a safe journey."

"We are sorry to leave," Ulyanov said, "and we are grateful to you and your wife for many kindnesses. We will not forget you. But you see, Herr Kammerer, we go so that we can make peace."

THE TRAIN

Caspar intervened quickly. "Your problem, comrade seated in von Dichter's office and trying to get a train. He spoke to officers of the Baden, Hesse, and Prussian State Railways; he spoke to Military Transport Officers of the First and Third Armies; he spoke to Romberg, to Under-Secretary Bussche and to Zimmerman. Finally he found himself talking to Freihen von Lersner, the Foreign Ministry Liaison Officer at General Headquarters. Now that Ulyanov had finally agreed to be transported through Germany, it was essential that he be removed from Switzerland as soon as possible.

But soon as possible could not be the evening of Friday, the sixth of April, von Lersner informed him. They were preparing a big offensive in the region of Arras, and neither men nor rolling stock could be diverted from that.

But Ulyanov could change his mind, Caspar protested.

In that case Herr Ulyanov could suck eggs in Switzerland till the war ended.

But peace on the Eastern Front—

Would have to wait. Even if rolling stock and the understanding officers Foreign Secretary Zimmerman had requested were available, they could not get to Gottmadingen that evening.

It's only two railway carriages, Caspar pleaded.

Sunday.

But that—

Sunday, definitely.

The afternoon brought the first, sharp showers of spring and another problem. Commissioner Hartmann wanted someone to call on him at the Hohnerstrasse for urgent discussions concerning the repatriation of the revolutionaries.

"You'd better go," von Dichter said. "You know more about it than I do, and you're much more reassuring."

Unable to find a cab, Caspar walked there. Spring rain was just as wet and misery-making as any other kind of rain.

"Working on your holiday. How tragic." Commissioner Hartmann sat very erect and very square before a large and empty desk in a large and gleaming office that looked as if it was scrubbed clean every hour on the hour.

"I understand you are proposing to relieve us of our Russian friends," Commissioner Hartmann said.

Caspar nodded, brightly. "That is correct, Commissioner."

"I also understand that you propose to allow them to cross the German Frontier without passports; indeed, without identification of any kind."

"The credentials of each of the exiles are being guaranteed by the Swiss Social Democrat Party."

"Indeed," Hartmann said, and favoured Caspar with a look of long-suffering patience. "And what if they guarantee a criminal? What if they guarantee one of their own people who is wanted for political offences in Switzerland?"

"I'm sure they wouldn't do that."

"It simply isn't good enough, Herr Ehrler. You must surely realise that anyone wanting to leave Switzerland illegally could get on that train simply by being nice to the Social Democrats." Hartmann looked at Caspar, keenly. "Even Rakovsky's murderer."

"If that were to happen, we would undertake to return him to you, forthwith."

"Provided," Hartmann said, "you knew who he was. Provided he did not make any attempt to stay in Germany or Sweden or wherever. Extradition costs money, you know."

"It is most unlikely," Caspar said. "Fritz Platten and his people are very thorough."

"But not as thorough as officials who customarily deal with these things. I am afraid I cannot allow these people to leave Switzerland without proper documentation."

"But most of them have no passports! And now there is no way that they can get them. The Provisional Government does not yet have proper diplomatic representation in Switzerland." That, Caspar thought, should do the trick.

"I can issue them with appropriate documentation," Hartmann said. "Have the revolutionaries come here on Monday."

Caspar felt himself sink into his chair. He couldn't imagine the revolutionaries agreeing to visit a Swiss police station. In a weak voice he said, "We hope to be gone by then."

Hartmann said firmly, "Without proper documentation, no one is going anywhere."

They discussed the matter for an hour. Hartmann's request was unfair, Caspar pointed out. Most of the revolutionaries were now in Berne; some of them having travelled there from Geneva and other places. For them to stay over in Zurich would cost money they didn't have, and besides, the train could not be held over indefinitely. If the revolutionaries missed this train, it could take weeks to organise another one. Also, as Hartmann well knew, the revolutionaries were nervous of official contact of any kind. His request that they should all gather at a police station might frighten them into abandoning the idea of going altogether, and then they would be in Switzerland till the end of the war.

Hartmann obviously did not want that, but he also wanted to ensure that proper procedures were followed and that there was no abuse of German laxity. He finally agreed to a compromise. If Caspar would provide him with a list of the travellers, he would check that against his own records. He would issue passes to all those who had not committed any offences in Switzerland, but without those passes, no one would be allowed to board the train. If Caspar gave him the list now, he promised to have the passes ready the following morning.

It seemed a reasonable solution. As he would be in Berne the following day, Caspar had Hartmann agree to Sonya's collecting the passes. After that he was free to worry whether all these complications would cause Ulyanov to change his mind.

The lounge of Zinoviev's apartment was full of animatedly talking revolutionaries eating and drinking and every bit of space that was not occupied by a person was filled with bags, suitcases, parcels, and baskets. It was like a party that had gone on too long, Caspar thought, as Ulyanov irritatedly hurried him and Platten through the lounge, across a narrow corridor, and into a small bedroom.

The bedroom, too, was crowded. There were baskets on the bed, a stack of books and papers on the floor, a paraffin stove wrapped in paper and tied with string, ready for transport to Petrograd.

"What is the meaning of all these postponements, Rihma? I demand to know. First it was Friday, then today, and now you say the train won't even be at Gottmadingen till Sunday evening!"

Caspar tried to sound reassuring. "The reasons are purely technical, to do with the availability of personnel and railway carriages."

"We are not asking for the Emperor's train. One railway carriage is all we need." Caspar could see Ulyanov's natural distrust rising to the surface. "Surely the magnificent German railway system can manage that?"

"On Sunday," Caspar said, "they will."

"As definite as all your other promises," Ulyanov snapped. He was tired and irritable. For two days he'd been surrounded by baskets and chattering revolutionaries. He hadn't had peace to think and there was so much he had to think about, so many directives he had to write. Now he was trapped for another twenty-four hours. What use could he make of it? No point canvassing approvals from fellow socialists. That had been a disaster. Three signatures of nonentities who were remaining in Switzerland, one thumb print and a gratuitous insult from Romain Rolland. Dangerous and cynical adventurer, indeed! When he got back to

Russia he would brand Rolland as a crypto-socialist.

If he got back to Russia.

Why were the Germans delaying the train? Didn't they realise that delay increased the risk of exposure; that whatever the effect of that exposure on the Germans, the effect on him, Ulyanov, would be fatal?

No, the approvals signed by Bronski on behalf of Poland, a journalist friend of Radek's on behalf of France, and by Platten himself for Switzerland, were not protection enough. He would have to make new conditions. By imposing proper conditions now, he would ensure that even if they were exposed, everyone would know they had travelled through Germany in total isolation. If they had not spoken or seen a single German on the way, how could they be accused of treason?

"We're not going," Ulyanov said.

"But, Vladimir Ilyich, we have the approvals," Platten blurted out. "It's only another twenty-four hours."

Ulyanov glared at Platten. "It is still too dangerous. In yesterday's *Le Petit Parisien,* Milyukov was reported as saying that anyone travelling through Germany would be hung for treason. It's impossible."

"Any alternative arrangements you make would take weeks, months even," Caspar said softly. "If you don't go now, you might never get to Petrograd."

An expression of extraordinary cunning crossed Ulyanov's face. "Why do you want us to return to Petrograd, Rihma?"

Caspar looked Ulyanov directly in the face. "The Germans believe you will make peace. I believe you will do much greater things than that."

Ulyanov appeared embarrassed by this affirmation of faith. "I will go," he rumbled, "but only on certain conditions."

"Conditions?"

"Yes, conditions." He rummaged amongst the books and handed paper and pencil to Platten. "Here Fritz, write."

1. *I, Fritz Platten, will conduct the carriage carrying political* émigrés *wishing to travel to Russia, through Germany, bearing full responsibility and personal liability at all times.*
2. *All communication with German organisations will be undertaken exclusively by Platten, without whose permission absolutely no one may enter the carriage, which will be locked at all times. The carriage will be granted extraterritorial rights.*
3. *No control of passports or persons may be carried out either on entering or leaving Germany.*
4. *Persons will be allowed to travel in the carriage absolutely regardless of their political opinions or their attitude towards the question of the desirability of war or peace.*
5. *Platten will buy tickets at the normal tariffs for those travelling.*
6. *As far as possible the journey shall be made without stops. . . .*

Caspar said, "I have no authority to agree to these conditions. I will have to discuss all this with Romberg."

Ulyanov smiled at him mockingly. "Romberg does not have any choice," he said.

In a bar near the Zurich Technische Hochshule, Badmayev sipped coffee and watched Boris down a

Steinhager. "What's happening with the train?" he asked.

Boris wiped his mouth with the back of his sleeve and grunted. "I don't know. First we were leaving on Friday, then Saturday, and now they say it's Monday afternoon."

"Why the delay?"

"They say Ulyanov is still negotiating with the Germans. He wants better conditions."

"And the Germans will agree to better conditions?"

"It might be that." Boris reached into his pocket and drew out the police pass Sonya had given him earlier that afternoon. "Or this."

Badmayev studied the pass carefully.

"The Karpinskaya woman gave it to me this afternoon. Apparently the police will not let us board the train without it."

Badmayev handed the pass back to Boris. "I'll want you in Zurich tonight," he said, standing up and throwing a few coins on the table. "We are going to stop that train."

In Berne, having despatched Platten to the German Embassy, Ulyanov went out for a walk. The continual comings and goings and chatter of the revolutionaries was making him nervous and had given him a headache. He needed peace and quiet and he liked walking.

He hurried under the vaulted roofs of the *lauben*, surrounded by placid, cowlike Swiss gazing calmly into the shop windows. He couldn't wait to leave this country and get back to Russia. March, and already it was spring. It was still winter in Russia. For twelve years he had missed those long, soulless Russian winters.

Winterlessness was a symbol of his exile, his separation from Russia. But soon he would be back.

He hurried along the Spitalgasse, boots squeaking on the cement. It was good to walk, feeling the muscles of his sturdy legs bunching underneath him. He felt better already. He could think. What, for instance, was the Swiss contribution to civilisation? Watches, cuckoo clocks, and fountains. He stared disgustedly at the Bagpiper Fountain in the middle of the street. Another twenty-four hours of this would be stultifying. He couldn't stand it; he couldn't stand the inactivity when there was so much to be done.

He wondered if Romberg would accept the conditions. Ah, but Romberg would have to. Romberg had no alternative. Except for the Bundists, all the other revolutionaries had refused to travel through Germany. He was the only one who was on their side. Nevertheless, what if the Germans refused to accept his conditions? He would be stuck here in Switzerland surrounded by uninspiring people and clocks while the revolution went on without him. That could not be allowed to happen. It must not happen. But what could he do? What concrete, practical thing could he do when there were only two ways out of Switzerland? France or Germany, and the French wouldn't let him through. So there was only Germany. Unless . . .

He hurried past the Church of the Holy Ghost looking for a public telephone. Woodrow Wilson was for peace. He had repeatedly called upon the belligerent powers to gather round a table and settle their differences amicably. America would support a Russian peace initiative. He must call the American Embassy now to arrange an immediate meeting with the Ambassador. Like Woodrow Wilson, he, Vladimir Ilyich Ulyanov, stood for peace.

The Ambassador would support someone who was aligned with his President. He would be able to arrange travel through France in a sealed carriage and provide an American destroyer, a neutral ship, for the journey from Cherbourg to Petrograd. For that he, Vladimir Ilyich Ulyanov, would give Woodrow Wilson what he wanted.

He found a telephone, rummaged in his pocket for coins, and dialled. He wished Zinoviev or Platten could have made this call for him, but there was no time. The Embassy would close for the weekend shortly and he couldn't wait till Monday. The phone burbled in his ear. He felt his mouth grow dry with apprehension. He couldn't stand the humiliation of a refusal.

A light, warm, pleasant girl's voice said, "American Embassy."

"I want to speak to the Ambassador. It is important."

The Ambassador would be some rich capitalist. Unlike in the Soviet states of the future, one could not speak to rich, capitalist ambassadors easily. The girl wanted to know what he wanted to talk about.

He wished Zinoviev were here. "I am Ulyanov—the Russian revolutionary. I want to talk to the Ambassador about peace. At once."

"I am afraid, sir, the Ambassador is engaged right now. I will put you through to Mr. Dulles."

Allen Welsh Dulles had arrived in Berne the previous week to join a team of cipher experts and lawyers who formed the nascent American Secret Service. Dulles had taken charge of Secret Service contacts with Russian exiles and other Slavic groups who congregated in Berne to plot the downfall of the Austro-Hungarian Empire. He'd heard of Ulyanov. The man was some kind of a nut. "What can I do for you, Mr. Ulyanov?"

Gutturally, disjointedly, in appalling English, Ulyanov told him. Sealed carriages, destroyers. Perhaps Ulyanov would like a marine band to play dance music on the way! In any case there wasn't much point to it. The reason for the increased activity of the American Secret Service was that within three weeks America would be at war. Dulles looked at his watch. He had a date to play tennis with Helene, whose family he had stayed with before the war and whom he had admired since he was fifteen years old. The date had been arranged with considerable difficulty. Ulyanov and his nutty peace mission could wait.

"The Embassy is closing now," he informed the revolutionary. "Come back first thing Monday morning."

"But—but—Monday—that is too late—I have to come now."

"Ten o'clock, Monday," Dulles cooed and replaced the receiver.

Sonya bounded up the stairs, shiny-faced, out of breath, booted legs kicking away the ends of her new, calf-length skirt. She'd spent all afternoon hurrying round Zurich distributing the passes that Hartmann had issued. Now, as she reached the top of the stairs, she saw, standing in the corridor outside the apartment, a familiar spindle-shanked figure, partly cloaked by a lumpy overcoat. Chernikov's knobbly face broke into a familiar, toothy grin as he saw her.

"Paul! What are you doing here?"

"I was hoping to see Caspar about two people who want to go on the train."

"Caspar is in Berne." She took out her key and opened the door. "Are you going on the train, too?"

"I'd like to, but travelling through Germany, however you look at it, it's treason."

He followed her into the apartment and stood patting his bulging pockets awkwardly.

Sonya saw that Caspar had returned and gone out again. There was an unfinished cup of coffee on the dining table and a hastily scribbled note. Caspar had gone to the Swiss Social Democrat offices in the Ramistrasse to meet Hartmann. She stifled a sigh of annoyance. She had been so looking forward to spending this last day alone with Caspar. She handed Chernikov the note. "Will you wait, Paul?"

"Wait? Oh, yes—yes. I'll wait. That is—if it isn't inconvenient."

"Of course it isn't inconvenient. Would you like some coffee?"

Again Chernikov hesitated, before saying, "Yes—yes, I would like some coffee. You go into the kitchen and make it."

Sonya threw her coat onto the sofa and went into the kitchen trying not to think of Caspar leaving with the others. That thought drove all else from her mind. She looked blank faced into the cupboard. After the next day or so, loneliness and blankness. And would there be Berlin afterwards? Even if there was Berlin afterwards, would it be the same? Frenetic, fornicating Caspar! War and revolution! What a time to fall in love!

She'd come to the kitchen to make coffee. Paul Chernikov was waiting in the lounge. Suddenly she was sure he'd gone out again. "Won't be long now," she shouted. Where the hell had Caspar put the coffee? Strange, however solidly apartments were built, they were always noisy; imaginary footsteps that were really expanding floorboards and opening doors that were the rumble of gas meters. Ah, there was the coffee, where Caspar usually left it. Open, lying on its side, on the second shelf of the larder, beside the cheese. If he'd left his coffee unfinished, he couldn't have been expecting a summons from Hartmann. He'd drunk a glass of Stafner, too, before he'd left. She was going to miss him a lot. Too much. Putting the glass into the sink, she felt like having a little Stafner herself. Better not, though, with Chernikov lurking in the lounge. Even revolutionary women did not drink alone, and certainly not before dinner—already there was enough gossip amongst the exiles about her liaison with a German agent.

The water boiled. She poured it into the coffee jug and went out to the lounge. "Paul, how do you like—"

There were three other men in the room with Chernikov—one tall, one short, and one medium, but only in relation to each other. They were all Russian, and they were all big.

"I didn't—didn't know you'd brought friends. Would you people like—"

One of the men walked quickly round behind her, standing between her and the kitchen.

"Paul, what is going on?"

Chernikov's smile was bleached. "It's all right, Sonya. It will all be explained later. Now don't make a fuss. Come with us, please."

Sonya screamed. Sonya tried to run for the door. Two bodies, solid and implacable as rock underneath the heavy overcoats, blocked her. Hands clawed at her. Her face was pressed against rough cloth. A palm closed about her gaping mouth. Choking, she beat at the men with her fists. Her flailing arms were grasped at the wrists and pulled away from her body. The man behind her braced his body against hers.

Then someone hit her. Someone hit her again, hard and low in the stomach. Her body slammed into that of the man behind her, her legs flying epileptically upwards from the heels. A fist grazed her face, rings cutting open the flesh of her cheek. She pulled her hands free, struggling, beating at the men. To her right she could see Chernikov, looking disturbed but doing nothing to help her. A fist crashed into her chest. She began to feel sick. Desperately she kicked out at the men. Someone got hold of her foot. She wrenched it free. Another blow, solid and breath shattering. She kicked again, weakly. The man behind her swept her foot away. For a brief moment she felt herself lifted into the air, then she was being borne down to the carpet by the combined weight of the men.

They held her there, her face pressed into the pile, unable to turn her head, unable to breathe or scream. One, possibly two of the men were lying across her, heavy and unrelenting as sacks of cement. She heaved helplessly against that massive inertia, trying impossibly to wriggle as her arms were pulled behind her and bound.

"Not a sound," someone said as they rose, helping her to her feet. One of them grasped her by the hair. There was a hard, dull ache in the pit of her stomach and her mouth felt dry and acrid.

"Don't struggle," Chernikov pleaded. "Please don't make a fuss. It will be worse for you if you do."

There was some sense in that, Sonya thought as they draped her coat over her shoulders and led her out of the apartment to a waiting car.

* * *

An hour later Caspar returned to the flat, worn out from a day of argument. Romberg had refused to agree to Ulyanov's conditions and had forwarded them to Berlin for approval. Ulyanov had muttered darkly that unless the conditions were accepted, none of the revolutionaries would travel. Then he had rushed out of Zinoviev's flat and gone for a long walk. When Caspar returned to Zurich, he'd found yet another urgent message from Hartmann.

A sudden exodus of *émigrés* had left a variety of small, dark, cold, and frequently dirty rooms suddenly empty, and a clutch of land-ladies complaining that even a revolution was no excuse for failure to give proper notice or pay proper compensation therefor. Hartmann would not allow any of the exiles to leave unless each of them produced appropriately verified statements that all their liabilities in Switzerland had been settled and that all their library books, which after all were the property of the state, had been returned.

It had taken Caspar an hour of strained argument to persuade Hartmann that the production of such statements was impossible. In the end Hartmann had agreed that the total liabilities of all the exiles could not possibly exceed a thousand francs each and had agreed to accept a bank guarantee in the sum of forty thousand francs from the Handel Bank. Procuring a bank guarantee late on a Saturday afternoon had been even more tiresome and taken even longer, and now Caspar went wearily into the kitchen and poured himself a glass of Stafner.

Sonya had been and gone. The wine glass he had used that morning had been put into the sink, and there was a full pot of coffee and two cups by the stove. The coffee was cold and bitter and had obviously been standing there for some time.

Carrying his drink, Caspar went back to the lounge. He picked up a copy of Bismarck's autobiography, which had caused a sensation when published soon after the Iron Chancellor's death, and, placing the bank guarantee between its pages, settled down to read.

That night, he and Sonya would dine at the Veltliner Keller.

A wheel locked and the car skidded slightly as it braked to a stop outside the shuttered house in Meilen. One of the three men crushed into the back with Sonya opened the door and motioned to her to get out. They crowded round her, wrapping her coat about her, and with one man gripping each elbow, she was led into the house and up the stairs to a classroom on the first floor.

From an upstairs window Badmayev watched the procession, and, as he recognised Sonya, his soft brown eyes gleamed with a strange brightness. Revolutionary scum! So she was going to deliver Russia to the usurpers of the Tsar! He watched her walk up the steps: bloody whore in a short skirt; traitorous slut who slept with Germans. This time, Badmayev promised himself, it would be different from Kiev.

In the classroom the chairs had been put away neatly in a corner, and on the desk was a basin and a jug of water. Beside the door was a camp bed.

"What is the meaning of all this?" Sonya cried. "I demand an explanation."

The three Russians who had accompanied her into the room remained silent. Chernikov, who had sat in the front passenger seat, pointed head staring fixedly at the snow-lined, potholed road all the way from Zurich, had disappeared the moment they entered the house.

"What is going on? You must tell me!"

The medium-sized Russian with the large eyes said, "It will all be explained in due course."

"Who are you?"

The man stood before her, silent.

"Okhrana?"

No one replied.

"For God's sake, you people are finished! There's been a revolution in Russia, or don't you know?"

Without speaking they forced her into a chair and tied her to it. Before they left, the one with the large eyes turned the chair round so she could look out of the window. There was some kindness in that.

In the room upstairs Badmayev asked Chernikov, "What about the German?"

"He wasn't there. He was with Hartmann and we didn't know how long he would be. So we took the girl."

"You did well," Badmayev said. It was better taking them separately.

"Shall we go back and get the German?"

"Later. I want to speak to the woman first."

He went downstairs to the room where Sonya was held.

She heard the sound of the door being unlocked behind her, the sound of light footsteps. Badmayev came round and stood between her and the window.

She looked up at that tall, lean figure, that flawless face and the mild brown eyes, and she remembered the horror of being splayed out on the table in Kiev, the agony of the blows raining down on her defenceless back. Panic welled within her and she struggled desperately against the ropes, feeling them cutting into her flesh. Oh, God, she was helpless and the panic was rising fast within her. She couldn't help it–she screamed.

The sting of Badmayev's open palm against her cheek shocked her into silence.

"There is nothing to scream about," Badmayev said, "as long as you co-operate."

Clicking his tongue with annoyance he took out a pocket knife and cut the rope that held her to the chair. Then, drawing a chair up to her, he sat astride it, leaning forward against its back. "What do you know about the train?" he asked.

Sonya looked past him at the window. "Nothing," she said.

"You must know something. After all, your lover arranged it."

"He doesn't discuss his work with me."

"But you help him. Today, for instance, you distributed police passes."

"I only do what I am asked. I have no interest in politics."

"Yes," Badmayev smiled. "I am aware of that. Why are the Germans helping Ulyanov?"

"I don't know," Sonya said.

"When is the train coming?"

"I don't know."

"Will it come to Zurich or wait on the border?"

"I don't know."

"Why have there been delays?"

"I don't know."

Badmayev stared at her in silence. Very softly but with great authority he said, "Stand up."

Sonya stood. He reached across from behind the

chair and with a few rapid strokes of the knife freed her wrists.

Sonya began to rub them gratefully, feeling the blood surging to the tips of her fingers.

"Does that feel better?"

"Thank you. Yes."

"If you want to return to Russia, I can arrange it," Badmayev said.

Sonya smiled. "There's the small matter of a different government."

"That's only temporary. As soon as the counterrevolution succeeds I can send you back." Badmayev smiled. "You'd like that, wouldn't you?"

Sonya nodded.

"Why don't you be reasonable, Sonya? Why don't you tell me what you know? You needn't be afraid of the revolutionaries."

"I've told you all I know," Sonya said, flatly.

For what seemed an eternity Badmayev stared at her, those dog-like eyes bathing her in a weird warmth. Then, still speaking softly, he said, "Take off your clothes."

"But–"

He flicked at her dress with the knife. "There are four men outside who would be glad of the opportunity."

Sonya shuddered at the thought of being forcibly stripped by Boris and the other Russians. Slowly she stooped down, unbuttoned her boots, and pulled them off. Then she unfastened the tops of her stockings and peeled them off her legs. She unbuttoned her blouse and slipped out of her new, calf-length skirt. She stood facing Badmayev in her slip and brassiere, her toes curling against the cold floor.

"I said, take your clothes off."

"Please, I've told you all I know."

Badmayev stared at her with that curious, warm impersonality. "Remove the rest of your clothes," he ordered.

Sonya unfastened her brassiere and stepped out of her petticoat. She rolled her knickers down her legs and placed them by her shoes.

Badmayev got to his feet. "Come with me."

Jabbing her lightly with the point of his knife, he took her down the stairs to the cellar. The three men who had brought her to Meilen were there, with Chernikov and Boris. She saw them move away from the wall and turn and stare at her. Boris reached out and cupped a hand around her breast.

Badmayev flicked Boris' hand away. "None of that nonsense," he snapped.

In the centre of the room was a plain wooden table. Sonya felt her breath catch in her throat, threatening to choke her. She fought to suppress a cry of fear.

"You know what to do," Badmayev said from behind her. "Go on. Do it."

Looking trancelike straight ahead of her, Sonya climbed onto the table and laid herself face down upon it, with her arms and legs dangling over the sides. The two Russians seized her wrists and bound them to the table legs. She felt Chernikov and Boris do the same with her ankles. The sound of her thudding heart filled her head, its incessant pounding seeming to reverberate off the table. Her mouth was dry and acrid. Badmayev came round and stood in front of her, looking down at her with those warm, impersonal eyes, just as he had done that day in Kiev.

"It's exactly like before," he said softly. "Only this time, you know what to expect."

Sonya closed her eyes and tried to prepare herself

for the beating. There was the sound of movement behind her, followed by silence. Then she heard the lash whistle through the air. It landed across her back in a vivid stripe of fire. She felt her body arch, felt the ropes sawing at her limbs. Her body was a seething liquid mass. She heard the thud as her hips cannoned back onto the table and she screamed. She lay there sobbing, feeling her body relaxing against the wood, fighting the sobs till the pain of the blow became a dull, slow burn.

She heard the lash whistle through the air again, felt her back grow taut. Then it coiled around her body in a tearing kiss of fire. This time her lips were clenched between her teeth, her moans stifled. This time she would tell them nothing. This time she would give them no satisfaction. She knew she could do it, this time. Oh, God, how long before she would faint?

The lash rippled across her body. She could feel the flesh swelling around it. It had taken ages in Kiev before she fainted, and afterwards she'd barely been able to stand. Badmayev was still looking at her with those warm, spaniel eyes.

She heard the sound of the lash being raised. Her back felt raw and open. It was worse this time. Much worse. Her back was ablaze with pain. She heard the lash cutting through the air, heard it land on her body with a wet thwacking sound. Oh, God, she couldn't stand it any longer. Her mouth was open and the saliva was streaming down her cheek. "The train leaves on Monday afternoon!" The voice was hers, but she hadn't spoken. "Everyone with police passes will be allowed to board the 3:24 from Zurich. The German train is at Gottmadingen. It will arrive there on Sunday evening." She was sobbing now, and Badmayev was squatting down before her, unfastening her wrists.

"Yes, Sonya," he was saying soothingly. "And how many carriages will there be on the train? How many guards?" Looking tearfully at the top of Badmayev's curly head, Sonya began to tell him all.

A while later Caspar began to worry about Sonya. She'd never stayed away all evening before, and to-night they were to have gone out to dinner. Bismarck, vindictive and discursive, was hardly soothing and Caspar put the book down and walked from the lounge to the kitchen and back. She couldn't still be delivering the passes. On the other hand the exiles were a suspicious and disorganised lot. She might have had to persuade one or more of them that the passes were necessary. But surely she would have phoned.

Perhaps she'd met with an accident. Caspar found he had taken the polished stone Easter egg that Sonya had given him from the mantelpiece and was walking about the lounge tossing it from palm to palm. Her love would endure as long as the stone, Sonya had said, and next week when he was in Germany or Sweden or wherever, he should place her egg amongst his other Easter presents and remember. Caspar smiled wryly. The damn thing was so heavy he could hardly forget. But where the devil was Sonya?

There was a light knock at the door. Pocketing the egg, Caspar hurried across the lounge and opened it.

"Boris, what happ–"

Three big Russians moved into the drawing room behind Boris, crowding into the apartment.

"German, come with us."

Boris reached out to grab him. Caspar elbowed Boris in the face and tried to slam the door shut. They charged, and in his confusion, Caspar turned and ran back across the lounge.

By the kitchen, Caspar turned. There was nowhere to run. He aimed a punch at Boris and caught him on the side of the head. Boris grunted, seized his arm, and dragged Caspar into the centre of the room. Caspar hit out, aiming low and hard, felt his knuckles bounce against the hard muscles of Boris' stomach. One of the Russians grabbed him by the shoulder. Caspar turned and swung, his whole weight behind the blow. He caught the Russian high on the head and felt him float light and easy on the end of his arm. The Russian crashed against a chair, then spun and kicked over a table.

Boris had him by the waist now. One of the other Russians was approaching him with a vicious glint in his eye. Caspar raised his feet and kicked. The Russian half turned and caught the blow on his hip. Caspar jerked backwards, the force of his movement tearing him free from Boris. He turned, staggering, and realised that he was free. There was no one between him and the door except the smallest Russian.

Caspar raced for the door. One step, two, a long, long stride. Suddenly his feet were swept from under him. His breath caught as he hung suspended. Then he saw the carpet and the sofa looming up at him. He was going to hit the sofa. Desperately he turned his head. Something cracked against the side of his face. He felt a rush of brilliant pain.

Then everything went dark.

Caspar came round, his mouth full of vomit, his head full of a sick, dull pain, his face feeling as if it had grown another skin. He was in a tiny, cheerless cubicle, and a medium-sized Russian with heavy, sad eyes was looking at him with concern.

"How do you feel?" the Russian asked.

Caspar swallowed. "Terrible," he croaked.

"You'll feel better soon. Let me get you some coffee."

The Russian padded away and came back moments later with a steaming cup of black coffee. Caspar drank it and felt excruciatingly sick.

"You will feel better soon," the Russian promised.

"Where am I?"

"You're with friends. You had an accident last night, but you will be better soon."

Caspar remembered Boris and the Russians charging into his apartment and realised with gratitude that Sonya hadn't been there. "I feel well enough to return to my apartment."

"You aren't strong enough yet," the Russian said, gently. "But we will take you back when you are well. Also, there is someone who wants to talk to you." He looked enquiringly at Caspar. "Do you feel better now?"

"A little," Caspar admitted.

"Good, good." The Russian took the empty coffee cup and padded away. Caspar heard the sounds of a telephone being taken off the hook, the subsequent conversation drowned by other Russian voices. The man with the sad eyes was obviously not alone in the house. Caspar quietly stretched himself. They had only removed his shoes and loosened his tie. He was still fully dressed under the sheet, and Sonya's Easter egg dragged at his pocket. The swelling above his temple began to throb.

The Russian returned carrying a bowl of soup. "Drink this and you will feel better." He sat at the end of the bed and watched Caspar drink. "The man who wants to speak to you is on his way. After that, you can go home. And once you get home, you must rest."

He said his name was Poidvosky and that Caspar spoke Russian very well. Caspar told him he'd learned it in Petrograd.

"Really, my home is in Petrograd."

They spoke desultorily about Petrograd for a while and then one of the other Russians, a tall, bearded man much bigger than Poidvosky, entered the room. "I heard voices," he said with apparent surprise.

Poidvosky smiled amiably at him. "We were talking about Petrograd. The German has lived there." He pointed to the intruder. "This is Igor."

Igor looked angrily down at Caspar. "If he is awake, we'd better make sure he can't escape."

"Don't be ridiculous, Igor. He can't escape. He's weak as a newborn kitten."

Which, Caspar thought sadly, was true.

A while later there was the sound of opening doors and tramping feet. Poidvosky waddled in nervously and said, "He's come," and helped Caspar sit up.

A rigid shaft of pain sliced through Caspar's head as he moved. He gasped, feeling the room spin around him, sank back onto the pillows, and waited until the dizziness had stopped and the pain had become a mild throbbing. Then, supported by Poidvosky, he went out of the cubicle into a sunny lounge. His eyeballs exploded at the sudden brightness and his legs felt hopelessly weak. Gently Poidvosky lowered him into a chair.

The lounge was small with a sofa and three armchairs, a bookshelf, a drinks cabinet, and a radio. It looked little used. Through the sun-bright window Caspar had a view of a river on whose further bank there was a small path. He looked at the man seated in the armchair opposite him. "What time is it?"

The man opposite was smartly though conservatively dressed, with a thick head of curly hair, a dimpled chin, and unblinking brown eyes. He looked more European than Russian, more like an actor than a secret agent. "It is two minutes after twelve," he said. "And it's Sunday."

Sunday, Caspar thought. How long had he been unconscious?

"I'd have liked to speak with you earlier," the young man opposite him said, "but"—he shrugged charmingly—"accidents happen. My name is Peter Badmayev."

Caspar froze. Peter Badmayev, the man who had flogged Sonya in Kiev.

"I am a Deputy Director of the Okhrana," Badmayev said. "The fact that we are both in this room demonstrates that the Okhrana is not yet finished."

Caspar swallowed, dry mouthed. Badmayev gestured to Poidvosky to give him a glass of water.

"I know everything about the train," Badmayev said, "when it will arrive, how many people will accompny it, which of the revolutionaries propose to travel and so on. I also know what you intend to do with Ulyanov." He leaned forward and looked directly into Caspar's face. "At this moment, you have a choice. You can force me to kill Ulyanov or you can stop the train."

Caspar made himself think. Twelve o'clock Sunday, and he should have been at Hartmann's at nine with the bank guarantee. By now Hartmann would surely have called von Dichter and von Dichter would have gone round to the apartment and found that something was very wrong. If von Dichter hadn't Sonya would have given the alarm. "Stopping the train is impossible," he said. "Arrangements have already been made."

"Cancel them."

"Only Foreign Secretary Zimmerman can do that."

"What about von Dichter?"

"Like me, only a cog in the machinery."

Badmayev took the Luger out of his pocket. He placed it against Caspar's temple and said, "Call Minister Romberg and tell him to stop the train or Ulyanov will be killed."

Igor placed the phone within easy reach of Caspar. Caspar called the operator and asked to be connected with Berne, while Badmayev picked up an extension.

Badmayev said, "If you give Romberg any warning, you're dead."

Caspar hoped that Romberg would be out. But he wasn't.

"What is it, Ehrler?"

"There is a rumour, Excellency, that the Okhrana plan to kill Ulyanov before he boards the train."

"Rumour! We can't stop the train because of a rumour! Besides, there isn't an Okhrana any more."

"Should we take a chance on that?" Caspar asked.

"Do you have any specific facts?"

Caspar looked at Badmayev. Badmayev shook his head. "No, Emcellency, there is only rumour."

"In that case, Ulyanov must take his chances. We've had enough postponements already. Anyway, it is impossible for me to cancel the train now. Any cancellation must come from Zimmerman."

"Yes, Excellency," Caspar said. "I am so glad you said that."

Badmayev put down the extension. "So you told me the truth. That is a splendid beginning. Now, tell me something else. What are you going to do with Ulyanov in Berlin?"

"What will we do with Ulyanov in Berlin? Nothing! Ulyanov has made it a condition that he should not speak to any Germans on the journey."

"Yes, yes, I know all that. But surely you aren't going to all this trouble just to help Ulyanov."

"Of course not. We hope that when Ulyanov returns to Russia, he will do his best to secure peace."

"That's a little haphazard and totally unlike the German Secret Service. Let me ask you again. What are you going to do with Ulyanov in Berlin?"

"We have been forced to accept his conditions."

"How can you guarantee that he will do what you want?"

"We have no guarantees, only expectations."

Badmayev leant back in his chair. "Tell me about the Reptile Fund."

Caspar went silent. "I don't know what you're talking about."

"Ulyanov does," Badmayev said. "I do. Your girl friend Sonya Karpinskaya does."

Caspar forced himself to remain calm. "Where is Sonya?"

"She is with me. At present she is well and comfortable and being looked after. Unless you co-operate, she will rapidly get less well."

Caspar thought Badmayev was looking for confirmation. After all, enough people had known about Quadriga. The exchange of the marks for the roubles hadn't exactly been a secret and the operation had been open from the very beginning. "I will tell you all about the Reptile Fund," Caspar said, "but first I must be assured that the girl is safe."

Badmayev looked at him thoughtfully, then smiled

and nodded. "It is agreed." He picked up the phone, dialled a number, and spoke rapidly to someone in Russian. The girl was to be set free. In five minutes she was to call and confirm that. He placed his hand over the mouthpiece and looked at Caspar for confirmation.

Caspar nodded.

Exactly five minutes later the phone rang. Badmayev picked it up and wordlessly passed it to Caspar.

"Sonya, darling, are you all right?"

"I'm fine."

She sounded listless.

"Are you hurt?"

A silence, as if she was considering the matter. Then, "I'm fine."

"Are you free now?"

"Yes, yes, I am free."

"Are you alone?"

A long hesitation. "No—"

There was a crackling sound on the other end, then a man's voice came on the line. "Caspar, this is Paul Chernikov. Sonya is with me. Two men left her at the Institute a few minutes ago. She is upset, but otherwise she is all right."

"Can I speak to her?"

"It might be better a little later. I'll have her call you."

"All right," Caspar said. "Thanks." Caspar put down the phone.

Badmayev smiled at him. "Well?"

"What do you want to know?" Caspar asked.

Badmayev's smile widened. "Everything."

When Caspar had finished, Badmayev said, "Do you know something, I believe you have saved Ulyanov's life. I think Ulyanov should go to Berlin and meet with your people. Then when he gets back to Russia, we can hang him for treason." He got to his feet and walked to the door. "I'm afraid I will have to detain you until the train leaves. Igor and Poidvosky will see that you are comfortable." He waved cheerily. "Good-bye! It's been a pleasure dealing with a professional."

When by two o'clock that afternoon the German agent had not come, Hartmann became concerned. Ehrler had struck him as a conscientious and determined young man, and if there had been any difficulties with the guarantee he would have telephoned or come round and argued his case. The fact that Hartmann had not heard from Ehrler or von Dichter intrigued him. The Germans were simply not like that. Jamming his hat firmly on his head, he went down to the street and took a cab to the Konradstrasse.

The apartment was in what had once been a large house in a rundown area of Zurich. Hartmann pushed open the street door and went briskly up the bare cement stairs. There was an air of neglect about the place. At the top of the stairs he made way for a large woman carrying laundry.

Hartmann strode along the dingy corridor and stopped outside the apartment. He knocked. No answer. He knocked again. Silence. Looking quickly up and down the corridor, Hartmann took out his skeleton keys and tried them on the lock. The third one fitted. He went in and stared at the disordered lounge with a professional calm.

Two upturned chairs in the middle of the room, a small table lying on its side, a broken glass, rucked carpets, and the sofa pushed awry. So a struggle had taken place. He walked into the kitchen. A cold pot of coffee, cups, a dirty wine glass. On the mantelpiece, Bismarck's memoirs. Inside it he found the bank guarantee.

So Ehrler had been ready to see him that morning, when he had been kidnapped. Kidnapped or murdered? No, not murder, yet. Whoever had taken him away had left the lights on. If that sort of person wanted to kill, he would have done it in the apartment. No, it had to be a kidnapping and something to do with that confounded train.

Next question, who were the kidnappers? Not the English. He had closed them down. Not the French either. It wasn't the way they operated. It could hardly be the Germans, which left only the Russians.

Hartmann went to the phone and called Zurich Central Police Station. He gave orders for a team of plainclothesmen to place the Russian house in Gessner Allee under surveillance, and for a team of investigators to be sent to the apartment in the Konradstrasse to enquire into the circumstances of the kidnapping. Then he called von Dichter and asked him to come to Zurich Central, where Hartmann would take charge of the operation.

Sonya sat on the end of the bed, her chin cupped in her hands, staring at her booted feet. She felt drained and helpless and full of shame. She had not been ill-treated since the flogging and they had left her free to move about the room.

From time to time that day Chernikov had kept her company. She'd been grateful for that. Chernikov told her that he had been a revolutionary once and that he had been arrested three times. The last time, a man called Kuryakin had beaten him with a knout and broken him. There was nothing to be ashamed of, he said. The human body and spirit could only take so much.

Badmayev, too, had been kind to her. He'd seen that her wounds were dressed and that she'd had enough food. Last night he'd sent her a bottle of wine and told her she would soon be free. Before he'd left for Zurich that morning, he'd come and rehearsed her for the phone call. She'd been so mindless, so helpless in his presence, that she'd agreed to do it; later, even the sound of Caspar's voice had not been enough to make her refuse.

Now she heard the sound of Badmayev's footsteps on the landing outside and her heart quickened. His nearness brought on feelings that she could not analyse. She was frightened of the man, she hated him, and yet the sound of his footsteps made her shiver with pleasurable anticipation.

Now he came in and stood in front of her. "You did well, he said, and Sonya felt pleased.

"How is Caspar?" she asked in a small voice.

"He is being looked after by Igor and Poidvosky."

Why didn't she feel any sense of betrayal? "You didn't hurt him?"

"That wasn't necessary."

Badmayev drew up a chair and sat down beside her. "I want you to do something for me."

Again she felt this strange excitement, this strange revulsion.

Badmayev held out Boris' pass. "I want you to prepare one of these for me. I want to get on board that train."

She looked directly into his eyes, looking for the person behind that strange impassivity. "What will you do on the train?"

Badmayev hesitated, then gave her a cursory smile.

"I suppose you will kill Ulyanov and everybody else?"

Badmayev looked away.

"I won't do it," Sonya said.

Badmayev said, "I have everything you will need—card, paper, even the purple ink Hartmann used to sign these."

Sonya said, "I won't do it."

Badmayev reached out and ran a hand down her back. Sonya, wincing with pain, trembled at his touch.

"Stand up," Badmayev said softly.

Sonya stood.

"Take off your clothes."

She began to fumble with the buttons of her blouse.

"It will be worse now," Badmayev said, "because you broke down the last time."

Sonya could hardly see her fingers for the tears in her eyes. "Please," she said, "don't make me do it."

"This last time," Badmayev said softly. "After I get on the train, you will be free."

Sonya buttoned up her blouse and sat down. She wasn't quite sure she wanted that.

All through that long, tedious, sunny afternoon, Caspar wondered about Hartmann and if he had gone to the apartment and when he would arrive. As the afternoon lengthened, Caspar's thoughts became more morbid. In less than twenty-four hours Ulyanov would be back in Zurich and Badmayev would kill him.

He had told Badmayev about Quadriga, secure in the knowledge that he could not get aboard the train, and that even if he did, there was nothing he could do in Germany. Even as he'd spoken, he'd known that whatever Badmayev would do would be in Zurich, and Caspar had been more than hopeful that Hartmann would have found him before the end of the afternoon.

Now with the grimy half-light of evening enveloping the windows, he faced the fact that Hartmann had failed. Ulyanov's life and Quadriga depended on him. He had to act.

All afternoon he'd sat in the lounge with Poidvosky and Igor. He was tired of watching Poidvosky doze and Igor read. He was sick of his own smell and irritated by the stubble round his chin. Everything was torpid and mind-emptying.

Once he had asked Poidvosky to show him round the house. They had eaten toast and butter and cake, and Caspar had tried separating them by asking one of them to go out and buy beer or wine or even vodka. He had to act. Whatever had happened to that great brain of his? What good was brain against two sprawling hulks within reach of the doorway? He would have to use speed. And stealth. He would have to do something soon. Now.

From the tour Poidvosky had given him of the house, Caspar knew the lounge was on the first floor, and round it were doors leading to a large bedroom, the cubicle where he had slept, a bathroom, and a landing. Above them, uncarpeted wooden stairs reached out to three more bedrooms. Below them, the stairs led to a small lobby, behind which there was a corridor, a second set of bedrooms, a lounge, a dining room, and a kitchen. At the front of the lobby was the main door with steps leading down to the street and freedom.

Caspar slumped low in his chair, fixing the image of

the house in his mind. Forget upstairs. He'd have to go down, through the front door, and out.

He hoped.

Poidvosky was asleep in his chair, his lips fluttering as he snored. Igor remained awake, reading an old Russian newspaper for the seventh time. *Victory Forecast in Galica.* Caspar had read that headline seventeen times, translated it into English, French, and German. Victory forecast—well, he hoped he'd have better luck than the Galicians. It was time to go.

He stretched and stood up on stockinged feet. Stockings for speed and to allay suspicion. Igor looked up enquiringly. Caspar pointed to the bathroom. Igor nodded and returned to his newspaper. Caspar hoped Igor was aware of the dangers of letting off firearms in confined spaces. He walked across to the bathroom door, stood before it a moment, then whirled and rushed for the door that led to the landing.

The padding of his feet made Igor drop his newspaper. Caspar wrenched at the door. The bloody thing was warped. Behind him Igor was rising, hand reaching for the gun. The door came open with a crunch. Caspar leapt out onto the landing, pulling the door shut behind him. The wood above his head splintered with the charge of a heavy bullet. Igor had no inhibitions about discharging firearms in a confined space.

Caspar hared down the landing, down the stairs, hearing the door open behind him, feeling the landing tremble from the pounding of Igor's booted feet. Down the stairs, swinging himself round the turnings, feet skipping lightly over wood, one more turn, and the foot of the stairs six steps away. Caspar jumped, feet jarring as they landed on cement, and kept on running, streaking through the lobby. He pulled open the front door, moved sideways, and stopped.

Massive pounding of feet behind him, massive rushing of breath, massive Igor charging through. Caspar stuck out a foot. With a yelp of surprise and a nasty, audible crack, Igor bounced spectacularly down the steps, his gun skittering along the road.

Caspar dropped his hand into his coat pocket. A lighter tread. Heavier breathing. Poidvosky paused in the doorway, white-faced, open mouthed. Caspar slammed him in the face with Sonya's stone egg and felt bone crumple under its solidity. He moved quickly indoors against an already reeling Poidvosky and shut the door behind him.

Poidvosky moved away, pulling bloody hands away from his face, making strange sucking noises from between suddenly sunken cheeks. His nose was crooked and flattened, the lower part of his face drenched with blood. He opened a very oddly-shaped mouth and tried to scream. Blood poured out, carrying with it white, hard fragments of tooth. Still moving forward Caspar slammed him on the side of the head with the stone egg, allowed Poidvosky to fall with a blood-wet squelch, turned, and ran back upstairs. Somewhere in Poidvosky's room was a gun.

He found it in the drawer of a bedside table, checked that the magazine was full, rushed down to the front door and opened it. Igor was stumbling dazedly about the pavement, cradling one awkwardly angled arm, looking for his gun. Caspar raised his own weapon with both hands and spread his feet wide apart, bracing himself, the way he had been taught in Infantry School. "Igor," he called.

Igor made a shambling turn, then stared dumbfounded at Caspar.

"Where's Badmayev?"

Igor shook his head.

"Three seconds and you get it through the kneecap. Three, two—" Caspar's fingers tightened round the trigger. He had every intention of shooting.

"They're in Meilen. At the Institute."

Caspar waved Igor up the steps and ushered him into the house. "Your friend Poidvosky has had an accident."

Igor looked at Poidvosky's shattered face with horror.

"Help him," Caspar said.

Igor knelt down, stooping over Poidvosky. Quickly Caspar reversed his grip on the gun and hit Igor viciously across the back of the neck. With a harsh grunt, Igor collapsed over Poidvosky.

Caspar went upstairs, collected his coat, put on his shoes, and, leaving the door on the latch, walked out of the house. The streets had a Sunday-evening look of emptiness and Caspar hurried along the Gessner Allee to the Bahnhof. There were more people there, some of them eyeing him strangely. He hadn't shaved, and there was Poidvosky's blood on his jacket. His overcoat hung clumsily from the weight of the pistol. He telephoned von Dichter and, getting no reply, decided to go on to Meilen alone. Somehow Badmayev had to be stopped.

At Zurich Central Police Station, Commissioner Hartmann put down two phones. His men had observed the incidents outside the house, and two of them had gone in and found two seriously wounded Russians. A third man had followed Caspar to the station and watched him buy a ticket to Meilen.

The investigation earlier that afternoon had revealed that not only had Caspar been kidnapped but that the Karpinskaya girl was also missing. Obviously, had she been held at the house in Gessner Allee, Caspar would not have left without her. Equally obviously, he was going to Meilen with the lunatic idea of rescuing her.

Hartmann picked up an internal phone and barked instructions. When all the arrangements were completed, he buckled on his revolver and asked the patiently waiting von Dichter to accompany him to the station courtyard where three squad cars filled with armed policemen awaited them.

In an upstairs room at Meilen, Badmayev finished checking the equipment Boris had constructed. "Are you sure it will work?"

"It will work all right. One pound of TNT will generate a terrific blast. But the blast is a funny thing. I cannot be sure what effect it will have. If it were set off in this room, both of us would be killed instantly and the windows blown across the street. There wouldn't be much left of the room, but Paul and Constantine in the next room could well be left unhurt because the walls which intenisfy the blast in this room could protect them. On the other hand, it mightn't do that, or it might destroy the wall and kill them with falling rubble."

"The chances are," Badmayev said, "that I will be using it on a train."

"Wood and glass," Boris said thoughtfully. "That will increase the blast area but diminish its potency. There'll be flying splinters as well. You're certainly going to injure a lot of people if you use it on a train. If the explosion is set off low enough, it will lift the carriage off the rails, and if the train is moving at speed—" Boris made a gesture of farewell.

"What is the certain area of lethality?" Badmayev asked.

"I'd say that under any circumstances, anyone standing within fifteen feet of the explosion would be killed."

"That's good enough for me," Badmayev said. He looked searchingly at Boris and hesitated, as if he wanted to thank him. Instead he said, "Ask the others to come in."

While Boris went to fetch the others, Badmayev poured out four glasses of vodka and set them on the now bare table. The room was bare too, as it always had been. He had never accumulated much in the way of personal possessions. His suitcase stood packed beside the neatly made-up bed, and his coat with the equipment Boris had constructed hung on the back of the door.

Boris came back with Chernikov and the big Russian, Constantine. A trifle awkwardly Badmayev went and stood before the table. "A farewell drink," he said. "On behalf of the Okhrana, I want to thank you for everything you have done. I have given Boris my personal testimony of your devoted service. He will present it to the Head of Section Four on your return to Russia. There will be work available for you and, I hope, formal recognition of your services." Badmayev studied their faces carefully. "I will be leaving shortly for Berlin, where I will be taking Boris' place amongst the revolutionaries returning to Russia. All of you should take instructions from Boris, and I want you all to keep out of circulation until you know that the train has been stopped. The news, I promise you, will be sensational. Boris has been provided with funds and documentation which will get you back to Russia. I leave it to you to choose the appropriate time."

Chernikov asked, "You mean to kill Ulyanov?"

"Yes. Ulyanov will die."

"Here in Zurich?"

"I mean to kill Ulyanov in Berlin." Badmayev gave them all a cold smile. "I regret, gentlemen, that it is unlikely I will see any of you again." Affected by their embarrassment, Badmayev kept talking. "The girl and the German agent must be kept in custody until my mission has been completed. Then you can do with them whatever you feel is necessary."

"It would be simpler to kill them now," Constantine said.

"No. A murder enquiry could result in all of you being arrested and, more important, in the train being stopped by the Swiss. The train must get to Berlin." He looked at each of them and said, "If there are no more questions. . . ." Badmayev pointed to the drinks.

Each man took a glass.

"To the Tsar!"

"To Holy Russia!"

The glasses shattered against the wall. Badmayev gave them all a wintry smile. "Now, if you will excuse me, I have a personal matter to attend to."

Seated on the bed, Sonya heard the sound of Badmayev's footsteps and the rattle of the key in the lock. Again she felt that weird mixture of excitement and fear, and she was beginning to tremble when he entered the room, shut the door behind him, and leant against it. From the light of the single lamp by the bed his face looked pale and taut, and for once there was an expression of uncertainty in his eyes.

She heard him turn the lock behind him, and her

hands flew up to her throat. He'd never done that before. Trapped between fear and a strange kind of desire, she watched him walk to the centre of the room, very tall, very erect, and turn and look at her.

"Stand up," he said in a low voice. "Take off your clothes."

"But I've done everything–"

"Stand up and take off your clothes." The voice, as always, was low and authoritative. His face was in shadow now and she couldn't see the expression in his eyes. Sonya stood up and, as she had done twenty-four hours ealier, stripped, and stood naked before him.

"You're beautiful," he said hoarsely. "You're very beautiful."

She clenched her fists to control the trembling that seized her. She felt a wild urge to reach out and touch him.

"You're very beautiful," he said again.

She wanted to turn his head so that she could see his face when he said it.

He came and stood before her, looking down at her nakedness.

"Perfect," he murmured and lowered his head.

Sonya felt his lips close on hers as his arms clasped her body. Then she reached up and drew his head to hers, staring at his closed eyes. Her whole body was trembling and she did not know if it was from relief or fear. All she knew was that she wanted Badmayev, she wanted him to use her again and again. She knew it was horrible and demeaning, but she wanted him. It had nothing to do with love or Caspar. She wanted to hold Badmayev in her arms, to look into his face as he took her and to feel him grow helpless in her arms.

Lips still fixed on his, Sonya stepped backwards and drew him down to the bed. He drew his lips away, pressed her shoulders onto the sheets, and lifted her legs onto the bed. She heard a rustle of clothing, and then his lean, hard body was over hers, his mouth all over her face.

She began to tremble violently as he penetrated her, filling her with deep, savage thrusts. Her flayed back was alive with pain that intermingled and became one with the pleasure of her loins and grew so intense that she thought she would die of it. He placed a hand across her mouth to muffle the cries she did not know she made, conscious as she was only of that life within her, hard and urgent, searing her flesh. She wished it would go on forever and forever and forever.

Afterwards he lay slumped across her, the expression in his eyes soft and human. She reached up and kissed his cheeks, his mouth and the flat, hard muscles of his chest. Then suddenly he rose, dressed, and walked out of the room.

It was as if part of her went with him. She knew she would never see him again and that certainty filled her with an overwhelming sadness.

For a long while after Badmayev left, Sonya lay on her side, staring blankly at the wall. She felt curiously unsynchronised, as if her body were no longer a part of her and that everything that had happened, had happened to someone else. She felt neither remorse nor betrayal. She was soulless, and even the smell of Badmayev's body only recalled a remote memory of desire.

She thought of Caspar and hoped he was safe. It didn't matter if she never saw him again. Parvus, the train, the fact that Caspar would be on it, nothing mattered. It was as if everything that had happened before had happened in a different world and she'd been reborn without feelings and memories. She remained staring at the wall, mindlessly suspended in time. It was strangely comforting.

The crash of the opening door and a rush of footsteps roused her from reverie. She sat up, turned, and pulled the sheet over her shoulders. Boris stood by the bed grinning at her. She could smell the alcohol on his breath.

"Don't cover them up, sweetheart!" He reached out and tore the sheet away from her quailing body.

"Boris, leave me alone!" She spoke loudly, firmly, shielding her breasts behind crossed arms.

Boris was sweating and there was a violent glitter in his eyes. "Come on, darling, give us a kiss! Don't save it all for Germans and senior officers of the Okhrana." He grabbed at her.

Sonya shouted, "Get away!" And, as he brought his head close to hers, she jabbed her finger into his eye.

Boris wheeled away, hand clutching his eye, letting out a roar of pain and anger. Sonya leapt off the bed, evaded his groping arms, and ran to the door. Constantine stood there, massively solid. "Please," she cried. "Help me!"

Constantine came into the room and moved sideways to block her. He grabbed her by the arms and forced them shoulderwidth apart.

"No," she cried. "Please, no! Paul, help! Paul!" She heard the tramp of Boris' boots behind her and felt his breath scorch her neck. Then he slapped her across the back and she screamed, as Constantine pushed her into the room. She struggled helplessly against his massive grip, then gasped as Boris bent down and lifted her clear off the floor.

"Paul!" she screamed as they swung her onto the bed.

Boris hurled himself across her stomach, holding her down with his weight. Constantine pulled her arms above her head and fastened them to the bedhead. She heard Constantine give a satisfied grunt, and Boris stood up. Lying spreadeagled on the bed, she glared defiantly at them.

"Me first," Boris said, throwing off his coat and lowering his trousers.

Sonya felt her stomach heave with revulsion. As he fell on her, she pressed her knees together and twisted her body sideways. Boris clawed at the tops of her thighs, nails twisting into the soft flesh. "Spread your legs, bitch!" There was a smell of stale sweat about him, a heavy rancid odour mixed with alcohol. "Spread your legs, German whore!"

She fought him, uttering soft moans, fought desperately as he twisted her onto her back. "Stop it! Stop it! Stop it!"

There was the patter of feet on the stairs, going away from her. The sound of the front door opening.

Boris smashed her in the face and, as she jerked with the shock of it, forced his body between her legs.

There was a strangled shout from Chernikov. The room vibrated as Constantine ran onto the landing.

"Boris!" Constantine shouted, and suddenly Boris' weight was removed from her.

Sonya lay there gasping for breath, staring wide-eyed at the ceiling.

From outside the room came the crack of rifle shots, the shouting of men, and the sound of heavy boots thudding up the stairs. She opened her mouth but no sound came. Her mind went blank.

* * *

Caspar ran quietly up the steps of the Institute and pressed the bell twice. The windows were shuttered and not a glimmer of light fell into the street. The doorbell had rung hollowly, and he wondered if Igor had lied.

He pressed his ear to the door. The creaking and rumbling he heard were the sounds of an empty house. Igor had lied. But there was a regularity about the sounds, a pattern. Footsteps. Someone was behind that door. A whispered voice asked, "Who is it?"

"It's Igor," Caspar whispered back.

"Igor! What are you doing here?"

"Let me in, quick. Ehrler has escaped."

The door swung open. Caspar glimpsed Chernikov standing there, peering into the darkness, wearing his toothy grin. Chernikov! So he was a traitor, too! And Sonya was somewhere in the house! Caspar hit him hard in the face with the stone egg, feeling the teeth crumple under the power of the blow and the nose bone smash with a sound like crushed pebbles, blood welling round his hand.

Chernikov gave a strangled shout and reeled backwards. Caspar went in after him, watching him raise his hands to his broken face and seeing blood spout from behind Chernikov's twisting fingers. Caspar hit him again, hard and viciously on the head. Chernikov moaned and fell.

Caspar tossed the stone egg to his left hand and took out Poidvosky's gun with his right. A light blazed at the top of the stairway. One of the Russians stood there, leaning over the bannister, a rifle cradled in his hand. He saw Caspar and fired from the hip.

Caspar dived across the stairs. Tripped. Fell. His head bounced off something and began to sing. Through the grey haze in front of his eyes he saw the gunman above him take aim carefully. Caspar's hand scrabbled wildly for his own gun.

There was a shot. The gunman looked down at Caspar with surprise, his rifle wavering. Another shot. Still surprised, the gunman bent slowly forward, made a deep obeisance over the bannister, and fell lifelessly down the stairs, his rifle clattering uselessly behind him.

The house filled with the pounding of feet on steps, on stairs, on landings. Through the haze Boris emerged, tugging at something in the pocket of his greatcoat. Booted, uniformed legs raced through the open doorway and up the stairs. There were shots. Rapid shots. Six of them. Boris wheeled, with blood streaking out of his mouth, slumped, and fell. There were men everywhere, running along the landing, up the stairs, shouting. Slowly Caspar dragged himself to his feet.

Someone had an arm around him. Von Dichter. Von Dichter was talking to him. "Well done, lad. Are you all right?"

Sonya, Caspar thought. He had to find Sonya. He pushed himself away from von Dichter and ran up the stairs.

He slipped and fell, hauling himself up again with his arms, dragging himself up the stairs, across the landing, and up the next flight of stairs. He ran along the landing, breathing stertorously, the mist around him growing thicker, as he tried all the doors. He stopped at one that was locked and heaved his shoulder against it. A policeman eased him out of the way and fired at the lock. Caspar threw himself against the door and then went in, his knees beginning to tremble.

He was in a darkened room with chairs neatly stacked up in one corner, and a bed in the other.

Sonya lay on it, naked, her hands bound to the bed-post above her head, her slender legs still in the position they had left them. Caspar wrenched at the ropes with his fingers. She was staring mindlessly at the ceiling and tears were running down her cheeks. As her hands fell free, she turned on her side, revealing the ugly weals on her back and shoulders and the soiled bedclothes underneath her body.

Caspar reached down and pulled a sheet over her, then stooped to lift her up, the mist around him growing steadily darker. He could feel his legs trembling, the room moving.

Someone had an arm round his shoulders, and Sonya was looking at him strangely. She was a dead weight in his arms, and he could feel his knees buckling.

"Sonya . . . Sonya. . . ."

She was smiling at him now, a strange, distant smile.

Caspar's knees went and he felt himself falling forward across her into a growing black cloud.

"You all right?"

Daylight was streaming through a window. There was a lovely smell of fresh coffee, and at the foot of the bed stood von Dichter, in braces and shirt sleeves, carrying a tray.

"Where am I?" Caspar asked.

"In my apartment. They wanted to keep you in hospital but I brought you here. Have some coffee." Von Dichter came round beside the bed and held out a steaming cup. "What happened to you? Knock yourself out with excitement?"

Caspar sat up slowly and sipped the coffee. His head throbbed and there was a small lump above his ear.

"I tripped, trying to get out of the way of the rifleman. What happened at the house?"

Von Dichter told him how Hartmann had kept the house in Gessner Allee under surveillance and how they had followed him to Meilen.

"Sonya?" Caspar asked.

"She is in hospital. Apart from bruising and shock, she is all right. She will leave hospital in two or three days."

Caspar recalled her stretched out on the bed and the damp stain underneath her body. "Was she violated?" His voice shook with helpless anger.

"It seems we got there in time to prevent that."

Caspar let out a long sigh of relief and swung his feet off the bed. "Where is she?"

"She is at the Kantonspital," von Dichter said. "We'll go there as soon as you've dressed." He poured out coffee for himself. "She's still in a state of shock. Don't be upset if she is listless and doesn't want to talk to you. The doctors assure me she will be completely recovered in a few days."

"I won't be upset," Caspar said, throwing on shirt and trousers, then stooping down to put on socks and shoes. "What happened to Poidvosky and the others?"

"They are under arrest and in a prison hospital. Neither Chernikov nor Poidvosky will ever talk normally again."

That was some satisfaction for what Sonya had suffered.

"Ehrler," von Dichter said, "in spite of everything that has happened to you, you must still get on the train with the exiles. You won't have much time with Sonya, I'm afraid. The train leaves in an hour."

"An hour," Caspar repeated helplessly. He'd been

asleep or unconscious for nearly fifteen hours. "You should have woken me," he protested.

"It was better that you rested. You won't be able to spend much time with Sonya anyway. She mustn't be disturbed for too long. She will be well looked after." He told Caspar that he had arranged a private room for her in the Kantonspital and had arranged for her to be given some money when she left hospital. At that time, if she wanted to, she could stay with a family he knew in Zurich, who were very hospitable and had two daughters her own age. "It is essential that you do not let your concern for Sonya affect Quadriga," he said. "The whole outcome of the war depends on getting Ulyanov to Russia."

"I realise that," Caspar said, fumbling with his tie.

"I had your case packed and brought here," von Dichter said. "It's downstairs, in the lobby."

"Let's go," Caspar said.

In the cab to the hospital Caspar asked, "What happened to Badmayev?"

Von Dichter raised bushy eyebrows. Caspar told him about Badmayev.

"There was no one else in the house or at the Institute," von Dichter said. "He must have left before we got there."

Caspar looked at him, aghast. "If Badmayev is free he will kill Ulyanov, here in Zurich. The train must be stopped."

"It is too late for that. All of them arrived from Berne two hours ago, and they are now having a farewell lunch at the Zahringerhof. Ulyanov will not stand for a postponement at this stage. Nor will Zimmerman."

"A postponement is better than shipping a dead Ulyanov to Berlin."

"There is no chance of that," von Dichter said. The other Russian exiles had organised a demonstration against Ulyanov travelling through Germany. That, combined with the events of the previous evening, had made Hartmann assign a squad of armed bodyguards in plainclothes who had kept Ulyanov under discreet surveillance since he arrived in Zurich. There would be more guards at the Bahnhof. "Hartmann wants an assassination in Zurich as little as we do," von Dichter said. "And once Ulyanov is on the train, he is safe."

Von Dichter waited outside while Caspar went into Sonya's room. There was a large basket of flowers by her bed and she lay on her side, facing the wall, the stream of raven hair across the pillow and the dark, bruiselike smudges under her eyes heightening the pallor of her face.

"Sonya, darling," Caspar said as he walked up to the bed.

She shuddered and kept facing the wall. She didn't want to see Caspar. She wanted to be left alone with the emptiness inside her head.

"It's all over," Caspar said. "Finished. You are safe, my love. Safe."

She felt him looking at her. He spoke too loudly.

"I can't stay long, my sweet. You must rest and I have to go to Berlin. When I get there, I'll send for you."

She shook her head hopelessly. She would never go with Caspar to Berlin. Not after her last betrayal.

"You will feel better soon. Von Dichter will look after you. Ask him for whatever you need, and if you want to, you can stay with some friends of his after you leave hospital."

Sonya turned her head and looked at him.

Caspar was shocked at the despair on her face. He kissed her lightly on the cheek and she turned her head away. "The doctors say you will be better soon."

Her body would heal, but she would never forget what she had done with Badmayev. She would never forget the sensation of his hard, lean body pressing down on hers or the shape of his face and that strange light in his eyes. If Badmayev walked in now, she would let him use her, want him to, let him take her again and again. She stared at the wall without blinking. If she did that long enough her mind would go blank.

Caspar said, "I still have your Easter egg. I still love you."

She had betrayed their love. Love was an empty, horrible word. The wall was shimmering before her eyes. Soon, soon, there would be blessed oblivion. Caspar's voice was already growing distant.

"I'm going with the exiles on the train."

The exile train. Badmayev was going on the train. She'd forged the passes for him. She felt her body come alive as it had done when he'd walked into the room at Meilen. Her breathing became rapid and shallow. Badmayev, who had bathed her in fire. Her need for him made her tremble.

She felt Caspar's hand on her shoulder. Forget the train. Stare at the wall. Soon all feeling would go away. Soon there would be nothing.

"Von Dichter is waiting for me outside. The train leaves in fifteen minutes."

The train. Caspar and Badmayev together on the train. One of them would kill the other. She stared at the wall. The wall began to shimmer. Soon, soon—She turned violently, her lacerated back flaring with pain. "Caspar, don't go!" Her voice was hoarse and loud.

"I have to, my love. I must get Ulyanov to Berlin."

"Forget Ulyanov! Forget Quadriga! Forget your idiotic dreams!"

He took her hands between his own. "I am a soldier and we are at war. I am under orders, I have to go."

She stared at him wild-eyed from behind the curtain of hair over her face, staring at his rumpled figure, his drawn face and bloodshot eyes. The face she had once drawn and which was like Ulyanov's. It was not she who had betrayed Caspar, it was Caspar who had betrayed her, Caspar who had violated her far worse than Boris or Constantine could have done. It was Caspar with his wild dreams of an ideal socialist state who had given her to Badmayev, who had made her less than Badmayev's whore. "You fool!" she croaked. "You'll never get Ulyanov to Berlin!"

His face hardened. "Why not?"

Her mouth broke into a crooked smile. Oh, no, it wouldn't be as easy as that. She would not betray Badmayev. She belonged to Badmayev. Her head was swimming, and, remembering Badmayev, she closed her eyes and sank down against the pillows and turned her head to the wall. She had to get alone again. She had to go where no one could be with her. She had to return to that comforting oblivion.

She'd forgotten Caspar and Badmayev completely when she heard him say, "I'm leaving now. I will send for you from Berlin." She felt the dry touch of his lips on her burning cheek.

Caspar was going on the train. Badmayev would be on the train. She opened her eyes. Caspar was already at the door. "Ba—Ba—Caspar, don't go!"

Caspar turned and waved. "Till Berlin."

Her mouth opened and closed soundlessly as the door swung shut behind him. "Ba–Ba–Ba–" She couldn't say his name out loud. Badmayev. Badmayev. Badmayev. Her back blazed with pain as she flung herself out of the bed. Her legs felt weak, the room was airless and closing in on her. Caspar. She loved Caspar. Swaying wildly, she made for the door, tears streaming down her cheeks, her body shaking with huge sobs. Caspar. Caspar, my love. Don't go. Caspar, my love, forgive me, do anything, but don't go on that train.

She felt her legs fold underneath her, saw the floor rise up to meet her and felt its coolness against her cheek. She struggled to crawl to the door. Caspar, Caspar. Her mouth opened and closed without a sound. Caspar.

She fainted.

Caspar got to the station as the exiles streamed raggedly into the Bahnhofplatz, everyone carrying baskets and cases, the men wearing dark, shabby suits and wide-brimmed hats, the women ungainly and dowdy in their sombre skirts and scarves. Ulyanov walked in the centre of the curving line, surrounded protectively by Nadya and the Zinovievs.

About a hundred or so Russians had gathered on the steps of the station and along the sides of the Bahnhofplatz. As they spotted the exiles, the jeering began. Shouts of "Traitors!"–"Spies!"–"German lackeys!" filled the air. Home-made banners were raised. ULYANOV IS A BOLSHEVIK PIG!—DEATH TO THE TRAITORS!—TO THE PETER AND PAUL WITH THE BETRAYERS OF SOCIALISM!—BRING BACK NICHLAS! BETTER A TSAR THAN TRAITOR!

The demonstrators crowded round the exiles, separated from them by a thin line of policemen. Caspar looked desperately for Badmayev.

They approached the station and went up the steps in a rowdy, abusive throng. "I know you get two hundred francs a month from the Germans!"

"Stay with the Kaiser! Russia does not want you!"

Replies from the exiles. "It is much easier to stay in Zurich than fight for Russian workers!"

"Cease fighting the imperialist war!"

"Bastards!"

"Pigs!"

"Spies!"

"Traitors!"

An enraged Bolshevik attempted to hit a demonstrator. A scuffle broke out. In the middle of all the shouting and jeering, Ulyanov walked, surrounded by Nadya, Inessa, and the Zinovievs, walked with his head down, staring at the pavement as if none of these things were happening.

Caspar hurried before the mob and onto the platform. The train was already drawn up, and before the two carriages which the exiles were to occupy, Hartmann stood with two small teams of policemen, waiting before the single open door of each carriage, to examine the passes.

Shouting, pushing, waving banners and sticks, now shoving at the exiles, now being shoved, snatching at their baskets and cases, crowding between the policemen, the crowd surged through the picket barrier onto the platform. Caspar saw Platten holding a bloodstained handkerchief to his face, Ulyanov, white-faced and still protected by the cordon of women and the Zinovievs, hurrying slightly ahead of the mob. Caspar kept looking for Badmayev, looking at Ulyanov, as the crowd swarmed round him.

He saw Ulyanov almost break into a run as he approached Hartmann. The other policemen turned their backs on the train and faced the crowd, while Ulyanov produced his pass and that of Nadya and accompanied by a chorus of hoots and jeers and cries of "Shame!" went on board the train.

Caspar saw him disappear into a compartment and let his shoulders slump with relief.

Ulyanov was on board. Ulyanov was safe. He pushed his way through the mob and joined the queue of exiles waiting to board the carriage behind Ulyanov's.

As the train prepared to leave and the Bolsheviks finished boarding, the shouts and jeers grew to a crescendo, magnified by the arched roof of the platform. All along the train, doors slammed and the engine hooted and puffed a cloud of steam.

A man broke from the crowd of demonstrators and ran to the carriage behind Ulyanov. There were cries of "Another traitor!"—"Stop him!" Someone tried to gram the man but was elbowed away. The man dodged quickly through the crowd and reached the barrier of policemen.

Hartmann looked at the man's chiselled features and friendly brown eyes. "These are reserved carriages. Find a place for yourself elsewhere."

The man reached into his leather jacket and produced a pass. Hartmann examined it. Peter Pripevsky. Pripevsky?

On the platform, the demonstrators stamped their feet and chanted, waved their banners, and beat at the iron pillars with their sticks. The engine hooted and belched steam; streams of smoke floated over the front end of the platform.

Hartmann looked back from the pass to the man. He had an easy confidence and a ready smile. Hartmann knew that though it was his signature on the pass, he had not signed it. The demonstrators were converging on the train now, beating at the carriages with their sticks. The guard was leaning impatiently out of his wagon at the end of the train. Hold the train or hold the man?

The devil with it, Hartmann thought. Why should it be his problem? The Germans and the Russians had caused enough trouble in his country. Now let them go and raise hell somewhere else. He twisted open the door of the carriage and let the man pass.

The guard blew his whistle. The demonstrators began to run alongside the train, beating at the carriages with their sticks, shouting and whistling and jeering.

Good bloody riddance, Hartmann thought.

Caspar, leaning forward in a corner seat by the door of the compartment, stared through the window beyond the corridor and saw the platform scud past and the angry shouting faces recede. Inside the carriage there was a ragged attempt at the *Marseillaise*. A few red pocket-handkerchiefs were waved. A hand slid before his face and opened the door of the compartment. Caspar nearly jumped upright with surprise. There, standing in the doorway and dressed in stained trousers and a leather workman's jacket, was Badmayev.

* * *

As the train rumbled through the Zurich suburbs, Badmayev beckoned Caspar into the corridor.

"I want to show you this," he said, and took out the metal, flask-shaped grenade that Caspar had last seen in Boris' basement at Meilen. Badmayev showed him the rubber tube that led from the top of the flask to a hole in the pocket of his jacket. "Boris fixed that up. This grenade is set off by a pressure fuse, detonated by this." Badmayev drew a rubber bulb out of his pocket attached to the length of tube. "All I have to do is squeeze the bulb once."

Caspar knew the flask contained a pound of TNT which, if exploded in a moving train, would kill everyone within fifteen feet of it and blast the carriage off the track, so that those who were not injured by the blast would be maimed by the subsequent derailment.

"If you betray me," Badmayev said, "or if I think you have betrayed me, or if I think anyone is threatening me, I'll press it." His eyes shone mildly over Caspar in the fading evening light.

"That would be pointless," Caspar said. "Boris and one of your Russians are dead. The others are under arrest."

"That doesn't make any difference," Badmayev replied. "The important thing is I am here."

Platten came down the corridor busily distributing pieces of paper. Badmayev dropped the flask and the bulb into their respective pockets, keeping his hand firmly on the bulb. "Your passports for entry into Germany," Platten said, and gave them two pieces of paper bearing numbers thirty-two and thirty-three.

"Couldn't it go off accidentally?" Caspar asked when Platten had passed through into the compartment.

"It could. That is a chance we'll all have to take."

"If you're going to use it, why not use it now and get it over with?"

Badmayev smiled, turned on his heel, and went into the carriage.

Caspar remained at the window, looking out into the undulating Swiss countryside with its snow-covered farms dotted with triangular-roofed houses, spotlessly white against a background of mountain and rock and sky.

Zinoviev bustled down the corridor. "If you're coming with us, you must sign the declaration."

Caspar read the document. It was an acknowledgement that the traveller was aware of the conditions agreed with the German Legation and was aware that his journey was only guaranteed as far as Stockholm. The traveller undertook to obey the orders of travel leader Platten and assumed personal responsibility for the political consequences of his journey.

All the Bolsheviks had signed the document. Ulyanov had used his *nom de guerre,* Lenin, and Caspar was amused to note that the signature was in Zinoviev's hand. At some time the great leader might have to deny his presence on the train. So might he, Caspar thought, and signed "Charitonoff."

Then he wondered what to do about Badmayev.

The light was going fast when they reached Neuhausen on the right bank of the Rhine. Towards Germany was the Bellevue Hotel and beyond that the German station with a long, black goods train pulling into it from the direction of Waldshut. On the other side of the train were the falls, a majestic, sweeping cascade of water crowned by a castle and a railway bridge.

The train followed the Rhine past the Swiss station, joining with the German railway system just before the Kasino Parade and rumbling into Schaffhausen. But there was no time to gaze at the medieval town with its patrician houses and oriel windows. No sooner had the train stopped than Swiss Customs Officers surrounded the exiles' carriage and herded them onto the platform.

There, in full view of all the other passengers, they were made to open their baskets and cases. Platten protested, Zinoviev protested, Kharitonov protested; Ulyanov did not protest but stood silently by his women with a look of defiant resignation on his face.

The Swiss were undeterred by the protests and soon they had discovered that the exiles were taking out more food than they were allowed. They were no party to any agreement between Platten and the Germans. They laughed as they confiscated the food.

Caspar wondered if he should tell the Swiss Customs officer leafing suspiciously through his books that Badmayev had a bomb in his pocket. He looked carefully at the impassive face before him. Tell that man about Badmayev and he would panic. Or he would rush Badmayev. Either way, there would be an explosion.

Badmayev was standing casually near the Ulyanovs and Zinovievs. They would certainly be blown to pieces. So also would a number of innocent passengers now crowding the windows to look at the tawdry possessions of the Bolsheviks spread on the platform below them.

Five miles further on at the Swiss customs post at Thayngen they were made to get out again. At least this time, the other passengers had to get out. The Customs officers ignored Platten's protests that they had already been examined, and ignored his threats of complaint to higher authority. They found precious little amongst the Bolsheviks' baggage, as most of the food had been confiscated at Schaffhausen.

Once again Caspar thought about warning the Swiss customs men about Badmayev. Once again he did nothing.

"Never seen such a scruffy lot," Caspar heard one of the customs men say as he climbed aboard the train. "Good riddance."

The train rumbled slowly into Germany, climbing the hill that overlooked Gottmadingen Station, moving past the old and faded Bahnhof Hotel and finally wearily coming to a halt with a prolonged hiss of steam. The platform at Gottmadingen was empty except for two German officers in high boots and pale green uniforms.

For the last four miles the exiles had sat like doomed men awaiting execution. Now the sight of the German soldiers brought on a kind of silent panic. Tight lipped and silent, they filtered out of the carriage and into a waiting room. Everyone was certain that they had been trapped. Caspar walked with Badmayev, hoping that if Badmayev did feel threatened he could somehow wrench his hand away from the bulb.

In the waiting room they were separated into two groups. The Bolsheviks became alarmed. Ulyanov rushed against the wall and the others surrounded him, grim and frightened in their black hats and overcoats.

One of the officers came up to Platten, asked him for his number, and enquired who had the money for the fares. Then, having collected the money and making them identify their baggage, he requested them to board the train that now awaited them.

It was not much of a train: a green carriage with eight compartments, three second-class and five third-class. Attached to it was a baggage wagon. The last third-class carriage was allocated to the German officers, and Platten drew a chalk line across the floor. No one but he would cross that line.

With a great deal of relief the exiles distributed themselves through the carriage. Ulyanov and Nadya had the end second-class compartment to themselves; next to them were the Austrian journalist Radek, Olga Ravich, Inessa, and another married couple. The Zinovievs and the other women had the next second-class compartment, and the single men distributed themselves along the hard wooden benches of the third-class. Caspar made sure he was with Badmayev in the compartment nearest the German officers.

Someone insisted that the external doors at the side of the platform should be locked, and when that was done, the carriage moved away, to isolated refrains of the *Internationale* and the *Marseillaise*.

They took half an hour to cover the next ten miles to Singen, where they were to spend the night.

In the motionless carriage the atmosphere became festive. As a gesture of goodwill the German officers had bought sandwiches and beer which they scrupulously left on the chalk line for the exiles to collect. Over the first glasses introductions were made. Caspar found that, in addition to Badmayev and Aisenblud, he was sharing the compartment with a journalist named Linde and a big, boisterous, elderly Caucasian called Mikha Tskhakaya.

While the others spoke about dialectics, life in Switzerland, and their revolutionary pasts, Badmayev spoke to Caspar.

"What happened last night?" he asked.

Briefly Caspar told him.

Badmayev gave him a quiet smile. "I'd never have thought you were capable of physical violence."

"I was in the German Army," Caspar said. "I fought in East Prussia."

"What about your girl friend?"

Caspar told him she was in hospital.

As Badmayev remembered the passion with which she had made love, an expression of sadness crossed his face. Then he said, "She is well out of this," and Caspar was surprised at the sincerity in his voice.

Badmayev leaned forward. "There was nothing personal in what I had done to her. I would like you to understand that. I had to make her talk."

And she had talked. With less persuasion Caspar, too, had talked. As a result of all that talk, Badmayev had decided not to kill Ulyanov in Zurich but to join the train. "How did you get a police pass to board the train?" Caspar asked.

"Your—I used Boris'," Badmayev replied.

"Why did you board the train?" Caspar asked. "Surely you could have stopped Ulyanov in Zurich?"

Badmayev smiled. "I could have done that but I prefer to do it nearer home."

Did he mean Russia? But the Okhrana were finished and Russia was a long way from anywhere.

Almost as if reading Caspar's thoughts, Badmayev said, "By the time we get to Russia, there will have been a counterrevolution."

Conversation in the carriage became more animated and clear thought impossible. Caspar found himself talking more and more to Badmayev. Badmayev asked him about his military service and told Caspar something of what he had done in Paris. He and Badmayev were both outsiders, Caspar thought. Spies. And though they were enemies, they had more in common with each other than with the exiles.

There was plenty of beer and plenty of singing. The exiles moved cheerfully from compartment to compartment. Introductions were made, people hugged each other, great passionate Russian kisses were exchanged. Caspar and Badmayev drank steadily but not to excess.

At about ten o'clock Zinoviev appeared at the carriage door and complained. "It is nor fair, comrades. Your cigarette smoke is spreading through the carriage. You know how Ilyich feels about smoking."

"Drinking without smoking is like shitting without peeing," Tskhakaya cried.

"What do you want us to do?" Badmayev asked. "Go to Germany for a cigarette?"

"It's upsetting Ilyich," Zinoviev said. "He cannot work."

"Working tonight? Tonight we celebrate!"

The party and the smoking continued. From the second-class compartment next to Ulyanov's the laughter was loudest and the singing most raucous. It was occupied by Radek, an impish Austrian with side-whiskers that met underneath his chin, and who later on did a turn in the corridor, imitating Ulyanov. Ulyanov himself made a brief, dignified, embarrassed appearance, clutching a glass of beer as if it were a time bomb, and then disappeared into the comparative quiet and privacy of his compartment.

Much later there were about eight or ten people in their compartment when Zinoviev appeared, serious faced. "Smoking must stop," he announced. "It is impossible for those of us who do not smoke to do anything."

"You were always good at doing nothing," Radek cried.

"All those who wish to smoke must do so in the toilet," Zinoviev ordered.

Immediately there was a rush from the carriage, some who wanted to smoke, some who wanted to make fun of Zinoviev's order, and some who wanted to use the toilet.

"We'll use the German toilets," Radek cried.

Zinoviev became hysterical. "No," he screamed, "no. Under no circumstances. Everyone wait here. I insist that everybody wait here, as a matter of party discipline."

Ten minutes later he was back, carrying passes showing two levels of priority. The first level was for those who wished to use the toilet for its intended purpose. The second for those who wished to smoke.

"That's what I mean by a socialist state," Badmayev said softly. "You have to get written permission to take a pee."

However, Zinoviev's protocol did not inhibit the festivities. Throughout the carriage people sang, danced, and shouted cheerfully to one another. The Ravich woman's high-pitched laugh could be heard all through the carriage, and Radek did much to stimulate it.

In Caspar's compartment the drinking became heavier and the conversation louder, more disjointed, and argumentative. Heads close together, Badmayev and Caspar discussed political alternatives. Suddenly from the opposite corner of the carriage, Linde shouted, "What are you two whispering about?" His narrow, peaked face was quite flushed and his sharp eyes had a reddened, watery look.

Caspar saw that quite unwittingly he and Badmayev had become separated from the other Bolsheviks, all of whom were looking at them with wary interest.

"We were talking about Russia," Caspar said. "Home." Badmayev had been telling him that the Provisional Government could not last, that it would be supplanted by monarchists or revolutionaries and that if it were the revolutionaries, there would be civil war.

"Where are you from, comrade?" one of the visitors to the compartment asked.

"We're from Petrograd," Caspar replied.

"Where did you live in Switzerland?" one of the others asked.

"Zurich," Caspar said.

"How long have you been away from Russia?"

Caspar hesitated slightly and said, "About three months."

"What's the matter with your friend," Linde asked. "Can't he speak for himself?" He looked challengingly at Badmayev.

Badmayev sat leaning sideways against the corridor partition, one hand resting lightly in his coat pocket, gazing at the assembled Bolsheviks with deceptive calm. "My friend has told you what you want to know," he said.

"But I didn't hear you say it, comrade. I didn't hear you say it." Linde was on his feet now, his little chest puffed out, moving excitedly from one foot to the other. "Where do you come from? What have you been doing in Switzerland? I have a right to ask. I have never seen you before." He looked at the comrades and gave a nervous laugh. "For all we know, you may be a police spy."

Caspar looked quickly at Badmayev's hand. There was nothing he could do before Badmayev squeezed the bulb.

Badmayev said easily, "I could say the same about you, friend."

"You could, comrade, but all these others know me. I was at Kienthal, I have taken part in party conferences, I have written for the paper. Everyone here knows me, don't you, comrades—Ivan Linde, the journalist."

The comrades affirmed their recognition of Linde with low rumbles of approval and shouts of "Of course we do."—"Who could forget you!"—"Known you too damn long."

Linde turned to them, "But does anyone here know this comrade?"

There was much shaking of heads and cries of "No!"

Linde smiled nastily. "Then I suggest, comrade, you tell us all about yourself so that we know you are not a police spy."

Idiots, Caspar thought furiously. Small-minded, bigoted, drunken idiots. In a split second they could all be blown to pieces. And while their lives were insignificant, Ulyanov could be killed, too; if Ulyanov died, a whole world would die with him.

Mikha Tskhakaya lumbered between the seats and stood between Caspar and Badmayev, blocking the door. The atmosphere in the carriage was brittle with the excitement of the hunt. "Now tell us who you are, where you come from, and what your function is in the party. Tell us what you were doing in Switzerland." Tskhakaya looked menacingly down at Badmayev.

"Comrades, what is this?" Caspar cried. "An inquisition?"

"Yes," Linde replied. "We have a right to know whom we are travelling with."

"The comrade is a courier," Caspar said quickly. As long as he kept talking, Badmayev would not detonate the bomb. Caspar's palms were damp with sweat and he could feel clammy moisture in the small of his back.

"Let him speak for himself," Tskhakaya rumbled. "What work did you do as a courier?"

Sonya, Caspar thought. If he was going to die, he wanted to die thinking of her.

"Distributing propaganda," Badmayev said.

Badmayev had nerve, Caspar thought, gratefully. He would keep fighting till there was no alternative but to blow them up.

"Tell us what you distributed," Linde sneered. "Tell us the name of the paper?"

"*Sotsial Demokrat,*" Caspar said.

"He must speak for himself," another of the visitors to the compartment piped up.

"*Sotsial Demokrat,*" Badmayev said.

"When did you join the party?" Linde's voice was strident.

"Three years ago."

"Why did you come to Switzerland?"

"I was sent."

"Who sent you?"

"We do not discuss these things in public."

"This is not public," Linde snapped. "This is a closed session of a Bolshevik committee conducting an investigation. You have to tell all."

For the first time Badmayev looked worried. Then he said, "Kamenev and Stalin sent me."

Linde laughed harshly. "Where did you meet Kamenev and Stalin? For the last six months they have been in Siberia."

Caspar intervened quickly. "Your problem, comrade Linde, is that you have been sitting too long in Switzerland and getting fat on the money we send you and acting like a revolutionary. Meanwhile, we professional revolutionaries have been risking our lives and freedom every day in Petrograd. Of course there are ways of getting directives to and from Siberia. There are even ways of getting directives to and from Zurich."

Linde said, "We're all professional revolutionaries here. We are all Bolsheviks, and I have risked as much for the cause as you." He leaned forward from the waist and made a show of peering closely at Caspar. "In any case, who are you, comrade, to talk of revolution? I have never seen you before."

"I have," Aisenblud said drowsily. "Comrade Rihma has been helping Vladimir Ilyich to organise this train."

An expression of painful surprise crossed Linde's face. The others looked at Caspar with sudden respect. Tskhakaya asked, "Is that true, comrade?"

"It's true. My friend here was sent from Petrograd to help us. I am sorry that Vladimir Ilyich did not consider comrade Linde of sufficient importance to invite him to join us in the planning."

Tskhakaya reached across the compartment and picked up two half empty bottles of beer. "Drink, comrades," he said, handing the bottles to Caspar and Badmayev. "We welcome you into our midst. We support the confidence Vladimir Ilyich places in you and are grateful for what you have done to organize our journey."

There was a smattering of applause and a frantic search for more beer.

"Now that's over," Aisenblud grumbled, "let's go to sleep."

From across the narrow passageway Badmayev looked at Caspar and gave him a happy, conspiratorial wink.

Caspar lay awake in silence, his head slightly fuzzy from the beer. Across the compartment from him Badmayev dozed. Tskhakaya snored. Aisenblud muttered in his sleep. Caspar decided to use the toilet for its intended purpose.

There were toilets at each end of the carriage, one in a small corridor behind their own compartment alongside the chalkline, the other at the further end in the second-class section beside Ulyanov's compartment. Caspar walked up the corridor. He knew he would be in that carriage for at least three days, and it was as well to take what exercise he could.

As he walked softly along the dark corridor, he wondered if he should reveal his identity to the German officers. But he had no proof of his Foreign Office connections, and the Germans were obviously plain and simple soldiers under orders to keep the Bolsheviks happy. They would be most reluctant to make an arrest, and in the time it took for them to make up their minds, Badmayev could well get suspicious and blow them all up.

Caspar buttoned his trousers and walked back along the corridor. The carriage was filled with the noises of sleep. Suddenly there was a different noise. A rapid whirring in front of his face. Then a thin cord snapped round his neck and he felt himself being yanked backwards, the cord biting into his throat in a narrow band of fire. He could feel his flesh swelling round it, feel his breath catch in his throat. He tried to gasp but couldn't. He felt blood spurt and reached backwards with his hands trying to grap his assailant. His mouth opened. His lungs gasped for air.

Desperately he pulled at the cord and tried to reach Badmayev. Never mind the bomb. He was being murdered. His arms flopped uselessly. A red haze spread before his eyes. He could hear a violent, frantic throbbing in his head. Caspar knew he was dying, dying in a second-class railway carriage at Singen.

His face was bathed in a damp sweat. His chest was stiff and unmoving. The darkness was closing in on him. He felt his legs turn to rubber and then from far away someone screamed.

There was light and he was lying on the floor. His head was surrounded by heavy workmen's boots. They would kick him, he thought, gasping for air as he tried to sit up. Hands grasped him under the arms and helped him to his feet.

Zinoviev, Radek, and two others were standing before him. Badmayev was holding him up.

"What's the matter?" Zinoviev demanded angrily.

Caspar tried to speak but only succeeded in gulping agonizingly. His bruised and swollen throat seemed to be on fire. It was Badmayev who said, "The comrade has had too much beer."

"Try to control youself," Zinoviev snapped. "You've woken up everybody. Go back to your carriage and be quiet."

Leaning on Badmayev, Caspar lurched back to his

compartment and let himself down slowly onto the wooden seat.

Badmayev sat quietly opposite him.

As silence descended on the compartment, Badmayev whispered, "That was a mistake, friend. Forgive me."

Caspar massaged his throat.

"I thought you were Linde," Badmayev hissed.

That confusion of identity made some kind of sense. "If you had killed Linde," Caspar whispered, "everyone would have known it was you."

"I realise that," Badmayev said. "I thought Linde was going to see Ulyanov to confirm our stories. I thought I had to stop him."

"Next time don't act so damned fast. Linde will never go to Ulyanov. Look how remote Ulyanov is from the ordinary Bolsheviks. He is a difficult man to approach. Leave Linde alone."

"I will," Badmayev promised. "Now go to sleep. I'll watch over you."

Caspar leant his head against the wooden back of the seat and closed his eyes. Badmayev would watch over him, he thought. After all, Badmayev needed him.

Kuryakin sat on the deserted, glass-screened terrace of the Café Huusniemi, a dark, hunched, solitary figure staring broodingly through the snow-spattered glass at the harbour with its few ships trailing the colours of the Baltic Fleet and the gray walls of Vyborg Castle beyond. From time to time Kuryakin looked from the battle-scarred walls of the castle and the harbour to the flight of stone steps to the right of the terrace along which his visitor would come. He had been waiting over an hour, but he had no doubt the appointment would be kept.

Thirty minutes later he came, a short man not much over five feet, dumpy in the army-style greatcoat, his fur hat pulled down over his large head, limping slightly as he climbed the steps. At the entrance to the terrace he stopped and hesitated; then, seeing Kuryakin alone, he limped quickly past the deserted tables.

"Koba," Kuryakin said. "It's good to see you."

His visitor took off his hat and coat and threw them over a chair. He was in his late thirties with a fine head of dark hair and a heavy moustache. His skin was pockmarked and faintly olive. His eyes in the wide, imprecisely defined Asiatic face were bright, keen, and curiously immobile. One of his arms was shorter than the other.

"No more Koba," he said sitting down. "It's Stalin now." Kuryakin frowned. Dzhugashivili had been known by that name only to the Okhrana and a few intimates. Everyone else knew him by his other alias of Koba.

Koba's teeth flashed under the moustache and he pounded his good arm on the table as, with cocked head, he looked challengingly at Kuryakin. "Man of steel. You like it?"

"It's a good name," Kuryakin said. "You have a lot to live up to. What news of Petrograd?"

While food and vodka were brought, Stalin told him. Things were quiet. The Provisional Government ruled with the help of the Soviet. The revolution was permanent.

"And what of the Bolsheviks?" Kuryakin asked.

"The Bolsheviks support the government."

"And you must be quite important now."

Stalin's smile was cursory. "They don't seem to put me in charge of anything much. I edit *Pravda,* jointly with Kamenev."

"And Ulyanov? What is his attitude?"

"He sends us directives from Zurich, telling us not to co-operate. But then Ilyich has been away a long time. He does not know the situation in Russia."

"He is coming back?"

Stalin looked at him flatly and said, "Yes."

"With German help."

"I don't know about that."

"I do," Kuryakin said. "The information is on my files."

"What other information do you have on your files?" Stalin asked quickly.

"Enough information to make or break the Provisional Government. Enough information to make or break the Soviet. Enough information to smash the opposition to any new government."

Stalin licked his lips. "You have information about me?"

Kuryakin nodded. "The files are safe, Josef, as long as I am safe. If anything happens to me. . . ." Kuryakin shrugged.

Stalin blinked nervously. "What do you want?"

"I want to return to Russia. I want to work for Russia. If you say the revolution is permanent, then I want to work for the revolution. Have you ever thought, Josef, that given a good intelligence system, a small, dedicated party can seize power?"

Stalin's eyes fixed on him, shiny, immobile. "This is not the right time," he said.

"Have you ever thought that with the right information, one man could control a small party? Josef, you have a greater destiny than being joint editor of *Pravda.*"

Stalin looked at him thoughtfully and lit a black Russian cigarette. "We both have a great destiny," he said, "but Ulyanov's shadow is long." He gave Kuryakin a humourless smile. "However, the sun moves and with it the shadow. At noon a man's shadow is very short."

Kuryakin remembered that when Stalin had been training for the priesthood, he'd published romantic poetry. "I could release my information on Ulyanov."

"Unwise. A short-term advantage. We need Ulyanov in Russia now. The more important he becomes. . . ." He looked directly at Kuryakin. "All the time the sun moves and men's shadows grow shorter."

"I can't wait for that," Kuryakin snapped. "I am needed in Russia now. It is I, Josef, who have made you what you are. It is I who made the arrests and ordered the executions. You need me, Josef."

Stalin brought his enormous head closer to Kuryakin's. "We need each other, Dimitri. But for now, you must be patient. We must be practical. But in time . . ." He told Kuryakin that the Bolsheviks were only a small party and the only man with the intellectual stature to lead them was Ulyanov. It was Ulyanov who gave the party significance, not the other way round. Ulyanov was ambitious. Ulyanov was stubborn and ruthless. Given the right opportunity, Ulyanov would dominate the Soviet as he dominated the Bolsheviks. From dominating the Soviet, it was but a small step to dominating Russia. But only Ulyanov could do that.

"Afterwards," Stalin said, "there will be changes. But first, we must seize power. And we cannot do that without Ulyanov." He got to his feet. "I must go now.

I will not forget you or your files. Very soon, I hope, we will work together again."

Gloomily Kuryakin watched Stalin limp past the empty tables. Stalin was right, but the one thing he didn't have was time.

Seated in the office that had once been Bismarck's, flanked by Under-Secretary Bussche and Ulrich von Ketteler, Artur Zimmerman worried. According to information sent by von Dichter, the Okhrana had taken it into their heads to stop Ulyanov. If Ulyanov were to be killed before he reached Petrograd, the resulting scandal would be far greater than that resulting from the telegram to Mexico. Zimmerman knew he would not be lucky with the Reichstag a second time. Already there were calls for an enquiry into the subterranean workings of the Foreign Office. If anything happened to Ulyanov, he would be finished.

Bussche cleared his throat and said softly, "Excellency, we must deal with the *émigrés'* conditions."

Oh, yes, the *émigrés* were imposing conditions. So far as Zimmerman knew, even though the conditions had not yet been agreed to, the journey was still going ahead. He took Romberg's cable from Bussche and read it again. *I have the honour to present the enclosed draft of the conditions for the passage of Russian* émigrés *from Switzerland to Stockholm, given me by Herr Platten.*

Zimmerman read the conditions. There were nine of them, most of them self-evident and already agreed to by implication. Quite obviously the whole purpose of the conditions was the Ulyanov would have a record of the circumstances under which he'd travelled through Germany. So be it. "Have Romberg inform the *émigrés* that all Platten's conditions are accepted," Zimmerman said, "except number two." Condition two was that only Platten should communicate with Germans. "Have Romberg tell them that the journey was only agreed to because of pressure put upon us by the German Trade Union Movement. Tell him that a representative of the Trade Union Movement, Jansson, will meet the exiles in Germany."

Zimmerman turned to von Ketteler. "We're ready to hear your plan for outwitting the Okhrana," he said.

Von Ketteler picked up his briefcase and unrolled a map of Western Europe. He had considered the problem with Imperial Intelligence Bureau East all weekend.

"There are only two places where Ulyanov can be attacked," he announced. "Here in Switzerland"—placing his finger in the middle of Europe—"or here in Scandinavia." Ulrich's finger traced a narrow semicircle skirting the Gulf of Bothnia. "It is too late to do anything about Switzerland, so we must concentrate our effort on Scandinavia. What I propose is that the carriage should be accompanied from Berlin by five members of the Finnish Jaeger Battalion. They are familiar with local conditions and can accompany Ulyanov to the Russian border."

"Two questions," Bussche said. "How are you going to get them into the carriage with Ulyanov? And how are you going to get them into Finland without their being arrested at the border and shot as traitors?"

"The Finns will travel in a separate compartment," Ulrich explained. "They will be masquerading as war-wounded being repatriated. Their weapons will be hidden by the dressings over their wounds. With Your Excellency's permission, I shall acompany them myself to the Finnish border."

Zimmerman was looking at Ulrich with barely concealed surprise. "Permission granted," he said wonderingly.

Dawn broke, appropriately red-eyed. With great sighings and stirrings and stretchings and yawns the carriage came awake. Voices asked the time and where they were. In fact they were being shunted back towards Switzerland, but only Mikha Tskhakaya recognised the fact. "Comrades, the revolution is over. We're going back." But no one took him up on that. Everyone was too stiff, too sleepy, too hung over, or too emotionally exhausted.

With a great deal of puffing and hooting and grinding they were joined onto a train and the journey through Germany began. Linde and Aisenblud took their washing kits and joined the queue in the corridor. Badmayev looked straight at Caspar and winked.

Overnight Badmayev had lost his remaining traces of elegance. His curly brown hair was tousled, his eyes were pouched, and ugly brown stubble dotted his cheeks and chin. Only the smile remained, and the doggy gleam in the eyes. Badmayev sighed and stretched. Then, leaning back against the straight wooden seat, he smiled again at Caspar and closed his eyes.

The train moved through the German countryside with its sloping meadows, fir woods, and village after village that looked exactly like Gottmadingen, climbing all the time.

Tea was brought from the Ulyanovs' compartment where Nadya had a stove. Stale sandwiches and rolls were produced. Caspar ate and then washed, but he decided to postpone the luxury of shaving until he got to Berlin and unlimited supplies of hot water. In the compartment Badmayev was asleep, his hand wedged tightly into his coat pocket. Thank God they were still climbing and the train was travelling slowly.

They passed the volcanic peaks of the Hegau. Around Caspar desultory conversations began, meandered, and died. Aisenblud, separated from Rosenblum, stared sadly out of the window. By the time they came to the Danube, Caspar was sleeping.

He woke with a start, feeling a certain loss of motion. From opposite him Badmayev welcomed him into wakefulness with a smile. They were stopped at a station. Caspar walked into the corridor and looked. They were at Tuttlingen and being transferred from the Baden State Railway to that of Wurttemberg. Back in the compartment, Badmayev continued to look happy.

They travelled through the wide valley of the Neckar, and Horb with its Gothic church and high walls. Outside it was a lovely spring day. Inside the carriage was beginning to smell of sweat and humid feet. Caspar closed his eyes and wondered what to do about Badmayev.

The problem was brutally simple. Badmayev had two weapons. Caspar had none. Before he could do anything about Badmayev that had to be remedied. The only way to remedy Badmayev was with a gun, a heavy enough bullet, and a shot of such accuracy that Badmayev would die instantaneously, without a convulsive twitch of his right hand. Difficult to guarantee under the most favourable circumstances. Under the present circumstances, impossible.

The Swiss customs search had revealed that none of the revolutionaries carried any weapons, and he could not hope to buy even a toy pistol at a German railway platform. It was an insoluble problem. Insoluble, irremediable. Caspar dozed, dreaming fitfully of Sonya, and the Tiergarten, and large cannons.

Sonya was saying it was time to wake. Caspar shook his head, opened his eyes. Not Sonya; Tskhakaya was shaking him, holding a hunk of stale bread before his face. The sun was a high, small, shiny ball. Lunchtime, Tskhakaya was saying, and Caspar hadn't brought any food. He took the bread and gnawed at it. Badmayev smiled and gave him some of his sausage. Linde began talking about continental trains. Before the war he'd travelled from Paris to Constantinople in one. Once more, tea was brought from the Ulyanovs' compartment, and soon afterwards they were hissing down through the Hasenberg woods to the old town of Stuttgart.

Stuttgart was the first major German station the exiles had seen, and they crowded into the corridor, peering out of the windows, commenting how quiet everything was. A few people got off; even fewer got on.

One of the German officers beckoned to Caspar. "There is one Herr Jansson of the German Social Democrat Party who wishes to speak with Herr Ulyanov. We have instructions to let him into the carriage."

"Let me check," Caspar said.

Zimmerman obviously did not understand that Ulyanov would not meet with insubstantial politicians like Jansson and that even the presence of Jansson in Stuttgart could prejudice the meetings in Berlin.

"There is a German Social Democrat who wants to see Vladimir Ilyich," he told Platten. "He will undoubtedly broadcast to the world who is on this train."

Platten came charging down the corridor, pushing exiles out of his way. "It is impossible," he cried, five feet away from the chalk line. "Herr Ulyanov will not meet with any German. Not even Herr Jansson."

"We have been told that everything has been agreed with Berlin."

"Definitely not." Platten pulled out a copy of the conditions. "Here, see for yourself."

The officer looked at the paper and handed it back to Platten. "I will inform Herr Jansson of your wishes."

It was just as well, Caspar thought, that he had not solicited their assistance in apprehending Badmayev.

A few minutes later the officer was back to face Platten and a crowd of exiles, who were no longer looking at Stuttgart but at him. "Herr Jansson says that he has instructions from Berlin to meet with Herr Ulyanov and that he proposes to enter the carriage."

"He'd better not," Platten said.

"Tell him he's not welcome," Zinoviev said.

"If he comes in here, we will beat him up," Tskhakaya shouted.

Caspar looked around for Badmayev. He was standing in the corridor with a strange smile on his face.

In the end Jansson did not come.

The train moved slowly out of the Nord Bahnhof and into the Prag Tunnel. Caspar sat alarmed in the sudden darkness, clenched fists held up in front of his body, but nothing happened. As they clattered into the light, Badmayev greeted him with a polite nod.

The train meandered through the unremarkable Wurttemberg countryside. Caspar dozed fitfully, dreaming of Sonya, of weapons, and of breasts like bombs. Once he came awake and saw that Badmayev, too, was sleeping and leaning heavily to his right. Caspar straightened him gently and, as he was doing so, asked himself, If Badmayev's only weapons were the garotte and the bomb, how was he going to kill Ulyanov?

The bomb was too imprecise and overly destructive. It would not kill Ulyanov but most of the train's passengeres as well. On the other hand, the garotte, as the previous night had shown, was difficult to use efficiently, especially as Ulyanov was never alone. If the garotte was inefficient, strangulation was even more unlikely. So how did Badmayev plan to do it?

Push Ulyanov off the train? Too risky. Poison? He couldn't get near Ulyanov's food. A sudden, killing blow? He would have done that already. Was he going to barge into Ulyanov's compartment and announce he was from the Okhrana in the hope that Ulyanov would have a heart attack?"

No, Badmayev would do none of those things. The awful, chilling certainty struck Caspar. Badmayev was going to use the bomb. That was the only possibility that made sense.

But why hadn't Badmayev blown them up already? Why was he waiting? Caspar remembered Badmayev's strange look when Jansson had tried to come aboard. In Berlin no one would ask the exiles' permission to enter the carriage. They would come—Zimmerman, high-ranking German officials, representatives of the military. A perfect time for Badmayev to explode his bomb. Even that would not be the end of it. The fact that the cream of the Foreign Office, high-ranking military officers, the foreign secretary, and a gaggle of Russian revolutionaries were plastered all over the Potsdam Station would be sensational news. No amount of censorship could suppress that. Germany would be laughed out of the war.

Badmayev had to be stopped. Somehow Caspar had to find himself a weapon. The only persons in the carriage who had weapons were the German escorts. Caspar stepped across Badmayev's motionless legs and went out into the corridor. Standing on the Russian side of the chalk line, he began a conversation with the Germans.

They told him his German was excellent, that he spoke it like a native, and became interested when he told them he'd once lived in Hamburg. They asked him what he would do in Russia. Free the people, Caspar said, speaking loudly and clearly in case Badmayev woke and became suspicious.

As he chatted, Caspar peered into their compartment. It was identical to his own: two rows of slatted wooden benches and clumsy overhead racks. The officers themselves were obviously from Military Intelligence, selected no doubt for their qualities of tact, understanding, and sense of compromise and, though neither of them had given signs of it so far, their knowledge of Russian. So they were Eastern Front veterans, infantrymen.

With an overwhelming sense of relief Caspar spied the rawhide valises and cloth-covered helmets on the overhead racks. Like all German soldiers on escort duty, they had to be ready for instantaneous transfer to a combat unit. Which meant that somewhere in that compartment were Mauser '98 rifles, saw-edged bayonets, ammunition pouches, and, of course, the 9mm Parabellum Mauser pistols strapped to their waists. A veritable plenitude of weapons. But how to get them, and what to do with them once he'd got them.

Caspar kept chatting to the officers. They were once more on the Baden State Railway, on a branch line to Karlsruhe. The more direct route through Pforzheim, one of the officers said, was filled with military trains. The Entente was launching a big offensive near Arras.

The officers said they would be stopping at Frankfurt for the night, and Caspar asked if they would buy him some food, some harsh Wurttemberg red wine, and dry Franconian white. He was aware, he said, of the smoother and milder Niersteiners, but tonight, Caspar informed the officers, he wanted to get drunk.

They bought him the wine and food at Karlsruhe, and afterwards the train crossed the bare, flat Baden plain which stretched for miles all around them, a vast, snow-covered emptiness. Some of the travellers had begun to sing revolutionary songs like "Don't Cry Over The Bodies Of Fallen Fighters" and "They Didn't Marry Us In Church." Some also sang the "Internationale" and the "Marseillaise."

With an uncharacteristic show of temper the German officers insisted that the *Marseillaise* be proscribed.

At Mannheim the engine was changed again. Afterwards they travelled along the Prussian-Hessian State Railway, across bare plains to Frankfurt.

They reached Frankfurt around six o'clock. The train stood at the platform for about twenty minutes, while Caspar wondered how he could get into the officers' compartment and steal their weapons. Soon afterwards their carriage was disconnected and shunted to a siding, and a little while later Radek danced down the corridor He was going into the town, he said, to visit an old friend. (He was not Russian and therefore not subject to quarantine.) Platten, being Swiss, was similarly exempt; and, soon afterwards, wearing the more outrageous of his hats and a vivid scarf, he, too, left the train.

An hour later, looking extremely smart in dress uniforms of field grey with red piping and high red collars brocaded with gold, the two officers marched away.

Afterwards, in the compartment, food was produced and Caspar opened all twelve bottles of wine. Nothing like open wine bottles to make people feel like drinking. Badmayev flashed him a glance of supercilious suspicion.

"Hah! You're a filthy capitalist!" Tskhakaya cried.

"No, just a filthy alcoholic!"

Linde suggested that they should share the bottles out amongst the other passengers. Caspar glared at the little swine in horror. Share the bottles out and everybody would have a couple of drinks and go to sleep feeling pleasant. Caspar didn't want any of his immediate companions feeling merely pleasant. He wanted them drunk; he wanted them leaden brained; he wanted them uncoordinated and somnolent. Most of all he wanted them deeply and soundly asleep. "I'm a filthy capitalist," he cried. "I want to get drunk."

"Why?" Aisenblud's enquiry was full of genuine interest.

Badmayev smiled.

"Because—because tomorrow in Berlin, I leave you."

That was sensational enough to make them all reach for bottles.

"Berlin is in Germany," Linde pointed out.

The officious little know-all obviously believed that he was the only one who'd had an elementary education. "So I've been told," Caspar said and took a swig from his bottle.

"Why are you leaving us in Berlin?" Tskhakaya

asked, darkly suspicious, the bottle of Wurttemberg red looking quite tiny in his massive hand.

Caspar hesitated. Ideally he would have liked to deal with one problem at a time.

"Comrade Charitonoff works for Parvus," Badmayev said smoothly. And, for the benefit of those who did not know, he added, "Parvus, the German agent."

Linde said, "If you stop off in Germany, you will never be able to get back to Russia."

Suddenly everyone was filled with didactic zeal. Caspar drank. "I won't be going to Russia, yet. From Berlin, I go to the Parvus Institute in Stockholm."

"Why leave the train, then?" Aisenblud asked. "We're going to Stockholm."

"There are certain publications to be collected in Berlin."

There was some relief in the compartment at that. They all knew that publications had to be printed in and collected from the strangest places. Thankfully Linde seemed to have forgotten about sharing out the wine.

They drank and ate the food. Conversation began to flow. As soon as he got back to Russia, Tskhakaya was going to walk barefoot in the mud. He wanted to feel cloying, sticky Russian mud all over him. There was no mud like Russian mud. They all raised their bottles and solemnly agreed. There was no mud like Russian mud, no earth like Russian earth. It was good to be returning home.

Linde said all censorship had been ended. All the revolutionary parties were publishing newspapers. He hoped Gorky would start another magazine.

The revolution could do with some culture, Badmayev said. Personally he had always admired Gorky.

Mikha Tskhakaya didn't. Gorky glamourised peasant suffering. He dabbled in serious matters and believed that human beings had souls. Gorky was a follower of Tolstoy.

"I always thought censorship was the worst aspect of Tsarism."

"How long before you leave Stockholm and join us in Russia?"

"Gorky once had a school for revolutionaries in Capri. Imagine that! Capri!"

"I've always said there cannot be a proper revolution without culture."

The conversation and the drinking became animated, simultaneous, cross-directional. Caspar came aware of a sense of physical isolation, especially when he looked up at the large yellow lamp in the middle of the carriage. He resolved to slow down on his drinking.

Tskhakaya sang "Marching Forward Together." Olga Ravich came to see what the noise was about, decided it was more fun there than in her own compartment, and stayed, snuggling next to Badmayev.

As if to celebrate, Badmayev started on a second bottle. Then he, too, sang, a sad, endless song about the Volga. No one quite understood it, but everyone looked suitably melancholy.

"Nothing should be censored. Not even pornography."

"Stalin waited on the pavement outside while we went into the bank."

Aisenblud said if nobody minded he would sit by the window and get a little sleep.

Ravich, now sharing Badmayev's bottle, said she would sing a happy song. This she did in a high contralto, and Caspar watched in alarm as with her arm around Badmayev's neck she swayed and stamped her feet on the floor. Tskhakaya joined in the stamping and Linde kept time, beating an empty bottle against the side of the carriage.

Zinoviev came and stared disapprovingly at Caspar. Ulyanov was working and did not like to be disturbed.

"He's getting off at Berlin tomorrow," Tskhakaya cried, pointing to Caspar.

Zinoviev looked at Caspar as if to say good riddance.

His visit curtailed the singing. Caspar was relieved that since the Ravich woman and Badmayev had arms round each other's necks, they were not swaying so much. Olga Ravich said that Inessa didn't want to return to Russia either.

"So I prodded him with the end of the gun and said, give us the money."

"Only in very rare instances is censorship permissible."

Inessa had been happy at Clarens and felt her days as a revolutionary were over.

"Why is she going back, then?" Badmayev asked.

"Because of him." Olga pointed with her thumb towards the front of the carriage.

"The miserable bourgeois clerk was trembling so much, he could hardly hand over the money."

"Love," Caspar said sagely, "conquers all."

Olga Ravich didn't believe in love. "He needs her to fulfil his function as a revolutionary."

"Don't we all, don't we all," Badmayev said. Old Ulyanov was a straight-up-and-down man. He had that sort of mind. *Mens rea in corpore*—no, that wasn't it. Something about minds and bodies being alike. Badmayev did a bit of shoulder nuzzling. At least he was getting his two pfennigs worth. Good for Badmayev. Good for everyone. It was a great party.

Tskhakaya said, "And then we fired into the roof and ran."

The lights went out.

Everyone shrieked.

The lights came on again. It was going to be fun.

Zinoviev appeared in the doorway wearing his most formidable schoolmasterly expression. There wasn't going to be fun. That was an order.

Afterwards they sat quietly and finished the wine. The Ravich woman returned to her compartment, Aisenblud snored. Linde went out to wash his face. Tskhakaya stretched himself on the seat and, still babbling on about the bank robbery, went to sleep.

Caspar sat upright, pulling slowly at the wine. After a while he heard Badmayev place his own bottle on the floor and begin to breathe deeply and evenly. It was time to go. Soon the officers would be back. He got to his feet, stepped carefully over Badmayev's outstretched legs, and tiptoed out into the corridor.

There was a sharp clang followed by profound swearing in German and Russian. Caspar looked out of the window. Walking in tiny little circles outside the carriage was bloody Radek, three sheets to the wind, one over the eight, and unable to find the carriage steps. Caspar jumped down and helped him up.

"Hee! Hee! You're in Germany now."

"Shut up or Zinoviev will have you hung by your whiskers."

"Hee hee, that's good!"

"Shut up!"

Caspar helped him up the steps and steered him down the corridor.

Back in the compartment, Badmayev smiled at him sleepily.

Caspar waited half an hour. Badmayev's breathing

resumed its even rhythm. He'd just have to hope that Badmayev had fallen asleep again. Any moment now the officers would be back. At least the toilet was in the same direction as their compartment, and he had the excuse of drinking too much.

Once more he tiptoed into the corridor. No drunken Radek this time; no sign of returning officers either. Caspar moved quickly over the chalk line and into their compartment.

He could discern the rifles stuck behind the seats, the bayonets in their scabbards on the racks above. He reached up for a bayonet and stopped. Even if he left the scabbard, they would notice that the bayonet was missing. Caspar remembered something else, too. In order to use a bayonet as effectively as he intended to, one needed leverage behind it. One needed the length of a rifle behind it. He also remembered that in East Prussia even the four-foot-long Mauser rifles hadn't been long enough. In East Prussia many of them had used sharpened entrenching tools and short-handled pickaxes instead of bayonets.

He moved quickly across the carriage, climbed on the seat, and took down a rawhide valise, then laid it on the seat and unstrapped it. As he expected, in the rolled compartment was a spade-shaped entrenching tool and a standard issue, short-handled, narrow-bladed pickaxe. He ran his thumb along the point of the pick and the cutting edge on its obverse. Honed to razor sharpness. Bet it had seen action before.

In his case he wouldn't have the time to take the axe out of its sheath. He removed the axe, then replaced the sheath in the compartment, rolled it up, closed the valise, and put it back on the rack. Holding the axe behind him, he went into the toilet and arranged it carefully down the front of his trousers.

He would have to walk stiffly and a trifle awkwardly. He hoped Badmayev wouldn't attack him, or that he wouldn't fall. If he did, he would forever afterwards speak in a higher tone than the Ravich woman's contralto.

Quite early the next morning they left Frankfurt, nearly leaving behind group leader Platten, who'd been away all night lavishing neutrality on some luckless Frau. All that morning they travelled with great urgency, unattached to any train, speeding nonstop through Fulda and Hersfeld and Nordhausen.

One of the officers said that if they didn't get to Berlin early that afternoon, they would miss their connection to Sassnitz and that their carriage had been given precedence over all other traffic including military trains and that of the Crown Prince himself. The officer seemed quite impressed.

As they bumped and clattered through the heartland of Germany, Caspar sat dry mouthed and stiff legged, praying that Badmayev, doubtlessly similarly dry mouthed, would remain analogously stiff palmed. There was a distinctly hangdog atmosphere in the compartment that morning. Heads ached, eyes squinted dyspeptically at the sun, and throats were very dry. There was nothing to drink except morning tea from the Ulyanovs' compartment until they stopped at Halle.

While they were being connected to a train on the Prussian State Railway, the officers bought sandwiches and beer, to which Caspar added a generous contribution of Augustinerbrau.

"More farewells?" Aisenblud asked incredulously. "It's hot and we are all thirsty."

"*Spassibo,*" Tskhakaya said, drinking. "Capitalists like you, I could love."

The beer made everyone relaxed and sweaty. The compartment began to smell decidedly fruity. There was more conversation and less bleary-eyed sighing. The train drove relentlessly on to Berlin. Almost as fast as the train to Constantinople, Linde said. In Siberia, Tskhakaya said, trains travelled more slowly. He was longing to get back to a proper Russian train with a samovar in each carriage and wide compartments in which a man could stretch himself. On Russian trains there was none of this hurried clattering that made one's head ache. Caspar sat stiff legged by the corridor, careful to avoid castration as people wandered, with increasing frequency, to the toilet.

For once Badmayev looked pensive and sallow faced, with grey bags underneath his eyes. From time to time he wondered aloud how long it would take to get to Berlin.

They were well past Rosslau, closing fast on Berlin, when Caspar asked him in German, "Are you still going to stop Ulyanov?"

Linde, making his fourth trip down the corridor, stepped over Caspar's leg and said, "When you come to Russia, comrade, we shall make you Commissar of Festivals."

"And you shall be Chief Censor."

Badmayev waited till Linde had turned the corner and asked, in German, "You have an alternative?"

"Yes. Get off the train with me in Berlin."

"And become a prisoner of war? No thank you."

"Join our Intelligence Service."

"And spy on Russia? And what will you do with me after the war?"

"We'll find work for you to do."

Badmayev shook his head. "I am not like these others. I can never be an exile."

They travelled on, stopping more frequently as they neared Berlin. Ragosen, Golzow, Brandenburg. Less than an hour to Berlin. Caspar began to feel the first stirrings of panic.

Tskhakaya clambered by clutching a bottle of beer. Caspar looked uneasily at Badmayev. The Okhrana man must have a bladder made of elastic. For fear of revealing the pickaxe under his trousers, Caspar couldn't go until Badmayev went. They left Brandenburg. Next stop, Potsdam.

"Have another beer."

"*Danke.*"

"You've lived with these people two days. Can't you see they're harmless?"

"Mindless, you mean."

"So why not let them go home? They wouldn't make any difference to what has happened already."

"If you believe that, you wouldn't have made all this effort to get them back."

"All we want is peace."

Badmayev's lips curled contemptuously. "I know."

They travelled in silence to Potsdam. Once or twice Badmayev shifted encouragingly but remained seated.

"You should take a look at Potsdam," Caspar said.

"Why?"

Potsdam was a beautiful city with its town palace and the Palace of Sanssouci, its parks and gardens and Brandenburg Gate. Potsdam was the city of Frederick the Great, the cradle of the Prussian Army. Potsdam was where Frederick's greyhounds were buried.

"You will like it," Caspar said. "Go out and have a look."

"All railway stations are the same," Badmayev said.

Caspar felt quite frustrated. The train began to move out of the station. From here it would run nonstop, reaching Berlin in half an hour. Caspar felt desperate.

"What's wrong with peace? Our countries would be friends again, like before the war. Like it always was."

"It cannot be," Badmayev said. "You don't have alliances with the Ulyanovs of this world. They are not princes."

The train picked up speed, the platform buildings scudding past the windows. They swept rapidly past the parkland of Teltow and through the suburb of Nowawe, rushing to Berlin, Caspar in the grip of dire, painful urgency.

The beer was finished. Tskhakaya made one more belching passage and then returned to stare silently out of the window.

They crossed the Avus in a blur of crisscrossed steel railings.

"How will you do it?"

"Why? So you can prevent me?"

"No. I was wondering whether you were going to do it before Ulyanov met with the German High Command or after."

"I think I will wait until Petrograd," Badmayev said smiling. "And hang him from a lamppost outside the Finland Station."

Badmayev's eyes were still like a friendly spaniel's. Caspar looked out of the window. Nicholas-See, Wansee. They were on the outskirts of Berlin. Caspar said, "Beter have a piddle before we get there. It's illegal to do it on a waiting train."

Badmayev got to his feet.

Stiffly, Caspar rose. "After you."

Badmayev gave him a fast sideways glance and went

out into the corridor. There he asked, "What's happened to your leg?"

"Ever tried helping a drunk into a railway carriage?" Caspar braced himself against the side of the corridor with one hand, holding onto the front of his trousers and the blade of the pickaxe with the other. Christ, the blade was sharp. One sudden jerk and it would slice through his trousers and his fingers.

Badmayev turned the corner. Caspar hurried after him, feeling the sweat break out all over his body, his heart beginning to pound, his mouth going very dry and a queer wrenching pain in his stomach. Badmayev pushed open the lavatory door.

"What's it worth to me to help you?"

Badmayev turned in the doorway, frowning. "Why would you want to do that?" Deeply suspicious.

"Hurry up and have your pee. My bladder's bursting." As Badmayev moved inside, Caspar moved into the doorway. "The Foreign Office is acting against my recommendations. I've told them Ulyanov is not to be trusted. I've told them supporting socialists will only bring ruin to the rest of Europe. I know it will." The words poured out of him in a rapid, almost unintelligible stream.

Badmayev unbuttoned his fly and began to piddle audibly in the centre of the bowl.

"The right thing to do is make a separate peace with the Tsar. I've told them, it's the Tsar today, the Kaiser tomorrow." He looked at Badmayev standing with his legs apart, head down, hands in front of him.

"The Tsar will make peace just as well as Ulyanov." Caspar wrenched open the top of his trousers and drew out the axe.

"The families are related. The alliance would be honourable."

Badmayev was reaching a dripping conclusion.

Caspar hit him with the axe.

The force of the blow jarred his whole body. The sharp point crunched through the bone just above the hairline with a wet, thwacking sound. Blood and yellowish brain matter spurted as Badmayev fell forward, flinging up his arms.

Caspar released the axe and moved forward, blood and matter spewing all over him. Grabbing Badmayev under the arms and holding them aloft, he brought his head round to peer at Badmayev's bloodless face and ghastly turned-up eyes.

The noise of the train grew louder. Badmayev's body swayed backwards. The handle of the axe thrust against Caspar's chest, goughed itself out of the wound, and clattered against the toilet seat. Caspar felt himself being thrown inexorably off balance and stuck out a leg to brace himself. With a harsh, metallic grinding noise, the train stopped.

Caspar began to tremble.

Gently he lowered Badmayev to the floor, laying him on his left side. Then he shut the door and moved abstractedly into the corridor, standing there dazed, unaware of the cold air playing around his bare knees.

He had to leave the train. He had to get to the Jaegerstrasse. He had to tell someone. His face was covered in a clammy sweat and his breath came in rapid shallow gasps. Numbly he tried to move towards the carriage door but tripped over his fallen trousers and fell, bumping his head against the wooden panelling.

Badmayev was alive! Badmayev was after him! Caspar scrambled to his feet, yanked up his trousers, and rushed over the chalk line into the German officers' compartment. Caspar stared at them, wild-eyed, breathless. His mouth moved but words wouldn't come. One of them took him by the arm, gingerly avoiding the blood on his shirt front.

"Don't . . . don't. . . . Stop anyone getting near that toilet!" Caspar cried and launched himself out of the carriage. He hit the platform and rolled, scampered to his feet, and began to run. Behind him he heard shouts. Clutching the front of his trousers, he dodged round passengers and porters, glimpsed a figure in vivid blue and red uniform and burnished steel *pickelhaube*. He ran towards it, tears streaming down his face, lungs burning, concentrating only on that watery image.

Suddenly his ankle caught something. He flew into the air and crashed down on hands and knees, staying there, head between his bleeding palms, sobbing.

A hand drew his face upwards by the hair. Caspar gazed into a face topped by a burnished helmet and a single eye that beamed pitilessly down on him. The eye of God, he thought. Judgement.

"Ehrler!" a familiar voice shouted. "What the hell do you think you are doing?"

Caspar squeezed the tears out of his eyes with the back of a grubby hand, sat up on his haunches, and looked into the angry face of Ulrich von Ketteler.

Wearily he gestured to him to kneel down. Ulrich frowned, then did so. In hoarse whispers, Caspar told him what had happened.

"For God's sake, take him out of the carriage upright and, whatever you do, don't even breathe on his right pocket."

Ulrich had a whispered conference with some soldiers, and then five of them marched towards the train. Three others helped Caspar to his feet and walked with him quietly to a waiting room.

* * *

Caspar slumped in the chair feeling as if he had been seated there all his life. His eyes were heavy, his head dull, his tongue weighted with lead.

The grey-moustached, crewcut Prussian with the old, kindly eyes said, "And so you went into the corridor with him."

Caspar licked his lips and held up his mug. Comforting hands poured equal amounts of tea and whisky. Caspar was at the headquarters of Imperial Intelligence Bureau East. They had been questioning him for hours, mostly the older man with the kindly eyes, occasionally others, younger, sharper, less accommodating. Who was Sonya? Where was she now? State exactly, please, the nature of your relationship. What was your relationship with Badmayev? Her relationship with him? How did he get on the train? What was his cover name? Why Pripevsky? Wasn't it a strange name, even for a Russian?

Badmayev had been carrying two pounds of explosive in his flask. If he had managed to press that bulb, he would have blown up the whole carriage and killed everyone in it. Caspar shuddered.

You were very brave, the older man said. I wish I had your courage. But that didn't make Caspar feel any better.

Probably saved a few innocent passengers as well, someone else said. Caspar must remember that there was a war on and that he was a soldier. Soldiers killed!

Caspar couldn't help it. He began to shudder again.

Were there agents of Badmayev's still on the train? How many agents did Badmayev have in Zurich? Where were they now? Did Badmayev have contacts with the British? The French? Why had Caspar not insisted on delaying the departure of the train? Why had they allowed the train to depart, knowing that Badmayev was still free?

They had sent two sappers into the carriage to defuse the bomb and afterwards they had taken Badmayev out with his arms round the necks of two soldiers, as if he were alive.

One always felt bad the first time, the older officer said. But Caspar mustn't worry about it. It would pass. He might not believe it now, but it would pass.

Caspar stared listlessly around him. For the moment the interrogation had stopped. The officers stood in a corner of the room talking amongst themselves. Badmayev wasn't operating alone, they said. They'd found coded telegrams from Finland amongst his effects. Ulyanov was not safe yet.

Badmayev was only a professional doing his job. They'd got on well together, Caspar said, but no one listened.

Had Badmayev been particularly friendly with any of the exiles? Particularly unfriendly? Why hadn't Sonya travelled on the train? Yes, they knew she had been beaten up, but before that, hadn't she refused to go? Why? What did Badmayev talk about on the train? He sang songs. Yes, he probably was from the Volga. Was Caspar certain that he didn't mention anything else? He just sat there and smiled? Strange.

He was a professional, Caspar said again. It was unfortunate he'd been on the other side.

Had the other agents mentioned anyone, their superiors, for instance? Any organisation in Finland?

Caspar wished they would stop. He felt tired, ill, indescribably filthy. He wanted to go home; he wanted to bathe and shave and sleep. He wanted to sleep for years.

In a while, they said, in a short while. Now, please, answer the questions. When did Badmayev first come to Zurich? When did Caspar first know of his presence? Would Caspar please repeat exactly what Badmayev had said when he showed him the bomb? Would he describe the demonstration at the Zurich Bahnhof? Was the British agent Maugham there? Who had punched Platten?

"And so you followed him into the corridor with the axe. . . ."

Questions, questions, questions; Caspar's head throbbed with questions. His chin was sunk on his chest, his voice hoarse with answering. In a moment he would be allowed to sleep. In a moment. But now, please answer this, what about that, please describe this again, that again. We're sorry, it is still not clear. Did anyone else see the bomb? Why did you not inform the escort?

"And then you swung the axe. . . ."

Caspar didn't hear the questions anymore, began answers that tailed off into silence. They shook him gently, gave him more whisky, asked him more questions. Caspar felt the room closing in on him, saw the older officer's face waver, start to float away.

"He's told us all he can," someone said. After that there was merciful silence. Caspar sank into the chair and closed his eyes. Someone held a glass to his mouth and allowed him to sip more whisky. For a long while there was peace.

The peace was broken by a hurried tramping of feet outside the door, much stirring about inside the room, and many heel-clicking and arm-snapping salutes. Caspar sat immobile, staring at his taped hands still grimy and stained with Badmayev's blood.

Someone touched his shoulder gently. A familiar

voice said, "Well done, my boy. We are all proud of you. Germany is proud of you."

Caspar raised a head that felt as heavy as cannon shot. Big, ginger-moustached, blue-eyed Artur Zimmerman was smiling down at him. Hurriedly Caspar got to his feet, swaying, clutching desperately at the top of his trousers.

"Audacity, courage, initiative. Herr Ehrler, you have our deepest admiration. And on behalf of His Imperial Majesty, I am honoured to inform you that it has been decided to award you the Order of the Red Eagle."

Caspar sat down again. It wasn't true. He wasn't the recipient of Germany's highest honour for valour. He struggled to his feet. Zimmerman was smiling at him, but it was all a dream. Just as the murder of Badmayev had been a nightmare.

"The award will be made at a private ceremony at the Stadt-Schloss in Potsdam."

So he was a hero. He thought of his parents, of Sonya, of old Hofer. He clutched his trousers tighter. He couldn't believe it.

"Of course, since you are a serving intelligence officer, the honour will not be made public until after the war."

Caspar cleared his throat. "Of course," he said thickly. He felt he should salute or click his heels, or something. He couldn't think what to do.

Zimmerman looked at his hands. "Are you all right, my boy?"

"Tired," Caspar said.

"Naturally. Well, if these gentlemen have finished with you, we had better see about taking you home and getting you to bed." His hand squeezed Caspar's shoulder warmly.

The door burst open. Ulrich von Ketteler marched

in, having changed out of his outrageous uniform and into formal frock-coat. "The exiles refuse to meet with Under-Secretary Bussche," he cried. "They are blocking the doors to the carriage and accuse us of breaching conditions."

"That condition was never agreed to," Zimmerman said.

"They insist it was. The only way we can get into that carriage is by force."

"That would negate the whole object of the exercise. Where's Bussche?"

"Still at the station, trying to persuade Platten to let him in."

Zimmerman walked thoughtfully round the room, then came back and stood in front of Caspar, rising and falling gently on his toes. Ulrich stood beside Zimmerman and glared balefully at Caspar with a kind of frenzied interest.

Caspar felt his stomach heave with panic. "I can't go back on that train! Can't you see! I'm covered in blood. I'm a murderer!"

"Someone has to go back on that train," Zimmerman said quietly. "Otherwise, Ulyanov will never reach Petrograd."

But Ulyanov had to reach Petrograd. Unless Ulyanov reached Petrograd, there wouldn't be peace; there wouldn't be a revolution that would change the world.

"For the sake of Germany and the lives of a million German soldiers," Zimmerman went on, "someone has to persuade Ulyanov to talk to us. You're the only one who can do it."

Caspar's head sunk onto his chest. "I'll go," he said.

* * *

The dimily lit carriage stood beside a remote siding with the shadowy figures of sentries standing beside rolls of barbed wire on the platform. Caspar was led through a gap in the wire and walked along the platform, alone, his footsteps echoing hollowly. He walked to the escorts' compartment, which was in darkness, and turned the handle, its clatter unnaturally loud. He climbed into the darkened compartment and walked towards the chalk line.

In the faintly lit corridor on the further side of the chalk line stood Platten, Tskhakaya, and a few other revolutionaries.

"Oh, it's you," Platten said relieved, as Caspar stepped into the light.

"Capitalist, are you all right?"

"I'm all right."

More revolutionaries were crowding into the corridor. "What happened?"—"What did they do to you?"—"Why did they take you away?"

Caspar screwed his eyes shut tightly, forcing himself to concentrate on what he had to do.

"Where's Pripevsky?"—"When are the Germans going to let us go?"

Zinoviev pushed his way through the crowd and came and stood beside Platten. "You're back."

Caspar nodded.

"Well, you'd better come and explain everything to Ulyanov."

The revolutionaries fell back as Zinoviev cleared a path for him and Caspar and led him up to Ulyanov's compartment. Ulyanov was seated opposite the door, reading. He looked up at Zinoviev and Caspar, marked his place in the book, closed it, and asked, "Where's Platten?"

Platten was right behind them. The three of them entered the compartment.

The compartment was similar in size to the one Caspar had shared. The only difference was that the bench seats were padded and the overhead racks slightly larger. Along the seat from Ulyanov was a basket full of papers and books, and two more baskets lay on the racks. In the space between the benches was the kerosene stove.

Caspar moved round the stove and sat opposite Ulyanov. The others sat beside Ulyanov, immediately giving the carriage the atmosphere of a courtroom.

Caspar decided to get Zinoviev and Platten out of the way quickly.

"Pripevsky was an Okhrana spy," Caspar said, giving them Badmayev's Okhrana card. "Deputy Director of the External Bureau, no less."

The three exiles peered closely at the document.

"It's a forgery," Zinoviev announced. "It's a German trap to arrest us."

"It's a device to make Vladya talk with them," Platten added disconsolately.

Ulyanov looked up from the documents. "How did you find out?" he asked, ignoring Zinoviev and Platten.

Caspar told him about the mock trial the night they'd left Switzerland. "I became suspicious of him then. He was never quite one of us, if you know what I mean."

Ulyanov knew.

"Once, when he went into the toilet, I examined his baggage and found this."

"Have you examined anyone else's baggage?"

"Yes. I have examined the baggage of everyone in my compartment."

"Comrade Rihma," Zinoviev cried, "that is most reprehensible. You have been behaving like a police spy."

"It doesn't matter how he behaved," Ulyanov said. "It's what he found out that's important. Now shut up, Gregori, and let me get on with this." Ulyanov turned back to Caspar, a mocking glint in his eyes. "And Tskhakaya, Aisenblud, Linde, they're not Okhrana spies?"

"Not as far as I know," Caspar replied.

"What happened this afternoon?"

"We had been drinking a lot."

Zinoviev nodded vehemently in confirmation.

"I felt I had to do something about Pripevsky. Just before Berlin we went to the toilet together, and I told him that I knew he was an Okhrana spy and that the Okhrana was finished. I told him he should surrender himself to the comrades or to the German authorities. Then he attacked me with a knife." Caspar held up his taped hand.

The three men opposite him turned quite pale. None of them was used to violence. "I managed to hit him, and he fell, hitting his head on something and knocking himself out. I panicked and ran and I told the first German officers I met."

"No," Ulyanov corrected. "You didn't tell the escorts, did you?"

"I told them to guard the toilet. I thought they would need reinforcements."

"A number of men came to take Pripevsky away," Platten said wonderingly. "They wouldn't even let us watch."

"I suppose they were concerned that they would be attacked by other Okhrana spies in the compartment."

"There are no Okhrana spies in this carriage," Zinoviev said.

"Not anymore," Ulyanov said.

"What happened between you and the Germans?" Ulyanov asked.

"They questioned me."

"About us?"

"No. Only about Pripevsky."

"You have done well, comrade," Ulyanov said. "We are grateful to you. Now I must get on with my work."

"I must talk with you alone," Caspar said.

Ulyanov looked at him suspiciously. "What about?"

Caspar said, "It is for your ears alone, Vladimir Ilyich. After we have spoken you can decide who else should know."

"I will," Ulyanov said.

Vladya," Zinoviev warned, "he might have a knife or a gun."

"Don't be absurd, Gregori. Comrade Rihma has already proved his loyalty." Ulyanov waited for Zinoviev and Platten to leave the compartment.

Caspar became aware of being closely scrutinized, of Ulyanov's deep-set eyes boring into him from under beetling brows. "What is it you wish to talk about?"

"Foreign Secretary Zimmerman wishes to meet with you."

Ulyanov smiled mockingly. "I do not have time for social engagements," he said.

"It isn't social," Caspar said.

"Zimmerman knows the conditions under which we are travelling. I will not meet with any German. I will not set foot on German soil."

"I am German," Caspar said. "I work for Zimmerman."

Ulyanov's nostrils flared. A red flush rose from the

depths of his beard to the top of his forehead. "Leave the train immediately," he snarled. "Get out! Now!" He pointed to the door.

"It makes no difference whether I leave the train or not," Caspar said, forcing himself to remain seated. "You are already compromised. No one will believe you didn't know I was an officer in German Intelligence."

Ulyanov pointed his finger at Caspar. "Traitor! he cried. "You and Parvus and Ganetsky have betrayed us! You have led us into a trap. Gregori! Fritz! Mik—"

"This train does not move until you see Zimmerman," Caspar snapped.

It was as if he had hit Ulyanov in the pit of the stomach. Ulyanov crouched back in his seat like a wounded animal, frustrated, ready to counterattack. The colour drained from his face. His expression grew thoughtful.

"We are prepared to keep you here until the end of the war," Caspar added.

"It is a breach of the conditions," Ulyanov said, half to himself. "We have been betrayed and I must deal with the consequences of that betrayal." He looked directly at Caspar and, once again, Caspar felt nearly paralysed by Ulyanov's penetrating gaze. Here was a man who was afraid of nothing, a man who would risk everything to impose his will on the world.

"What does Zimmerman want to see me about?" Ulyanov asked, gutturally.

"He wants to talk to you about your plans for Russia."

"Let him talk to Ganetsky."

"Ganetsky is in Stockholm. Besides, Zimmerman will not deal with minions. He wants to talk to the leader of the Bolshevik Party."

Ulyanov's brows knitted together and he stared past his own reflection out of the window. "I will not see him," he muttered.

"The meeting will be very discreet," Caspar said. "No one will know. Zimmerman is waiting for you at the Hotel Adlon. It is less than a thousand metres from here. There is a car outside. We can be there and back before anyone even knows you've gone."

"And at the Adlon, I suppose, there will be photographers, men from the newsreels, all kinds of people from the Foreign Office." He looked nastily at Caspar. "And more spies."

"No," Caspar said. "There will only be the two of you. We will go in from the service entrance. There will be some soldiers but they will not know who you are."

"No," Ulyanov said. "It is too dangerous."

"Zimmerman wants to offer you the support of the German government."

"And what is the support of the German government worth? I am a revolutionary, not an imperialist pig."

"All we want to do is give you Russia," Caspar sighed.

Ulyanov stared at him, eyes wide with shock. Above the untidy beard his cheeks were pimpled with sweat. "Me?" he asked gutturally. "Why me?"

"Because you are here," Caspar said, "and you're the first of the revolutionaries to pass through Germany."

"You don't know what you're talking about." With stubby fingers he combed his beard. "Russia. . . ."

"Talk to Zimmerman."

"You people wouldn't give me anything," Ulyanov rumbled.

"I've read all you've written," Caspar said fervently.

"I believe you can change the world and I believe Zimmerman can give you the means to do it with."

"Your idealism is sickening," Ulyanov said. "Above all, Rihma, the revolutionary must be practical. Who are the other revolutionaries who are travelling through Germany?"

"I don't know yet. But after you've shown that it is possible, there will be others."

Ulyanov looked down at the floor of the compartment. "You will give them money, I suppose. You will have Parvus sell drugs on their behalf."

"Talk to Zimmerman," Caspar urged. "You've nothing to lose. By sitting in this carriage, you are compromised. Whether you do or not, your enemies will say that you met with German agents. Why lose a substantial advantage for such a tiny risk?"

"Where is Parvus?" Ulyanov asked.

"In Stockholm."

"You're sure about that? You're not lying to me, Rihma?"

"Parvus is in Stockholm. Zimmerman will see you alone. If you do not like what he says, you will be free to leave. On the other hand, if you refuse to see him, you might have to remain longer in Germany than you would wish. And that will give rise to all kinds of speculation and be far more dangerous."

Ulyanov beat at the top of his thigh with a clenched fist. "Let me think about it," he said.

Two hours past midnight. The train in the siding was in darkness. Caspar and Ulyanov tiptoed along the corridor to the door Caspar had left open and climbed down onto the platform. Caspar stood there allowing his eyes to get accustomed to the darkness.

Then, taking Ulyanov's arm, he walked quietly to the first reel of barbed wire. "Quadriga," he whispered to the sentry.

Noiselessly the roll of wire was moved. A shaded torch faintly lit their way past the other sentries by the ticket office and through the door of the station. A black Mercedes waited at the foot of the steps.

Its engine coughed into life, and no sooner had they got in than the car surged away, racing across the deserted Potsdamerplatz, past the dark mass of the Furstenhof. They rushed along the Koniggratzer Strasse, swaying across the tram lines. Lights burned in the offices of the Chancellery and the Foreign Ministry on the right, and on the left was a dark vastness that was the Tiergarten. In the reflected light of the car's headlamps, Caspar stole a glance at Ulyanov, crouching low on his seat, his face covered by an enormous woollen scarf, a flat workman's hat jammed well down on his head so that only the glint of his eyes could be seen. Despite Caspar's assurances that if they had wanted to kill him, they'd have let Badmayev do it, Ulyanov looked as if he were being taken for execution.

At the end of the Koniggratzer Strasse, the car turned right, between the floodlit, Doric columns of the Brandenburg Gate, into the Pariserplatz. They drove rapidly down a small alley at the back of the Hotel Adlon and stopped. Ulyanov drew breath sharply. There were armed soldiers everywhere. "It's all right," Caspar whispered, patting his arm. "They're only here to protect you." He got out of the car and spoke to the soldiers at the service entrance, who opened the door and brought the elevator down to ground level. Then, pushing Ulyanov before him, they ran through the entrance, along a corridor beside the empty kitchens, and got into the elevator.

On the third floor there were more soldiers lining the carpeted corridor all the way to the Kaiser Suite.

"Lights," Ulyanov whispered hoarsely, not moving from the elevator. "Have them turn off the lights."

A few moments later the entire Adlon was plunged into darkness, and Ulyanov and Caspar scampered along the corridor to the suite. Caspar knocked loudly at the door.

"Who is it?"

"Ehrler."

The door opened. They stepped into darkness. As they shut the door behind them, the room blazed with light.

The Adlon was Berlin's newest and most magnificent hotel, and the Kaiser Suite was sumptuous. Vivid Oriental rugs were scattered over thick pile carpet; deep sofas and armchairs were lined with silk and leather. In the middle of the room was a mahogany table inlaid with rosewood, and tall windows looked out over the Pariserplatz and the floodlit, copper Quadriga of Victory above the Brandenburg Gate. The room was lit by chandeliers suspended from a carved ceiling, and, beside the table, Zimmerman and von Futran stood, both immaculately clad in evening clothes, their white gloves lying on the table beside them.

"My dear Ulyanov," Zimmerman said striding forward, one large hand outstretched, his heavy face radiating welcome. "I can't tell you how much we have looked forward to meeting you." He betrayed absolutely no surprise at the shabby, leather-jacketed, muffled, carpet-slippered figure before him.

Ulyanov did not move to take the outstretched

hand. From behind his muffler he said, "I have come under protest."

Zimmerman stopped and lowered his hand, still beaming radiance. "Under protest, my dear fellow?"

"I was told we would not be allowed to leave Berlin until I met with you."

Zimmerman clicked his tongue in annoyance. "Sometimes my subordinates are a trifle overzealous. There was never any question of your not leaving Berlin. You have always been free to leave whenever you wanted to, subject to train schedules, of course." He endeavoured to put his arm around Ulyanov's shoulder and lead him to the chairs arranged before the blazing fireplace.

Ulyanov wriggled away. "I was told this meeting would be private."

"Of course," Zimmerman said. With pointing finger he asked von Futran and Caspar to leave.

"I want Rihma to stay."

For a moment, Zimmerman looked perplexed; then he said, "As you wish."

After von Futran had left, Zimmerman went to the sofa and sat down, waiting while Ulyanov selected a straight-backed chair away from him. "A drink, Herr Ulyanov? Some food?" He pointed to a trolley covered with bottles, a tray of canapés and a bottle of champagne in an ice bucket.

"I did not come here to eat," Ulyanov snapped.

"Yes," Zimmerman said, peering hard at the muffled, defiant figure as he walked across the room and poured himself a glass of champagne. Sitting down again he asked, "What will you do when you get to Petrograd?"

"My policy has already been laid down in my speeches and in my letters."

"Unfortunately, I have not had the time to read them. Perhaps Ehrler would—"

"My policy is no compromise," Ulyanov said quickly. "No support of the Milyukov-Gutchov clique. I will nationalize the banks and the large estates. I will abolish the army, the police, and the Tsarist bureaucracy. I will create a People's Militia."

"Meanwhile the Milyukov-Gutchov clique is in power," Zimmerman remarked quietly.

"Their bourgeois revolution will die out. The only true revolution is a revolution of the proletariat. That is the inevitable, historical process. That is what I will work for, in Russia."

"Is it possible to speed up that process?" Zimmerman asked.

"Impossible. If you had read Karl Marx at all, you would know that the laws of history are unchangeable."

Zimmerman sipped his champagne. "What kind of support do you have in Russia? A million? Two million? Ten million?"

For the first time Ulyanov looked uncomfortable. "Enough," he said. "We have enough people."

"But not enough to carry Zimmerwald. Not enough to carry Kienthal. Not enough to fill a train with supporters to accompany you through Germany."

"I have not come here to indulge in socialist gossip," Ulyanov said.

"Quite so. Quite so. Tell me, Herr Ulyanov, how will you transform the small, argumentative, extremist Bolshevik Party into a large, powerful party that dominates Russia?"

"The means are within our control, and we have everything we need. Organisation, support, people. All we need are more people totally dedicated to revolution, more people prepared to listen to directions. But don't worry, Mr. Foreign Secretary Zimmerman, we will do it. We have more support than the Mensheviks."

"You have the organisational ability and you have some support. But you do not have money."

"Money!" Ulyanov flung his hands into the air. "If you want to talk about money, go and talk to Parvus. I am a socialist. What do I want with money?"

"You think that you will control the Soviet by issuing directives telling people how to vote?"

What else could he do? The Bolsheviks were a small party. He did not know how many members they had in Russia. He was relieved that as many as thirty were prepared to travel with him through Germany. What could he do other than what he had already done?

"We will give you money," Zimmerman said.

Ulyanov shook his head. "Give it to Parvus. He likes money. I am an international revolutionary." Look what they had written about him after Zimmerwald. He had made his name there. He could not associate with the likes of Zimmerman and Parvus. "I do not want to be contaminated with your money."

"Money buys power," Zimmerman said. "In twenty years, what have you achieved with your pamphlets and letters and directives and resolutions? What did you achieve in Zimmerwald? At Kienthal? Whole days and nights spent in discussion and intrigue for the satisfaction of seeing your resolutions passed with appropriate amendments? You call that being a revolutionary leader?"

"Grimm let us down," Ulyanov cried, angrily. "He was too weak. We could have carried Zimmerwald if not for Grimm."

"And then what? More resolutions, more directives,

more articles, more pamphlets, more words? Herr Ulyanov, the revolution has taken place in Russia. Words are no longer necessary. It's action that's needed now, and whatever you say, you cannot act effectively without money. This is an opportunity that you will never have again. I am offering you the support of the German government to replace the revolution of Kerensky with that of Vladimir Ilyich Ulyanov."

"Offering me support?" Ulyanov's eyes glinted mockingly. "Why are *you* offering *me* support?"

"Because you are the only man who can bring peace between Germany and Russia," Zimmerman said. He stood up and began to pace agitatedly about the room.

"What do I care about peace between imperialists?" Ulyanov demanded. "What do I care about the money you will pay to soothe your conscience?"

"You need money," Zimmerman cried, pausing momentarily in his pacing. "Without money you cannot do anything."

Ulyanov grunted scornfully. "I don't need your money."

Zimmerman had lost his nerve, Caspar thought. He had shown Ulyanov how much he was needed. Ulyanov did not care about peace; he did not care about money. He had to be cajoled, not bought, and Zimmerman's anxiety had only made Ulyanov suspicious.

"All we want is peace, Vladimir Ilyich," Caspar said, "peace that you want for Russia, peace that will enable you to build a new Russia, and us, to recreate a different Germany. Vladimir Ilyich, please, take the money, not for the Bolsheviks but for the Russia and the Germany you can and will build."

"Ideals," Ulyanov muttered and glared suspiciously at Caspar. Then, frowning heavily, he asked, "How much money?"

"Unlimited amounts," Zimmerman cried. "Money to spend on what you please. One hundred million gold marks, just for a beginning."

"One hundred million gold marks," Ulyanov repeated mockingly. For me, for us, he thought, for the Bolsheviks. Despite his apparent calm, his head was throbbing, his heart racing. Money. The things he'd had to do for money. Bank raids when the Social Democrats were against him. Forcing one of his young men to marry the Mozorov heiress so that her inheritance would come to the party; tolerating cretins like Gorky so that they would contribute a few measly roubles; lecturing to watchmakers about the Paris Commune. Money. One hundred million gold marks. He could buy newspapers, publish articles, staff a propaganda office, publish books and pamphlets. One million gold marks. With that he could conquer the world.

"What do I have to do for this money?" he asked.

"Ensure there is peace with Germany."

Above the outrageous scarf, a mocking glint came into Ulyanov's eyes. "And if not?"

"If not, we will take Russia apart piece by piece. And then we will deal with you."

"You realise that my attitude to peace is not because I love Germany. You realise that the only reason I advocate peace is because this is an imperialist war; all the participants are capitalist, monopolist oppressors."

"I am not interested in your philosophy," Zimmerman said drily. "All I want to know is whether you will work for peace with Germany?"

"Yes, Ulyanov said. Then he added, "The money must be clean."

"It will be as clean as we can make it. It will be made available to you through Parvus, in Stockholm."

"Not Parvus," Ulyanov said. "You must realise that

for a socialist with my principles to be seen to work with him is impossible. The money must be channelled through Ganetsky."

"However you want it," Zimmerman said. "Ehrler will attend to the details."

However he wanted it! That could easily be arranged in Sweden. They would form an International Bolshevik Information Centre. Radek would run it. He was a journalist after all. He could run it with Ganetsky. All party contributions would go through the information centre, so the German money would be properly laundered. He would have to talk about it with Ganetsky, of course. But Ganetsky knew how to deal with these things. A hundred million. A hundred million, and that was only the beginning.

"We cannot wait for the bourgeois revolution to work itself through," Zimmerman said. "We want peace in three months."

"If all goes well, you may have peace in two months."

Zimmerman held out his hand. Ulyanov took it. Both men said, "We are agreed."

After that, all that was left was to make suitable adaptations to Marx.

The next day the combined organisation of the Foreign Office, the Army, Section IIIb, and the Imperial Intelligence Bureau East ensured that other trains were held, that the lines were cleared, and engine changes were made rapidly. All that day the exiles raced across Germany. They reached the port of Sassnitz that afternoon and immediately boarded a Swedish ferry. That the man who was being paid by the Germans to bring defeat upon England should travel on a boat named the *Queen Victoria* was an irony that only Caspar appreciated.

The journey was rough, and many of the comrades were seasick, most of them gathering miserably in the bows of the ship and turning a most unrevolutionary green. Ulyanov remained on deck most of the time, walking briskly round and round, holding his bowler hat in front of him with his voluminous coat flapping around him in the chill wind. From time to time he would talk to a wandering comrade, while Caspar alternated between seasick comrades, Ulyanov, and the bar. Once Caspar spotted von Ketteler shepherding his Finnish wounded, and cheerily raised a Steinhager, without getting a response.

It was after dark when they got to Trelleborg, but there was a crowd of Swedish socialists and newspapermen on the quay to greet them, most of them carrying copies of *Politikien* with a large picture of a young-looking Ulyanov on its front page and a headline describing him as the leader of the Russian Revolution. To Caspar's amusement, copies of this photography were shown to the customs men, who, after a close look at Ulyanov, allowed the now euphorious rabble through without any further questioning or examination.

They gathered noisily outside the customs house, struggling with baggage, clapping each other on the shoulders, and introducing themselves to the patient Swedes. They could hardly believe that they had crossed Germany and that nothing had happened. Now, at least till they got to Petrograd, they were safe.

Caspar walked up to where Zinoviev, Radek, and Platten were forming a barricade against the newspapermen. "No comment, no comment," Zinoviev was crying. "A full press statement will be issued in Stockholm tomorrow."

Ulyanov, standing with Nadya a little away from them, looked disturbed.

"I am leaving for Stockholm now," Caspar said.

Ulyanov looked at him in surprise. "Now? But I will see you tomorrow? We are staying at the Regina Hotel."

Caspar grinned mischieviously. "If we miss each other, you can always find me through Parvus. He is staying at the Grand."

Ulyanov frowned. "I will have no contact with Parvus," he said and turned away.

Caspar looked warmly at the stocky figure in the large hat and oversized raincoat. Ulyanov looked less than ordinary, but was more than human. Now that he was safely in Sweden, the revolution was secure.

Tskhakaya cried, "Capitalist! You can't go yet. They're giving a party for us in Malmo. With *zakuska*! Linde, we can't have a party without our commissar of festivities."

Casper left genuine regret at leaving the big boisterous Caucasian. "It's only till tomorrow," he said. "Enjoy your party. Tomorrow we will have another party, in Stockholm." He shook hands quickly with Tskhakaya and Linde and, picking up his case, hurried to the street, where he found a cab to take him to the station.

He bought himself a large meal on the train and consumed a bottle of prewar Burgundy before luxuriating in the privacy and relative comfort of a first-class sleeping betrh. He slept soundly, all the way to Stockholm.

COUNTERPASSANT

Hain sat drinking alone in the bar of the only hotel in Tornio. Here, as near to the Arctic Circle as made no difference, it was still winter, with short grey evenings and early darkness and nothing to do after the border was closed but sit in the hotel bar and drink and wonder why he had such bright ideas.

It had all happened because of the ambiguity and unpreparedness with which HMG had received news of the revolution. On the one hand, the alliance with the Autocrat of All the Russias, even though he bore a remarkable physical resemblance to his cousin George V, had become a little embarrassing. On the other hand, this new lot was still dithering about the war with Germany, and if they made peace, there was a good chance that His Imperial Majesty Wilhelm II might be able to divert sufficient men and materials to give the forces of his cousin George V, to whom he bore no physical resemblance whatsoever, a sound drubbing.

What made this seem more likely was the Provisional Government's decision to let anybody who wanted to come, enter Russia. They were letting in not only political exiles but all kinds of people, including German agents. Knowing that the Provisional Government had been worried about the loyalty of its border troops, who naturally had not been able to participate in the uprising in Petrograd, Hain had suggested to the Ambassador and the Ambassador had suggested to the Provisional Government that under the auspices of Allied Command, British troops should work side by side with their Russian—er—comrades in policing the border. As Hain was the only person in the embassy in Petrograd who spoke Russian, he had been despatched to Tornio to see that there were no incidents amongst the comrades, and particularly to ensure that any non-Russian who wasn't approved of by the British was kept firmly out.

So much, Hain thought, for bright ideas. He thumped his glass on the counter to be refilled, while pulling out the telegram that had been despatched early that evening fromTrelleborg. There was no need for him to read it again because the message was short and he knew what it said. But he liked looking at it. It made his mind focus on the problem. *Ulyanov returned this evening.*

What the hell was he supposed to do? Ulyanov was a Russian. Whether he was welcome or not by the British, he had to be let in. Diplomatic representations had already been made by the French and the Americans, and by the British. Ulyanov, they had said, had travelled through Germany; he was obviously an agent of the Germans and would strive to break the Entente. The Provisional Government had listened patiently and said again that all Russian political exiles, whatever their beliefs, were welcome home. After Ulyanov had returned and they had heard his explanation, then they would decide whether or not he had committed treason. By then, given German funds, Ulyanov could be the government. So what was Hain to do?

There was another bright idea that he'd kept suppressed, ever since he'd heard of Ulyanov's return through Germany. It was risky, personally disastrous if he was ever found out, but effective. He stared at his drink and thought, one had to take chances. If he succeeded, well, who knew? He finished his drink, put on his coat and cap, and walked shivering through the ankle-deep snow to the guardhouse at the bridge. There he woke a driver and asked to be taken in the three-ton Dennis to the hut where Kuryakin and his four Okhrana veterans lived.

Hain had brought Kuryakin and the veterans from Imatra when he'd been placed in charge of border security. It was mutually advantageous. They needed the work, and the only information Hain had on undesirables was from their files. Now, he thought, as the truck lurched over the rutted snow and roots of trees, perhaps they could arrange something else mutually advantageous.

The hut was only a few kilometres away, and Hain reached it in half an hour. It was in darkness. Asking the driver to wait, he walked up to the door. Before he could knock, it opened. A torch flashed into his face, and from the darkness behind it Kuryakin's voice said, "Walk straight in."

The door shut behind Hain. A lamp was turned up. In the dim yellow lighting Hain saw Kuryakin standing across the room from him, a loaded rifle in his hands.

"What is it?" Kuryakin asked.

Hain gave him the telegram.

Still cradling the rifle, Kuryakin read it. "So he'll be through here tomorrow or the day after."

"I suppose so."

"And I suppose you want him stopped?"

"Don't you want to stop him?"

Kuryakin smiled thinly. "I might have other ideas."

Caspar reached Stockholm at five o'clock in the morning, climbing sleepily from his secluded comfort onto a draughty, gaslit platform. At that time of the morning, Stockholm was dark and dreary, and there was a persistent drizzle as Caspar took a cab to the Grand Hotel and Royal.

Despite the unearthly hour Parvus was ebullience itself. Resplendent in a dressing gown of Chinese silk, brushing sleep from his fat little eyes, Parvus seized Caspar's hand in both his podgy ones and ushered him breathlessly into the suite.

"My boy, you gave me quite a shock. Your beard, your suit—what's happened to your customary elegance? Honestly, for a moment I thought you were Vladya come to reproach me for living in grandeur."

Caspar said, "Travel third class for three days and the first thing you lose is elegance."

"So Vladya insisted on travelling third class, did he?"

"Insisted on paying for it, too."

"Well, dear boy, the saints have always believed that mortification of the flesh was good for the soul, but as Vladya neither believes in saints nor souls, I wonder why he does it. What time will they be here?"

"Around ten or so, I should think."

"And everything's settled, is it?"

"All but the details. From our point of view, he's got to give us what we want. From his point of view, the money must be clean."

"Ganetsky will see to that. Ganetsky is very good at cleaning money. But you must be tired and hungry.

Sit down and tell me all while I get you some champagne and some breakfast. When shall I meet with Ulyanov?"

"You won't," Caspar said.

Parvus' face crumpled; his little, fat body seemed to sag.

"Ulyanov made it a condition of his agreement with us that he should not be required to deal directly with you. Zimmerman agreed to that condition."

"But why, Caspar, why? I've done nothing but help your government! I've done nothing but help Ulyanov! Why discard me now in this shameless manner?"

"Because Ulyanov wants it. That was the only condition he refused even to discuss. We need Ulyanov now. We must respect his wishes."

"And how do you think Ulyanov will achieve anything without my organisation behind him?"

"Ulyanov knows how reliant you are on Germany and that you cannot risk the official displeasure of the German government. Foreign Secretary Zimmerman wished me to remind you of the extraordinary lengths he went to in order to get you Prussian citizenship, citizenship which gives you the right to reside permanently in Germany."

"So if I don't work with you, someone will find an irregularity in my papers and I will be expelled from Germany?"

"No, that will not happen, because you are going to help us. Not because you feel threatened, but because you would rather see Ulyanov succeed than the Provisional Government. You will do it because you want the same things for Russia as Ulyanov does. You will do it because the more you help Ulyanov, the more he will be in your debt, and the more he relies on you, the more you can influence him."

"You are a charming advocate," Parvus said, and poured out two large glasses of champagne. "Let us drink to the success of Ulyanov!"

Breakfast was brought in on a trolley. While they ate, Caspar told Parvus how Sonya and he had lived together in Zurich and that he was in love with her and was going to take her back to Berlin to marry her.

"You bring nothing but bad news," Parvus cried in mock anger. "First you kick me out of Quadriga. Then you take my Sonya away from me." He waddled over to a roll-topped desk and came back waving a cheque. "Proof of my disappointment. Let me be the first to give you a wedding present."

Caspar said, "Keep it until the wedding. You might have to give the bride away."

With a brusque knock on the door, Ulrich von Ketteler came in and, despite his civilian frock-coat, stood solemnly in front of Caspar and saluted.

"Forgive me, Caspar," Ulrich said. "I did not hear the news till after you'd got on the train."

"News?" Parvus enquired.

Ulrich explained about the Order of the Red Eagle and the reasons for it. After congratulating him, Parvus made him recount everything that had happened in Zurich and on the way to Berlin.

"So the Okhrana still exists," Parvus said moodily, topping up their glasses. "Ulyanov cannot leave Sweden." Parvus explained that the entrance to Finland, at Tornio, was now manned by British troops, and, from the manner in which certain people had been arrested and others refused entry, he suspected the British had access to secret Okhrana files. This fact was amplified by rumours that some members of the Okhrana had escaped into Finland and were trying to stage a counterrevolution from there. Everything Caspar and Ulrich had told him confirmed that the Okhrana were not only active but would stop Ulyanov entering Russia.

Ulrich explained about his bodyguards.

Parvus wasn't impressed. He didn't quite trust Finns who'd fought for Germany. Even if they did go with Ulyanov, that was no guarantee that the Okhrana wouldn't kill him. "All it needs is one carefully aimed bullet," Parvus said, "and everything's finished."

Caspar thought about that for a while. All that time, all that effort, all those risks—all would be useless if Ulyanov could not enter Russia. And without Ulyanov, there would not be a revolution.

"I'll go," Caspar said.

Ulrich asked, "What do you mean, Ehrler?"

"I'll go instead of Ulyanov. Everyone tells me I look like him, even you, Parvus."

"A younger Ulyanov," Parvus said, thoughtfully. It was an interesting idea. If Ehrler, masquerading as Ulyanov, got into Finland without being harmed, he could be got out easily enough. It would prove that Ulyanov had nothing to fear. On the other hand. . . .

"It could just work," Caspar explained excitedly. "Ulyanov has not been back in Russia for twelve years and then only briefly. It is unlikely that any of the men on the border would recognize him."

"They have files and records," von Ketteler pointed out. "And photographs."

"When was Ulyanov last publicly photographed? When we came into Trelleborg last evening, they let Ulyanov through on the basis of a newspaper photograph that was fifteen or twenty years old."

"It could work," Parvus said, "so long as they do not have someone on the border who knows Ulyanov."

"If you are found out," Ulrich said, "you could be shot as a spy."

"Better me than Ulyanov," Caspar said. "In any case, Herr von Ketteler, I am expecting you and your Finns to masquerade as Bolsheviks and protect me."

Before von Ketteler could protest, Parvus said, "It's crazy, but it's possible. I think you should do it."

For the next hour they discussed the arrangements. Caspar, Ulrich, and the Finns would leave Stockholm as soon as possible for the Swedish border town of Haparanda. There they would make the land crossing to Tornio. Parvus would arrange for someone to meet them on the train and take the arms across the border. After they had entered Finland, they would be met at Kemi by another guide, who would walk them across the ice to the island of Seskaro; from there they would return to Haparanda by sledge. The way Parvus outlined it, nothing could be simpler.

Having looked at the map and finalized the procedure, Caspar took Parvus to a corner of the room and said, "My only worry, if anything goes wrong, is Sonya."

"Let it cease to be a worry," Parvus said. "I will never be able to replace you in her affections, my boy, but, I promise you, I will look after her."

An hour and a half later, with entry permits stamped by the Russian consul, and accompanied by Ulrich and the five massive Finns all looking earnestly revolutionary in their hurriedly bought second-hand clothes, Caspar took the train that in sixteen hours would deposit them on the Finnish border.

They reached Haparanda early the next morning. From what Casper could see of it, it wasn't much of a town, a huddle of single-storeyed wooden houses, a large hotel, a few provisions and liquor stores, a small shop selling curios, streets laid out with logs. There were no sleds at the station, and they had to walk through the town to the bridge. The raised wooden slats were covered with snow, and occasionally they slipped.

At Karungi, some thirty kilometres before Haparanda, two furtive-looking men in heavy furs had entered their carriage and, saying that they were from Parvus, taken the Finns' weapons, promising to deliver them in Tornio. Since then, the Finns had been more than usually silent and looked more than usually taciturn; now, as they walked in a circle around Caspar, they looked distinctly worried.

At least they were big, Caspar thought with relief, and it was too dark for sniping. Perhaps they would get to Kemi before it was light, and then he could be satisfied that Ulyanov would be safe.

They left the town and walked along the riverbank, beside lines of tarpaulined equipment waiting to be taken across the river. There was a whole fleet of lorries, shrouded 75mm guns, American-built Holt tractors, Vickers machine-gun motorcycle combinations, and boxes that looked as if they contained small arms and ammunition. Weaponry for use on the Eastern Front, Caspar reflected, provided by the Entente and America; weaponry that, hopefully, would never be used.

They reached the bridge with its striped barrier and guardhouses glowing dimly from within. The Swedes were carelessly friendly and, having checked that everyone had entry permits, waved them across. "Don't know if the Russkies are awake yet," they cried.

The bridge shuddered under their combined weight,

the sound of their boots muffled by the heavy snow but still sounding ominous and clumsy. Halfway across was a barred gate beside an empty sentry box. The gate was open and they went past it, walking closely together in silence as they approached the further end of the bridge. On the far side the Russians were awake.

At the end of the bridge was a large, fenced compound, whose gates, leading into the town, were manned by two armed sentries. Within the compound was an enormously wide wooden guardhouse beside whose door an indistinguishable flag drooped. The sentries shouted at them to go into the guardhouse; leaving their cases outside the door and dashing the snow from their boots, they did.

On one side of the building was a large room with desks arranged in rows of three, an ikon, and a picture of the Tsar still on the wall. A door led off from this room to what looked like a row of cells. There was a similar room on the opposite side, busy now with sentries picking up rifles, getting into furs, and talking sleepily to each other while a samovar bubbled in a corner. They brushed past the waiting travellers, asking them to go into the office.

One row of the desks was manned by a round-shouldered, round-faced British sergeant with an untidy, drooping moustache, a cap stuck through his epaulettes, and an air of mildly dismayed surprise. Beside him and a little behind him sat a swarthy, bearded Russian, also in klaki and, Casper was surprised to notice, with British shoulder flashes on his sleeve.

"Yes, gentlemen," the sergeant said.

One of the Finns, speaking Russian, said they wished to cross into Finland and had entry permits.

The Russian beckoned him forward. The Finn went, pulling out the permit as he did so and opening the human circle that surrounded Caspar. The Russian looked past the advancing Finn. For a moment his eyes met Caspar's. There was a flash of surprise, of recognition; then the Russian was opening a drawer in the Englishman's desk and taking out a large folder. He kept turning over its pages while the Finn handed over his permit to the Englishman.

Caspar felt his mouth go dry and his breath become light and inadequate. The Englishman looked from the permit to the Finn and waited for the Russian to ask the appropriate questions. The Russian looked up from the folder, tapped the Englishman on the shoulder, and made him look at the folder. And then both of them looked up at Caspar.

With a crooked finger the Russian beckoned him forward.

Caspar went with measured, hollow footsteps, feeling his stomach quiver with apprehension. In the folder was a copy of *Politikien*, with Ulyanov's photograph on its front page.

"Are you Russian?"

"Yes," Caspar said.

"How long have you been away?"

"Many years. I left Russia illegally."

"Why?"

"I am a political exile. I have been living in Cracow, London, Paris, and, most recently, in Zurich."

"What is your occupation?"

"I am a journalist. I am also a lawyer, but I have not practised law for many years."

The Russian looked back at the folder, turned over a couple of pages, then, picking up a form from the desk, pushed it across to Caspar. "Complete that."

Caspar did. He put the date and place of his birth down as Kazan, twenty-third September 1884, and recorded his religion as Orthodox. He wrote that he had no intention of stopping in Finland and gave his address in Petrograd as c/o Maria Ulyanova, Shirokaya Street 48/9, Apartment 24.

The officer scrutinized the form carefully. "Belenin, is that your real name?"

"It's the name by which I am known."

The Russian looked down at the copy of *Politikien*, then turned it so that Caspar could see it, too. "These people are with you?"

"We have travelled together from Zurich."

The Russian put away the folder and the newspaper, slamming the drawer shut. "Welcome home, comrade," he said. "Here, have the others complete these forms and then you can go through."

It was much easier than Caspar had expected. He didn't even have to explain to the border guard that Ulrich, fearsome in a black wig, was a dumb Swede. Caspar distributed the forms amongst the Finns and, when they had completed them, took them back to the desk. The Russian was standing up, ready to go somewhere. Without even looking at the forms he scooped them up and bundled them into a desk drawer. "You have luggage?"

"Outside," Caspar said.

"Bring it in here and I will have an officer examine it."

While they brought their luggage in, the Russian left the compound behind the wheel of a muddy, brown Dennis truck. The customs officer, when he came, was far less co-operative. It took them an hour and a half before he was satisfied and they were allowed through the barred gate into Finland.

* * *

Serge Chudnovsky pounded the truck along the rutted path, ignoring the protesting groans from its suspension, the flexing squeals from its body, and the way it bounced and chattered and slid over the potholes and ridges of snow. He raced into the clearing before the house and slewed to a stop. Leaving the engine still running he flung open the door and ran to the house.

"Ulyanov's arrived," he said as soon as Kuryakin opened the front door. "He's come with six others."

Kuryakin frowned. "Our reports indicate that more than six people were travelling with Ulyanov. Are you sure it's him?"

"Well, if he's not, he bears a remarkable resemblance to the photographs we have," Serge replied. "He also fits the physical description in our files: short, stocky, bearded, balding, and red headed. He also said he was a political exile and hadn't been in Russia for many years. He gave his name as Belenin, one of Ulyanov's aliases. The name and address of his next of kin and his known occupation corresponded exactly with the files."

"All right," Kuryakin said, "let's go and get him."

Tornio was a pleasant little town of squat wooden houses, with snow-covered fields reaching right up to their back doors. The travellers walked past the school and a small Russian church, with its belfry separated from the main building as a precaution against fire, and found Tornio's only hotel without difficulty. The two men who had met them at Karungi were waiting outside with three sleds. They would have to drive fourteen *versts,* as far as Ylelulias, because the railway had been damaged and trains were not running into Tornio that day.

They breakfasted at the hotel and set off, one of the men and two Finns in the first sled, Ulrich driving Caspar with a certain panache in the second, the three other Finns and the second man bringing up the rear. After a bridge and almost two hundred yards of wide flat road, they came to Tornio station. A man in a dark uniform embroidered with the gold lettering of the Societetshuset confirmed that trains were running only as far as Ylelulias. The line might be fixed by the afternoon, but, as they had sleds, they'd do better to go straight on.

The road was good, following the coast in sweeping curves. The grey morning light became roseate as the sun rose above pine forests, a great red globe bloodily illuminating the peak of Aavasaka behind them. The air was brisk and the motion of their passage soothing. Casper threw his head back and laughed with the sensation of it. He hadn't ridden in a sled for years; there was something exhilarating about the jangle of harness, the sight of heaving, glowing flanks before him, the sensation of slipping loosely along the snow, the breeze tugging at his hat and reddening his cheeks. He looked sideways at Ulrich. Ulrich was enjoying himself, too.

They left the coast, ascended a slight incline, then plunged into the sudden gloom of a pine forest, the horses rushing through the half-dark with a sudden spurt of fear. If anyone wanted to kill Ulyanov, it would be in a place like this, Caspar thought, peering worriedly at the dappled light between the trees, feeling quite vulnerable and exposed. He needed big Finns all around and over him.

The horses galloped out of the forest and they were in listless sunlight again. The sun had disappeared into the faintest of blue skies and the light was harsh and very clear. Caspar rubbed his hands together, warming them inside the fleece-lined gloves. The road flattened out as they moved out once again beside the railway and the sea. Ylelulias, then the train to Kemi, the smallest town in Finland, or so one of the Finns had said, then across the ice with the two men who'd promised to stay with them till Haparanda. Now that he was actually doing it, things seemed a lot easier than they had in Parvus' suite at the Grand. In less than three hours he would be on his way back to Stockholm. If nothing happened. They crossed a small river and plunged through another pine forest. Nothing happened.

Nothing happened till they were about fifteen minutes from Ylelulias, plunging through the now familiar semi-darkness of a forest. Caspar saw a tiny orange flash ahead and, to the right of him, one of the Finns travelling in the sledge ahead raised his hands to his throat and tumbled off, the thwack of his body hitting the snow coinciding with the sharp crack of a rifle shot. No flash the next time, just a sharp crack, a low-pitched, fast buzzing, Ulrich gasping once, the reins slipping from his fingers. Caspar threw himself at the reins as Ulrich slumped sideways, found them, grasped them, then felt the pull of the horses against his slipping fingers. The Finn in front of him was clambering to the back of the sled, rifle raised. Two shots in sharp succession and the Finn fell face down into the back of the sled. One of the leading horses was hit, too. The sled slewed across the track in a flurry of snow, raising itself slowly, almost elegantly, on one gleaming runner before smashing onto its side, crushing the driver underneath it and tipping out the body of the fallen Finn.

Casper's own horses swerved. His sled slid wildly and crashed sideways into the sled in front of him, with a horrible splintering of wood. Ulrich lolled against him, one gouged-out bloody eye staring out of the frame of a shattered monocle, his black wig askew revealing the grey Prussian stubble underneath.

Ulrich was dead, there was firing all round him, but Caspar felt no emotion, no fear. Reacting instinctively, he threw himself out of the sled, rolling over and over into the snow until he reached the safety of the ditch.

When the sled behind him had stopped, the Finns and the driver threw themselves flat on the road beside it. Two spherical, metallic objects hurtled from the trees and landed in the middle of the sled. There was a second of awful silence. Then the sled erupted orange. Wood and metal, parts of human body and horse, flew up in the air surrounded by a ring of smoke and snow. Caspar cowered in the ditch and watched it smoulder.

They'd got everyone but him, and he was unarmed. The firing had died down and he wondered if he could make it to a sled and find a weapon. He decided against it! He would be exposed, and no weapon could be seen. Far better to make it back along the ditch, escape through the forest, find the road by the coast, and somehow make his way back to Haparanda. Crouching, wet, his feet sinking into a sticky mixture of snow, mud, and ice, he crawled along the ditch and past the sleds. He crawled till he thought he was well clear of the ambush, then stormed up the bank and made for the forest.

He'd picked the wrong place to go up the bank. It was steep, almost vertical; six feet up and he lost his grip and plunged backwards into the ditch. He lay there shivering, trying to get his breath back. He had to go along the ditch and risk crossing the road to make for the forest on the other side. He crawled a little further, wet and bedraggled, his breath wheezing in his throat. He could hear voices now coming down the road towards him and the crunch of cautious footsteps. Slowly he raised his head. He was round a curve in the road now. He climbed out of the ditch onto the road and stood there getting his bearings. There was a dull throbbing noise from round the corner and, as Casper reached the centre of the road, he heard a shout, A shot winged high into the trees. He turned and ran down the road. Distance was as important as cover. He raced round the corner on skidding feet and stopped.

There, grinding towards him like some monolithic monster, tiny, low set headlights glowing a pale yellow, was the khaki-brown, mud-stained, three ton Dennis truck, from whose open door a figure leaned, pointing a long-barrelled Mosin-Nagant rifle unsteadily at him.

"Wait there," the figure shouted.

The footsteps behind him drew closer. Caspar turned and hesitated, standing there trapped.

The footsteps behind him grew nearer. Three men, all armed, all wearing camouflage.

"Vladimir Ilyich Ulyanov," shouted the man in the truck, "welcome to Russia."

They bound his hands behind his back and tossed him uncermoniously into the truck. Three men climbed in after him; then the truck reversed into the forest, turned round, and went back towards Tornio. Caspar lay shivering, cold and helpless, his shoulder bouncing against the metal floor with each lurch of the truck over the broken snow. The three men ignored him completely, bracing themselves against the truck's movement, squatting together behind the driver's cabin.

They were obviously army of some sort. The way the ambush had been staged and their familiarity with weapons told him that. But what army? Their common-flage uniforms were devoid of insignia; apart from the border patrol, there weren't Russian units so far north. Trying to protect his shoulder from the merciless bouncing. Casper realised that the men were renegade members of the border patrol. Hadn't Parvus said something about the loyalty of the border troops being suspect? Well, here was proof, and they were about to make an example of Ulyanov.

The truck turned off the main road and the bouncing and bucking got worse, accompanied by the harsh scrape of branches against the tarpaulin roof. Caspar rolled about the floor in jolts of sudden, bruising pain. Aeons later they stopped, the patient clatter of the truck's engine fading into an abrupt, heightened silence. The men ran past him, kicked down the tail-board, and dragged him out of the truck onto his feet.

They were in a small clearing surrounded by deep, dark, silent forest. In front of Casper was a large two-storeyed wooden house with a sharply pointed roof and curious S-shaped scrolls about its windows. Some-one pushed him by the neck towards it.

They went up a log ramp to a massive front door, up dusty wooden stairs to a room on the top floor. The windows were shuttered and the room was dark, cold, and empty except for a large table in the centre and a shrouded line of chairs against a wall. Two men arranged themselves on either side of Caspar, while a squat, savage-looking man with heavy Tartar features walked to the head of the table. He looked dispassionately at Caspar.

"Well, Vladimir Ilyich, what have you to say for yourself?"

What could he say? That he was not Vladimir Ilyich but a German spy? That he was a German spy masquerading as Vladimir Ilyich? In his best Vladimir Ilyich tones, Caspar said, "I demand an explanation," and shivered.

The man at the head of the table smiled. He gestured to one of the others to free Caspar's hands. "It is you, Vladimir Ilyich, who owe us an explanation. What will you do when you get back to Russia?"

Caspar hesitated. What specifically would Ulyanov do when he got back to Russia? "Preserve the revolution," he said.

"With a handful of Bolsheviks!" the man laughed scornfully. "Tell me, Vladimir Ilyich, exactly how will you seize power?"

"There are many alternatives," Caspar muttered.

The men walked round the table and stood in front of Caspar. He pressed two fingers under Caspar's chin and raised Caspar's head, looking keenly into Caspar's face. Then, wordlessly, he ripped away Caspar's shirt and jacket. "The exile years have treated you uncommonly well," he said softly.

He walked back to the table and stared thoughtfully at Caspar. "Much too well," he muttered, and nodded to the two men standing behind Caspar. "Flog him."

The two men took Caspar by the arms and walked him to the table, then bent him face down over it. Holding him there by the shoulders, they ripped away his sodden trousers and beat him on his bare bottom with what felt like a leather flail. If not for the sting of the blows, Caspar would have been amused.

Afterwards they led him from the room to a small bedroom, empty of all furniture. They unfastened his hands, took away his shirt and jacket, gave him a rough blanket, and left him.

Caspar walked to the window and opened it. Naturally it was barred, and of course the door behind him was locked. Wrapping the blanket round him, he sat in a corner opposite the door and tried to think.

If he told them he was a German spy, they would shoot him and go after Ulyanov. That way both he and Ulyanov would be killed. On the other hand, if he pretended to be Ulyanov, then at least Ulyanov might get away. And perhaps when the real Ulyanov walked through the guardpost at Tornio, by some miracle he would be freed.

Caspar pulled the blanket tight round him. At least he could stand the pain, and they had left him alone. He began to drowse. For the moment, clad as he was only in a blanket and locked in a room guarded by five rugged men, escape was impossible.

He'd just slipped off to sleep when a kick in the ribs sent him sprawling on the floor. The Russian who had allowed him through the border that morning was standing over him, shouting, "How dare you sleep! You must get permission to sleep! On your feet! Stand to attention!"

Caspar got to his feet, slowly.

The man hit him savagely and kicked his ankles away from under him. "Quicker!" he shouted.

Two more men had come into the room. Caspar jumped to his feet and was hit about the head and thrown to the floor again. "Faster, and this time I want you to salute." Casper tried. His arm was nerveless and he could only raise it halfway before the pain grew too much.

"Call that a salute!"

He was lying on the floor again, feeling the salty tang of blood welling into his mouth. Desperately he willed his aching arms and legs to move. Wearily he climbed to his feet. Even more wearily he saluted.

The Russian looked at him and smiled. "I'll be back in ten minutes. Keep practising. I want to see you jumping up twice as quick as that."

They went.

Caspar was alone, his body a throbbing weal of agony.

Kuryakin, Serge, and Tihon sat at the table on which Caspar had been beaten. "He's not Ulyanov," Kuryakin said.

"He must be," Serge protested. "He fits everything we have on our records."

Kuryakin looked at Tihon.

"I think not," Tihon said.

"We agree then that he isn't Ulyanov." Before Serge could protest, Kuyakin continued. "He may fit in with our records, Serge, but that doesn't mean he's Ulyanov. It could simply mean tht our records are out of date. Ulyanov is an old man, almost fifty. The body of our prisoner is that of someone of half that age. Not all his walking in the Swiss mountains could preserve Ulyanov's body to that extent."

"But why would anyone pretend to be Ulyanov?" Serge asked.

"That's what we have to find out." Kuryakin turned to Tihon. "Unfortunately, the telegram to Kerensky has already been sent. We will have to break this prisoner quickly. What's the fastest way to do that?"

"We will need twenty-four hours or so. For this man to come into Finland masquerading as a dangerous revolutionary, he must be highly motivated. If we were to threaten him directly, he would resist very strongly. I feel we should accept this story and treat him as if he were Ulyanov."

A while later Caspar was taken back into the room where he had been beaten. The Tartar sat on one side of the table, between the bearded man who had been at the frontier post and a younger, clean-shaven man whom Caspar did not remember seeing before.

It was this last man who spoke. "You're a mindless little shit, Ulyanov. No one wants you back in Russia. No one wants your second-hand ideas or your boring books. You're a cretin, Ulyanov."

Someone spat in Caspar's face. He moved to avoid a glass of water thrown at his head, and someone else slapped him.

"When we are talking to you, don't bloody move!" someone shouted.

The clean-shaven man behind the table continued speaking. "So you're the great revolutionary." All the men laughed. "What are you doing standing naked in this room? You are no revolutionary, Ulyanov. You are a muddle-headed, small-minded meddler. You think you and your Bolsheviks farting round in Zurich mean anything? Do you think anyone cares about your conferences and resolutions? Even if they wanted to pay attention, you're so damn boring. Do you think anyone even likes you? You're only a putrid little half-man. . . ."

They continued for two hours, laughing at his achievements, ridiculing his body. They pushed him and prodded him. They made him stand on one leg and imitate a crane. They slapped him. They taunted him about Inessa and made crude jokes about Nadya. They made him kneel and they kicked him. They forced him to kiss a picture of the Tsar and took him outside the house and rolled him in the snow.

Caspar was overwhelmed by their viciousness and hatred for him. He found himself ceasing to believe in what he was doing and began secretly looking for ways to earn their approval. But nothing he did or said affected them in any way. Sometimes they abused him for doing what they wanted; at other times they cheered his refusals. Everything was disconnected and illogical. Their questions frequently had nothing to do with anything, and sometimes they insisted that his answers be equally without point. He was sometimes accepted, sometimes ignored, kicked and slapped and always humiliated. As the treatment went on, Caspar became hopelessly confused, and withdrawn.

Suddenly the clean-faced young man said, "Because you're such a revolting, useless son of a bitch, we are going to flog you." He gestured to the others. "Give the tiresome Ulyanov six strokes."

There was nothing Caspar could do about it. He was placed face down on the table and bound to it. The strokes were placed with loving efficiency, all the way down from his shoulders. They were also applied with a good deal more strength than previously, each lash coiling like liquid fire round his body. And to make matters worse they counted.

"One."

"Two."

"Three."

Caspar heard himself scream, felt tears, hot and frustrated and angry, pour out of his eyes.

"Four."

"Five."

Caspar waited, tense. The lash whistled. His body flexed against the bonds, jerked as the lash hit the table beside him. He subsided, waiting, sobbing.

"Take him back to his room," the leaders said.

They freed him and led him back, shut the door behind him and locked it. Casper pulled the blanket round him, and was made to sit, then remained half-squatting. He was too frightened to sit. The bearded, swarthy Russian might come in, to force him to stand up and salute.

Suddenly he realised what they were doing to him. To Ulyanov. They were cracking his mind.

Saturday afternoon and the whole of Petrograd was in the thrall of the Lenten Fast, the tension building up remorselessly, punctuated by the regular, monotonous dirge of bells from the churches of Petrograd, Kazan, St. Isaac, St. Catherine, St. Nicholas, and the Monastery of Alexander Nevsky.

The bells of St. Cosmos and Damien sounded almost directly outside Kerensky's private office in the Tauride Palace. But Kerensky's thoughts were not on the long Easter service which would start at ten o'clock that night and climax in candelit processions and joyous cries of "He is risen!," the exchanging of three-fold kisses, and the eating of sweet *kulitch* cake. Sitting behind his desk, nervously shredding wastepaper, Kerensky wondered what to do about the telegram.

It had arrived an hour earlier, marked for his attention only, written in the secret code of the Tsarist

Ministry of the Interior. Kuryakin had kidnapped Ulyanov. Kuryakin wanted a meeting in Imatra within the next forty-eight hours. Kuryakin wanted to exchange Ulyanov for the Tsar, and an amnesty for himself and four of his men.

Kerensky got up from his chair and began to pace about his silent office. The strain of the past few weeks showed in his drooping shoulders, in his long face, devoid of colour, and in skin that was waxed and dried like old parchment glued to bone. The exchange that Kuryakin contemplated was unthinkable. Public knowledge of even that demand for such an exchange would inflame the Soviet, make them renew their demands for the Tsar's trial and execution, and ruin Kerensky's own plan for the exile of the Tsar and his family to England. A pardon for any member of Section Four of the Okhrana was inconceivable.

The only course of action was to find Kuryakin and persuade or force him to yield Ulyanov. He picked up the telegram and looked at it again. It had been despatched from Tornio shortly after noon. Did that mean the Border Guard supported Kuryakin? That Kuryakin was starting a counterrevolution in Finland?

Before he could act, before he could summon the ministers from their Easter holiday, before he could risk facing conflicting demands for an immediate rescue or a compromise for leaving both Ulyanov and the Tsar to their fate, he had to ascertain the facts. He called the telephone exchange and put a call through to the commander of the Border Guard. He picked up the telegram and looked at it again.

Noon. Tornio. His information showed that Ulyanov had only arrived from Sweden on the Thursday night. Ulyanov must have been in an almighty hurry to get back to Petrograd. Strange, also, that if he had been kidnapped, the Bolsheviks weren't beating down his door demanding that whole divisions of the Russian Army be sent to Finland.

He called the Kshesinskaya Palace which the Bolsheviks had appropriated as their offices. Being materialists, they were not concerned with Easter. Stalin came on the phone directly. Yes, Ulyanov was on his way back to Petrograd. He had spent all of Friday resting from his journey in Stockholm, and they were expecting him within the next two days. They were also planning a massive welcome at the Finland Station.

If Ulyanov had spent Friday in Stockholm, not even he could have been at Tornio by noon on the Saturday.

Kerensky was intrigued. If there had been incidents of any kind at Tornio, the British would know.

The British didn't know of any incidents in Tornio. Ulyanov had not arrived at the border yet. Yes, they fully understood that he was to be allowed entry. If the Minister of Justice insisted, they would reinforce that understanding with an immediate telegram to their liaison officer at Tornio.

The commander of the Russian Border Guard came on the phone. Everything was very quiet in Tornio, with the troops preparing for the Easter celebrations. Ulyanov had not passed through yet, and he would once again inform the British that Ulyanov was free to enter Russia.

By the end of the afternoon Kerensky was still intrigued. Either Kuryakin had made a daring raid into Sweden or he was lying. He couldn't have seized Ulyanov without seizing fifty of sixty other Bolsheviks as well. If he'd done that in Sweden, the news would be public knowledge by now. So perhaps Kuryakin was lying; perhaps the strain of exile was driving him mad.

Kerensky shrugged. He would wait and see.

Caspar stood naked and shivering, staring at the wall, his legs and arms and the back of his shoulders filled with pain as he tried to force his body to remain still. If he kept still for one more minute, three more minutes, five more minutes, they would let him sit. If he remained still they would even let him lie down. Perhaps they would even let his sleep.

"Who organised the journey through Germany?"

"Parvus."

A quick flip of a wet towel against his flayed back. An explosion of surging agony.

"Wrong answer. Keep still. You're moving. Now you will have to stand there for three more minutes."

Silence.

Caspar forced his trembling limbs into a semblance of quietude. The last time he'd told them it was Parvus who'd organised the journey, they'd allowed him to sit. He could feel himself starting to tremble again. He mustn't let himself tremble. Mustn't move. Think of the time. Count the seconds. How many seconds were there in three minutes. One, two, three, three sixes were eighteen, nineteen, twenty-two. He couldn't count. Best not to count.

"You're moving!"

"No!"

"Don't answer back!"

A quick snap of the towel, pain flaring his back.

"Two extra minutes."

Oh, God, no. They'd let him alone only for minutes

at a time, waking him up each time he drowsed, making him run in the snow each time he collapsed.

It was the unpredictability of it all that he couldn't cope with. An hour, two hours ago they had given him food, sat round the table and talked with him like human beings. The leader was called Kuryakin and the bearded, swarthy one was Serge. The one with the young-looking face was Tihon. He'd only got as far as that when they'd taken the food away from him and set upon him, beating him with their fists, not hard enough to mark but hard and repeatedly, abusing him all the while, telling him he was a thief, a liar, a traitor.

What had he said or done? They'd been talking about the weather in Zurich. It was absurd. Why should the weather in Zurich upset them? It must be something else. Something he had said, something he had done. What?

"Who organised your journey through Germany?"

Parvus, he thought, but that was not the answer they wanted. Whose name could he use, quickly, quickly, before they hit him with the towel again.

"Foreign Secretary Zimmerman."

The towel snapped out again, a blaze of pain along his back that made his legs tremble. "Liar! It was Parvus. You know it was Parvus. Why are you lying to us? You moved again. One more minute."

From somewhere behind him a voice counted off the seconds. "Sixty, fifty-nine, fifty-eight, fifty-seven. . . ."

Caspar forced himself to concentrate on the wall, the grain of the wood. He wouldn't move. He mustn't move. In a short time, in a very short time, they would let him sit, they would leave him alone. The muscles of his legs were like branding irons.

"Thirty, twenty-nine—you moved. Two minutes."

"No!" Caspar cried. He was trembling. The wooden wall in front of him was trembling, his body was uncontrollable, his teeth chattering in his head. "No," he cried again, the wall closing in round him, his body shuddering in huge spasms. "No! Please!" He could feel his body swaying, a faraway, high-pitched voice, screaming, pleading, footsteps behind him, arms taking hold of his body. They were going to make him run in the snow again. No, please God, no.

"You may sit," someone said.

Caspar sat, his body shuddering, his shoulders heaving in uncontrollable sobs.

All that day the border had been busy. With the approaching Easter holiday, Swedes had been going to Finland, Finns to Sweden, and Russian exiles had arrived from everywhere. On top of everything, Sergeant Harris told Hain that Kuryakin and his Russians had gone AWOL.

Early that morning Ulyanov had crossed over, accompanied by a party of six. Serge had authorised the entry; then taken the Dennis truck and disappeared.

It wasn't serious, Hain assured Sergeant Harris. They would all be back after the holiday. It was, he said, the Russian temperament.

Soon afterwards, full of Russian vodka and Russian temperament, the Russian commanding officer turned up at the guardhouse. He had been telephoned by the Minister of Justice himself. He was under orders to ensure that under no circumstances would the British prevent Ulyanov entering Finland.

Ulyanov was already in Finland, Hain pointed out reasonably. He'd crossed over early that morning and had been admitted without any fuss.

The Russian commander hesitated, looking suspiciously round the guardhouse, and said as long as the British understood that was all right.

Soon afterwards there was a telegram for Hain from the British Embassy, saying much the same thing.

Soon afterwards there was Ulyanov, accompanied by about thirty exiles.

They streamed across the bridge in an untidy mob, carrying bags and baskets, wearing dark overcoats and black hats, looking like a party of workmen attending an important funeral. The Russian soldiers greeted them warmly, and soon everyone was chattering excitedly, some of the men even kissing each other.

The first priority, Hain decided, was to enforce discipline. He had the exiles herded into a room and made them complete immigration forms. They had no passports, so each of them was to be individually questioned. For all anyone knew, they might be Germans. Then they were to be searched. They might be carrying weapons. Their luggage was to be scrupulously examined.

While all that was going on, Hain ordered a car and drove to Kuryakin's hut.

There was no one there.

Hain had no doubt what had happened. By some weird mischance, Kuryakin had snatched the wrong people. And no doubt, by now, he would have discovered his mistake and would be lurking in the dark somewhere between Tornio and Ylelulias, waiting to grab the right ones.

Hain shuddered. If Kuryakin succeeded, there would be a most god-awful fuss. Having bungled so spectacularly once, Hain would not be able to keep secret his part in one or both abductions. There was no help for it. Kuryakin must be found and stopped.

But there was no hope of finding Kuryakin in the dark. Hain had to buy time. He spoke to the Russian commander. It was dangerous for Ulyanov and his party to travel to Ylelulias by sled at night. Apart from the natural hazards of travel, there were rumours that the line between Ylelulias and Tornio had been sabotaged. He had also been informed by the Embassy that there was a conspiracy to prevent Ulyanov reaching Petrograd. Now if it was the conspirators who had sabotaged the line. . . .

It wasn't his problem, the Russian commander said. All he had been instructed to do was to see that Ulyanov was allowed to enter Finland.

It wasn't his problem, Hain agreed. It was their joint responsibility. Obviously both Kerensky and the British wanted Ulyanov in Petrograd. If something happened to Ulyanov in territory which was under their control, how could they avoid being responsible?

The Russian commander pondered that seriously. What did Hain suggest?

Hain suggested that the Russain commander persuade Ulyanov to remain in Tornio for twenty-four hours. Within that time he would ascertain whether the rumours of conspiracy had any substance; if they had, he would have Kerensky send an armed guard to escort Ulyanov back to Petrograd. What happened after that would not be their responsibility.

The Russian commander spoke to Ulyanov. Ulyanov spoke to Zinoviev and Nadya and Inessa. They agreed unanimously that after all their vexations, to risk everything for the sake of twenty-four hours was pointless. They would wait till the following evening, but if they were delayed beyond that, they would protest.

They, accompanied by Sergeant Harris, Hain went to the hotel in Tornio, where they clearly remembered the party of seven men who had breakfasted there earlier that day. There had been three sleds waiting for them, and after breakfast they had set out for Ylelulias.

The Station Master at Ylelulias did not remember a party of seven in three sleds. There hadn't been any passengers going as far as Petrograd that day. Back at the hotel, in Tornio, Hain checked again. Yes, the three sleds had been waiting for the men when they arrived. Yes, there had been baggage in the sleds.

Hain relaxed. Perhaps Kuryakin had not snatched anybody at all. Perhaps the seven men who came over were members of his counterrevolutionary movement who had smuggled weapons over the border. He had been foolish to worry.

He finished his drink and ordered another. Foolish to worry? Now that he knew who the men were, he knew what they had come for. Kuryakin could not hope to capture thirty or so exiles with only five men. The men who had crossed the border early that morning were reinforcements.

Tomorrow, Hain decided, would be soon enough to find Kuryakin.

Pain and darkness and cold. Shoulder sockets that were racked with agony. He would do anything, anything if they would only release his arms and allow him to rest the weight of his body on the floor.

Caspar did not know how long he had been strung to the rafter. He did not know how long they had been questioning him or how long it was since he had been captured. He had no clear recollection of anything. Fragments of questions penetrated his consciousness; garbled answers poured from his quivering lips. From the damp darkness beyond, the Prussian officer with the kindly eyes was asking, "And what are you?"

"A journalist."

"A revolutionary journalist?"

"No."

"No, what?"

"Not a revolutionary–"

The freezing water cascaded over his shrouded head, filling the mask, filling his nostrils, filling his gasping mouth, gurgling into his lungs as he coughed and spluttered and writhed wildly, each desperate swing of his body yanking at his arms, sending waves of jarring pain all the way to his shoulders.

From the darkness beyond hands reached out and steadied him. Caspar hung gasping, cold, shivering, trying to breathe through the waterlogged hood.

"You mustn't use that word again."

"No," Caspar said.

"Not ever."

"Not ever."

"What word?"

"Please," Caspar said, "You know."

"What will you campaign for in Russia?"

"For change."

Caspar bit his lip and waited, bracing his body for the chilling shock of freezing water. Change. They didn't like that word, either.

Nothing happened.

"What kind of change?"

"Ch–for responsible government."

"And what will happen if you forget what you have learned?"

"You will find me, wherever I am."

"What else?"

"You will keep me like this forever. You are all-powerful."

Kuryakin looked at Tihon. Tihon nodded. Caspar was cut down and led away to his room.

After Caspar had gone, Kuryakin asked, "Is that it?"

"Not yet," Tihon said. "Let him start thinking the worst is over, then we will start again."

The truck drove slowly in the middle of the road, Hain and Sergeant Harris peering out of the windows, examining both the icy road ahead of them and the snowbanks on either side. Hain had little hope of the road. It had been churned up and any tracks long ago obliterated. But he had no alternative but to go on looking. After all, three sleds and seven men could not just vanish.

When they came to the first patch of forest, he made Harris drive slowly down the middle, while the platoon of soldiers behind them walked along the sides of the road and on the snowbanks. Their progress was agonizingly slow and made no provision for the possibility that men were Kuryakin's accomplices or that whatever had happened had happened deep in the forest.

At the end of the first patch of forest the men climbed back into the truck and drove on again, still looking and not finding.

Another patch of forest, another careful search beside the road. Nothing. Hain was beginning to get discouraged. Perhaps it hadn't happened like this at all. Perhaps it had happened elsewhere. They went on.

It took them nearly an hour to find the tyre tracks where the Dennis had turned. Minutes after that to find blackened snow, as if something had burned, broken snowbanks, and three sleds hidden amongst the trees, near the road.

They found the bodies half an hour later.

In the darkened room at the top of the house, Caspar was suspended from a rafter, his head covered by the black hood, and murmuring on oath of loyalty to the Kaiser. He'd been murmuring that oath for fifteen minutes, and nothing they did would make him stop.

Once again Kuryakin had him cut down and taken away to his room, still murmuring his oath. They had taken it in relays to keep torturing Caspar all night. Apart from the stripes on his back, he was physically sound, but now it seemed his mind had snapped.

"We've gone too far," Kuryakin said.

"He'll recover. If he is left alone and allowed to sleep, he will recover."

"Are you sure?"

Tihon shrugged. "One can never be sure, but he wants to survive. That is obvious from the fact that he has reverted to his true German identity."

"Let him have as much sleep as he needs," Kuryakin said.

Hours later Caspar was woken from an exhausted sleep, dressed, and brought back to the room. Only Kuryakin and Tihon were there. He began to tremble.

"Sit down," Kuryakin said, pointing to a chair opposite him. Cautiously, Caspar sat and watched frozen faced as Kuryakin pushed a glass of tea towards him. Warily, expecting the scalding liquid to be poured over his face, Caspar picked up the glass with both hands and drank.

"How do you feel, Herr Ehrler?" Tihon asked softly.

Caspar dropped the steaming glass. For a moment he watched, cowering, knowing they were going to beat him.

Then Kuryakin said, "Leave it," and pushed his own glass across.

"You have no need to be frightened or ashamed," Kuryakin said. "No one could have withstood what you have been through. We know you work for the Foreign Office Intelligence Bureau East. We know you arranged the money and transport for Ulyanov. Now, please relax, take your time, and tell us all about it. Begin at the beginning, and don't worry, no one is going to hurt you whatever you say."

Caspar picked up Kuryakin's glass of tea with a hand that trembled violently and pressed the glass against his lips. His chest burned. He gave a strangled cry. He couldn't help it. The tears were rolling down his face. He began to talk.

Hain knelt by the tracks where the Dennis truck had turned. It was obvious that they had gone back towards Tornio, but he wasn't thinking about that now.

With six deaths and the wrong man in Kuryakin's hands, the matter would not pass away. And if Kuryakin were arrested, Hain's own involvement would not be allowed to pass away. He thought about the problem, staring blankly at the tyre tracks. It would all depend on whether Kuryakin gave in peaceably or not.

He went back to his truck and asked Sergeant Harris to drive towards Tornio, instructing the men behind to keep a sharp lookout for tyre tracks on side turnings.

They found a probable turning twenty minutes later, and not because of the tyre tracks. One of the men who had not so long ago been a boy scout had noticed a line of broken branches.

Kuryakin and the others were seated round the table in the upstairs room eating when they heard the sound of the approaching truck. Kuryakin gestured to them to remain still, picked up a rifle and went to the window. He saw the truck emerge into the clearing and stop. Khaki-clad figures peeled out of the truck and disappeared into the forest. Then he saw Hain climb out.

"Kuryakin!" Hain shouted.

Kuryakin put down the rifle and opened the window. "Tell your men to hold their fire. I'm coming out."

He left the rifle and went down the stairs, then ran down the log ramp and across the clearing to Hain. "What are all the soldiers for?"

Hain looked past his shoulder. "I can't help you anymore," he said tightly. "Not with six murders. And the man you've got in there isn't Ulyanov."

"I know that," Kuryakin said. "The man in there is the German agent who is running Ulyanov. The others were spies. I have a signed statement. Why don't you come inside and read it."

Hain followed Kuryakin inside where he was introduced to Caspar and read the statement.

"Well," he said, "I'd better take him into custody. And go back to the hotel and arrest Ulyanov."

"Not yet," Kuryakin said. "I must talk to Ulyanov first."

For a moment Hain stared at him keenly. Then he said, "I suppose you've earned that privilege."

Ulyanov paced the hotel room restlessly, his large head thrust forward, his thumbs hooked into his waistcoat. From the window he could see the shadowy outlines of the army trucks and he knew there were sentries posted discreetly round the hotel. Sentries for what? To prevent enemies from getting him or him from getting out? He had been foolish to agree to stay twenty-four hours, but there hadn't been much of a choice and last night it had seemed a good idea. He stopped and peered through the window. He couldn't see them, but he knew the troops outside were British. That worried him. He began to pace again. What were they waiting for? Fifteen of the agreed twenty-four hours had gone, and there was no word from anyone, only politeness, consideration, and vagueness.

From the bed Nadya said, "Vladya, it's not good for you to worry yourself like this. Please try to relax."

"I can't help worrying," Ulyanov replied. "I'm responsible for all of you." He walked up to the bed. "I don't trust the British."

"I know," Nadya said. Ever since that year in London, they hadn't liked, trusted, or understood the British. Vladya, she remembered, had been particularly horrified by Parliament. "Why don't you read?" she asked.

Just then there was a knock at the door. Ulyanov cried, "Who is it?"

"Lieutenant Chudnovsky for Mr. Ulyanov."

With a mixture of suspicion and relief, Ulyanov opened the door.

A big, bearded man wearing a military uniform stood outside, his cap and swagger stick clasped firmly under his arm. Immediately he recognised Ulyanov; he saluted. "I am Major Kuryakin's adjutant. We are to escort you and your party to Bieloostrov. Major Kuryakin presents his compliments and would be grateful if you could spare him a few minutes to finalize the arrangements."

"An armed guard? Why is that necessary?"

"There are bands of Tsarist counterrevolutionaries in Finland."

"I don't believe that. You are placing us under arrest."

"No, sir. Most definitely not, sir. Our orders are very specific on that. They are from Minister Kerensky himself. We are to protect you. Major Kuryakin will show you the telegram."

Ulyanov was convinced. He turned and rushed excitedly into the room. "Nadya, what do you think! Kerensky has sent an armed escort for us. Isn't it wonderful. They're not going to arrest us in St. Petersburg."

"I don't trust Kerensky," Nadya said.

Ulyanov got into his jacket and came to the door. "I'd better get Zinoviev."

"Mr. Zinoviev is already with Major Kuryakin, sir. This way, please."

Ulyanov walked down the corridor, beside the officer. "What regiment are you from?"

"The Preobrajensky, sir. We were the second regiment to come out in support of the revolution."

"*Molodetz!* What are you doing in Finland?"

"There have been attempts by the British to subvert the Border Patrol and prevent certain of the political exiles returning, sir."

"You'll have to get out of the habit of calling people 'sir.' "

"I'm sure I will, sir."

They were at the end of the corridor, facing the solid wooden door which led outside. They were flanked on either side by smaller doors leading to rooms. The officer knocked cursorily on one of them and opened the door. Ulyanov went in.

He was in a small room that was in total darkness, except for the light of a desk lamp which only illuminated the plain wooden desk. In the gloom behind it was a bulky figure whose uniform buttons glinted weakly in the dimly reflected light.

"Major Kuryakin?" He peered into the darkness, looking for Zinoviev.

"Yes, Mr. Ulyanov. Please come in."

Ulyanov walked cautiously up to the desk. He couldn't see Zinoviev. "You wished to discuss our travel arrangements."

"Yes. Sit down." Kuryakin swung forward. His hand reached across the desk. In his scarred fist was a gun. "Sit down," he repeated. There was no politeness in his voice.

Staring uncomprehendingly at the gun, Ulyanov sat, feeling his heart lurch and the familiar shock wave of pulse through his temples. His mouth became very dry. "What—what is the meaning of this?" His voice was an indignant croak.

With a sudden movement Kuryakin swung the desk lamp away from him. Instinctively Ulyanov followed its sweep and saw—Rihma!

"A prodigal returned to the fold," Kuryakin said.

Ulyanov felt the blood pounding in his head and had a mad urge to get up and run. His mind was completely blank, focussed on the implacably levelled gun. No, he could not run. There was only one thing to do. Deny everything. "Who is this man?" Struggling to get the words out.

"His name is Caspar Ehrler. He is an agent of the German Foreign Office. He has arranged your transport through Germany, and through Parvus and Ganetsky he is arranging to make available one hundred and twenty million marks to the Bolshevik Party. You see, Mr. Ulyanov, you needn't bother to lie. We know everything."

"I have never seen this man before in my life," Ulyanov said. Deny and keep on denying, wear them down with denials. His will and stamina were greater. As long as he kept denying they could not do anything to him.

Caspar looked away from the light and Ulyanov.

"I have a signed statement from Ehrler," Kuryakin said.

"The Germans will say anything if it suits them. Have you corroboration?"

"All the circumstances corroborate Ehrler's statement."

Ulyanov said, "This is a Tsarist plot to compromise me."

Kuryakin said nothing.

In silence Caspar watched the two men seated opposite each other. The German peace plan was in ruins. There would be no peace on the Eastern Front and the Americans had already joined the Entente in the West. It was the end for Germany, the end for Ulyanov, the end for Parvus, Ganetsky, Zimmerman. The end for him, too.

Ulyanov leaned forward peering closely at Kuryakin. "Who are you?"

"Count Dimitri Kuryakin, former head of Section Four of the Okhrana."

"Former head," Ulyanov repeated, acidly. The man had no power. The Okhrana was finished. He dabbed fiercely at his face with a handkerchief.

"You have taken German money and agreed to make peace with Germany. Have you anything to say before I hand you over to the British to be shot?"

It was a trap. He was suspected Parvus and the Germans all along. They disliked him, envied him; now they were getting rid of him. "I am not a traitor," Ulyanov said, and repeated, "I am not a traitor." Somehow he had to convince this policeman that he was a patriot. "Everything I have done has been for Russia." Not only he and Nadya would be shot. His entire party would be liquidated. "Throughout my years in exile, I have been a patriotic Russian. I have opposed the war because it has senselessly wasted Russian lives. You can see for yourself. The Russian Army, is it strong, well organised, proud?"

"No," Kuryakin said, "it is weak, disorganised, and without morale."

"If you don't have an army that can fight, I submit it is sensible to make peace. There is no treachery in that. Only the saving of life." He peered at the shadowy presence on the opposite side of the desk, hoping the man opposite understood the need to save soldier's lives.

"Yes." Kuryakin's tone was flat, uncompromising, the voice of a man who had no intention of getting involved in debate. "What are you doing with the German money? What are your plans for peace with Germany?"

Ulyanov thought rapidly, carefully. He had to get this right. He brushed his sweating palms against the top of his serge trousers. "Peace with Germany is necessary, only because it is necessary for Russia. It is necessary for Russia because the war cannot be won, and the resources devoted to war must be diverted to building a better Russia." He felt more confident now. Kuryakin was letting him talk, and as long as he could keep Kuryakin's interest, he could convince him. "The transfer of power that has taken place in Russia," he said slowly, "is irreversible." He peered again into the gloom behind the desk. It was important that Kuryakin realise that his class was finished, that for him there was no going back. "Nothing can change that. Not war, not peace, not the execution of myself and my supporters. The revolution has transferred state power from one class to another. That is a fact."

"An obvious fact," Kuryakin said, drily.

"You accept it. Good!" He had to be careful not to antagonise Kuryakin, not to talk above his head. "Because of the peculiar circumstances under which this transfer of power took place, power is presently shared by a duality—the proletariat, as represented by the Soviet, and the petty bourgeois, as represented by the Provisional Government." Kuryakin, the secret policeman, the oppressor of the people, was allowing him to speak. What could Kuryakin know of the class struggle? Yet he was listening. "The two forces cannot work together forever. Sooner or later one must exterminate the other."

"Exterminate," Kuryakin said musingly. "Tell me, who will exterminate whom?"

"According to the immutable laws of history, we will exterminate them," Ulyanov said. "The petty bourgeois, Kerensky, Lvov, and others have power only because the proletariat has ceded power to them. That will not last."

"Not if you are permitted to return to Petrograd with German money."

"I will use the German money to educate and inform the proletariat, to fund newspapers, to create a propaganda machine, to criticise and point out the mistakes of the social chauvinists who call themselves the government of Russia. I intend to use German money for Russia and for the Russian workers. That is not treason."

"So you are returning to Russia to educate the workers." A cigarette glowed in the darkness beyond the desk. "But you are not an educationalist, Mr. Ulyanov. You are a professional revolutionary. You are returning to Russia to seize power for the Bolsheviks."

"I am returning to Russia to preserve the revolution."

"With German money?"

"With whatever means are at my disposal."

"The end justifies the means?"

"According to Marx–"

"If all you are concerned with is seizing power, then Machiavelli is as valid as Marx."

"The Bolshevik party is a Marxist party. We reject other philosophies."

"But you would not refuse power if you were offered it by a Machiavellian?"

"No."

"And you would not refuse an opportunity to seize power?"

"The true revolutionary is always willing to seize power."

"And so, the only principles that are valid are those that result in success. The unalterable fact, Mr. Ulyanov, is that you will not achieve power only through propaganda and education. To control Russia you need arms, you need trained soldiers, you need a proper intelligence system."

Ulyanov peered into the shadow beyond the desk. "In time, we will acquire what we need."

"In time," Kuryakin repeated, softly. Then, raising his voice, he said, "I am prepared to place at your disposal now a hard core of professional soldiers and the complete information system of the Okhrana."

Ulyanov sat silent. With that and one hundred and twenty million marks—"And what do you want, Count Dimitri Kuryakin?"

"Is it true that everyone apart from Zinoviev and yourself are travelling without passports? That your only means of identity are numbered slips of paper?"

"That's correct."

"I want you to issue me and my men numbered slips of paper. I want you to get us into Russia."

"And then?" Ulyanov asked mockingly.

"Then I will create the militia you will require to seize power. I will construct the secret police you will need to keep power, once you have seized it."

Caspar felt numb with shock and an awesome sense of failure. Ulyanov could not accept the help of a man like Kuryakin. The Kuryakins were corrupters, predators. There was no room for them nor for their foul secret police in the socialist state Ulyanov would found. It was better to abandon everything than make such a compromise.

Ulyanov was seated very upright in his chair, transfixing Kuryakin with those all-seeing, all-knowing, fearless eyes. "And if I refuse?"

Kuryakin picked up the revolver from the desk, drew back the hammer with a loud click.

"If you refuse, you will be dead." Kuryakin levelled the gun at Ulyanov.

Ulyanov sat silent, lost in concentration.

He was preparing to die, Caspar thought. It was the only choice he could make. He eased slowly forward in his chair.

"If you kill me, Count Kuryakin," Ulyanov said softly, "how will you ever get back to Russia?" There was triumph in his voice, that familiar mocking gling in his eyes.

"I might find another opportunity," Kuryakin said. "A dead man does not get a second chance." He allowed an ominous silence to intervene. "However, let us not talk of killing." He put the gun down on the desk. "The fact is that we can be useful to each other. The fact is that you need me, and I need you. As the end justifies the means, why should an alliance with the Okhrana be any different from an alliance with the Germans?"

"The only morality," Ulyanov said softly, "is that which contributes to the triumph of the revolution. The only immorality is that which stands in its way."

"NO!" Caspar cried, the sound of his rage and disappointment filling the room. Nechayev was wrong. Ulyanov was wrong. Better the old ways than this. Still screaming, Caspar flung himself across the desk and grabbed Kuryakin's revolver. Kuryakin swung at him and caught him on the shoulder as he rolled off the desk onto the floor. Twisting round, Caspar squatted on his haunches. Kuryakin advanced towards him, big, massive, solid.

Caspar fired.

Kuryakin shouted, spun round, bounced against the wall.

Caspar twisted himself upright and stood bracing

the gun against his body with both hands, aiming it at Kuryakin's heart.

"Rihma! Stop! This man is useful to us!" Ulyanov was on his feet, his face under the red beard flushed and sweating. "We need him, Rihma." Ulyanov repeated. "We need him to save the revolution."

Caspar turned the gun on Ulyanov. Sonya had been right all along. The man Ulyanov was nothing like his ideas. The only world Ulyanov would build was a dictatorship far worse than the Tsar's. "Vladimir Ilyich," he whispered, choking, "you bastard!" His finger tightened on the trigger.

The chair caught Caspar on the side of the head, knocking the gun from his hand and sending him crashing to the floor. His head singing, Caspar pushed away the chair and stretched out a hand for the gun.

Ulyanov's booted foot kicked it away, towards Kuryakin.

Desperately Caspar tried to rise. Kuryakin's foot caught him on the side of the head, spinning him across the floor. He could feel the hot wetness of blood running down his face, and through red haze he saw Kuryakin stoop for the gun.

Caspar skidded across the floor towards him, then felt his teeth crunch loose as Kuryakin kicked him in the mouth. Caspar rolled behind the desk, using it to lever himself upright.

"Kill him!" Ulyanov cried. "I order it! To save the revolution!"

Kuryakin had the gun now and was pointing it at Caspar. Caspar curled himself into a ball and hurled himself through the window. Glass exploded all round him, sharp splinters tugging at his face and body. Then he bounced onto the snow and rolled, slid, staggered to his feet and ran clumsily, feeling the blood dripping down his face, his teeth loose in his head, slipping and sliding, sucking in great gulps of freezing air.

He heard shouting behind him and the whistle of a bullet through the darkness. He forced himself to run faster, harder, breath searing his lungs, heading towards the deeper shadows of the trucks. He had to find Hain. He had to tell Hain what Ulyanov and Kuryakin were planning. He had to stop them.

His legs felt weak and rubbery; ribbons of pain shot along his calves and thighs. Once he turned and saw two figures behind him. Then hands reached out and grabbed him by the shoulders. Caspar stopped, panting.

Hain's voice said, "Don't move or I'll shoot you."

"I'm not trying to escape," Caspar panted. "Kuryakin is—"

From behind them there was a shout, "Ehrler!"

Caspar broke free from Hain and began to run. He heard the shots explode behind him and felt the bullets tear into him, lift his body, wheel it round, and hurl him onto the snow. He lay there choking, hardly feeling the chill or the wet. He couldn't breathe. Fluid was pumping up his throat and filling his nose. The snow round him was black with blood. He remembered the Order of the Red Eagle that would never be publicly acknowledged. Quadriga. The revolution. The new world that would now never be built. Hamburg. He glimpsed the house in Petrograd where he had lived as a boy.

Sonya—

Hain ran up to where Caspar lay; then knelt down beside him and turned him onto his back. Ehrler's eyes stared unblinkingly at the night sky. He heard footsteps behind him and Kuryakin lurched out of the darkness, one hand clutching his shoulder, the other trailing a gun.

"You didn't have to kill him," Hain said.

"He shot at me." Kuryakin knelt down beside the body and looked.

"He's dead," Hain said. "Our only witness."

"Yes," Kuryakin said and placed his arm, as if for support, round Hain's shoulder.

"I suppose I'd better arrest Ulyanov anyway," Hain said.

Kuryakin remained silent.

After a while he said, "Hain."

"Yes. . . ."

Hain turned his head and felt the cold muzzle of the revolver press against his ear.

Kuryakin pulled the trigger.

CODA

Along the Simbirskaya Ulitza the crowd waited pressed six deep against the buildings from the jammed steps of the Finland Station to the cruciform, granite walls of Kresti Prison. They had collected in the early evening, street sweepers, peasants, workers from the diesel and telephone factories nearby, delegates from outside Petrograd, their fur hats and jackets dusted with snow, the ground under their feet slushy from constant movement. The centre of the street was blocked with vehicles, exhausts pluming smoke into the chill air. The noise of the crowd and the throb of engines reverberated off the walls, the deep staccato clatter of armoured cars counterpointing the soft burble of passenger vehicles. All the street lights had been damaged in the uprising, and flags and bunting fluttered from the darkened lampposts, illuminated by the orange glow of communal fires and the sharp yellow glare of searchlights mounted on mobile platforms.

Inside the station the slender, branching columns that supported the cavernous roof were draped with red, and magnificent gold and red banners formed row upon row of triumphal arches proclaiming THE CENTRAL COMMITTEE OF THE BOLSHEVIKS. The station was small, provincial, its single platform lined with benches dulled by continual waiting. On the side opposite to that on which the trains came in were the waiting rooms, a greasy-windowed buffet displaying trays of pastries and stale cake, baggage and ticket offices, and, behind ornate doors of heavy glass, a solitary touch of grandeur; the waiting room of the Tsar.

The platform was crowded. Delegates wearing red armbands and clutching red flags pressed together in the centre of the platform, looking tiredly self-important. Two columns of soldiers lined the platform, standing stiffly at ease, looking impassively in front of them. Stalin and Shlyapnikov walked between the rows of soldiers, heads bowed in conversation, but stopped now and then to look up at the decorations, to listen to the sound of the crowd outside, and to look up at the windows of the building blocked by human bodies and backlit by the searchlights.

"Don't you think it's a splendid show?" Stalin said for the fifteenth time. "Don't you think it's splendid?"

"The train is late," Shlyapnilov said, looking at his watch. The train was three hours late. It was nearly midnight.

"Who was that who went into the waiting room?"

"Sukhanov."

"Representing the Soviet or writing his diary?"

"There are only delegates from the Soviet in the waiting room."

"The Provisional Government should have sent someone."

"The other parties, too."

"After all, we sent a representative to greet Plekhanov. Don't you think we've put on a splendid show?"

It was a conversation they'd had many times that night.

The train arrived with a harsh clatter of metal against metal, a piercing hiss of steam, a giant headlight gleaming out of the snowflecked darkness, a hard jarring sound that reverberated through the station.

"Present arms!" There was the stamp of booted feet and the slap of palms against rifle butts.

Shlyapnikov and Stalin, now joined by the other delegates, stood between the line of soldiers peering into the carriage whose windows were filled with gently heaving figures. The carriage door opened. There was a sudden silence. Then five men jumped out, dressed in khaki with red bandanas round their foreheads and massive red armbands above their elbows. With levelled rifles they surveyed the platform, then stepped back to form a very private guard of honour.

The band broke into the *Marseillaise*. Ulyanov, short, aggressive, booted, stepped down from the train.

From outside the station came the sound of cheering and racing engines, the sharp crack of fireworks and rifle shots; the vivid yellow beams of searchlights danced against the windows. An embarrassed little girl came out from the knot of delegates and presented an equally embarrassed Ulyanov with a large bunch of red roses. The delegates clapped, then came up and shook hands. Later, clutching the flowers, Ulyanov stepped between the ranks of soldiers. Nadya and Zinoviev crowded in on either side, while Stalin rushed ahead, crying, "Comrades, please make way. Comrades, please give us room."

Ulyanov, excited, overwhelmed, walked faster and faster. He was nearly running when he reached the waiting room of the Tsar where the four delegates from the Soviet awaited him.

While inside the waiting room brief speeches were exchanged, the noise outside the station grew to a crescendo. Cries, explosions, a sustained roar of engines filled the air. Suddenly, with a great pattering of feet, the crowd broke through the slim cordon of soldiers into the station, raced along the platform, and, crying excitedly, beat at the heavy glass doors. They began to cheer, repeatedly, monotonously, shouting the one word over and over again: "Lenin! Lenin! Lenin!" The cry echoed off the walls and resounded against the oval, metal roof. "Lenin! Lenin! Lenin!"

A group of soldiers pushed their way to the head of the crowd and pried people away from the doors. A few scuffles broke out. Using their rifle butts the soldiers cleared a passage before the door. An officer marched along the cleared space, opened the doors, and saluted.

Lenin came to the door and stood there, still clutching the bouquet of roses. "What's this?" he asked.

"The workers, the people, and the revolutionary soldiers welcome you to Petrograd." He dropped his arm and leaned forward to whisper that Lenin should say a few words.

Lenin walked forward and took off his bowler hat. "Comrades, I greet you without knowing yet whether or not you have been decieved by the Provisional Government. . . . The people need peace; the people need bread; the people need land. And they give you war, hunger, no bread. . . . We must fight for the social revolution, fight for the complete victory of the proletariat. Long live the world revolution!"

The cries of "Lenin!" grew deafening. The crowd burst through the military cordon, placed him on their shoulders, and took him outside. The beams of the searchlights danced along the platform, and from the street there was a frenzied uproar of cheering, drowning the band's *Marseillaise*. The crowd moved excitedly through the station doors, followed by the band and the delegates.

In the street they placed Lenin on top of an armoured car. With searchlights crisscrossing the street and the rubber-grey façade of the Finland Station, he began to speak.

Inside the station the lights had been turned out. Kuryakin stood beside the silent train, watching the beams of the searchlight dart across the darkened platform, illuminating tattered banners and flagpoles, torn bunting, and abandoned drapery. Lenin's voice echoed under the vaulted roof, strident and much magnified by loudspeakers.

"The worldwide socialist revolution has already dawned . . . any day now the whole of European capitalism may crash . . . we must have peace now . . ."

Over the sound of Lenin's voice, Kuryakin heard footsteps sounding hesitantly along the platform. He saw Stalin's lumpy, greatcoated figure, picked out by the searchlight beams, limping over the tattered decorations.

"It was a good show, wasn't it?"

There was only the voice, the figure lost in sudden darkness as the searchlight tracked away.

"Yes."

"I'm glad you have come back. We can work together again."

From the street outside, Lenin's garbled words came through, harsh, broken, distorted, didactic. "Imperialist warmongers . . . capitalist hyenas . . . liars . . . frauds . . . "

"It is his hour," Stalin said "But already the sun has begun to move."

At that moment the searchlight illuminated his face. With a sudden, frightening awareness, Kuryakin looked into it, wide, smiling, moustached, inscrutable, Asiatic.

At Brest-Litovsk on the third of March, 1918, the government of Vladimir Ilyich Ulyanov signed a peace treaty with Germany. In August, 1918, pursuant to a supplementary protocol to that treaty, the Soviet government repaid Germany, in gold roubles, its investment in peace.

He who establishes a dictatorship and
does not kill Brutus, or he who founds
a republic and does not kill the sons
of Brutus, will only reign for a short time.

—Machiavelli, *Discorsi.*